The Last Secret of the Deverills

Santa Montefiore

The Last Secret *of the* Deverills

Published by Simon & Schuster

New York   London   Toronto   Sydney   New Delhi

First published in Great Britain by Simon & Schuster UK Ltd, 2017
A CBS COMPANY
This Canadian export edition published 2019
Copyright © Santa Montefiore, 2017

1 3 5 7 9 10 8 6 4 2

Simon & Schuster UK Ltd
1st Floor
222 Gray's Inn Road
London WC1X 8HB

www.simonandschuster.co.uk

Simon & Schuster Australia, Sydney
Simon & Schuster India, New Delhi

A CIP catalogue record for this book is available from
the British Library.

Paperback ISBN: 978-1-4711-7237-3
eBook ISBN: 978-1-4711-7284-7

Typeset in Bembo by M Rules

To my darling Uncle and Godfather Chris,
with love

Castellum Deverilli est suum regnum

A Deverill's castle is his kingdom

Ballinakelly Deverills of Castle Deverill

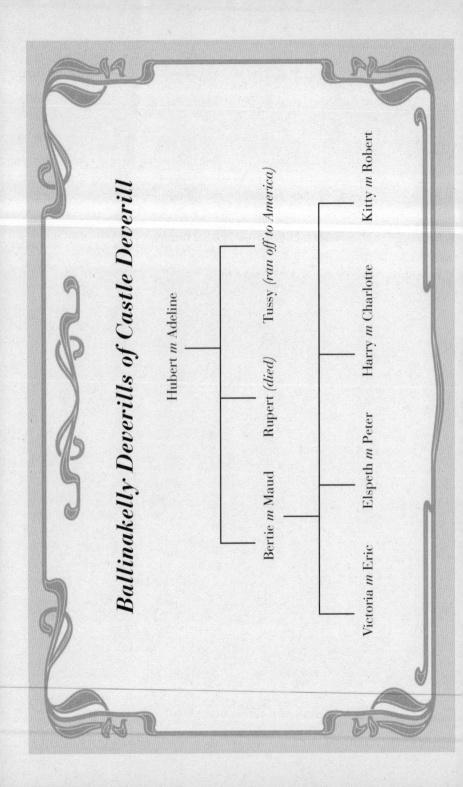

Hubert *m* Adeline

Bertie *m* Maud — Rupert *(died)* — Tussy *(ran off to America)*

Victoria *m* Eric — Elspeth *m* Peter — Harry *m* Charlotte — Kitty *m* Robert

London Deverills of Deverill House

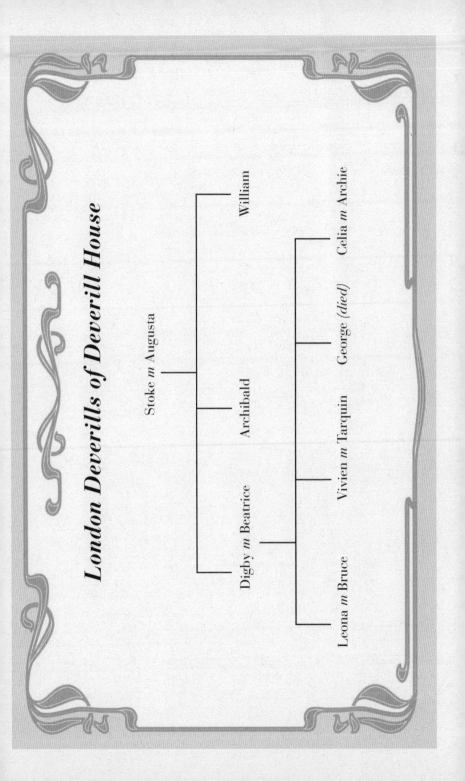

Stoke *m* Augusta

- William
- Archibald

Digby *m* Beatrice

- Leona *m* Bruce
- Vivien *m* Tarquin
- George *(died)*
- Celia *m* Archie

Maggie O'Leary

Some said she was born on the feast of Samhna, when the people of Ballinakelly celebrated the harvest with a feast, but others said she was born *after* sunset and *before* dawn, when the malevolent pookas, banshees and faeries joined the spirits of the dead to roam freely among the living during the hours of darkness. Whichever the case, the reality was that Maggie O'Leary came into the world on the first day of November 1640, when a dense mist gathered in the valleys and a light drizzle dampened the air and the wind smelt of heather and grass and brine.

There was a restlessness about the O'Leary farm that night. The cows mooed and stamped their hooves and the horses snorted agitatedly and tossed their manes. Inky black crows gathered on the roof of the farmhouse where Órlagh Ni Laoghaire paced her bedroom with her hands on the small of her back, anticipating the impending arrival of her sixth child with more than the usual apprehension. She was as restless as the animals, moaning and suffering with the extent of her labour, for the first five children had arrived easily and in haste. Every now and then she glanced out of the window, searching for the flush of dawn in the eastern sky. She hoped her baby would hold on until All

Saints Day and not arrive during these dark and haunted hours.

Not far away Órlagh's children were enjoying the feast with the rest of the community in a large barn in the heart of the village. The doors and windows of every dwelling had been flung open to allow both the ghouls and the friendly spirits to wander freely and the fires had been quenched. Outside the golden glow of bonfires warmed the air, which was cold with the presence of those malevolent beings who played havoc in the darkness.

It was not a night to come into the world, but Maggie came anyway.

Just before dawn, after a difficult labour, Órlagh was delivered of a healthy baby whose shrill cries tore a hole in the sky, releasing the first ray of light. But with the birth of a new life came the death of an old one. Órlagh was carried into the beyond but not before she whispered weakly to the babe in her arms, '*Céad míle fáilte, Peig*' a hundred thousand welcomes – thus giving her child a name and blessing her with a kiss.

Maggie was a child whose beauty was strange and arresting. Her hair was as black as a raven's wing, her eyes were a bewitching shade of green and her lips were full and sensual and curled with knowing. Maggie was uncommon in many ways, but nothing separated her more surely from her family and community than her unusual gift: Maggie saw visions of dead people, sometimes even *before* they were dead.

Such was Maggie's gift that her brothers and sister teased her for being a witch until their father told them in a low and trembling voice what became of witches. Father Brennan, the local priest, crossed himself whenever he saw her and tried to coerce her into confessing that the things she claimed to see were invented in order to get attention; the people of Ballinakelly stared at her with wide and frightened eyes, believing her to be under the influence of the ghosts who had been present at her birth, and the old women muttered, 'That child has been here before, as true as God is my judge.' Even Maggie's grandmother said that if she hadn't seen her slither out of Órlagh's body with her own eyes she would have believed her to be a changeling sent by an old pooka to bring misfortune into the house.

But misfortune came anyway, whether or not Maggie was a changeling.

For Maggie, however, there was nothing unusual about seeing the dead or predicting death. For as long as she could remember she had seen things that were beyond the senses of other people. And she wasn't wicked. *She* knew that. Her gift was God-given. So she escaped to the hills where she could be at one with all creation. With the wind in her hair and her skin damp with drizzle, she enjoyed striding through the wild grasses towards the edge of the earth where the sea rolled onto the sand in glistening waves. Beneath the wheeling gulls she'd wrap her shawl about her shoulders and throw her gaze across the water, and occasionally she'd spy the sails of a vessel on the distant horizon and wonder at the vastness and mystery of the world far from her shores. But it was high up on the cliffs, in the ancient stone circle known as the Fairy Ring, that she played with the nature spirits no one else could see, for there, in that magical place, no one feared her or judged her or castigated her: there was only God and the secret pagan world that He permitted her to see in all its wonder.

However, as Maggie got older the spirits grew insistent. They demanded more from her. They had messages, they said, which they wanted passed on to those they had left behind. Maggie's father reminded her of the penalty of witchcraft, her older sister begged her to keep quiet and her grandmother predicted nothing but doom, yet still the voices did not quieten or leave Maggie in peace. She believed she had a higher purpose. She believed it was God's will that she relieved the consciences of the dead. She was convinced that it was her duty to do so.

Times were hard and the O'Learys were poor. Maggie's father and four older brothers were farmers, as generations of O'Learys had been before them, keeping watch over the sheep that grazed on their land overlooking the sea; the beloved land that had been theirs for as long as anyone could remember. But there were eight mouths to feed in the O'Leary farmhouse and food was scarce. Out of desperation Maggie's father relented and slowly, secretly, he began to charge for a sitting with his daughter. Maggie would pass on these messages she claimed were from the dead and he would collect the money in order that they could eat. By and by word spread and the bereaved and troubled came in droves, like dark souls with outstretched arms, searching for the light. Those who could not pay with coin brought anything they could, be it milk, cheese, eggs – even the odd hen or hare. But the fear spread also, for surely such a gift was the Devil's work, and Maggie grew up without a friend save the birds and beasts of the land.

Maggie was nine years old when Oliver Cromwell arrived with his army to conquer Ireland. Her brothers joined the Royalists and even with her gift of sight she could not foresee whether she'd ever lay eyes on them again. The war was vicious and tales of Cromwell's brutality spread throughout Co. Cork like the plague and famine that swept the land in its wake. The siege of Drogheda and the massacre that followed were woven into Ireland's history in a scarlet thread of blood. Cromwell's soldiers put thousands to the sword and burned to death those who had fled to the church to seek refuge in God's house.

Word reached Ballinakelly that Cromwell would show no mercy to Catholics, even if they surrendered. So it was, with a mixture of outrage and fear, that Maggie's father joined the rebels and took to the hills to fight with whatever weapons he could lay his hands on. He was brave and strong, but what was bravery and strength against the might of Cromwell's well-armed and highly trained soldiers? King Charles II withdrew his support. He abandoned his armies in Ireland in favour of the Scots and the defence disintegrated. The Irish were beleaguered and alone, cast aside and betrayed, left to die on the hillside like helpless sheep ravaged by wolves.

Maggie's brothers came to her from the other side of death with messages for her sister and grandmother, standing with the other poor souls at the window to this world, recounting their deaths by fire, bludgeon and sword. Maggie's father died in the hills, cut down like a hare in the heather, and his womenfolk were left with no one to look after them. Indeed they were as helpless as beggars. Most of their sheep had been plundered. There was no charity to be had for the war had razed the land and the local people were starving or slowly dying of the plague. But Maggie had her gift and people continued to come knocking, with what little they had, to receive messages from their loved ones. And the O'Leary women grieved in silence because they had to remain strong for each other; because their grief would get them nowhere; because their survival depended on their resilience.

However, all was not lost. They had their land, their precious, beautiful land overlooking the sea. In spite of the violence of war nature flourished as it always would. The heather blossomed on the hillsides, butterflies took to the air, birds twittered in trees burgeoning with bright green leaves, and the soft rain and spring sunshine gave birth to rainbows that bestrode the valley in dazzling arcs of hope. Indeed, they had their land; at least they had that.

But Barton Deverill, the first Lord Deverill of Ballinakelly, would take it from them; he would take all they had and leave them with nothing.

PART ONE

Chapter 1

Dublin, February 1939

Martha Wallace skipped along the path that meandered through St Stephen's Green. She couldn't walk, she simply couldn't. Her heart was too light. It lifted her body with every step, giving her a buoyant gait as if she were walking on clouds. Mrs Goodwin hurried behind her with small, brisk steps, struggling to keep up. 'My dear, you're racing along. Why don't we find a nice bench and sit down?' she suggested, catching her breath.

Martha swung round and began to skip backwards, a few paces in front of her elderly nanny. 'I don't think I could sit, even for a minute!' She laughed with abandon. 'To think I came here to find my mother but I've lost my heart instead. It's too ridiculous, don't you think?' Martha's American accent was in stark contrast to Mrs Goodwin's clipped English vowels. Her pale Irish skin was flushed on the apples of her cheeks and her cocoa-coloured eyes shone with excitement. She had taken off her hat and consequently invited the wind to play with her long brown hair. This it did with relish, pulling it from its pins, giving her a wild and reckless look. It was hard for Mrs Goodwin to believe, watching the seventeen-year-old girl now dancing in front of her, that only a few hours before she had left the Convent of Our Lady Queen of Heaven in tears after having been told that there were no records of her birth to be found and no information about her real mother.

'Now let's not get carried away, Martha dear.'

'Goodwin, you're so serious suddenly. When you know, you know, right?'

'You've only just met and for no more than an hour. I'm only saying it would be prudent to be cautious.'

'He's handsome, isn't he? I've never seen such a handsome man. He has the kindest eyes. They're the prettiest grey and they looked at me so intensely. Am I wrong to think he liked me too?'

'Of course he liked you, Martha dear. You're a lovely girl. He'd be blind if he didn't see how lovely you are.'

Martha threw her arms around her old nanny, which took her so much by surprise that she laughed. The girl's ebullience was irresistible. 'And his smile, Goodwin. His smile!' Martha gushed. 'It had such mischief in it. Such charm. Really, I don't think I've ever seen anyone with such a captivating smile. He's even more handsome than Clark Gable!'

To Mrs Goodwin's relief, she spotted a bench beneath a sturdy horse chestnut tree and sat down with a sigh, expanding onto the seat like a sponge pudding. 'I must say, they were both very polite,' she said, recalling the boy's father, Lord Deverill, with a rush of admiration. She was flattered that a man of his standing had treated her, a mere nanny, with such politeness and grace. She knew that he had invited them to join their table for tea on account of his son, who had clearly been taken with Martha, but Lord Deverill had extended Mrs Goodwin every courtesy, when he hadn't needed to, and for that the old lady was extremely grateful. 'Lord Deverill is a gentleman in every sense of the word,' she added.

'I think I lost my heart the moment he came into the tea room,' said Martha, thinking only of the boy.

'He couldn't take his eyes off you. How fortunate that his father took the initiative, otherwise you might never have had the opportunity to meet him.'

'Oh, will I ever see him again?' Martha sighed, wringing her hands.

'Well, he knows where we're staying and if we delay our trip to London a day, that might give him time to come calling.'

'I'm so excited I can't stand still,' said Martha, clapping her hands together. 'I don't want to go home. I want to stay in Ireland forever.'

Mrs Goodwin smiled at the naivety of youth. How simple life seemed to be in the rosy glow of first love. 'I don't wish to bring you back to earth, my dear, but we have a mission, do we not?'

This gentle reminder deflated a little of Martha's enthusiasm. She sat down beside Mrs Goodwin and dropped her shoulders. 'We do,' she replied. 'You can be sure that nothing will distract me from that.'

'Perhaps JP can help us. After all, the aristocracy all seem to know one another.'

'No, I don't want to share it with anyone. It's too painful. I couldn't admit that my real mother didn't want me and abandoned me in a convent.' Martha dropped her gaze onto the path as a red squirrel scurried across it and disappeared beneath a laurel. 'I'm only just coming to terms with it myself,' she said softly, her exuberance now all but dissipated. 'I won't lie to him; I just won't volunteer the truth. As you say, we've known each other no more than an hour. We can hardly expect to bare our souls.'

Mrs Goodwin folded her gloved hands in her lap. 'Very well. We'll stay in Dublin for another day and then make our way to London. I'm sure we'll be able to find the Rowan-Hampton family without too much difficulty. There can't be many Lady Rowan-Hamptons, after all.' She put her hand on Martha's and squeezed it. The fact that the name on Martha's birth certificate was an aristocratic one made their task much easier than if it had been a common name like Mary Smith. In that case Mrs Goodwin wouldn't have known where to start. 'No doubt we have a rocky road ahead,' she said. 'We might as well enjoy ourselves before things get serious.'

Martha glanced at Mrs Goodwin and bit her lip. 'Oh, I do hope he comes calling.'

JP Deverill stood by the open window of his room in the Shelbourne Hotel and gazed out over St Stephen's Green. The smoke from his cigarette curled into the air before the wind snatched it away. His vision was trained on the lattice-work of branches rising out of the Green, but he didn't see them; all he saw was Martha Wallace.

JP had never been in love. He'd been attracted to girls and kissed a few but he'd not cared for any of them. He cared for Martha Wallace, even though he had only spent an hour in her company. But what an hour it had been. He wanted to give her the world. He wanted to see her smile and to know that her smile was for him. He wanted more than anything to hold her hand, look deeply into her eyes and tell her how he felt. He dragged on his cigarette and shook his head in disbelief. Martha Wallace had pulled the rug out from under his feet and set him off balance. She had been a bolt of lightning that had struck him between the eyes, an arrow launched from Cupid's bow straight to his heart. Every cliché he'd ever read now made sense to him and he didn't know what to do.

Thankfully Bertie Deverill knew exactly what to do. He had patted his son on the back and chuckled in a manner that left JP in no doubt that his father had once been quite the lady's man. 'If you want to see her again, JP, you must act quickly. Didn't they say they were headed for London? Why don't you buy some flowers and call on her at her hotel? You could show her the sights of Dublin. I'm sure she'd be thrilled to see you.'

JP replayed every second of their encounter in the tea room downstairs. The first moment they had caught eyes Martha had been watching him from the table where she sat with her companion by the window. He hadn't noticed her at first, so busy was he greeting people he knew and settling into his chair at the table a short distance from hers. But then her gaze had attracted him and like a homing pigeon he had alighted there and something magical had happened. She wasn't beautiful, she wasn't striking and she certainly wasn't the sort of young woman to draw attention to herself, but JP was astonished to discover that he did not want to pull his eyes away. It gave him a frisson of pleasure now to remember it. She hadn't looked away either but remained locked into his gaze, unblinking. Her cheeks had blushed and a surprised look had swept across her face. It had almost been a look of recognition, as if she had seen something in his countenance and was startled to discover that she knew it. Poetry told of this kind of love at first sight, but JP had never given it much thought. He hadn't ever considered or pursued such a thing. But now *love* had found *him* and he felt as if it had cast a net and caught him in it.

Poetry also told of the peculiar feeling of having known someone for the whole of eternity, of staring into the eyes of a stranger and seeing a familiar friend. JP had never given *that* much consideration either, but as they had sat at the table, their hands touching over the cake stand as they made for the same egg and watercress sandwich and the same piece of chocolate cake, he had felt as if they had somehow known each other before. There was a bond, a connection, an understanding and they only had to look at each other to see it. He *knew* her and she *knew* him and suddenly all those poems he had deemed quite silly spoke a language that he understood. He had crossed a threshold and what was previously hidden was now revealed in wondrous colour and vibrancy. He stubbed out his cigarette and decided to do as his father suggested.

He bought a bunch of red roses at a stand around the corner from the hotel and set off through the Green at an impatient pace. There was no time to delay. She could be packing her bags this very minute, preparing to leave for London. If he didn't hurry he might never see her again. The sun was low in the sky, slowly completing its daily descent, and the tangle of bare branches cast long damp shadows across the path before him. Blackbirds and crows squawked as they settled down to roost and squirrels took to their nests, but JP didn't notice any of the things that would normally give him pleasure, so intent was he on his mission.

He was uncharacteristically nervous. He knew he was considered handsome even by those who weren't normally attracted to men with red hair, and his half-sister, Kitty, who had raised him in the place of the mother he didn't have, never ceased to remind him of the *Deverill* charm in his *Deverill* smile so that he had grown up believing himself special simply for being a Deverill. But suddenly, in the face of actually caring what another person thought of him, he doubted himself.

The small, inexpensive hotel where Mrs Goodwin and Martha were staying was not far from the Shelbourne, but when JP reached it he was out of breath from having walked so fast. The rosy-cheeked receptionist looked up from behind the desk and smiled at him warmly, her eyes brightening behind her glasses at the sight of such a tall and fine-looking gentleman. 'Good afternoon,' he said, feeling a little foolish for carrying a bouquet of roses. 'I'm after a Miss Wallace,' he said, leaning on the top of the desk. The receptionist didn't need to look in the book for she knew very well who Miss Wallace was. The young lady and her friend had enquired about the Convent of Our Lady Queen of Heaven that morning and she had given them directions.

'I'm afraid she and her companion are still out,' said the receptionist in her gentle Irish lilt, dropping her eyes onto the flowers. 'Would you like me to put those in water for you?'

JP's disappointment was palpable. He tapped his fingers on the wood impatiently. 'But they will be coming back?' he asked, frowning.

'Yes indeed,' the receptionist replied. She knew it was incorrect to divulge any more of their arrangements but the young man looked so sad and the gift of flowers was so romantic that she added quietly, 'They've changed their booking and will be staying another day.'

At this he cheered up and the receptionist was pleased to be the cause of his happiness. 'Then I shall leave these with you. May I have a piece of paper so I can write a note?'

'I can do better than that. I can give you a little white card with an envelope. Much more elegant,' she said with a smile. She turned round and pretended to look through a pile of letters to give the gentleman some privacy. JP tapped the pen against his temple and wondered what to write. He was good with words usually, but suddenly he didn't even know how to begin.

What he wanted to say was most definitely too forward. He didn't want to frighten off Martha before she had even had the chance to get to know him. He wished he could remember a line from a poem, or something witty from a novel, but his mind had gone blank and he remembered nothing. Of course his father would know exactly what to write but he was at the Kildare Street Club, where he would no doubt be discussing racing and politics with his Anglo-Irish friends, as was his custom when he came to Dublin. Kitty would know what to write too, but she was back at home in Ballinakelly. JP was on his own and he felt useless.

Mrs Goodwin and Martha returned to the hotel a little after seven that evening. They had spent the rest of the afternoon wandering around the city enjoying the sights before settling into Bewley's in Grafton Street for a cup of tea. With its sumptuous crimson banquettes, stained-glass windows and warm, golden lights the café had a distinctly European feel which delighted the two women, tired from walking in the cold. They warmed up on tea and restored their energy with cake and watched the other people with the fascination of tourists in a new city who delight in every new flavour.

JP Deverill dominated Martha's thoughts, but every now and then she'd turn a corner and find herself wondering whether the elegant lady walking on the other side of the street, or the one sitting on the bench, could possibly be her mother. For all she knew she could have passed her a dozen times already. A small spark of hope that perhaps Lady Rowan-Hampton was looking for *her* ignited in her heart and her thoughts continually drifted off into the cliché of an emotional reunion.

The receptionist smiled when they stepped into the foyer of their hotel. 'Good evening, Miss Wallace. A gentleman came by this afternoon with flowers for you.' She turned and lifted them off the floor. 'I took the liberty of putting them in water.'

Martha caught her breath and pressed her hand to her heart. 'Oh my, they're beautiful!' she exclaimed, reaching for them.

'They certainly are,' Mrs Goodwin agreed. 'My goodness, what a gentleman he is.'

'He wrote a note to go with them,' said the receptionist, thinking Miss Wallace the luckiest girl in the whole of Dublin.

'A note!' Martha declared excitedly, lifting the small envelope out from among the roses.

'What does it say?' asked Mrs Goodwin, leaning over to smell the flowers.

Martha pulled off her gloves and put them on the reception desk, then slid out the card with trembling fingers. She smiled at his neat handwriting and because she now had something of his to treasure. '*Dear Miss Wallace,*' she read. '*I am usually good with words but you have rendered me hopelessly inept. Forgive my lack of poetry. Will you allow me the honour of escorting you around our beautiful city? I shall call on you at your hotel tomorrow at ten. Yours hopefully, JP Deverill.*' Martha sighed happily and pressed the card against her chest. 'He's coming tomorrow at ten!' She widened her eyes at Mrs Goodwin. 'I think I need to sit down.'

Mrs Goodwin accompanied Martha up to their room, carrying the vase of red roses behind her like a bridesmaid. Once inside Martha sank onto the bed and lay back with a contented sigh. Mrs Goodwin smoothed her grey hair and looked at her charge through the mirror which hung on the wall in front of her. 'Of course I will have to come with you,' she said firmly. Her soft heart did not in any way undermine her sense of responsibility. Even though she was no longer in the employ of Martha's parents, it was her duty to look after their daughter as she had done for the last seventeen years. Nonetheless, she felt as if she and Martha were a pair of fugitives running from a crime scene and was determined to see that, once Martha had found her birth mother, she was returned safely to the bosom of her family in Connecticut.

Martha giggled. 'I *want* you to come with me, Goodwin,' she said, propping herself up on her elbows. 'I want you to witness everything. It will save me having to tell you about it afterwards. What shall I wear?'

Mrs Goodwin, who had unpacked Martha's trunk, opened the wardrobe and pulled out a pretty blue dress with a matching belt to emphasize her slender waist. 'I think this will do,' she said, holding it up by the hanger. 'You look lovely in blue and it's very ladylike.'

'I shan't sleep a wink tonight. I'm all wound up.'

'A glass of warm milk and honey will see to that. If you want to look your best for Mr Deverill, you must get your beauty sleep.'

'Mr Deverill.' Martha lay down again and sighed. 'There's something delightfully wicked about that name.'

'Because it sounds like "devil",' said Mrs Goodwin, then pursed her lips. 'I hope that's the only similarity.'

*

Even after a glass of warm milk and honey Martha was unable to sleep. Mrs Goodwin, on the other hand, had no such difficulty and breathed heavily in the next-door bed, her throat relaxing into the occasional snore, which grated on Martha's patience.

Martha climbed out of bed and went to the window, tiptoeing across the creaking floorboards. She pulled the curtains apart and gazed out onto the street below. The city was dark but for the golden glow of the street lamps, and she could see a fine drizzle falling gently through the auras of light like tiny sparks. It was quiet too, and above the glistening tiled roofs the clouds were heavy and grey. There was no moon or star to be seen, no tear in the sky through which to glimpse the romance of the heavens, no snow to soften the stone, no leaves to give movement to the trees which stood stiff and trembling in the cold February night, but the thought of JP Deverill rendered everything beautiful.

Mrs Goodwin had suggested she write to her parents to let them know that she had arrived safely in Dublin. Dutifully, Martha had set about the task with a mollified heart. As she crossed the Atlantic she had had time to think about her situation and her horror at having discovered that she was not her parents' biological child – unlike her little sister Edith who had taken such pleasure in telling her so – had eased and she now felt nothing but compassion. Her parents were simply two people who had longed for a child. Unable to have their own they had adopted a baby from Ireland, which was where her adoptive mother Pam Wallace's family originally came from. As perhaps any loving parents would do they had kept it secret in order to protect Martha. She didn't blame them. She didn't even blame Edith for spilling the secret. However, she was hurt that her aunt Joan could give such a sensitive piece of information to a child who was too young to know how explosive it was.

So, Martha had written a long letter on the hotel paper, laying bare her feelings, which her first note, left on the hall table in the house for her parents to find after she had gone, had failed to do. Now she believed they needed more of an explanation. She couldn't have confronted them about the truth of her situation because it was too painful. She loved them so much that the reality of not really belonging to them was like a knife to the heart. It was unspeakable – and until she came to terms with it she would not talk about it to anyone else but Goodwin. Had she asked them for permission to go she doubted they would have given it. There was talk of a possible war in Europe and Pam Wallace was notoriously overprotective of her two daughters. *I need to unearth my roots, whatever they may be,* she wrote. *You will always be my mummy and daddy. If you love me back please forgive me and try to understand.*

Now she reflected further on her predicament and a tiny grain of resentment embedded itself in her heart like a worm in the core of an apple. She reflected on the pressure her mother had always put on her to be immaculate: immaculately dressed, mannered, behaved and gracious – nothing less would do, and often being immaculate was somehow not enough to satisfy Pam Wallace. When she was a little girl her mother had minded so badly that she impress Grandma Wallace and the rest of her husband's family that she had turned her daughter into a sack of nerves. Martha had barely had the courage to speak for fear of saying something out of turn. She remembered the horrible feeling of rejection one hard stare from her mother could induce if she fell short – and most of the time she wasn't even sure what she had done.

Even now the memory of it caused her heart to contract with panic. It hadn't been the same for Edith. Martha's sister, six years her junior, had come as a surprise to Pam and Larry Wallace and now Martha understood why; they hadn't thought they could make a child. Consequently, Edith was more precious than Martha and her birth had been celebrated with such exhilaration it could have been the Second Coming.

The truth was that Pam Wallace had to mould Martha into a Wallace, but Edith didn't require any moulding because she *was* a Wallace. *That* was why they had been treated differently. It all fell into place now. Martha's adoption was the missing piece in the puzzle that had been her childhood. Edith could behave with impunity and Pam did nothing to discipline or reprimand her. The two sisters had been treated differently because they *were* different. One was a Wallace and the other was not and no amount of moulding or hard stares could ever make Martha into what she wasn't. As a seventeen-year-old girl with little experience of the world this fact convinced her that her parents loved Edith more – and from her lonely contemplation now by the window that conclusion was indisputable.

Martha wondered about her real mother, as she had done so often since finding her birth certificate at the back of her mother's bathroom cupboard. Lady Rowan-Hampton was her name and Martha had constructed a character to match. She imagined her with soft brown eyes, much like her own, and long curly brown hair. She was beautiful and elegant as an aristocratic British lady would most certainly be, and when at last they were reunited her mother would shed tears of joy and relief and wrap her arms around her, whispering between sobs that now they had found each other they would never be parted.

Suddenly Martha began to cry. The surge of emotion came as such a surprise that she put her fingers to her mouth and gasped. She glanced at the bed to make sure that she hadn't awoken her nanny, but the old woman was sleeping peacefully beneath the blanket, which rose and fell with her breath. Martha threw her gaze out of the window but her vision was blurred and all she saw was her own distorted reflection in the glass staring forlornly back at her. Who was she? Where did she come from? What kind of life would she have had had her mother not abandoned her at the convent? Would she ever know? There were so many questions, her brain ached. And she felt so rootless, so alone. Only Mrs Goodwin was who she claimed to be. Everyone else had lied. Martha's shoulders began to shake. One moment she had been a young American woman from a well-connected, wealthy family, secure in the knowledge of her family's love, dutiful, biddable and obedient. The next an outsider, purchased from a convent on the other side of the world, rebellious, disobedient and defiant. Where did she belong and to whom? What could she believe in any more? It was as if the structures within which she had grown up had collapsed around her, leaving her exposed and vulnerable, like a tortoise without its shell.

She wiped away her tears and closed the curtains. Mrs Goodwin sighed in her sleep and heaved her large body over like a walrus on the beach. Martha climbed back into bed and pulled the blanket to her chin. She shivered with cold and curled into a ball. As she drifted off to sleep at last it wasn't her mother who played about her mind or the unanswered questions that had so depleted her energy, but JP Deverill emerging through the fog of her bewilderment like a dashing knight to rescue her from her growing sense of rejection.

Chapter 2

JP had barely slept. He was a sack of nerves. All he could think about was Martha Wallace. Everything about her fascinated him, from her mysterious reserve to her shy and bashful smile, and he could only guess at the life she had lived on the other side of the Atlantic. He wanted to know everything about her, from the mundane and trivial to the big and important. Their chance meeting in the tea room at the Shelbourne had been so momentous it was as if the very plates beneath the earth's surface had shifted, changing the way he saw himself and the world. Ballinakelly had always been the centre of his universe, yet now he felt as if he had outgrown it. Martha smelt of foreign lands and sophisticated cities and he wanted her to take him by the hand and show them to him.

He breakfasted with his father, who was always up early. Bertie Deverill was a busy man. Ever since he had sold Castle Deverill and given most of what he had to his estranged wife Maud – who had swiftly bought a sumptuous house in Belgravia from where she entertained lavishly with her portly and exceedingly rich lover, Arthur Arlington – he had set about exploring new ways to make money. So far nothing had quite come off but Bertie was always cheerful and enthusiastic and confident that, in time, one of his schemes would eventually succeed. Looking at him now, sitting in regal splendour in the dining room of the Shelbourne, one would not have imagined that he had a single financial concern.

'You look bright-eyed and bushy-tailed this morning,' he said to his son. 'I don't suppose it has anything to do with that pretty girl you met yesterday?'

JP grinned and the freckles expanded on his nose and his grey eyes gleamed. 'I'm going to show her the sights,' he said.

'Ah, so you took my advice, did you?'

'I did. I left flowers at her hotel with a note. I hope to meet her at ten.'

Bertie took his watch out of his waistcoat pocket. He had to hold it out on its chain in order to see the little hands for his eyesight was deteriorating. 'You have two hours to kill, JP.'

'I know, and they'll be the slowest two hours of my life.' He laughed and Bertie shook his head and put his teacup to his lips.

'It doesn't feel so long ago that Maud made me feel like that.' He took a sip and his eyes misted. 'Hard to believe now, isn't it?' JP had noticed that a certain wistfulness had begun to seep into his father's recollections when he spoke about his wife. From the little JP had gleaned from listening to his half-sisters Kitty and Elspeth, Maud was snobby, cold-hearted and selfish and their marriage had been a desert for years. Maud hadn't forgiven Bertie for publicly recognizing JP, the bastard child he had spawned with one of the house-maids, or for selling the castle, which was their own son Harry's inheritance. She had stormed off to London and, as far as JP could tell, everyone was very relieved, especially

Kitty and Elspeth. But recently Bertie's attitude towards Maud had begun to change. A thawing seemed to be taking place. A melting of old resentments. A healing of wounds. Her name was creeping into his sentences and the sound of it no longer jarred.

JP rarely thought about his birth mother. He included her in his prayers every night and he sometimes wondered whether she was in Heaven, looking down on him. But he didn't really care. Kitty had always been a mother to him, her husband Robert rather like a stepfather. JP considered himself lucky to have two fathers. So many had none, for the Great War had done away with almost an entire generation of men.

He wasn't nostalgic about the past or romantic about the story of his birth. He knew he had arrived in a basket on the doorstep of the Hunting Lodge, where his father and Kitty lived, with a note that asked Kitty to look after him as his own mother had died. He wasn't curious to know more. He didn't feel inadequate as others might for he was confident that Kitty loved him as if he were her own child and he had never desired more; it wasn't in his nature. JP was a happy, positive young man, living fully in the present; a man whose heart was spilling over with gratitude.

'I'll meet you back here at 5.30 then,' said Bertie. 'We'll take the evening train down to Ballinakelly. I told Kitty you'd be back in time for supper.'

JP's face fell. 'I was rather hoping I might stay an extra night,' he said.

Bertie shook his head. 'Doesn't she have to go to London?' he asked, referring to Martha Wallace.

'I don't know when ...'

'Why don't you see how today goes, eh? You might find

you don't like her as much as you thought you did,' he said. JP knew that wasn't going to happen.

When at last it was time to leave, JP had read every word of the *Irish Times*, twice. He placed his hat upon his head, threw his coat over his jacket and straightened his tie in the mirror that hung in the hotel lobby. It was cold outside and misty. The trees in St Stephen's Green looked thin and miserable in the fog, the birds earthbound and hungry, pecking the sodden ground for worms. Yet, nestled in the grass, were the emerging shoots of snowdrops, ready to bloom as soon as the winter sun shone.

JP walked through the Green with his hands in his coat pockets, whistling a merry tune. But as he neared the hotel his nerves began to get the better of him. What if she wasn't there? What if she didn't want to see him? What if he had imagined her interest? Doubts flooded his mind and he stopped whistling and slowed his pace. Was it arrogant of him to assume that his feelings were reciprocated? Perhaps she had smiled at him only out of politeness. Perhaps his ardour had blinded him to that fact. He kicked a stone across the path and sighed. Then with his usual optimism he reasoned that he wouldn't know until he saw her and if she declined his invitation he would simply return home on the evening train having learnt a valuable lesson in restraint.

He arrived at the hotel and strode in. He ran his eyes around the small lobby but saw only a couple of old ladies in hats and coats sitting expectantly with their handbags on their knees. But he was a little early so it was no surprise that she hadn't come down. After all, it was unseemly for a lady to be seen waiting for a gentleman.

He stood by the window, pulled out his gold cigarette case from the inside pocket of his jacket and flicked it open with his thumb. He popped a cigarette between his lips and lit it. Then he waited, trying not to let his nervousness show.

Suddenly he felt the air in the lobby change and turned round. There, standing at the reception desk in a pretty blue dress and hat, her coat draped over her arm, was Martha Wallace. Hastily JP stubbed out his cigarette and walked over to greet her. When she saw him she smiled and her cheeks flushed, which he took as a good sign. He recognized attraction when he saw it and he was relieved. 'I'm so pleased you decided to come,' he said, believing her even lovelier than she had been the day before in the Shelbourne.

'I couldn't very well refuse after you delivered such a beautiful bouquet of roses,' she replied and she was surprised at how calm her voice sounded when on the inside she was trembling like a young fawn.

'I'm glad you liked them,' he said.

'Oh, I did, very much. Thank you.' Just then Mrs Goodwin stepped round the corner in her coat and hat, a pair of gloves loose in her hand.

'Good morning, Mrs Goodwin,' said JP, a little disappointed that Martha's companion had decided to join them. He had hoped they might be given some time alone together. 'Well, shall we get going? There's a lot to see. I thought we could start with Trinity College and then wander up to the General Post Office. How much do you know of Irish history?' he asked as they walked to the door.

'I know nothing,' Martha replied.

'Then allow me to be your guide and tutor,' said JP importantly, taking Martha's coat and helping her into it. 'But don't worry, I won't test you over lunch.'

JP offered to take a taxi to Trinity College, an offer which Mrs Goodwin would have accepted with gratitude for it was a damp and foggy morning and her legs were still aching from the day before. But Martha wanted to walk through the Green as much as JP did and they set off beneath the trees. The elderly nanny walked a discreet distance behind, hoping that they might stop for a cup of tea once they got to the College.

It wasn't long before JP and Martha shed their nervousness and settled into an easy conversation. He asked her about her home in Connecticut and she asked him about Ballinakelly and both omitted to reveal the truth about their parentage. Martha's omission was more deliberate because of her recent discovery, the subject being too raw to broach, whereas JP was so used to the unusual circumstances of his birth that he didn't think them worth mentioning.

Talking about all the positive things in her life came to Martha as a welcome respite. She didn't mention that she and Mrs Goodwin were as fugitives on the run. Instead she told JP that her parents wanted her to see a little of the world and where better to start than in Ireland where her mother was born, which was partly true, for Pam Wallace's family, the Tobins, came from Clonakilty.

By the time they reached Trinity College Mrs Goodwin was pink in the face and panting. 'I really must sit down,' she said, relieved to see a little restaurant on the corner. Then, noticing Martha's expression, she added, 'Why don't you two go on without me? I'll settle into a nice chair and have a rest while you look around the College. Don't worry about me. I'll be perfectly fine with a cup of tea. Nothing like a cup of tea to restore one's energy.' JP didn't forget his manners and escorted her inside, making sure she was given a table by the window.

He sauntered out of the restaurant with a bounce in his

step. Now he was alone with Martha and the feeling was intoxicating. She felt it too and her laughter came more readily. 'Goodwin has been with my family since I was a baby,' she told him. 'She's been my nanny and my friend and I'm so grateful to her for everything she has done for me. But I can't help feeling a little thankful that the walk tired her out.' She grinned and her freckles spread across her nose in the same way that JP's did. 'It makes me self-conscious to feel that I'm being watched.'

'You're not the only one,' said JP. 'Now I can be myself.'

Martha raised her eyebrows. 'And what is that exactly?'

'A scoundrel and a reprobate!' he teased.

She laughed. 'Your face is too gentle to be either of those things.'

'A rascal?'

She shook her head. 'Not that either.'

'A rogue?'

She laughed and walked on.

Then he took her hand. 'A romantic?'

Martha caught her breath and froze. No man besides her father had ever held her hand before. Her lips parted and she gazed at him in alarm then glanced over her shoulder, fearful that Mrs Goodwin might have changed her mind and followed them after all. In a second she came to her senses and pulled her hand away. Her skin seemed to burn beneath the glove. 'Really, JP, you are forward.'

'I'm sorry. I shouldn't have,' he muttered. 'Kitty used to tell me off as a boy for not knowing when I'd gone too far.'

'Please don't be sorry,' she said, suddenly feeling bad for having overreacted. 'We were having such a nice time. I don't want to spoil it.' She laughed at her own foolishness. 'After all, you were only teasing.'

'I can't pretend I don't want to hold your hand,' he said seriously.

'But I shall pretend that I don't want you to. Isn't that the way a lady should behave?'

'Indeed it is. You are absolutely right. I shall give it time and then try again.'

'Perhaps next time you will be more successful,' she said coyly, astonished to find that she was flirting.

'I can live in hope,' he said, thrusting his hands into his trouser pockets and walking on. 'Now let me show you around the College where I shall be attending lectures this coming September.'

Her face lit up with admiration. 'Really? You're going to study in this beautiful place?'

'I am,' he said proudly.

As they wandered around the College Martha noticed that JP drew the attention of females everywhere. Young girls glanced at him and then glanced at him again. Ordinary women watched him admiringly, some even quite brazenly, while grand ladies in fur coats stole the odd peek from beneath the brims of their hats. He had a charming, mischievous smile and sparkling grey eyes, but it was his charisma that attracted them, as if he somehow shone a little brighter than everyone else. Martha felt good being in his company, for a little of his light shone on her, giving her the confidence to be a bit more extrovert. She was no longer under the scrutiny of her mother. She could allow herself a freedom of movement and speech that she had never been permitted before. At first it was unsettling, for her patterns of behaviour were so ingrained and her reserve second nature. But as JP made her laugh she realized that, with him, she could be a truer version of herself.

By the time they returned to the restaurant to find Mrs Goodwin they were chatting away as if they were old friends. Mrs Goodwin was restored and ready to join them on their visit to the General Post Office, which had been at the very centre of the Easter Rising in 1916. However, of much more interest to her as they walked up the street was the remarkable change in Martha. The girl seemed to have become another person in the hour that she had spent with Mr Deverill. In fact, they had settled into each other's company like a perfectly harmonious melody. This wasn't meant to happen, Mrs Goodwin thought to herself. They had come all the way from America to complete a mission and this was very distracting. Mrs Goodwin had hoped that they would find her mother as soon as possible so that Martha could return home to the Wallaces, who were no doubt worried sick at their daughter's sudden disappearance. But now Martha had seemingly fallen for Mr Deverill, what was she going to do?

As JP and Martha laughed and teased each other as if she wasn't there, Mrs Goodwin kept her reservations to herself. She was grateful that she was no longer in the employ of the Wallaces for she doubted Mrs Wallace would think very highly of this budding romance, even though Mr Deverill's father was a lord, which might go some way towards pacifying her. They certainly wouldn't thank *her* for having witnessed it and done nothing to prevent it. On the other hand, Mrs Goodwin knew that Mrs Wallace was highly competitive with her two sisters-in-law so Martha bagging a future lord, if the boy was indeed the eldest son, could trump them all.

As Martha and Mrs Goodwin had already had tea at Bewley's the day before, JP invited them to the Gresham for lunch. JP was not partial to the formality of the place but his father liked to go there and all JP had to do was sign the bill. Mrs Goodwin had intended to leave them alone while she went and browsed the shelves in Brown Thomas, but she was so enjoying herself that she quite forgot and the two young people had to include her in their conversation when they would have much preferred to talk to each other.

While Mrs Goodwin gabbled on, Martha and JP communicated their amusement in surreptitious looks that passed silently between them. Although Martha felt marginally guilty for allowing her beloved nanny to become a figure of fun, she relished this wordless conversation that was more like the secret communication of long-standing conspirators than the frustrated glances of two people who had only recently met. By the time lunch was over they truly felt bonded.

Neither JP nor Martha wanted the day to end. But the sky grew dark above them and the wind blew damp and cold through the streets of the city. The yellow glow of electric light blazed through the thickening fog, reflecting on the wet pavements like spilt gold. Mrs Goodwin was keen to return to the hotel, reminding Martha that they had to pack their suitcases in order to leave promptly for London the following morning, but Martha was in no hurry to draw to a close probably the most wonderful day she had ever had. 'Why don't you go back in a cab, Goodwin, and I'll follow shortly,' she suggested.

'Allow me to pay for the cab,' interjected JP who was disappointed that he too would have to leave for home. 'You look weary and I give you my word that I will see that Martha is back at the hotel by five. I have to be at the Shelbourne at half past to meet my father, so I will drop her off on the way.' He smiled his most charming smile and added, 'I will look after her, Mrs Goodwin. I promise.'

Mrs Goodwin's legs ached and her feet were sore. If she hadn't been so tired she might have declined his offer and stuck it out until the very last, but as it was she was barely able to climb into the cab. She hoped to God that JP was a man of honour.

As they watched her cab disappear around the corner JP turned to Martha, a sudden sorrow flooding his heart. It was as if he was about to lose something enormously precious. 'There's one more thing I want to show you,' he said.

He led her up the streets to the River Liffey that glistened like a black serpent sliding through the mist. Straddling the bridge that crossed it were two iron arches crowned with lamps that shone weakly through the fog. It was a beautiful sight and a lump lodged itself in JP's throat at the thought of having to leave her. 'This is Ha'penny Bridge,' he said softly. 'It's tradition to toss in a coin for luck.'

They walked to the middle then stood gazing into the glossy darkness below. JP put a hand in his pocket and pulled out a couple of pennies. 'Make a wish,' he told her, handing her a penny.

Martha frowned. 'Can I have two wishes?'

'No, you're only allowed one,' he replied.

'But I have two,' she protested, smiling feebly because she really did have two and she couldn't choose between them.

'Well, I have only one,' he said firmly, tossing his coin into the water below. They listened for the plop but nothing came. It simply dissolved into the mist. He closed his eyes and made his wish: *I wish that I will see Martha Wallace again.* As he spoke those words inside his head he realized how passionately he meant them. 'Your turn,' he said, leaning on the iron railing and looking at her with an intensity that made something inside her stomach flutter.

'All right,' she said. She squeezed her eyes shut and wondered how she could get two wishes into one without it being disqualified. She remained a moment thinking very hard. At last it came to her. *I wish that I find my mother and she leads me back to JP.*

She still had her eyes shut when she felt his hand take hers. She opened them and looked down to see her glove in his. She gazed at him and he gazed at her and the realization that they would soon be parted stole their breath.

Slowly and deliberately Martha took off her glove. Understanding immediately, JP took off his. Smiling shyly, she gave him her hand. It was delicate and warm with long fingers that tapered prettily. As he touched her she felt a frisson ripple across her entire body as if he hadn't just taken her hand, but her whole being.

'I will write to you in Ballinakelly,' she said, no longer feeling the need for caution.

'You must let me know where I can write to *you*,' he replied.

She didn't want to think about returning to America. She didn't want to think of anything that would take her from this man who had slipped so easily into her heart. It was as if he had always been there. 'I will find a way,' she replied.

Reluctantly they set off back down the bridge, hand in hand. JP would return to Ballinakelly on the evening train with his father and Martha would travel to London in the hope of finding her birth mother. But both knew that their chance meeting at the Shelbourne had changed everything.

Chapter 3

Ballinakelly

In the dim light of the Doyles' farmhouse, Old Mrs Nagle lay dying. She had been expiring for days now, seeming to resist the call with a ferocity of will astonishing in such a minute and feeble woman. Her family, weary of the long- drawn-out wait, stood around her bedside, anticipating her final breath.

There was her daughter, Mariah Doyle, who pushed the well-worn beads of her rosary through fingers coarsened from having known only toil and hard winters. Her face had been set into a scowl for thirty years now, ever since her husband had been murdered by a tinker, and her only comfort was her religion and its promise of eternal rest. There were her grandsons, Michael and Sean, two very different men in both looks and character. Michael was tall and broad with thick curly hair as black as his eyes and a powerful charisma that repelled and attracted in equal measure, while his younger brother Sean was fairer of hair and lighter of skin with kind hazel eyes and a smile that was full of all the charm his brother lacked. Rosetta, Sean's wife, and mother of their five children ranging in age from four to thirteen, had grown fat and slothful and her beauty had faded. But there was sunshine in her melodious Italian vowels and a sweetness in her nature that ensured her husband's eye never strayed, and if on occasion it wandered that it always came back. Rosetta stood by Old Mrs Nagle's bed and prayed for her soul – and hoped that God would take pity on them all and release them from this daily vigil so that they could leave this uncomfortable little farmhouse and go and live up at the castle with Sean's sister Bridie, who, to everyone's surprise except Rosetta's, was its new owner.

The wind rattled the window panes and the rain clattered against the glass and the February skies hung low and heavy and dark. The cows were restless in the cowsheds, their breath rising into the damp air to create a fog as dense inside as it was outside and the gulls huddled together against the rocks as the winter gales battered the shore. Yet, as Bridie was driven down the valley towards the farmhouse where she had grown up, she felt only nostalgia, which came in waves, sweeping in memories she had so far managed to ignore. She had been in Ballinakelly a week now and every day, when she came to visit her grandmother, she found she retrieved a little bit more of herself.

Old Mrs Nagle turned her head to the door as her youngest grandchild walked in. Her raisin eyes lit up with intent and her mouth, a black cavern of toothless gums, opened and closed like a fish as she tried, and failed, to speak. She attempted to lift her hand and Bridie pushed past her brothers and knelt beside her, taking her bony fingers in her hands as if cradling a little bird. Old Mrs Nagle gazed into her granddaughter's eyes and Bridie longed to tell her what she had been through. That she hadn't left Ballinakelly all those years ago because she'd been offered a better life in America but because she had been seduced by Lord Deverill at the castle, forced to give birth in a convent in Dublin and persuaded to leave forever so that Bertie Deverill could pretend that the tawdry affair had never happened. She wanted her grandmother to know that she had had to endure the agony of losing her son not once but twice, because her brother Michael had stolen the child from the convent and left him on Kitty Deverill's doorstep in order that she, the baby's half-sister, could raise him as her own. When Bridie had returned some years later to Ballinakelly and discovered that her boy was in Kitty's care she had been forced to accept that she had lost him all over again.

Kitty had told JP that his mother was dead. He had no idea that she now lived at the other end of the estate in the castle that used to belong to his father. Bridie would have to endure the sight of him, knowing that she could never tell him the truth. She could never wrap her arms around him, hold him close and tell him that she loved him, because Kitty did that in her stead: Kitty Deverill, once her greatest friend and now her most hated enemy. Bridie wanted her grandmother to see her pain and her animosity and to understand. The secret was gnawing through her insides and the burden of hiding the hurting was becoming too much to bear. If only she could share it with her beloved grandmother; then her grandmother would take it to her grave.

No one besides Michael knew the seedy truth behind Bridie's triumphant return. The rest of the family saw only what she had acquired: a dashing husband who was a count, their young son Leopoldo, the mighty Castle Deverill, her fine clothes and jewellery, her shiny motor car and the chauffeur who drove it in his gloves and hat. Not even Michael knew how much she had lost. And she could never tell.

Bridie longed for her grandmother to know her sins, *all of them*, and for her to love her in spite of them. Suddenly, it mattered to Bridie more than anything else in the world that her grandmother should know the truth. She leaned closer so that she could smell the old lady's sour odour – the odour of a body already in decay. 'I never wanted to leave you,' she whispered softly, releasing a trail of tears. She pressed her grandmother's hand to her wet cheek. 'It was beyond my control. I did some terrible things and I had to leave. But all I wanted was to come home, to you and Mam. All I wanted was to share ... and for you to love me ...' Her whispering became a rasp. Her grandmother's eyes seemed to look past the woman she had become to the scrawny little girl she had once been, with knotted hair, bare feet and a rumbling belly that was never satisfied. And in the reflection of her gaze, Bridie saw her too. How she wished she could be that girl once more and live it all again. How different it could have been.

'It won't be long now, God help us. 'Twill be a happy day for her,' said Mrs Doyle, blessing herself.

Bridie's throat tightened and her vision blurred. Unable to speak, she simply stroked her grandmother's white hair and tried to smile so as not to alarm the old lady with her fear. As Bridie gazed into her eyes, Old Mrs Nagle seemed to be saying, *Don't forget who you are, child. Don't ever forget who you are.*

'Why is she holding on?' asked Rosetta.

'Because death, when it comes, is a leap into the unknown, however strong your faith,' said Michael, who had so successfully transformed himself into a devout and spiritual man that few remembered the ruthless rebel he had been during the Troubles twenty years before and the atrocities he had committed in the name of freedom.

'She doesn't want to leave us,' said Sean. Rosetta leant her head against her husband's shoulder and tried not to let her impatience show.

Mrs Doyle's bottom lip gave a sudden tremor before she stiffened her jaw and brought it under control. 'God knows you've earned your rest. You can go now and rest in peace with the Lord and reap your eternal rewards,' she said. 'A cross in this life; a crown in the next.'

Old Mrs Nagle stared at Bridie and her eyes grew dim. *Don't forget who you are.*

At last her spirit departed and her small body expelled a final breath then stilled. Mrs Doyle gasped and pressed her hand to her mouth. In spite of having prepared herself for this, the finality of death was a shock. Bridie sank onto the floor and dropped her head against the mattress. It was over. Her grandmother was gone and Bridie had never got the chance to tell her the truth.

At length Bridie stood up and went to open the window to release her grandmother's spirit. For a long moment no one said anything. They stood around the bed, bowing their heads in respect, awed by the emptiness of the body before them. Presently Mrs Doyle turned to Sean. 'Go and get Father Quinn,' she said. 'And knock up Mrs O'Donovan and get a pound of rashers and a black pudding and two noggins of whiskey. 'Tis the done thing to put something on the table for the laying-out women. Ask her if you can use the telephone to put the death in the *Cork Examiner*.' She turned to Michael. 'You go and get the two Nellies and tell them to bring out the linen and the Child of Mary rig.'

'I can go up to the castle, Mam, and bring back the food, whiskey and linens,' Bridie suggested, wanting to help.

'No, Bridie,' her mother retorted sharply. 'We are simple,

God-fearing people and we don't want any displays of grandeur in front of the people. Nanna wouldn't like it. I can hear her now saying that we were full of *eirí-in-áirde*. There'll be no showing off in this house as long as I'm alive.'

Bridie was stung. She remembered the day her father was killed by the tinker, when Lady Deverill gifted her a pair of dancing shoes and the girls in Ballinakelly had mocked her for putting on airs. She turned away so her mother would not see her blushing with shame or know how unworthy she had made her feel.

The room had darkened with the day in spite of the candles that flickered on every surface. Bridie had offered to pay for electricity but Old Mrs Nagle had been appalled by the very idea of it. It was enough to have a wireless, which they kept under a lace cloth on the dresser and considered something of a miracle, for where in God's name did the music come from? What on earth did they need electricity for when they had natural light in the day and candlelight in the night? It would only lead them into temptation for surely material wealth was the Devil's ploy for enticing souls away from the simplicity of God.

But Bridie craved her mother's admiration. She fought back tears and put her arms around her, hugging her tightly. The years had done much to distance mother from daughter and Bridie was determined to retrieve the closeness that had been lost. 'You must come and live with me,' she said. 'I'll see that you never want for anything again.'

But Mrs Doyle stiffened and pulled away. 'It is easier for a camel to pass through the eye of a needle than for a rich man to enter the Kingdom of God,' she said gravely. 'I will remain in this house until I die, Bridie. It was good enough for your father therefore it's good enough for me. You might be a wealthy lady now, Bridie, with all your airs and graces, but it's not right that you should be mistress of Castle Deverill. It's as if you've turned the world on its head. I'm only happy that the previous Lord and Lady Deverill, God rest their souls, aren't alive to see it. I would die of shame. You weren't born to that kind of life. God knows I didn't raise you that way. There, I've said it now.' She lifted her chin and pursed her lips. 'I only hope you haven't forgotten your faith.'

'I haven't forgotten my faith, Mam,' Bridie replied, defeated. 'I give thanks to the Lord every day for my blessings. Surely it is God's will that I have married well. I have a husband I love and a son I love even more. If I am blessed it is because the Lord has blessed me.' *And by God, after all that I have suffered, I deserve to be happy,* she thought to herself. Mrs Doyle pressed her handkerchief to her mouth to smother a sob.

Bridie turned to Rosetta, her old friend whom she had met during her first lonely winter in New York and brought back to Ballinakelly, only to lose her to her brother. 'Surely, *you'll* come, Rosetta. This place is much too small for five children and you and Sean can have the east wing of the castle to yourselves.'

Rosetta was quick to accept. 'With Mariah's blessing we will come,' she said tactfully, knowing that her mother-in-law could not deny them the comforts of the castle. Mrs Doyle gave a little nod.

'And Michael?' Bridie asked.

Michael shook his head. 'I will stay and look after Mam,' he said firmly and Mrs Doyle's shoulders shuddered as a wave of gratitude swept through her.

But the truth was that Michael Doyle could never live in the castle he had set alight that tumultuous Christmas of 1921. He could never reside in a place that carried the Deverill name after everything he had done to destroy it. Most of all he couldn't bear to walk those corridors that had once belonged to Kitty Deverill, knowing what he did to her in the farmhouse the morning after the fire. He would carry his shame along with his remorse in the sack of corpses that was forever slung over his back, for he could never be free of his guilt. Guilt for the tinker child killed in the fire he had lit in revenge for his father's murder, guilt for Colonel Manley's death on the Dunashee Road, when he and a small group of rebels had lured the Englishman to an isolated farmhouse and slayed him for the brutal way he had treated their fellow Irishmen, and guilt for the many others he'd slaughtered in the name of freedom. God had forgiven him of all his sins and washed his soul clean. He had vowed to lead a pious life. But Michael's guilt ran deep, like an underground river of tar; however beautiful the earth was above it, the water below would always be polluted.

'Very well,' said Bridie. 'I know you're a proud man, Michael, but now I am back in Ballinakelly, I will make sure that my family never wants for anything. If God has blessed me with great wealth, I will give thanks by looking after my own.'

Bridie left the farmhouse, hugging her coat about her body for comfort as much as for warmth. Her mother disapproved of her wealth, but how much greater would her disapproval be were she to know the whole truth? Material wealth was the very least of Bridie's transgressions; no amount of Hail Marys could make up for the gravity of her sins.

It was almost dark now. The afternoon had receded into evening and the rain was still heavy on the wind that blew in over the ocean. Bridie gazed out of the car window onto a landscape that never changed, in spite of what human beings did upon its soil. The green hills whose crests were now disappearing into cloud and the valleys where patches of mist were slowly gathering in pools were constant in their beauty and something caught in Bridie's chest as she looked upon them. All the while she had lived in America Ireland's gentle whispering had summoned her home and she had, for so long, chosen to ignore it. Yet, deep in her heart, she knew that she belonged here and *only* here and she would never truly be happy until she had chased all the demons she had left here out of the shadows.

As the car made its way up the drive that swept through rhododendron bushes, already budding through the winter chill, the castle loomed out of the fog. Golden light spilled out of the many windows, giving an enticing allusion to the splendour within, and the imposing walls, extravagantly rebuilt after the fire by Kitty's cousin Celia, who, for a short time, had sustained the Deverill inheritance, rose magnificent and proud just as they had when Bridie was a child. The car drew up in front of the grand entrance where the Deverill family motto was still carved into the stone: *Castellum Deverilli est suum regnum* – A Deverill's castle is his kingdom – and Bridie glanced up at the tall landing window above where she, Kitty and Celia had once stood as little girls to watch the guests arriving for the Summer Ball. They had been as close as sisters then, each born in the year 1900. She remembered the two cousins in their beautiful silk dresses with ribbons in their hair and patent leather shoes in the prettiest pink and blue on their stockinged feet, and she remembered her own grubby apron and scratchy dress, her pitifully naked legs and shoeless, dirty feet, and the thorn of resentment pierced her heart because while they had had everything she had had nothing. They had skipped blithe and carefree downstairs to the ball while *she* had returned to the kitchen below stairs to help her mother, who was the cook.

As the butler opened the door for Bridie Doyle, now Countess di Marcantonio, mistress of Castle Deverill, she couldn't help but feel a cruel sense of satisfaction that the Great Depression and Celia's husband's suicide had laid to rest the Deverill ambitions once and for all. *She* belonged here now and her son Leopoldo would grow up within its walls and one day inherit it. The castle would never again belong to a Deverill.

Bridie gave the butler her coat, gloves and hat and strode into the hall. There was a boisterous fire in the grate to lift her spirits and all the lights were blazing, giving the place a gratifying air of comfort and opulence, which only a great deal of money can buy. She dragged her mind away from the humble kitchen in the Doyle farmhouse where she had danced as a little girl in her father's arms, and reminded herself that her life was here now, that as much as it was natural for her to cling to the past, only the present could make her happy.

She found her husband in the library. Cesare was deep in conversation with a tall, artistic-looking man she had never seen before. When she appeared in the doorway they both stood up. 'Mr O'Malley, let me introduce my wife, Countess di Marcantonio,' Cesare said proudly, for Bridie's pallor only enhanced her prettiness. Bridie held out her hand so that Mr O'Malley could shake it. 'My darling, this wonderfully talented gentleman is going to make three fantastic bees out of stone to put above the front door. I have been explaining to him that my family is descended from the family of Pope

Urban VIII, Maffeo Barberini, and that the Barberini family coat of arms is three bees.' Bridie's fingers went straight to the gold bee brooch pinned to her dress that Cesare had given her on their wedding day. 'They are very particular bees so I am trusting into his care one of my precious bee shirt studs so that he can draw his design.' Bridie was a little surprised because Cesare had not discussed this with her first, but her husband was a man who knew his mind and she loved him more for that.

'I think it's a grand idea,' she said. After all, why shouldn't they replace the Deverill family motto? It was *their* castle now and how fitting to display the three Barberini bees above the door. If Cesare wanted more bees (since their marriage – and *her* money – Cesare had commissioned every type of bee to embellish himself and their home) he should have more. Pride was a weakness of his that she found endearing.

'I'm so pleased you approve, my darling. Family is important, no?' He shrugged. 'Not everyone can have a family as illustrious as mine, after all.' He threw his head back and laughed, big white teeth gleaming against olive-brown skin, and Bridie felt a surge of admiration and gratitude that this beautiful man belonged to *her*.

Bridie wanted to tell him that her grandmother had died, but Mr O'Malley didn't look as if he was going anywhere so it would have to wait. 'Very nice to meet you, Mr O'Malley,' she said politely. 'I look forward to seeing your designs.' She walked back into the hall as her husband sank into the armchair and continued to boast to Mr O'Malley about his family of Italian princes. Bridie stood at the bottom of the grand staircase, in the part of the house where as a child she had been forbidden to go, and felt a moment of uncertainty. She could almost hear Adeline Deverill in the drawing room and the tapping of claws on the marble floor as Hubert Deverill's wolfhounds came trotting in from their walk with their master, who had always looked shabby in threadbare tweed jackets and moth-eaten sweaters. She half expected one of the servants to reprimand her now for straying beyond the green baize door into the family part of the house.

Bridie couldn't wait for Rosetta to come and live here with her. She needed Rosetta's companionship again. As much as she relished her new position as chatelaine of Castle Deverill, it felt strange. It felt lonely and it felt *wrong*. But she wasn't going to sink now that she had risen to the height of her ambitions. She turned her thoughts to Kitty and Celia Deverill and her determination to find a sense of belonging grew strong again.

A sudden screech echoed in the depths of the castle. *Leopoldo!* With her heart in her mouth Bridie climbed the stairs at a run. She raced down the corridors, trying to ascertain where the cry had come from. The castle was vast and she had only been there a week so she still wasn't familiar with its endless corridors and many rooms. Dizzy with panic she passed long walls of paintings she had never seen before, sculptures that meant nothing to her and furniture whose value she couldn't even guess at, all chosen by Celia Deverill, and she felt even more the empty feeling of alienation. Would she ever know her way around? Would she ever feel she belonged? Would this castle ever be home?

At last, as she turned the corner into another long corridor, she saw, at the very end, her seven-year-old son Leopoldo, running towards her. She held out her arms and scooped him up. 'What's all that noise for, Leo?' she asked, hugging him tightly.

'I saw a ghost!' he exclaimed.

'Oh darling, there aren't such things as ghosts,' Bridie said, stroking the child's dark hair. But she went cold as she remembered Kitty telling her about the cursing of her ancestor Barton Deverill. According to family legend Maggie O'Leary, who had owned the land the castle was built on in the 1600s, had put a curse on the first Lord Deverill of Ballinakelly, confining his soul and that of all his heirs to a life of limbo inside the castle until the day an O'Leary returned to reclaim the land.

'I saw it, Mama.' The child was trembling.

'Where did you see it?' she asked.

'In the tower.'

She gasped in horror. 'God save us, Leo! What were you doing in the tower?' Kitty had once taken her up there with the intention of showing her the ghost of Barton Deverill. Of course, Bridie had seen nothing, but Kitty had spoken to the chair as if there had been a person sitting in it.

'I was exploring,' said the boy.

'Well, you shouldn't be exploring on your own. This is a very big castle and you might get lost. Imagine if we never found you!' She took the boy's hand and led him back the way she had come.

When they reached the hall Mr O'Malley had gone and Cesare was standing in front of the fire with his hands on his hips. 'Ah, there you are, *tesoro*,' he said and his Italian accent was so pronounced as to sound almost comical. 'Have you invited anyone for dinner?'

'No,' she replied. 'I haven't.'

A shadow of irritation swept across his face. 'Then you must begin. You must be the greatest hostess in Co. Cork,' he said emphatically. Bridie was now sufficiently well-acquainted with the stiffening of his jaw to know when a suggestion had become a command. 'We must entertain. We must throw dinner parties and lunch parties. We must invite everyone. It is not enough to live in the castle; we have to dominate the county too. We are the first family of Ballinakelly and *you*,' he said, lifting his son into the air, 'are an Italian prince. Count Leopoldo di Marcantonio, descended from Pope Urban VIII.' The little boy squealed in delight, forgetting all about the ghost.

'I will organize entertainment for you,' said Bridie, desperately wanting to please this dashing, charismatic man who had chosen *her* out of a cast of thousands.

'I know you will. But why the sad face, my darling?' Cesare put his son down and settled his mesmerizing green eyes onto his wife with concern.

'My grandmother died this afternoon,' said Bridie.

'That is a great pity,' he replied carelessly. 'But she was old. She is in a better place now.'

'I know, but I feel—'

He broke her off mid-sentence. 'You must let your sorrow go, my darling. It will not get you anywhere and you have lots to do. I have had my fair share of grief but I have risen above it like sunshine. Life is too short to waste time in mourning. Life must go on. You have to keep yourself busy then grief will have no space to occupy.'

'My brother and Rosetta are coming to live in the east wing,' she said. 'I hope you don't mind. I know we've just moved in but—'

'Of course they must,' he said enthusiastically, as if it was the most wonderful idea he had ever heard. 'And what about your mother? Will Mariah be joining us too?'

'She won't be moved and Michael has decided to stay with her.'

'Your mother is a proud woman. But Leopoldo will have cousins to play with,' he said, smiling at the boy. 'But don't forget that they are not princes like you, Leopoldo. They are simple country children and will be guests in your home, so you must be nice to them.' Neither Cesare nor Bridie ever noticed that Leopoldo was so spoiled that he was *never* nice to anyone.

'Now I will go out,' said Cesare.

Bridie was a little hurt. 'Now?'

'As you have not invited anyone to entertain me, I have to find entertainment elsewhere.'

'Will you be back for supper?' she asked, watching him stride towards the door where the butler stood ready with his coat and hat.

'No.' He thought of the baker's daughter's plump thighs and knew that, once between them, he'd be in no hurry to leave. 'I'll most likely be back late.' Then he was gone, leaving Bridie wondering how she could make his home more attractive so he would be inclined to stay.

Chapter 4

'Did you really have to frighten the boy?' said Barton Deverill, slouching in the armchair with his feet on a stool as he had done for the best part of two hundred and seventy years. Although free to roam the castle, Barton had chosen the room at the top of the western tower and only a small handful of ghosts were permitted to join him there – most avoided it on account of his bad mood, which had prevailed now for nearly three centuries.

'This Doyle woman does not belong here,' his son Egerton retorted crossly. 'She's a usurper and must be forced to leave.'

'I want her to go as much as you do, but frightening a small boy is not the way to do it.'

'He's odious,' Egerton snarled. He walked over to the window and looked out onto the lawn, which was sparkling in the sunshine with a light sprinkling of frost. But Egerton was not the sort of man to be moved by the beauty of nature. His heart had been calcified long ago and the years imprisoned in this limbo had only softened it a little. 'He throws sticks at birds, pulls the legs off spiders and kicks the dogs.'

'You did a great deal worse when *you* were a boy,' Barton reminded him.

'And look at the man I became.' He grinned grimly at his father.

'You have paid for your sins,' said Barton. 'And I have paid for mine.'

'When we get out of here I doubt I'll be going to the same place as you. I never treated anyone with any respect or kindness when I was alive.'

'Trust me, son, whatever you have done I have done worse.'

'That cannot be true, Father.'

Barton gazed at Egerton, the corners of his mouth turning down into bitterness. 'You don't know the half of it.'

'Then tell me.'

'If I've held my tongue for over two centuries I'm hardly going to let it loose now.'

Egerton turned his attention to the gardens again. 'This castle belongs to the Deverills, not to the Doyles or anyone else.'

'Indeed it does. But you terrorizing a child will not bring the Deverills back.'

Adeline Deverill floated into the room, followed by her husband Hubert, who had been a jocular, cheerful man in life but was now a dark energy full of regrets and self-pity. 'You're not *still* going on about Bridie Doyle, are you?' she said, folding her arms. 'There is no point descending into unpleasantness. You have to accept what *is* because you can't change it.'

'It's all very well for you, Adeline. You can come and go as you please,' said Barton.

'But I choose to remain here with all of you. Goodness, what was I thinking? I could have floated up to the light. But no, it's much more fun down here listening to you all complaining of your lot.'

'If it was *your* lot, you'd complain worse than us, I dare say,' he added.

'You have to learn to accept the things you cannot change,' she said, wandering around the edge of the room where she had spent the last years of her life. In spite of the extravagant rebuilding, this western tower still held on to its original charm.

'Egerton thinks he *can* change it, by haunting the child,' Barton growled.

Adeline shook her head disapprovingly. 'That's not very nice, Egerton.'

'Being nice won't get rid of them.'

'And if you *do* get rid of them, who do you think will come in their place?' she asked. Egerton did not like to be disputed, especially not by a woman. He scowled into his beard. 'Your freedom is in the hands of an O'Leary and it doesn't look like any of them have the means to buy Castle Deverill. Perhaps an O'Leary daughter will marry this Leopoldo,' Adeline said reasonably.

'If he continues the way he's going no one will want to marry him,' said Barton.

'Women are very stupid,' Egerton added pointedly. 'There are many who would gladly have a man with a castle, even if he's a tyrant and a bully.'

'You should know,' said Barton.

Egerton grinned wickedly. 'My wife was the stupidest of the lot!'

Hubert sank into the other armchair, opposite Barton, and folded his hands over his belly. 'Let's face it, we're never getting out of here,' he said gloomily.

'Darling, it's not like you to be so pessimistic,' Adeline replied, trying to rouse him out of his depression. 'You were always a cheerful, optimistic fellow.'

'In life, Adeline. This kind of half-death is very disappointing and as far as I can see, endless! What are the chances of an O'Leary coming to live here now that that housemaid has got her hands on it? A housemaid, I ask you! How the devil did that happen? In our day a person knew where he stood. He was happy to remain there, too. The ambitions of this woman are beyond belief.'

'She married a very rich count, my dear,' said Adeline, crouching by his chair and putting a hand on his.

'She'll not hold on to him,' Egerton added. 'They've been here but a week and he's already seduced one of the pantry maids.'

'There's nothing new about that, Egerton,' Adeline retorted. 'I'm sure *you* didn't behave much better when you were master of the castle.'

Egerton took that as a compliment and grinned raffishly. 'It was my right to enjoy the servant girls. They would have been mightily disappointed had I not.'

'Human nature will never change,' Adeline said wisely. 'Modes come and go, but human nature remains the same. Beneath the trappings of civilization, we are closer to the animal kingdom than we realize.'

'What nonsense,' Barton scoffed. 'You should concentrate more on getting us all out of here and less on the complexities of human nature. Leave that to the philosophers. If I have to spend the next two hundred years in this dastardly limbo I shall go mad and then see what havoc I will wreak on the inhabitants of this castle! It's a wonder that I haven't already. Unfortunately, I cannot kill myself because I am dead already.'

'Don't be such a misery, Father,' said Egerton. 'It was *you* who got us into this mess in the first place.'

'And with all the will in the world, Egerton, I cannot

get us out. How many times do I have to tell you? Only an O'Leary can by reclaiming the land.'

Hubert dug his chin into his chest and stuck out his bottom lip. 'And that's as likely as a man on the moon,' he said.

Adeline smiled indulgently because her love for her husband was both profound and patient. 'My dear, if a housemaid can rise to be lady of a great house, so too can an O'Leary.'

'Man on the moon,' said Hubert grumpily and he would have liked more than anything to pour himself a large glass of whiskey. If he'd known then what it was like to be dead, he'd have drunk a great deal more of it when he was alive.

Since Bridie had moved into the castle Kitty had been in a fever of outrage. It was unbelievable that her childhood friend had swiped her family home right from under her nose. Unthinkable that, after their altercation at the bottom of the garden fourteen years before, when Bridie had returned to Ballinakelly and accused Kitty of stealing her son and threatened to take him, she should come back now and buy the castle. Surely, it was an act of revenge, Kitty reasoned. Bridie couldn't lay claim to her child but she could have everything else – and she wanted Kitty to know it. She wanted to lord it over Kitty as Kitty had once lorded it over *her*. Kitty wondered whether Bridie had forgotten the bond they shared, the years they had played together as equals, the fun they had had when Bridie was Kitty's lady's maid. But their friendship was in ruins and no amount of money could rebuild it. JP stood between them like an unscalable wall. They both had a right to him, but it was Kitty who had raised him and she honestly felt that she had done the best for her friend. She couldn't help the way things had turned out.

And what a mess it all was. JP had no idea that Bridie was his mother and Bridie could never tell him. He believed his late mother had been called Mary, because that's what Kitty and Bertie had agreed to tell him. The truth must never come out. Never. But now the truth had moved in only a few miles across the estate.

Kitty's father had reassured her that it wouldn't be too hard to keep Bridie and JP apart. There was no chance of them meeting socially, Bertie said, even less chance of them being introduced on Sundays for they attended different churches, and if they passed each other in the street, they would be strangers. Besides, JP would soon be leaving for Dublin to study at Trinity College. Bertie had returned the day before from Dublin and reported that JP had fallen for a girl he had met in the tea room at the Shelbourne. This was welcome news to Kitty. The sooner he left Ballinakelly the better – not that she wanted him to go, but he was a man now and it was natural for a man to make his own way in the world. She had held on to him when other boys his age had been sent to England to be educated (partly because they didn't have the money to send him to Eton and partly because her husband Robert, who had been Kitty's tutor, was a more than adequate teacher). It was now time to let JP go.

JP could think of nothing else but this girl he had met. Kitty noticed the faraway look in his eyes and the agitated way he moved restlessly around the house. He took his horse out and galloped over the hills. How she remembered doing that herself when her own agitated spirit could only be quietened by the wind in her hair and the sound of thundering hooves in her ears. She watched him set off and saw herself not only in his red hair and wilful nature but also in his passionate heart. He was a Deverill and it didn't matter that he was also a Doyle because he was now a man and *she* had shaped him. As far as Kitty was concerned there was nothing of the Doyles in him.

Kitty often thought of Michael Doyle. The memory of the rape in the farmhouse, when, in a frenzy of anger she had left her blazing family home and gone to confront him about his part in the arson, only for him to accuse her father of raping his sister and inflict the same violent act on her, was now distant as if it pertained to another life. The anxiety of bumping into him in town had eased so that now she no longer sweated with nerves or dreaded turning the corner. When she did see him, which she inevitably did, she simply looked away, held her chin high and crossed the street. She would never forgive him and she would never acknowledge him as JP's uncle. As far as Kitty was concerned Michael did not exist, even in her nightmares, which had subsided too by the sheer force of her will. She had accepted the rape as part of her past and had buried it along with her love for Jack O'Leary. Both men were relegated to the dusty shadows of her being, one dark, the other light, but both once the cause of great anguish.

Kitty had got on with her life. Her daughter Florence was now twelve. She was like her father: studious, kind and gentle-natured. Unlike JP she had few Deverill characteristics and unlike Kitty she didn't have the gift of a sixth sense, which Kitty had inherited from her grandmother Adeline. Kitty loved her fiercely. Raising JP and Florence and being a good wife to Robert had fulfilled her. Once she had made the heartbreaking decision to stay in Ireland with Robert and Jack had left for America, Kitty had found a contentment she had never believed she could.

Jack O'Leary had been her great love ever since she was old enough to know her own heart. They had been children together, playing in the woods and down by the river, hunting for frogs and beetles and caterpillars, watching badgers and rabbits and mice. Then they had grown into young adults and had ridden out over the hills together, talking about their hopes for Ireland and their dreams of independence in the Fairy Ring of stone circles high up on the cliff top while the sinking sun set the ocean aflame. Jack had kissed her there and in that moment, when their lips had touched, Kitty had understood that she would know no finer love for a man. Her love for Robert was of a different kind. It was deep, certainly, and it was tender, but how could it compete with the love she felt for Jack whose history she shared?

The years of struggling for independence, the mutual love for their country, the risks they had both taken and the danger they had been in had bound them together in an unbreakable tie. Even though Kitty had relinquished her dream of being with Jack, she knew that Jack still held the roots of her heart, right down deep in the place where she had first learned to love. But she had taught herself to ignore the pull and to withstand the ache and over time she had managed to accommodate both.

Kitty barely saw her mother Maud, for whom she had no affection, or her oldest sister Victoria, Countess of Elmrod. Maud, icily beautiful with slanting blue cat's eyes, alabaster skin and white-blonde hair cut into a severe bob which emphasized the determined line of her jaw. She had never asked Bertie for a divorce but for a woman so concerned about what 'Society' thought of her it was extraordinary that she should be so indiscreet. Equally beautiful and insufferably entitled, her eldest daughter Victoria also lived in London but had the advantage of a grand estate in Kent where she retreated when the London season drew to a close. Her husband was the dullest man in England and one of the richest, which was of greater value than character to Victoria who tolerated him in exchange for the life her mother had dreamed of for her. Kitty was close to her other sister Elspeth, who had not been blessed with beauty but was sweet-natured and modest with the temperament of a loyal dog. She had surprised everybody by defying their mother's social ambitions and marrying Peter MacCartain, an Anglo-Irishman without title or fortune, and going to live in his cold and dreadfully uncomfortable castle a short distance from Castle Deverill. Hard-up but happy, Elspeth was Kitty's dearest friend and her three children were only a little older than Florence. In Elspeth she found a loyal, serene and unexcitable companion, which was what she needed now after years of drama and heartbreak.

It was a bright February morning when Kitty and her sister Elspeth drove into Ballinakelly. Gulls wheeled beneath blue skies and the sun managed to melt the frost although it clung to the ground in the shadows and on the hilltops where the air was colder. Wound up by Bridie's underhand purchase of Castle Deverill, Kitty had been persuaded by Elspeth to go into town to do a little browsing to take her mind off it. A new milliner from Dublin had opened a small atelier on the main street. In fact, Kitty and Elspeth's great-aunts, Laurel and Hazel, affectionately known as the Shrubs, had been sporting two of the milliner's creations at church on Sunday and everyone had admired them. The scandal those two elderly women had caused by inviting Grace Rowan-Hampton's father, Lord Hunt, to live with them in a very shocking *ménage à trois* had not abated with the years and the people of Ballinakelly still gossiped about it and wondered how on earth it worked. Kitty and Elspeth had done as much gossiping as the rest of them, but were less shocked. In a family such as theirs, a *ménage à trois* was hardly world-shattering.

'I'm sorry to go on, Elspeth, but I'm devastated about the castle,' said Kitty as they drove into town in Elspeth's small Baby Austin. 'I wish Celia hadn't sold it. I wish it still belonged to our family. But it's gone forever and I can't bear it.'

'There's no point in wishing. There's too much to wish for: that the financial world hadn't crashed, that Britain hadn't been plunged into recession, that Archie hadn't lost all his money, that he hadn't committed suicide, that Cousin Celia hadn't found herself not only a widow but a *poor* widow and been forced to sell the castle. It's infuriating, I agree, but Grandma would say that if you can't do anything about it you should let it go.'

'And she's right. But I'm beside myself.' Kitty put a gloved knuckle in her mouth and bit on it.

'You're like a dog with a bone. You'll drive yourself mad.'

Kitty couldn't tell her about her anxiety for JP. Besides her father Bertie, her husband Robert, Michael Doyle who had brought the baby down from Dublin, and Grace, in whom Kitty had confided after she had found the child on her doorstep, no one else knew that Bridie was JP's mother. Elspeth couldn't imagine why Kitty minded so much that Bridie now lived on the other side of the estate and Kitty was not going to enlighten her. Instead, Kitty put it down to the unnatural order of things. 'I'm paying rent to her!' she seethed. 'It's all wrong. She's the daughter of the cook, for goodness' sake.

It's not right that she is now mistress of Castle Deverill. It's not right at all!'

'You must put it into perspective, Kitty,' said Elspeth wisely and a little firmly because, in Elspeth's opinion, Kitty was overreacting. 'No one is sick or dying. The castle is just a castle. I know it means more to you than that, we *all* know how much you love it, but it is only a building made of stone. Ah, here we are,' she said briskly. 'Let's go and have a look at some hats. That will cheer you up.'

They entered the boutique to find a large assortment of hats exhibited on stands in the bay window and crammed on shelves with reels of ribbons, rolls of fabric and reams of lace and sequins and other trimmings. Feathers peeped out of boxes on the top of the counter and inside the display below, carefully arranged behind glass, were brooches and baubles that glittered enticingly. Pretty hat boxes were piled against one wall in neat towers and Kitty's eyes feasted on them with delight. Elspeth had been right to bring her. She was forgetting her troubles already.

At the tinkling of the doorbell a woman came out from a room at the back of the shop. Her big brown eyes took in the two ladies and she wrung her hands, out of nervousness, because she knew who they were and she was a little in awe. Everyone knew of Kitty Deverill; with her long red hair and singular beauty she was unmistakable. Indeed, the milliner had heard of Kitty Deverill even before she had married and moved to Ballinakelly.

'Good morning,' she said politely in her lyrical Irish brogue, giving only a small smile so as not to reveal her crooked teeth.

'Good morning,' said Elspeth cheerfully. 'What a beautiful atelier you have.'

'Oh, I would not use such a grand word for my humble business,' she replied.

'It is most certainly an atelier. Didn't I tell you, Kitty? Soon the whole of Co. Cork will be wearing your creations. Look at this one. Isn't it lovely?'

'Would you like to try it on?' asked the milliner.

'Yes please.' Elspeth watched the woman lift the hat off the stand.

'If you take a seat here in front of this mirror, madam, I'll help you.' Elspeth sat down and the milliner replaced the hat she was wearing with a very fine creation in a plum-coloured felt with a contrasting teal-coloured ribbon, which did much to lift the mousy-brown shade of her hair. 'This one is called a Florentine, madam, and it sits on the front of the head like this.'

'Very flirty,' said Kitty admiringly, cocking her head. 'And the colour suits you.'

'Oh, I adore it,' Elspeth gushed.

'I can make it for you in any colour. You can choose your ribbons over there.'

Kitty moved to the shelves to look at the fabrics and trimmings while Elspeth tried on another style with a wider brim. Soon Kitty was pulling out rolls of ribbon and laying them across different-coloured felts. 'I love this green. With my colouring I'm a little limited,' she told the milliner.

'I disagree. I think your colouring is so striking you could wear scarlet and get away with it.'

'Goodness, you don't think it would clash horribly, do you?'

'Not at all. I think it would be daring.'

As Kitty took Elspeth's place in front of the mirror another woman emerged from the room at the back. She was pretty with pale Irish skin sprinkled with freckles, blue eyes that were gentle and engaging and long curly hair the colour of sun-dried hay. When she saw Kitty and Elspeth she smiled in a friendly manner quite uncommon in a stranger. 'Good morning,' she said and her American accent was stark.

'Good morning,' said Kitty with a frown. She had never seen this woman before and her accent immediately aroused her interest.

The milliner was apologetic. 'Excuse me, ladies, I'll just see Mrs O'Leary out.'

Kitty stiffened. 'Mrs O'Leary?' she mumbled, forgetting to take a breath.

'Yes, my name is Emer and I'm new in Ballinakelly. My husband and I have just arrived from America.'

Although Kitty was sitting down the blood seemed to drain from her legs into her feet. 'And which O'Leary is your husband?' she asked, although she knew the answer. She knew it from the sudden pounding in her chest and the thumping against her temples. She knew it from the happy smile this woman wore upon her face and she was suddenly seized by a raging jealousy, as if a hand had grabbed her heart.

'Jack O'Leary,' replied the woman who did not notice Kitty's pallor or the haunted look that had deepened the shadows around her eyes. 'You might remember him. He used to be the veterinarian here before he left for America.'

'We do remember him,' Elspeth cut in. 'I'm Mrs MacCartain and this is my sister Mrs Trench.'

'It's very nice to meet you,' said Emer O'Leary. 'I'm having a hat made in the most beautiful blue. Mrs O'Leary, Loretta, is a cousin of my husband.' She turned to the milliner with a grin. 'Well, she is now that she's married his cousin Séamus.' She glanced outside. 'Ah, there's my husband. I'd better be

going or he'll get impatient. He's not very keen on shopping.'
With that she thanked her cousin and left the shop. The
little bell gave a tinkle as the door opened and then closed
behind her.

'So you married Séamus O'Leary,' said Elspeth to the
milliner. While the two women chatted Kitty got up and
moved slowly to the window. She peered through the glass
with trepidation, holding the hat she had just been trying
on so tightly that her knuckles went white. There, standing
a few yards away, was Jack. Jack O'Leary. *Her* Jack. He was
bending his head to listen to what his wife was telling him
and there was an intimacy in the way they stood, with their
bodies touching, that caused something in Kitty's heart to
snag.

Jack looked just the same. The years had been kind. His
hair, although mostly hidden beneath a cap, was curling at
his neck and at the temples greying a little, as was his beard,
which was not so thick that it covered the strong line of his
jaw or detracted from the angular line of his cheekbones. He
was even more handsome with age. Then, as if by default,
the pull of her gaze attracted his and those eyes, which
were so familiar, so *deeply* familiar, locked into hers. With
a flush of surprise he stared at *her* staring at *him* through the
shop window and the world around them stilled. Kitty's
lips parted and she gasped. Suddenly the hand that held the
roots of her heart pulled down hard and Kitty remembered
with a painful jolt her love and her sorrow in an excruciating recall of memory. In that short but seemingly endless
moment, the years that had grown up between them fell
away. Kitty searched for the silent communication in his
gaze that had always been there; the wordless understanding
of two people who knew each other's thoughts, who were

forever linked. But the world began to move again with a jerk and Jack pulled his eyes away. He put his hand around his wife's waist and led her up the street without a backwards glance. Kitty pressed her palm to her chest and suppressed the impulse to sob.

'Are you all right?' Elspeth asked, trying to see what her sister was looking at through the window.

'I'm feeling a little unwell suddenly,' Kitty whispered. 'I want to go home.' *I want to be alone,* she thought unhappily. *I want to throw myself beneath the quilt and cry into my pillow. Jack is back. Jack is back and he is married. God help me to endure this because I cannot endure it on my own.*

Elspeth accompanied Kitty out of the shop and helped her into the car. Kitty searched the street for Jack, frightened of seeing him again and yet wanting to so badly that her whole body ached. 'What is it, Kitty?' Elspeth asked again. But Kitty was used to lying and dissembling – the War of Independence had taught her to be a master of deceit – so she gave her sister a reassuring smile and replied that she hadn't eaten that morning, which had made her feel faint.

'We'll come back,' said Elspeth, putting her foot down and speeding out of the town. 'I have my eye on that plum-coloured hat.'

Chapter 5

London

Mrs Goodwin and Martha arrived in England on a rainy morning after a turbulent passage across the Irish Sea. They disembarked at Fishguard in Wales and travelled on the 'boat train' to Paddington Station in London. Martha had gazed out of the window of the train at the bleak English countryside, and wondered where on earth Wordsworth had got his inspiration from, for surely his poetry wasn't about this dull and sodden land? Mrs Goodwin had told her that when the sun shone there was no place more beautiful than England, but to Martha it just looked desolate. The hills were a dismal, dreary green, the forests dark and damp and shivering beneath foggy clouds. Hamlets nestled in the valleys, the smoke from their chimneys wafting cheerlessly into the mist, and on the hillsides sheep huddled together against the gale, their woolly coats a dirty off-white colour like the sky. Martha's thoughts were drawn back to Ireland, whose emerald hills seemed to have a deep and tender charm, even in the middle of winter. It didn't occur to her that Ireland's beauty was rendered all the more arresting because of JP Deverill's attachment to it. In any case, she longed to return. She did not want to be in London at all.

Mrs Goodwin's brother, Professor Stephen Partridge, was an historian who had taught at Cambridge University for thirty years before retiring and writing large, indigestible tomes on eighteenth-century France. He was only too happy to welcome his sister back from America and to meet her young charge, about whom he had read a great deal in his sister's regular letters home.

Professor Partridge was tall and thin like a reed with a balding head of grey hair, a pair of round glasses and a tidy grey moustache, which sat pertly above his vanishing top lip. He had never married and preferred his own company, leading a solitary life of books, which were his greatest pleasure. However, he had a couple of spare bedrooms and a maid who came daily to clean and cook and wash and iron, so his sister and Martha were no imposition, as long as they didn't stay too long. A couple of weeks would be more than enough. He wouldn't mind his routine being disturbed for a short and finite period. He trusted his sister to be sensitive to his need for solitude.

Martha was astonished by Mrs Goodwin's brother. She had imagined someone warmer, softer, more cheerful and much less austere. Goodwin was a cosy, maternal woman. Her brother was quite the opposite. He was stiff, dry like an old bone and brittle. His three-piece suit was clean and pressed, his shoes were polished and *he* seemed clean, pressed and polished in them. 'Welcome to my humble abode,' he said in a high voice that surprised Martha, for she had expected it to be much lower. His English accent was more pronounced than Mrs Goodwin's and his reserve more acute.

Martha had told Mrs Goodwin to explain her situation to her brother in private. She didn't think she could discuss it without getting emotional and she was loath to break down in front of a stranger. Judging by her first impression of Professor Partridge, she didn't think he'd be comfortable with a weeping woman. So, while Mrs Goodwin and her brother drank tea in the parlour, in front of a tidy fire, Martha sat at the little writing desk in her bedroom and wrote two letters. One to her parents to let them know that she was safe and well in London and the other to JP.

10 Ormonde Gate, Chelsea, London

Dear JP

I hope this finds you well. I have just arrived in London and my first impressions are nothing like as delightful as my first impressions of Dublin, but perhaps that is because I don't have the advantage of a good guide. It is raining, which Goodwin tells me is perfectly normal. I so enjoyed our day together in Dublin. I think it could have drizzled to its heart's content and we would still have found the sunshine in each other. You made it fun, JP, and for a girl enjoying her first taste of freedom far from home I am truly grateful.

I am staying with Mrs Goodwin's brother, Professor Stephen Partridge.

I send you my fond wishes
Martha

Martha read the letter more times than she could count. She did not want to come across as forward and yet at the same time she did not want to be too formal. They had shared something special in Dublin and she wanted JP to know how deeply it had affected her. She wished that he had written first, but that was impossible given that he did not know her address. Therefore, she had been left no choice but to put pen to paper and hope that she hadn't misread his feelings.

When she had finished, she went downstairs for supper. Mrs Goodwin was still talking to her brother in the parlour. Mrs Hancock, the maid, had put another log on the fire and taken away the tea tray. Mrs Goodwin was now drinking a small glass of sherry while Professor Partridge was enjoying what looked like a glass of brandy. Martha sat on the sofa and answered questions about her home in Connecticut, when Mrs Goodwin *allowed* her to answer. So excited was she to be showing Martha off to her brother that she frequently interrupted before Martha could speak, jumping in with elaborate descriptions of their life in America. Professor Partridge did not mention Martha's present predicament. It was only when they retired to bed after supper that Mrs Goodwin told her that she had discussed the matter with her brother and he had suggested they call on an acquaintance of his, a certain Lady Gershaw, who lived in Mayfair and knew 'everyone who was anyone', which would most certainly include a titled lady such as Martha's birth mother. 'We're getting closer,' said Mrs Goodwin with a smile. 'I'm feeling very positive about the whole situation.'

Martha was hopeful, albeit anxious that her expectations might not be met. She had imagined the reunion a thousand times. There were countless reasons why the mission might go wrong and Martha did not want to dwell on any one of them. But now that they were close to finding out who her real mother was, those reasons rose to the surface of her mind like little pins to pop the bubbles of fantasy there. 'Thank you, Goodwin. You are too good to me.' She embraced her tearfully. 'I don't know what I'd do without you. You've been my most loyal friend all through my life. I'm lucky to have you.'

Mrs Goodwin was so touched that she squeezed her lips tightly to hold back her emotions and embraced Martha in return. 'Whatever happens, Martha my dear, don't forget that you have a loving family back home in Connecticut. I don't blame you for wanting to find out who brought you into the world, and for all I know she might be looking for you too, but it's Mrs Wallace who has loved you and cared for you from the moment she held you. That's what being a mother is about.'

'I won't forget,' said Martha. 'But I won't rest until I know why my birth mother gave me away. Why she didn't want me. Why she couldn't keep me.'

The following morning the two women took the bus to Mayfair. The professor had telephoned ahead and Lady Gershaw had invited Mrs Goodwin and Martha for a cup of tea at eleven. They had devised a plan, because of course they could not reveal the real reason why Martha wanted to find Lady Rowan-Hampton. They were confident that their plan would be sufficient for Lady Gershaw to help them find her.

Lady Gershaw lived in a palatial white house a few streets away from Hyde Park. The two women climbed the wide steps leading up to large double doors with big brass door knobs and a heavy brass knocker and rang the bell. A moment later a butler in a pristine tailcoat and starched white shirt opened the door and peered at them. He looked from Mrs Goodwin to Martha and then said, in the accent of the King, 'Lady Gershaw is expecting you.' He invited them into the hall and led them across the shining floor to a grand and elegant sitting room, warm from the glow of a hearty fire. 'Lady Gershaw will be with you shortly,' he said and left them alone.

Martha was wringing her hands nervously until Mrs Goodwin stopped her by placing her own hand on top. 'You don't need to be nervous, my dear. Stephen speaks highly of Lady Gershaw.'

'I'm not nervous about *her*, Goodwin, but about what she might tell me.'

Just as Mrs Goodwin was about to reassure her again, a short, rotund woman of about sixty, with a cheerful round face, bright green eyes and a wide, confident smile strode into the room in a pair of sensible brown lace-up shoes and tweed suit, followed by three small fox terriers. 'How lovely!' she exclaimed, putting out a hand. 'You must be Stephen's sister,' she said, looking directly at Mrs Goodwin.

'Yes, I am,' replied Mrs Goodwin, shaking her soft, pudgy hand. 'And this is Martha Wallace, my charge from Connecticut.'

'Welcome, my dear,' said Lady Gershaw fruitily. 'Please, do sit down. Amy is going to bring us tea. I hope you like tea?' She turned to Martha and raised her eyebrows.

'Oh yes, I do, Lady Gershaw, thank you.' Martha waited for Mrs Goodwin to sit down on the sofa before taking the place beside her. Lady Gershaw chose one of the armchairs and the terriers, after sniffing the two guests with prodding, curious snouts, settled on the rug at their mistress's feet.

'I don't suppose Stephen has told you why we are friends?' Lady Gershaw said with a mischievous smile. 'Well, let me tell you. I wrote to him out of the blue, because I adore his work. You see, I'm an avid reader and history is my passion. I'm an admirer. That's how we met!' She shook her grey curls. 'Isn't that funny? I bet you couldn't have guessed.'

'No,' said Mrs Goodwin, genuinely surprised. 'I would *never* have guessed.'

'Professor Partridge wrote back to me. So sweet of him to bother and I wasted no time in responding. You see, I'm a persistent woman,' Lady Gershaw said with a coquettish grin. 'And I usually get what I want. In this case, I invited the Professor to tea, rather like we are meeting today, and, bless him, he came. I gather he is something of a recluse, but I did write an extraordinarily good letter. We discussed his work for much of the morning and *that* is how our friendship began. *He* is the teacher and *I* am the pupil and he is so fascinating, I could listen to him for days! I only wish I was able to drag him away from his books more often, but if I did, *I* would be the loser, for I'd have to wait even longer to read his work.' Martha controlled the smile that was about to break out on her face for it was clear that Lady Gershaw was in love with Mrs Goodwin's brother. Martha was certain that her ardour was not reciprocated. Professor Partridge did not seem like a man much interested in women. He seemed like a man who was only interested in books.

'So, you are his sister, Mrs Goodwin. Do tell me what it was like growing up with Stephen. Have you always been close?' Mrs Goodwin satisfied their hostess with stories from her childhood, while they sipped the tea the maid had brought in and ate the biscuits without noticing the three pairs of eyes that watched them greedily from the rug at Lady Gershaw's feet.

Martha wondered whether they would ever get around

to finding out whether Lady Gershaw knew of Lady Rowan-Hampton. Lady Gershaw was so gripped by Mrs Goodwin's stories it was as if Martha was not in the room. At last, when the old lady drew breath, Lady Gershaw turned to Martha.

'My dear, how long will you be staying in London?'

'I'm really not sure. I'd like to see as much of it as I can,' she said vaguely.

'You must go to the theatre, and the museums are wonderful. London is a treasure chest of delights. I only wish the sun would shine for you.'

'Lady Gershaw,' Mrs Goodwin interrupted, aware of Martha's growing impatience. 'I have a favour to ask you.'

Lady Gershaw was so enjoying talking to Professor Partridge's sister that she was prepared to do anything Mrs Goodwin requested of her. 'Please, tell me, what can I do for you?'

'Many years ago I worked for a family who introduced me to a certain Lady Rowan-Hampton, Grace Rowan-Hampton. She gave me something of value and now that I'm in England I would very much like to give it back to her. Might you know who she is and where I might find her?'

Martha's heart was beating very loudly now, pounding against her ribcage like a drumstick. She began to pick her nails and bite her lower lip, but Lady Gershaw was not looking at her. She was looking at Mrs Goodwin with a wide smile, delighted that she was in a position to help Professor Partridge's sister – delighted that she could boast of her wide and illustrious connections. 'My dear Mrs Goodwin,' she gushed. 'I know Grace Rowan-Hampton very well. She lives not far from here. However, she is not in London at present. She spends most of her time in Ireland.'

'Ireland?' repeated Mrs Goodwin. Martha's cheeks glowed red.

'Yes, she and her husband Sir Ronald have a house in Co. Cork. Ronald travels so much but Grace prefers to be there. She has a lovely house in a small town called Ballinakelly.' At the mention of JP's home town Martha's whole face flushed. She stared at Lady Gershaw over her teacup, afraid to put it down in case she dropped it.

'How very strange,' said Mrs Goodwin, with forced calmness. 'We were only just in Dublin and met a man and his son who live in Ballinakelly.'

'And who might they be? I bet I know them,' said Lady Gershaw and it was clear to Martha that this was a woman who made it her business to know everyone.

'Lord Deverill,' Mrs Goodwin replied.

'Bertie Deverill,' Lady Gershaw exclaimed happily. 'What a coincidence! Why ever did you not ask *him*?'

'I didn't think of it,' said Mrs Goodwin truthfully. 'I never thought for one moment that they would know each other. I never imagined that Lady Rowan-Hampton would live in Ireland.'

'*Know* each other? Why, they are the very best of friends.' She pulled a face to suggest that she was keeping a monumental secret and that it was all she could do not to divulge it. '*Very* best of friends,' she repeated with emphasis. Martha realized that her jaw was hanging open and swiftly closed it. 'Would you like me to arrange for you to meet her?' Lady Gershaw asked.

Mrs Goodwin glanced at Martha who was staring at Lady Gershaw with eyes so wide it was alarming. 'No, really, you're much too kind. Next time I am in Ireland I will pay her a visit.'

'She will be in London in the spring. She always returns for the Season and to see her sons, of course. You know all three are married with children?'

'No, I didn't know she had children,' said Mrs Goodwin.

'They don't much like Ireland. Ever since the Troubles they have lived here. I imagine the company is more exciting for young people in a vibrant, cosmopolitan city like London.'

'Of course,' Mrs Goodwin agreed.

'Do allow me to invite you all for dinner,' Lady Gershaw said in a sudden flourish of inspiration. 'I know Stephen rarely goes out but really, he should be more generous with his brilliant mind and share it with us lesser-gifted folk. Allow me to host a dinner for you. How about next week. What do you say?'

Mrs Goodwin was a little embarrassed. It didn't seem correct that an aristocratic lady such as Lady Gershaw should host a dinner for a woman who was of no social standing, even if she happened to be the sister of someone Lady Gershaw so greatly admired. But Mrs Goodwin had no choice but to accept. 'We'd be honoured, Lady Gershaw,' she replied.

'Good, that's settled then,' said Lady Gershaw with satisfaction. 'I will put together a small group of people you will like. Martha dear, how old are you?'

'Seventeen,' she replied.

Lady Gershaw narrowed her eyes. 'I might recruit a couple of young gentlemen for you. Tell me, what does your father do?'

Mrs Goodwin was so relieved that Lady Gershaw had asked a question to which the answer was going to be entirely to her approval that she jumped in and spoke on Martha's behalf. 'Mr Wallace is in the Foreign Service. He's one of the most well-connected men in Connecticut. Of course, the Wallace family is a very respectable, very distinguished *old* family . . .' Martha squirmed uneasily on the sofa but Lady Gershaw's eyes were gleaming.

As they left the house half an hour later, Lady Gershaw stood at the top of the steps and waved. When they were safely out of earshot Martha exploded. 'Goodwin, my mother is in Ireland. She lives in Ballinakelly, near the Deverills. Can you believe the coincidence? It's too much! We should have mentioned her to JP and saved ourselves the trouble of travelling all the way to London.'

'I'm astonished,' Mrs Goodwin agreed. 'It's extraordinary.'

'We must go to Ireland at once.'

'Not before we have dinner with Lady Gershaw.'

'But that's next week! Do we really have to?' Martha complained.

'My dear, we owe her everything. Thanks to her you might be reunited with your mother, after all.'

'She has three sons,' said Martha thoughtfully. 'Do you think she might be pleased to discover that she also has a daughter?'

'I don't know. She might not welcome you turning up out of the past. Remember she is married and has a family. She's a respectable member of the aristocracy. She'll have a reputation to uphold. Until we meet her there's no telling what sort of woman she is.'

'I think she's going to be happy, Goodwin. I can feel it,' said Martha with a shiver of excitement. 'And to think I'm going to see JP again! It's too wonderful. Come, let's not take the bus. Let's walk through the park and find somewhere nice to have lunch. I don't care that it's raining. Everything is going to turn out well. I just know it is.'

Mrs Goodwin followed after her, wondering how she was going to break it to her brother that he was going to have to have dinner with Lady Gershaw.

Chapter 6

Ballinakelly

Old Mrs Nagle was buried in the graveyard outside the Catholic church of All Saints and Sean and Rosetta moved into the east wing of the castle with their five children. As one era ended another was beginning. Bridie was grateful for Rosetta's company because Cesare spent little time at home. She didn't know where he went and she knew not to ask. The first time she had asked, not long after their wedding, he had answered that he had business to see to; although what business it was she couldn't imagine for Cesare was a pleasure-seeker with little money of his own and no interest in commerce. The second time she had enquired, he had snapped impatiently, 'Does a man have to explain where he goes to his wife?' and Bridie had been stung for he had never spoken to her like that *before* they were married. He had looked at her with an imperious expression and his beautiful green eyes had darkened with indignation and Bridie had been cowed. She hadn't seen that side of his character before and it had alarmed her.

Contrary to her expectations Cesare never took her to Buenos Aires as he had promised and she had never met his family. When she asked him about it he waved his hands in the air as if trying to clear away an unpleasant smell. 'My treasure, there is time enough for everything. I will introduce you to my family when the time is right.' But it never was.

Over the years that followed, Cesare had revealed himself to be a masterful, domineering and selfish husband, but Bridie loved him in spite of his faults. The very qualities that might have repelled another woman drew Bridie closer to him because his authority made her feel safe.

Rosetta, on the other hand, was more circumspect and she was not blinded, as Bridie was, by love. Yes, Cesare was undoubtedly blessed with beauty, and his charm, when he chose to be charming, was irresistible, but very quickly after meeting him Rosetta suspected that the man behind the mask was simply another man wearing a mask. There was something unknowable about him, as if he was made of many elaborate layers, and yet each seemingly substantial layer was paper thin and might at any moment disintegrate if touched. There was also something sly, which revealed itself in the moments when his face fell into repose, when he thought no one was looking, when he ceased to play a part. Then shadows would distort his features, that fine nose would look pointy, the full mouth petulant and his charm would fall away like fairy dust. He avoided going into any detail about his childhood in Italy and he avoided talking to Rosetta in their native tongue. However, the few sentences she had prised out of him had revealed something in the vowels that was neither Spanish nor Italian. It was something else besides, but Rosetta couldn't put her finger on what exactly it was. She was certain of one thing, however: she would never share her suspicions with Bridie because Bridie was blissfully happy in ignorance.

'Can I speak to you plainly,' said Bridie to Rosetta one afternoon not long after her Italian friend had moved into the castle. They were upstairs in Bridie's sitting room that was situated next to her bedroom with an interconnecting door. It wasn't large and imposing like the reception rooms downstairs with their elaborate and extravagant decoration, nor was it masculine like the library where Cesare liked to sit and smoke. It was small with two sofas and two armchairs arranged around a fireplace. Tall windows looked out over the garden and were framed by green-and-pink curtains that broke onto the rug, matching the green-and-pink floral wallpaper. It was the only room in the entire castle where Bridie felt comfortable. The rest of the place made her uneasy. It was much too grand and held too many memories she would rather not confront.

'Cesare wants me to entertain lavishly,' she said. 'But I don't know who to invite.' Bridie stood up and walked to the fireplace. She put her hand on the mantelpiece and stared into the flames. 'I'm neither fish nor fowl, Rosetta.'

Rosetta frowned. 'What do you mean?'

Bridie turned round with a sigh and Rosetta saw that her eyes were glistening with tears. 'I grew up in a farmhouse but I'm not that girl any longer because I'm a countess in a castle. But I'm not from that world either, the world of counts and countesses and castles. I fall somewhere between the two, but I don't know where that is. The Anglo-Irish who used to come here in droves won't come near *me*. They despise me for having bought the castle, which in their opinion should belong to a Deverill, and I'm a working-class Catholic, beneath them in every way. Then there are the upper-class Catholics who look down their noses at me because I'm not from their world either. The working-class farmers I grew up with are now suspicious of me and Cesare doesn't want to mix with the likes of them because they're ill-educated and unsophisticated and he's right. He's much too good for them. So, you see, I have no one to invite, and Cesare . . .' She took a staggered breath, suddenly overcome with emotion. 'Cesare wants me to fill the castle with people. He wants me to entertain like Lady Deverill used to do, but he doesn't realize that I can't. I don't know anyone. In New York I could be someone different. I could reinvent myself. But here I'll always be Bridie Doyle and the limitations imposed upon a girl like her will never change. Bridie Doyle should have married a farmer's son and raised a family in Ballinakelly. What am I going to do?' She began to cry.

Rosetta was sympathetic. 'I'm a simple girl from New York, Bridie. I don't know what you should do either.'

Bridie sat beside her on the sofa and her shoulders sagged in defeat. 'I don't want to be a disappointment to Cesare,' she said in a small voice and Rosetta had to fight the fury that rose in her because Cesare had turned her friend, who had once been so courageous and bold, into a coward.

Rosetta took her hand and squeezed it fiercely. 'You could never be a disappointment to anyone,' she said. 'Cesare is lucky to have you, don't ever think it is the other way round. You have a heart of gold, Bridie, and Cesare is lucky that you have given it to him. Just make sure you keep a little of it for yourself.' She had to bite her tongue to stop it from revealing what she *really* thought.

It wasn't long, however, before Bridie received her first visitor. To her surprise it was none other than Lady Rowan-Hampton, the very woman who had arranged her brief stay at the convent in Dublin and her subsequent passage to America; the very woman whom Bridie blamed for compelling her to leave behind her baby son. Bridie was so shocked when the butler announced Grace that she kept her visitor waiting for ten minutes in the drawing room while she composed herself upstairs in her little sitting room. She wished that Rosetta hadn't gone to visit her mother-in-law and that Cesare hadn't gone to play cards in O'Donovan's. She was obliged to entertain Lady Rowan-Hampton alone.

'My dear Bridie,' said Grace when Bridie appeared at last. The older woman held out her hands and Bridie was left no choice but to take them. She felt as if the castle didn't belong to her at all, but to this sophisticated, elegant lady who was so much more at ease than she was in this ostentatious drawing room. 'It is good to see you looking so well,' she said, running her soft brown eyes over Bridie's face. 'The years have been kind to you.'

'And to you, Lady Rowan-Hampton,' Bridie replied.

'Please, call me Grace. I should like us to be friends, Bridie. The past is water under the bridge. You are now mistress of this castle and a countess. You have been shrewd. I must say, when you left for America, I never imagined you would return in such style.'

Bridie didn't think she could ever be friends with a woman who had persuaded her to give up her child, who had arranged to send her to the other side of the world. But Cesare would be happy that she was entertaining a lady of importance, so she decided to let go her animosity and welcome Grace into her life as if she were a new friend. 'Please, do sit down,' she said. 'Would you like tea?'

'That would be lovely,' said Grace, settling into the sofa where she had so often sat when Adeline and Hubert had lived here. 'It's terribly cold and damp today.'

Bridie pulled a cord that rang a bell in the kitchen and a butler soon appeared in the doorway. Then she sat down opposite Grace and folded her hands in her lap. Bridie might have been mistress of the castle but it was Grace who led the conversation.

'I am sorry to hear that your grandmother passed away,' she said. 'Old Mrs Nagle was a sweet woman. I had the pleasure of meeting her when I used to visit your mother.'

'You used to visit my mother?' Bridie asked.

'Yes, I feel very at home in the Doyle kitchen.'

Bridie assumed that she had visited her mother out of charity. 'How kind of you to take the trouble,' she said.

Grace waved a hand dismissively. 'It was nothing but a pleasure. I gather she won't be coming to live with you.'

'No,' said Bridie. 'She won't leave the house she used to share with my father.'

'Ah well, that's understandable. And Michael?' Grace bit her bottom lip.

'He has chosen to stay with her.'

Grace shook her head and sighed, as if awed by the admirable qualities of the man. 'He's a good son. Truly he is.'

'I don't think he'd feel right about coming to live here,' she said and Grace understood that Bridie was referring to his bitter hatred for the British. Bridie wouldn't have known that it was Michael who had burnt down the castle and had his wicked way with Kitty the following morning when she had stormed over to confront him. She didn't know either that Grace and Michael had been lovers or that Grace had bedded Cesare when he had come to Ireland to buy the castle. Grace watched Bridie like a snake watching a mouse and wondered how well she really knew her oldest brother and her husband.

'How does Michael get on with his new brother-in-law?' she asked and she betrayed nothing of her deeper interest.

'I would say they are cordial at best,' Bridie revealed before regretting her indiscretion. There was something in Grace's gaze that punctured holes in her, causing her to leak like a sieve. 'They like each other,' she said weakly, trying to make up for her blunder. But Grace had already seized upon such tantalizing information and was gobbling it up greedily.

'They are very different, of course,' she said. 'I had the pleasure of meeting the Count when he came over to look at the castle. I didn't realize then that he was your husband. It was a great surprise when the Countess's identity was revealed. Though, there are some who are not too happy about it.'

'Indeed, there are bound to be,' Bridie said quietly.

'Have you seen the Deverills?' Grace asked bluntly. Bridie blushed. She didn't want to think about Lord Deverill, or Kitty, or the fact that her son was only a few miles away and yet a stranger to her, which caused her terrible pain.

'No,' she replied curtly. 'I haven't and I don't see any reason why I should.' Grace saw the softness in Bridie harden as she drew her defences around her like a cloak of steel. 'If the Deverills hate me for having bought their home then they should look more closely at themselves and see the part they played in my fate. If Lord Deverill had been a gentleman I would never have been forced to leave Ballinakelly in the first place. *He* set the ball rolling and now it has landed here. Some would say he has got his just deserts.' Grace was stunned by the girl's defiance. She wasn't the lost child she had been when Bertie had sent her up to Dublin pregnant and afraid. She had been meek and compliant then. Now Grace could see the resentment that burned in her eyes and she dropped her gaze into her hands as she recalled *her* part in Bridie's fate.

Both women looked to the door with relief as Cesare strode in, bringing with him an air of self-importance and vanity. He wore a sports jacket with exaggeratedly broad shoulders, an open-neck shirt and wide grey trousers that were meticulously creased down the centre and cuffed at the bottom. He took off his flat cap when he saw the ladies and raked his black hair off his forehead with strong fingers. Grace's face beamed with pleasure. Bridie looked down at her hands and found that they were shaking. 'What an unexpected pleasure,' he said, taking Grace's hand and bringing it to his lips. His heavy eyes looked at her knowingly and Grace felt a frisson of excitement hurtle through her limbs as he was so clearly recalling those nights of pleasure they had shared in her bed – and *she* recalled them too and the blood scalded her cheeks.

'My darling,' he said to his wife and Grace withdrew her hand, afraid that he might have given them away by looking at her like that. But Bridie seemed unaware of the tremor that vibrated in the air between them. 'Grace was a most generous hostess when I first visited Ballinakelly,' he told her. 'I was without a friend and this delightful lady took me under her wing and introduced me to her friends.'

'Which I will gladly do again,' Grace offered.

Cesare settled into an armchair and crossed one leg over the other, revealing brown-and-white two-tone shoes and brown socks. He had brought the glamour of America to Ballinakelly, Grace thought with admiration. 'I want to fill the castle with people. I want to entertain lavishly. In America we were the toast of New York. I do not want to die of boredom down here in Co. Cork.' He smiled, baring his big white teeth, but Grace, ever sensitive to the hidden currents that moved people, detected a sliver of a threat beneath his boasting. She was quite certain that if he didn't get what he wanted in Ballinakelly he would think nothing of hot-footing it back to Manhattan.

'Allow me to help you,' she said, turning to Bridie. 'I will be your guide in this matter. We must spread our net wider than Ballinakelly, for this is Deverill territory and you won't find many friends here.' Grace knitted her fingers and considered the Catholic world in Dublin that she had secretly penetrated and courted while converting. 'I know just the people to entertain you,' she said.

'Good. I want to host a ball,' Cesare rejoined. 'The biggest and grandest ball Castle Deverill has ever seen.' At the mention of a ball Bridie's heart lifted. With *her* wealth and Grace's help she would show the Deverills that a triumphant new era had indeed begun; an era that would outshine any before it in both glamour and grandeur. Uninvited, Lord Deverill and Kitty would be forced to watch the night's sky glowing above the castle with a thousand lights and realize that their destinies were entirely of their own making. As the Bible put it so beautifully: *Whatsoever a man soweth, that shall he also reap.*

After Grace's visit Bridie found the confidence to show her face in town. She went to Mass. The church of All Saints with its austere grey walls and soaring spire was the same as when she had been a child and Father Quinn had changed only in the greyness of his hair and skin and in his stoop. But Bridie *had* changed and now she sat in her finery in the front pew with Leopoldo and her dashing husband in his elegant brown suit and fur-trimmed coat. They were like a trio of golden pheasants next to moorhens for Michael and Mrs

Doyle, who shared their pew, looked sombre in their habitual black attire and Bridie knew that the only thing saving her from her mother's disapproval was Mrs Doyle's belief that Cesare was a papal count, a title granted by the Pope himself. Bridie had not enlightened her with the truth. Rosetta sat with Sean and their five children in the pew behind, aware that every eye in the church was trained on the Count and Countess who exuded an air of royalty, and the congregation was awed into silence.

Jack O'Leary took Emer's hand and smiled at her reassuringly. She smiled back from beneath the brim of the blue cloche hat that Jack's cousin Loretta had created for her. Jack looked into his wife's gentle face and kind eyes and tried to dispel the image of Kitty staring at him through the glass of the milliner's atelier which had haunted him ever since. He turned his attention to Father Quinn, who was directing his sermon at Bridie Doyle and her pompous-looking husband, and remembered creeping out of Bridie's bed without so much as a goodbye. What would she make of him now that they were once again thrown together?

Jack watched Bridie's hat move as she turned to whisper something to her son and knew that her occupation of Castle Deverill was the stuff of Kitty's nightmares. *Kitty Kitty Kitty* – he angrily rejected her name once again and tried to concentrate on the sermon.

Emer knew nothing of his life before they met. It wasn't that she was naïve. Her own father had been involved in criminal activity in New York and she knew that the work her husband had done for the Italian gangs was just as unsavoury. She knew too that Jack had been hired by the Mafia boss Salvatore Maranzano to deal with his rival 'Lucky'

Luciano and that the plot had been foiled, for they had fled to Argentina and lived in hiding for almost eight years before Jack had deemed it safe enough to start afresh in Ballinakelly. She knew too of the bounty on his head, of the gun he kept beneath his pillow and of the constant fear that someone would show up out of the past to claim that bounty.

But Emer knew nothing of his love for Kitty or his brief encounter with Bridie. She had already settled into life in Ballinakelly as if there had always been an Emer-shaped space waiting just for her. She had been embraced by Jack's large family of siblings and cousins and by his mother Julia, whose happiness was complete now that her son and grandchildren had come home at last. Everyone loved Emer on sight and the small community welcomed her into their midst as if she were already one of them, and they clamoured to raise their glasses in toasts to Jack as if he were a conquering hero.

When Mass was over everyone made their way outside to chat in the sunshine. Cesare escorted Mrs Doyle, who took his arm gladly and tried not to succumb to pride, while Michael walked with Bridie and Leopoldo. Behind them Rosetta and Sean followed with their children. Outside, Jack waited for Bridie to see him, but Michael saw him first. His face showed surprise as he spotted him through the crowd even though word had already reached him that Jack O'Leary was back in town with a wife and three children in tow. The last time the two men had met had been nearly fifteen years before on the track from Ballinakelly to the Doyle farmhouse. Driven into a blinding rage after having learned that Michael had betrayed him to the Royal Irish Constabulary, Jack had lain in wait for him in the darkness and the two men had fought almost to the death. That was before Michael had gone to Mount Melleray Abbey. Before he had sobered up and been forgiven of his sins. Now he was a respectable man of piety. He shifted his black eyes and Jack saw nothing of the jealousy that simmered behind them as once again the image of Kitty Deverill rose up between them like a ghost.

Then, as Bridie walked down the path towards the road, she saw him too. Her lips parted and her face paled and her eyes hid nothing of the hurt he had inflicted. For a long moment they stared at one another and it was as if she were walking through tar, slowly and laboriously, and getting nowhere. But it was Jack who dropped his gaze, out of shame for the callous way he had behaved, and Bridie lifted her chin and walked on.

Bridie did not wish to linger outside the church and quickened her pace, but Julia O'Leary had other plans. Ever since her late husband had told her the story of the first Lord Deverill of Ballinakelly building his castle on O'Leary land she had despised the Deverills. She knew, as only a mother could, about the way Kitty Deverill had tortured her son, playing with his heart like a cat with a ball of string, and she was determined to see that the woman came nowhere near Jack now that he was back. As she strode up to Bridie she couldn't help but notice the handsome little boy by her side who looked like he was the same age as Liam, Jack and Emer's boy, and only a little younger than their eldest daughter Alana.

'Bridie,' she said, her voice stopping Bridie in her tracks.

Bridie turned and knew that it would be impolite not to greet Mrs O'Leary, whom she had known as a child. 'Hello, Mrs O'Leary,' she said.

'Julia, please. We're old family friends. I was hoping to

see you today. I wanted to tell you that I know that your grandmother died and I'm sorry for your loss,' she said and Bridie was grateful for her compassion.

'Thank you, Mrs O'Leary,' she replied, emphasizing that she did not wish to be familiar.

'I can see her now in her chair by the fire, smoking her clay pipe.'

'I miss her,' said Bridie, but more than that she missed what the old woman had represented: a past that Bridie could never get back.

'I know you do, dear. When my Liam died it was as if someone had scooped out my heart with a spoon.'

'Yes, I heard about that. I'm sorry too. He was a good man and a wise vet.'

'I don't like change, but everything changes nonetheless. Look at you, now, mistress of Castle Deverill.'

'I bought it to save it from strangers,' Bridie said, suddenly feeling the need to explain to this woman who had always considered the Doyles to be beneath her why the daughter of the cook should want to purchase a grand castle.

But Julia O'Leary did not seem to think less of her for it. 'You acted wisely,' she said. 'It's heart-warming to know that that beautiful home is in the hands of someone who understands it; after all, you and your mother practically lived there. I'm proud of you, Bridie. I'm proud of what you've achieved in your life. Most never leave their home town but you went to America and made something of yourself. You're a fine example and Ballinakelly is fortunate that you've chosen to come back.' Bridie was disarmed by Mrs O'Leary's warmth and was lost for words. 'Have you met my daughter-in-law, Emer? She and Jack have just come back from Buenos Aires. She's the same age as you, I suspect, and has three children who would make lovely playmates for your boy.'

Bridie put her hand on Leopoldo's shoulder. 'He's seven,' she said.

'The same age as little Liam,' said Julia. She beckoned Emer with a wave. 'You'll love Emer, everyone loves her. Not a mean bone in her body.'

Emer's smile was like balm to Bridie's soul. She didn't look her over with suspicion or dismiss her for being above herself, she simply greeted her politely and shook her hand as if Bridie had always been a countess. For a fleeting moment Bridie felt like she was back in New York again where people accepted her for who she was *now*. 'We are both newly arrived in Ballinakelly,' said Bridie.

'And I've fallen in love with it already,' Emer replied. 'I like the peace and quiet here. New York and Buenos Aires are big, noisy cities but Ballinakelly is small and I like living by the sea. The sea is in my bones. I don't think I'm going to miss those cities because in a way I've come home to my roots. My family are from Co. Wicklow, you see.'

'She's Irish to her marrow,' said Julia proudly. 'May we visit you up at the castle?' she asked. 'I never desired to see it when it belonged to the Deverills, but now you are mistress there I would be curious to see inside.'

'I think we must leave the Countess to settle into her home before we descend on her,' said Emer, embarrassed by her mother-in-law's lack of restraint.

'Not at all,' said Bridie, suddenly thrilled to be in demand again. 'You must bring your children. My brother Sean and his wife Rosetta have five. We can have a tea. It'll be fun and I'd be delighted to show you around the castle. I'm still getting to know my way around myself!'

'Hello, Bridie,' said Jack, stepping in beside his wife.

'Hello, Jack,' said Bridie, lifting her chin. There was an awkward silence before Jack's mother broke it with another attempt to reinvent the past.

'Our families were so close, Emer. Jack and Bridie used to play together all the time as children.'

'Jack always loved animals,' said Bridie.

'Bridie was afraid of insects,' he said.

'Hairy mollies especially,' Bridie added.

'And rats.'

'No one likes rats,' said Bridie.

'Jack does,' interjected Emer with a laugh and they all laughed with her for Emer had the gift of radiating light into the darkest places. 'Isn't it nice that we've all come to live here at the same time?' she added, turning to her husband.

'It's grand,' said Jack. 'You've done well for yourself, Bridie.'

Bridie frowned for she didn't expect Jack's support, but then she remembered that Kitty had betrayed him and she smiled, hoping he would see the forgiveness in it, for Kitty was her enemy and, by all accounts, it appeared that she was Jack's enemy too. 'Why don't you all come for tea?' she suggested happily. 'I must tell you about our plans for a magnificent summer ball . . .'

Chapter Seven

Ever since Kitty had seen Jack O'Leary through the window of the milliner's shop she had been in a state of deep anguish, for never had she imagined that he would come home. She had finally managed to move on, finally found contentment with Robert, JP and Florence, finally learned to live without him. How she wished he were still in America where she could manipulate his image to her will. But he was here, now, in Ballinakelly, and he belonged to someone else.

Kitty hated herself for despising his wife and yet she couldn't help it. The fact that the woman possessed the serenity of someone whose happiness is complete made her despise her all the more. It made no difference to Kitty that it had been *her* choice not to run away with him to America, to stay with her husband, to have a child with him. It made no difference at all. She knew her arguments were irrational and yet she felt as if Jack had grabbed her by the heart that morning in Ballinakelly – and his hand was as cold and hard as his eyes had been.

Kitty moved about the house in a trance, barely hearing the demands of her daughter Florence or her husband's conversation at the dinner table. She could scarcely swallow her food for the tightness in her throat and she awoke in the middle of the night with her pillow damp with tears. How was she going to cope with Jack living in Ballinakelly? How could she pretend that everything was fine when Jack's fingers were squeezing the life out of her heart? She didn't think she had the energy for charades any more. She would simply have to stop going into town. She would remain in the house as much as possible and hope that by hiding out here she could avoid bumping into him.

Robert noticed his wife's wretchedness at once and assumed it was a reaction to the Countess di Marcantonio moving into the castle; after all, Kitty had been in a high state of agitation since hearing the news. But he was wrong. For the first time ever Kitty's feelings for Castle Deverill were overshadowed. Bridie's arrival paled in the light of Jack's return, and she laughed bitterly at the fuss she had made. All her life the castle had come first. Perhaps *that* had been her gravest mistake.

Robert was losing patience. He loved Kitty for her passionate nature, for the fact that she felt things deeply and visibly, but he had endured her fixation with the castle for too many years now and what had at first been charming and romantic was becoming tedious. Naturally she had suffered when much of the building had been destroyed by fire during the Troubles and later when her cousin Celia had bought it and rebuilt it – and Robert had been quick to lend her his sympathy and support. Indeed, he hadn't complained when she had talked of nothing else, when her distress had consumed her – when it had consumed them all. He had had the forbearance of a saint. But after Archie's suicide and Celia's decision to sell the castle, Kitty should have had the wisdom to let it go. She had a family to think about and a home of her own to run. Her attachment to her old home had turned into an obsession, Robert thought, and it was bad for her health and bad for their marriage. He decided he would allow it to continue for another week or so and then, if it hadn't abated, he would have words.

When JP received Martha's letter he thrust it into his pocket excitedly, saddled his horse and galloped up to the Fairy Ring. He tied his mare to a tree and sat on one of the smaller boulders which were scattered near the ring of much larger, monolithic stones. There, with the sea crashing against the rocks below him and the sky above a clear, icy blue, he pulled the letter out of the envelope and began to read it. As his eyes ran over the neat handwriting, his happiness swelled; she hadn't forgotten him. He pressed the paper against his heart and turned to face the wind. This was undoubtedly love! *This* was what poets tried to put into words; he knew now that their words fell short.

JP resolved to write back at once, to the address stated in the letter, and tell her that he would go to London, under the pretext of visiting his uncle Harry, as soon as he received word from her that she would wait for him. He could barely conceal his impatience to see her again. He raised his eyes to the sky and noticed a thick wall of cloud making its way in over the water. Closing his eyes he could feel a light drizzle on his skin. He didn't care about a little rain, or even a storm, for his spirit was warm with the memory of Martha's smile and the touch of her hand in his.

Alana O'Leary was ten years old, but, being the eldest of Jack and Emer's children, she appeared older. She was innately wise, opinionated, responsible and fiercely independent. Born in America and then raised in Argentina, where she had learned to speak Spanish like a native, Alana had been given the gifts of a broad mind and self-confidence. Her accent was hard to place, being a mixture of the three influences in her life: American-English, Irish and Spanish, and her character, shaped by years of living in two different cultures, was considered a little eccentric by the insulated children of Ballinakelly. But Alana relished being different. Where other children might have shrunk from those differences, Alana took her pleasure. Her parents had brought her up to be proud of who she was.

With her mother's fair hair and her father's pale blue eyes Alana was already striking. There was a vitality that shone through her features which separated her from the rest. She seemed more alert than other children, more curious and more daring, going wherever that curiosity took her, especially if it was into the unknown. The one thing she loved more than anything else, and which Co. Cork had in abundance, was countryside. Alana adored the sea, the rivers and streams, the thick forests and long grasses of Ireland and the host of creatures in it. It was all she could do to restrain herself and sit quietly at her desk in class while nature beckoned to her in whispers that were carried into the classroom on the salty breeze.

So, one morning she climbed the stone wall at the back of the schoolhouse, tearing the skirt of her blue dress on one of the flints, and ran down the narrow back streets of Ballinakelly and out towards the hills. The sky shone a cerulean blue and gulls wheeled beneath it, the tips of their white wings catching the winter sun and glinting. With her heart overflowing with joy Alana left the track and bounded along a path that cut through the heather until the schoolhouse and the nuns who taught there were far behind her. When she was sure she wasn't going to be caught she slowed her pace to a walk. With only her cardigan to keep her warm and leather boots to keep her feet dry, she began to relish her freedom without giving a thought to the cold February air and the heavy clouds making their way slowly inland.

The path led into the hills and Alana skipped along it, gazing around her in wonder. There were sheep grazing among the rocks and birds chirruping in the bushes. She noticed a pair of tawny hares that hopped off when she tried to approach them and the flash of a fox's tail as it disappeared behind the crest of a knoll. When she spotted a cat hunting in the long grass she followed it, straying off the path and wandering deeper into the wildness. At length she found a stream and knelt beside it, cupping her hands to drink the water there. She didn't notice that her dress was now stained with mud and that the ribbons had fallen out of her hair, for her adventure was wholly absorbing. She delighted in the trickling sound of the rivulet and in the distant roaring of the sea and when rain began to fall lightly onto her face she delighted in that too.

It wasn't until she began to feel cold that the adventure lost a little of its attraction. She looked for the way back to town but recognized nothing. There was no path, no track, only hills and fields and forests and the wind that was now blowing stronger as those grey clouds gathered ominously above her, darkening the sky. But Alana didn't feel afraid, only cross with herself for having got lost. She should have kept to the path, she thought, as she began to make her way down the slope, following the stream. Didn't all streams lead to the sea?

*

With Martha's letter folded into the inside pocket of his coat, pressed against his heart, JP walked his horse over the crest of the hill he knew so well. He'd ridden across this land, which had once belonged to his family, since he was a boy, and no other place on earth, in his opinion, was as beautiful. However, it seemed even more beautiful today in the light of Martha's letter. He glanced at the scudding clouds and blinked as the drizzle was blown onto his eyelashes, and yet there was beauty in its bleakness in spite of the darkening day. He took pleasure from the yellow gorse and large swathes of brown heather and stopped his horse to enjoy the moment. He'd bring Martha here one day, he resolved. He was certain that she'd love it like he did.

At that moment he saw a small figure in the distance, wandering slowly down the hill. He could see that it was a girl by her blue dress and long hair, and, by the unsteady way that she was walking, he sensed that she was in trouble. He squeezed his horse into a canter and made his way over the sodden ground towards her.

When Alana heard the sound of hooves she looked up and watched him approach. Too proud to let the stranger know that she was lost she lifted her chin and hid her relief behind a lofty gaze.

'Hello there,' he said, slowing down to a trot. Alana took a step back as the rider drew the horse to a halt. The horse snorted through big glistening nostrils and tossed its glossy mane. 'Are you all right?'

'Of course I'm all right,' Alana replied, sweeping her wet hair off her face with a muddy hand.

JP narrowed his eyes. He didn't recognize the child or her accent. She clearly wasn't from around here. 'Are you sure?' he persisted, for he could see that she was shivering. Suddenly aware of her appearance she glanced down at her torn and muddy dress, her waterlogged boots and dirty socks. 'What's your name?' he asked and when Alana looked at him again she noticed that he was smiling at her kindly.

'I was christened Rosaleen, but when I was little my mam called me Alana, which means "baby" in Gaelic, and everyone copied her. So I'm Alana, Alana O'Leary,' she replied.

He smiled in amusement at her long reply and at the confident way she had delivered it. 'Ah, you're an O'Leary, are you?' he said, his face creasing into a frown because she didn't sound like one.

'I've just arrived from Argentina,' Alana explained. 'My father used to be the veterinarian in Ballinakelly before moving to America. He's called Jack O'Leary.'

JP nodded, for he knew of Jack O'Leary. 'And what are you doing wandering the hills on your own? You don't even have a coat.'

Alana pulled at her cardigan for she felt suddenly shy in front of this stranger who didn't talk like the people she was used to. 'I forgot it. Anyway, it was sunny when I left the school.'

'I see,' he said, raising an eyebrow. 'You've run away from school, have you?'

Encouraged by his grin, which had more than a hint of mischief in it, she smiled and added, 'I don't like school.'

'I don't suppose anyone does. No one likes having to learn things. I was always much happier out here than inside, studying. But it's going to rain heavily soon, look at those clouds, and you're a long walk from Ballinakelly.' Alana looked forlornly into the valley. 'Do you realize you're walking the wrong way?' he said gently. She shook her head. 'If you continue walking *this* way you'll end up in Drimoleague.'

'I don't know Drimoleague.'

'Lovely place, but not for today.' JP dismounted and Alana was impressed by the ease with which he swung himself out of the saddle. She could see now that beneath the rim of his hat his eyes were a pale grey and very twinkly. He shrugged off his jacket. 'Put this on before you catch cold and I'll give you a ride home. You'll have to show me where you live.'

'I'm going to go on *that*?' she asked, looking up at the horse as he helped her into his jacket. It was much too big for her, nearly reaching her knees, but it was warm. She realized then how cold she was and shivered again.

'Have you never ridden?'

'No. Da rides horses but Ma is afraid of them.'

'You don't need to be afraid of Dervish, she's a gentle thing.' He put his hands beneath her arms. 'When I say jump, jump.' Before Alana had time to think she was being lifted into the saddle. The man handed her the reins then put his foot in the stirrup and swung himself up to sit behind her. 'Right,' he said, putting his arms around her to take the reins. 'You ready?' Slowly the horse made its way back up the hill. 'My name's JP Deverill: J for Jack, like your father, and P for Patrick, like the patron saint of Ireland. Your family and mine have been in Co. Cork for hundreds of years. Did you know that?'

'No.'

'How old are you, Alana?'

'Ten and a half,' she replied.

'Do you like Ireland?'

'I *love* Ireland,' she said and JP could tell from the enthusiasm in her voice that she truly did.

'Tell me, what was it like growing up in Argentina?'

She leaned back against his warm body and sighed. 'I lived

in America first. In New York. But I was only little when I left so I don't remember much about it. I remember our apartment and I remember the snow in winter. There was no snow in Buenos Aires and the sky was always blue. But I prefer Ireland. Do you know I saw a fox just now? Only the tail, but it was definitely a fox. I know all about animals because my father liked to tell me stories of when he was a veterinarian.'

JP let the child chatter on and was surprised by her maturity. She seemed older than her years. She wasn't shy in telling him about her life nor was she nervous about sitting on a horse. By the time they reached the town Alana had shared many of her experiences with JP and he had listened with amused interest, for she was a lively and unusual child.

With her torn and muddy dress Alana was in no condition to go back to school, so she directed JP to the house her father was renting while he looked for somewhere to build. It was whitewashed with a grey tiled roof and situated on the outskirts of town, a short distance from the sea. JP dismounted and then helped Alana down. 'Thank you for bringing me home,' she said. Then remembering that she was wearing his jacket, she took it off. 'I'm warm now,' she added, handing it back.

'Go and have a hot drink,' he suggested. 'And hope your mother doesn't send you back to school!'

As he was about to mount again the front door opened and a fair-haired woman with the same colouring as the girl stood in the doorway with a surprised look on her face. She swept her gaze over the ripped dress and dirty boots then looked at JP in bewilderment.

JP took off his hat, revealing a mop of red hair. 'I found your daughter wandering the hills like a fox,' he explained and when he grinned at Alana the child felt something respond with a leap in her belly.

'Wandering the hills?' said Emer O'Leary. 'Alana?'

'I don't like school,' the girl responded with a shrug. 'So I went in search of a different kind of education. Da would approve,' she added, glancing impishly at JP, knowing that her cheek would amuse him. JP was interested to see that it amused her mother too.

The corners of Emer's lips curled indulgently and she put her hands on her hips. 'Well, you'd better go in and clean up, hadn't you? I have company. Countess di Marcantonio is in the drawing room, so when you are presentable you can come and say hello.' Then she turned to JP. 'How can I thank you?'

'JP Deverill,' he said, extending his hand. Emer shook it and felt a blush flourish on her cheeks for the young man was very attractive.

'Mrs O'Leary,' she replied, and then felt a little silly because she was sure that Alana had already introduced herself. 'Are you sure you wouldn't like a drink? It's cold and wet out here and we have a boisterous fire in the drawing room and a fresh pot of tea. Have you met the Countess?'

'I haven't had the pleasure,' JP replied. He would have enjoyed meeting the infamous Countess di Marcantonio, the woman who had turned Kitty and his father into a lather of fury, but he knew that Kitty, at least, would not wish them to socialize. 'I really must be getting on.' He replaced his hat.

'You're very kind. I'm sorry to have troubled you.'

'It was no trouble, really,' said JP. 'Your daughter kept me entertained with stories of Buenos Aires all the way back down the hill.'

'I bet she did.' Emer shook her head at the thought of her loquacious child and JP mounted his horse and then set off back down the road.

When Emer returned to the drawing room Bridie was sitting beside the fire. 'That was Mr Deverill,' Emer told her new friend.

Bridie blanched. '*Mr* Deverill?'

'JP Deverill. He brought Alana down from the hills. She'd run off.' Emer laughed and Bridie feigned amusement while inside she suffered a stab to the heart. 'He's a handsome young man.'

'He is indeed,' said Bridie in a thin voice. She recalled the moment she had tried to lure him away with her when he was a little boy and turned her face to the fire so that Emer wouldn't see her cheeks burning with shame.

'Are you all right, Bridie?' Emer asked softly.

'It's nothing,' Bridie replied quickly. 'I think I might be a little hungry. Could I trouble you for a biscuit?'

'Of course.' Emer hurried out of the room, leaving Bridie alone with her thoughts for a blessed moment. She wished it had been *she* who had answered the door. She longed to see her son, to talk to him, for him to know her even though he would never know what she was to him. She wanted so very badly for him to acknowledge her existence.

Bridie stood up and went to the window. She hoped she might glimpse JP walking down the road but of course he had long gone. She stood gazing out onto the drizzle and realized that she couldn't go on knowing that he was living only a few miles from the castle and not being able to see him. She had to do something. She had to engineer a chance meeting. She'd think of something. She'd ask the Virgin

Mary to inspire her. After all, she was a mother; of all the saints, the Virgin Mary would understand the most.

Excited by the letter he'd received JP decided to pay his father a visit on his way home. Bertie was the one person JP could confide in about Martha because he had been present when they had met. He had also given him good advice. JP was sure that, when it came to matters of the heart, his father was the best qualified to advise. Of course, JP suspected Kitty knew that he had fallen in love, his half-sister was too savvy to miss that sort of thing, but he didn't feel ready to share it with her. He hadn't told Robert either, not because he didn't trust him, but because he knew he would tell Kitty and then there'd be no end to her prying. He wanted to keep Martha to himself for the time being.

JP reached the Hunting Lodge, which was an austere grey house with pointed gables and dark windows where Kitty had grown up while her grandparents lived in the castle. The air was cold for a dampness rose off the river that flowed past the house towards the sea. Kitty said it was always damp there, even in summer, and made no secret of the fact that she felt no fondness for the place whatsoever. JP handed his horse to one of the grooms then strode into the house. He found his father in the drawing room with his wolfhounds at his side, giving instructions to a couple of men who were taking down the portrait of Adeline. 'Ah, hello, young man,' said Bertie. 'Careful, Mr Barrett, it's heavier than it looks.'

'Yes, m'lord,' said Mr Barrett, turning red with exertion.

'Why are you taking Grandma down?' JP asked.

'There's a leak, *another* leak, and I want to protect the painting. It's a rather good likeness of her, I think.'

'She was beautiful,' said JP.

'She was. It's a pity you're too young to have known her.'

'She looks like Kitty.'

'Yes, she does. The same red hair and pale grey eyes and the same expression. Sometimes the likeness is so uncanny I have to pinch myself. I'll put the painting back as soon as the wall dries. Won't waste money on repairs. I dare say the eye will be drawn away from the stain by the picture.'

Mr Barrett and his helper began to stagger out into the hall. 'Careful now,' said Bertie again. 'There's no rush, Mr Barrett. Take your time. Molly here will show you where to put it, won't you, Molly? And do be careful to cover it. I don't want it to get dusty.'

'Yes, Lord Deverill,' said the rosy-faced maid in a white apron who had appeared in the doorway. She beckoned the men towards the library and, they hoped, to a rewarding drink afterwards.

'I tell you, JP, it's a miracle this place is still standing,' said Bertie, sinking into an armchair and shaking his head at the sorry state of the room. 'But there's no point despairing. We're lucky to have a roof over our heads.'

'Perhaps the Countess will repair it,' said JP, taking the other armchair. 'After all, she owns it now and you pay rent. It's up to her to make sure it's in good shape.'

Bertie huffed as if he didn't think much of the Countess. 'Better not mention her to Kitty or you'll get an earful.' He grinned. 'Now, what can I do for you?' JP's face beamed with a broad smile. 'Ah, you've had a letter, have you?' said Bertie, watching his son pull an envelope out of his jacket pocket. 'She likes you, does she?'

'I think she does,' said JP.

'Then you must go to London,' Bertie urged him.

'I was hoping you'd say that,' said JP with relief.

'My dear boy, when it comes to matters of the heart one doesn't want to waste time. Everyone else would caution you, after all, you're only seventeen, but I say go and find her. Nothing ventured, nothing gained and a man needs to sow his wild oats before he settles down.'

JP's face fell. 'I'm not going to sow my wild oats with Martha, Papa. She's not that sort of girl. I intend to marry her.'

Now Bertie looked alarmed. 'You've only met her once,' he said.

JP smiled. 'When you know, you know,' he said with a shrug and Bertie couldn't argue with that.

Chapter 8

Professor Partridge was horrified when his sister informed him of Lady Gershaw's dinner invitation. 'We will be returning to Ireland at the earliest,' said Mrs Goodwin, standing in the doorway of his study. 'But first we are obliged to accept Lady Gershaw's invitation. She was kind enough to give us the information we needed, so the least *we* can do is deliver *you* to her dinner table.'

Professor Partridge took off his glasses and rubbed the bridge of his nose, suspending his reading with obvious reluctance. 'I don't see how I can refuse,' he said after a while and Mrs Goodwin was relieved.

'You might actually enjoy yourself, Stephen,' she added with a small smile.

'There's a great danger in enjoying myself,' he replied drily.

'Danger?'

'If I enjoy myself *too* much I might be tempted to stray more often from my desk. Then I'd get no work done at all.'

'I suppose you're going to tell me that women are a man's undoing?'

'In Lady Gershaw's case, possibly.'

'She's very keen on you.'

The Professor replaced his glasses. 'When might you be leaving for Ireland?' he asked and his sister could tell that, one, he was keen to be rid of them and two, he was not prepared to discuss Lady Gershaw.

'Within the week. I will make the necessary arrangements and find us somewhere to stay in Ballinakelly.'

'Very well,' said Professor Partridge. 'Now, do me a favour and ask Mrs Brown to put another log on the fire and close the door behind you.'

A few days later Martha sat at Lady Gershaw's dinner table. On her right was the elderly vicar, Reverend Peter Dyson, who was a good-humoured man, a little mischievous even, with a full head of dove-grey curls and gentle eyes the colour of blue topaz. On her left was Lady Gershaw's nephew, a handsome young man called Edward Pearson, whose shiny dark hair was brushed off a wide forehead, revealing a distinctive widow's peak and startlingly beautiful green eyes most women would swoon over. However, his sulky mouth pouted petulantly as he surveyed the table with ill-concealed boredom. He didn't look at all happy to be there. Mrs Goodwin was seated on the other side of the vicar with another elderly gentleman, some lord or other whose name had already escaped Martha, on her right. Lady Gershaw had placed Professor Partridge next to her and was talking to him confidentially. She didn't look as if she had any interest in anyone else. Martha found it amusing that Lady Gershaw had gone to the trouble of inviting a party of ten, all for the purpose of having the pleasure of Professor Partridge. And what a pleasure it was, for her cheeks were flushed and her laughter came out of a very happy place.

Martha spent the first course, which was a delicious salmon mousse, talking to the vicar. He was delightful, entertaining her with colourful stories of his parishioners, and Martha's shyness melted away in the warmth of his humour. She liked his British accent and the gravelly texture of his voice and could have talked to him all evening. But when the second course was served and Lady Gershaw reluctantly turned to the gentleman seated on her left, Martha found herself having to turn too and face the unwelcoming man on her other side. She stared into her plate as the vicar struck up a conversation with Mrs Goodwin and wondered helplessly how to ignite a dialogue with such a sullen-looking man.

Edward Pearson sighed wearily and tapped his fork against the food unenthusiastically. 'It's always duck or pheasant,' he said and Martha understood from his tone that he liked neither. 'Aunt Marjorie loves heavy food with lots of sauce and potatoes. It's all much too heavy for my taste.'

He cut a piece off the duck breast and put it into his mouth. Martha did the same and was surprised to find that it was perfectly delicious. They chewed silently. 'Aunt Marjorie tells me you're from Connecticut,' said Edward finally.

'Yes,' Martha replied. It was going to be a long evening, she feared.

'What brings you to London?'

Martha didn't imagine he was very interested in her answer for his gaze was drifting across the room as if searching for something more compelling to focus on. However, she answered politely because she had been brought up to be gracious. How she would have loved to turn her back on him and join in the lively conversation Goodwin was enjoying with Reverend Dyson. An uncomfortable silence ensued once again as they ate their duck. Everyone else at the table was talking animatedly, even Professor Partridge who seemed never to be very animated about anything. Martha thought of JP and how charming he was in comparison to this petulant man and she smiled absent-mindedly, wondering what he would make of Edward Pearson.

'What's so amusing?' Edward asked. 'I'd be grateful if you shared it with me because I find little to amuse me here tonight.'

Martha started to laugh. She dropped her knife and fork onto her plate and put her napkin to her mouth. Edward frowned. But Martha was unable to stop. There was something so hilariously comical about him when viewed through the eyes of JP Deverill that she saw how ridiculous he was. 'I'm sorry,' she said at last, carefully wiping the corner of her eye so as not to smudge her kohl.

'Was it something I said?' Martha began to laugh again. 'It *was* something I said, wasn't it?' he persisted. 'But you're laughing *at* me, not with me. I should apologize, I'm not in a good mood this evening.'

Martha stopped laughing and felt ashamed. 'No, *I* apologize. I was so nervous coming here tonight . . .'

'Nervous? What's there to be nervous about?'

'I don't know. I'm new to London. I know no one and Lady Gershaw is a formidable woman.'

At this Edward's lips curled into an incredulous smile. 'She doesn't scare you, does she? Not Aunt Marjorie.'

'She might be Aunt Marjorie to you but she's Lady Gershaw to me. I've never met a lady before.'

'She wasn't born a lady, you know, and she's not scary, just pushy.' He leaned towards her and lowered his voice. 'What would you say if I told you that her father was in trade?'

'Trade?'

'Yes, my great-grandfather manufactured fabric and my grandfather opened a shop. His daughter, Marjorie, caught

the eye of a rich aristocrat and that was that. His younger
daughter, my mother, wasn't so shrewd, although she didn't
do too badly in marrying my father. But I can tell you, when
Aunt Marjorie sets her sights on something she usually gets
it.' He sighed theatrically. 'Poor Professor Partridge, he's like
a fox with his paw in the trap.'

'I don't think Professor Partridge is the marrying type,'
said Martha and they both watched him from the other side
of the table. 'I think he's more interested in books.'

'Which is why Aunt Marjorie wants him so badly, because
she can't have him. It's human nature to want what one can't
have.'

'What happened to her husband?'

'Died in a hunting accident in Ireland. I tell you, those
Irish are as wild as snakes.'

Martha felt as if an electric shock had passed through her.
'In Ireland?'

'Yes, a tiny place no one would ever have heard of were it
not for a very colourful family with a big castle.'

'Do tell me about them,' said Martha. Could it be possible
that he was talking about the Deverills?

'It's a small, rather insignificant place called Ballinakelly.'
Martha suddenly remembered to take a breath. 'Uncle
Toad – he was really called Tony, but he was big and portly
with an enormous belly and a penchant for living well, so
we all knew him as Toad, after—'

'*The Wind in the Willows*,' Martha interrupted. 'What a
beautiful book that is.'

'There was nothing beautiful about Uncle Toad, I can
tell you. Anyhow, he loved to hunt and the Ballinakelly
Foxhounds is famously perilous and Lord Deverill famously
generous with the port, so *that* was an invitation he looked

forward to with more relish than any other. Of course Aunt Marjorie loves to hobnob with the grandees although she doesn't hunt, which is lucky, because if she were as strident on a horse as she is off it, she'd be unbearable!'

'What happened in the hunt?' asked Martha, keen to steer the conversation back to the Deverills.

'Uncle Toad, Bertie Deverill and Bertie's mad cousin Digby used to compete. They were all at school together as boys and great rivals. Now we're talking twenty years ago, just after the war. Uncle Toad wasn't as young and fit as he had once been, but he was still reckless. They set off on a particularly soggy morning and he jumped everything in sight. Now, Uncle Toad could never compete with a Deverill in the saddle, those Deverills were born to it, you see, but Uncle Toad wanted to show that *he* could ride just as well as *them*. The silly man went for something ridiculously high and the horse decided at the last minute that he wasn't going to attempt such a daft hurdle and shied, slipping in the mud. Uncle Toad fell off and broke his neck.'

'That's dreadful!' Martha exclaimed.

'Sad for Aunt Marjorie, because she didn't have any children so she was left on her own. She's never married again, but she does go back to Ballinakelly every now and then.'

'How terrible for the Deverills to have *that* happen to one of their guests.'

'They've suffered worse, I can tell you. Their home was burnt down during the Troubles.'

'The castle?'

'Yes, the greater part of it burnt to a cinder. Hubert Deverill, Bertie's father, was killed in the fire.' When Edward saw Martha's shocked face he was encouraged to divulge more. 'Then there was a wonderful scandal when Bertie fathered a child with one of the housemaids. His wife left Ireland in a sulk and hasn't been back since. She lives in Belgravia and has a rich lover. It's really quite scandalous.'

'What happened to the child Bertie fathered with the maid?'

'Bertie acknowledged him and brought him up. Thought nothing of it. But that's Bertie for you. Nice chap, he is, the boy. Very Deverill, I'd say.'

Martha averted her eyes and breathed slowly. She barely dared ask the question, but her curiosity was too much for her. 'What is the boy called?'

'JP,' Edward replied. 'JP Deverill.'

Edward continued to divert her with stories of the Deverills. Warming to his subject he told her about Celia rebuilding the castle and then being forced to sell when her husband Archie committed suicide after losing all his money in the Great Crash, about her father Digby dying of a heart attack on the golf course and Celia running away to South Africa. 'How the mighty fall, eh?' said Edward as Martha was left reeling from his tales. 'Someone should write a book about them,' he chuckled. 'It would make a gripping read.'

Martha was disappointed when Lady Gershaw stood up and led the ladies out of the room so that the men could pass the port and discuss politics. After powdering her nose in an upstairs bathroom, she joined Mrs Goodwin in front of the fire. 'How was that good-looking young man?' Mrs Goodwin asked quietly. 'I was worried about you at the beginning but you seemed to be holding your own by the end.'

Martha gripped her arm. 'He knows the Deverills,' she replied. 'He knows JP.'

'I told you, didn't I? The English aristocrats all know each other.'

Lady Gershaw plonked herself into an armchair and grinned at Martha. 'So, Martha my dear, how was my nephew? He's a delight, isn't he?'

Later, when Martha was alone with Mrs Goodwin in her bedroom in Professor Partridge's house, she told her nanny everything that Edward had told her. Mrs Goodwin listened in fascination from the edge of the bed while Martha paced the room. 'Well, what can I say? Those Deverills are extraordinary.'

'I didn't ask about Lady Rowan-Hampton. I was too scared,' Martha confessed, stopping for a moment. 'I don't want to hear anything that might change the way I think about her.'

'You're going to find out for yourself very soon. I will make the necessary arrangements in the morning. Lady Gershaw recommended a charming little inn in the heart of Ballinakelly. I doubt it's very grand but it's inexpensive and convenient. Lady Gershaw says it overlooks the harbour, which will be nice, won't it?'

'I don't mind that JP is illegitimate. So am I, really,' said Martha, who had been thinking of little else. 'That's another thing we have in common besides liking our tea milky!' She pressed her hands against her chest and sighed with longing. 'I wouldn't care if his parents were peasants! I love him just the way he is.'

Mrs Goodwin smiled. 'You do realize that Lady Gershaw was matchmaking you with her nephew.'

'I'm sure she wasn't,' Martha protested.

'I knew it from the moment I started telling her about

your parents and how well-established the Wallace family is. Her little eyes were shining like a magpie spying a piece of silver. The vicar told me that Edward is a great worry to her because, as she has no children, *he* is her heir and so far he's only courted the most unsuitable girls.'

'Well, she's going to be disappointed,' said Martha, but Mrs Goodwin could see that she was flattered that anyone might consider her 'suitable'. 'My heart is elsewhere.'

'Of course it is,' said Mrs Goodwin, hoisting herself up from the bed. 'Now, it's time you went to bed. I think we've repaid Lady Gershaw for her kindness.'

'We most certainly have,' Martha agreed. 'Poor Professor, he was so reluctant to come.'

Mrs Goodwin narrowed her eyes. 'I don't think he's as reluctant as you imagine. I might even go so far as to say that I think he likes Lady Gershaw.'

'Really?'

'Indeed I do. She brings him out, you see, in every way. She gets him out of his house and brings out his humour. I think he's forgotten what it is to be young and carefree and Lady Gershaw reminds him.' She hesitated in the doorway. 'I do know that he'll be very happy to be rid of us.'

'I don't suppose he's used to having guests.'

'I think we're the first!' Mrs Goodwin smiled. 'Now, get some sleep. I think we're in for an interesting ride in Ballinakelly. You'll need all your energy for what lies ahead.'

'Thank you, Goodwin,' said Martha.

'Don't mention it, my dear. I wouldn't have missed this adventure for anything in the world.'

Martha was too excited to sleep. She couldn't stop thinking about JP and the Deverills. She imagined the great castle, burnt to the ground. She imagined the hunting and the parties and the glamour that Edward had told her about. Her world seemed so very conservative and dull by comparison: lunches at the golf club, tea parties in manicured gardens, polite, gracious, beautifully dressed people in beautifully decorated houses. There had been no tragic deaths, suicides, scandals or fires to add a little spice, to add a little *depth*, to what was perhaps a rather shallow existence. Nothing of any interest had ever happened in her life until Edith had divulged the secret Joan had told her and suddenly, overnight, Martha's reality had shifted, bringing with it a glimpse of an alternative existence. A glimpse of something else, something spicier. She felt that now, suddenly, she was swimming beyond the sheltered cove of her childhood, into a perilous sea of turbulent waves and treacherous creatures, and yet the danger of it thrilled her. She had never felt so excited before. She had shaken off the constraints of her youth, imposed upon her by her mother in particular, who wanted her to be something that she wasn't, not really, not deep down: a Wallace. No, she was somebody different and she couldn't wait to find out what that was.

Martha had found love and she was going to pursue it. She didn't know where it would take her, but she was eager because she knew that she and JP belonged together. She was certain of it. She felt as if all her life she had been waiting for him and, now that she had found him, she would never be lonely again. It was as if she had been missing some vital part of herself and had at last found it. Before meeting JP she had been half of something and then, all at once, she had become whole. Perhaps that was the sort of cliché one might hear in a badly written song, but it befitted *her*. It was entirely apt. Now she was going to go to Ireland and discover that she belonged in an entirely different world to the one she had known across the Atlantic. Maybe she belonged to this flamboyant Irish world that Edward had described with such gusto. She wondered whether JP had received her letter and whether he had written back. She'd leave before it arrived, of course, but she'd surprise him instead by turning up in Ballinakelly. Yes, she told herself emphatically, she'd *surprise* him and the thought of seeing him again made her chest expand with happiness. She lay in bed, blinking into the darkness, visualizing the look on his face when he opened his door and saw her there.

She thought of her *real* mother, of Grace Rowan-Hampton, and she didn't think about her parents in Connecticut and how they might be suffering. She didn't think about them at all.

Chapter 9

It was a dazzling morning when Kitty set off towards Dunderry Castle to visit her sister Elspeth. The sun shone vibrantly in a clear sky and seagulls spread their wings and seemed to relish the splendour of it too. Jack's return to Ballinakelly had shattered the peace that Kitty had worked so hard to find. The only remedy was to ride out over the hills, for there, among the wild beauty of the country she loved so deeply, could she recapture the lost sense of harmony she craved. Only on horseback, with the rhythm of galloping hooves beneath her and the bracing wind against her face, could she truly feel herself.

Kitty's heart lifted at the expansive view of rocky peaks and grassy slopes and the noise of crashing waves below grounded her in the present so that for a magical moment her mind stilled and she was aware only of her senses. Then the grim grey walls of the MacCartains' castle came into view and Kitty was dragged out of her reverie as once again she questioned how on earth her sister could live in such an unattractive place.

Dunderry Castle was not at all like Castle Deverill. It looked more like a fortress than a palace. The windows were small like mean little eyes on the face of a bitter old man who had long forgotten to smile. There were no gardens to soften it, only soggy grass and rocks, and even the ivy, with its voracious appetite for climbing walls, had recoiled from those slippery stones, leaving them bare and severe. As Kitty approached, big black crows cawed assertively from the turrets, frightening away the more gentle robins and wrens, so that the only sound was their forbidding banter. She decided that Elspeth must love Peter very much to put up with living there.

Kitty rode her horse round to the stable block at the back to find Peter and Elspeth on the cobbles talking to Mr Browne, the head groom. They were looking at a sturdy grey mare with worried expressions on their faces. When Elspeth saw Kitty, she pulled away from the group to greet her. 'Jezebel is lame,' she announced.

'Oh dear,' said Kitty, dismounting. 'Is it serious?'

'I hope not. She's been lame for a couple of days. I've called the vet.'

Kitty's breath caught in her throat. 'The vet?' she repeated. *Surely not Jack*, she thought.

'Yes, he's on his way. She was only shod a couple of days ago so Mr Browne suspects the farrier's done a rum job!' she added crossly. 'Mr O'Leary will know what to do.'

Kitty felt a rising panic in her chest. 'Well, I can see that you're busy,' she said, leading her horse away. 'I'll come back later.'

Elspeth laughed. 'Don't be silly!' she said, frowning. 'He'll only be a minute.'

'I have things to do,' Kitty blurted, knowing that Elspeth was thinking her behaviour irrational.

'Kitty!' But as Kitty was about to mount her horse the rattling sound of a car distracted them both and they turned to see a black Ford Model T making its way towards them. Inside, at the wheel, was the unmistakable face of Jack O'Leary.

Kitty walked her horse out of the way to let him pass as he turned the car into the stable yard. As she did so she caught his eye. He seemed as surprised to see her as she was to see him. They stared at each other and as they did so the blood rushed into Kitty's face to burn her cheeks. Her lips parted and she gazed helplessly as Jack's expression hardened, and it wasn't the face of the man she remembered but the face of the man she had left behind in the cottage, the man whose spirit she had broken, and she was overcome by a wave of remorse.

The car drew to a halt, the door opened and Jack climbed out. Kitty had no choice but to stay. She observed him from a distance and as she did so she suffered a searing sense of loss. This man whose skin had once felt as familiar as her own was now a stranger to her. There was a rigidity to him that had never been there before and she longed to wrap her arms around him and soften him with kisses. But she doubted her kisses would penetrate the hurt she had inflicted. He had a wife who kissed him now. She remembered the way he had wound his arm around Emer's waist and bent his head to listen to what she had to say and she felt her stomach cramp with jealousy. But Kitty only had herself to blame. She remained close to her horse, watching him warily, knowing that his rejection was exactly what she deserved.

Elspeth greeted him warmly. 'You remember my sister, don't you, Mr O'Leary?' she said innocently, for Kitty had never confided in her. Jack didn't look at Kitty directly but nodded and doffed his cap. Kitty nodded back and mumbled a salutation. Elspeth might have noticed her sister's embarrassment had she not already been making her way to her horse. With the horse Jack was himself again: confident, assertive and wise. He seemed to forget that Kitty was a few yards away, gazing at him with yearning. He bent down and ran his capable hands over the horse's leg – those hands that she had once known so well. How often they had caressed her body, bringing her to great heights of pleasure. How often she had thought of *that* in the years following his departure to America. Sometimes, when she and Robert made love, she would find herself drifting into her memories and the intensity of her pleasure would be increased because of Robert's hands being substituted for Jack's. She put her fingers to her lips and stroked the skin there absent-mindedly.

Jack lifted the horse's leg to examine the hoof. He was completely absorbed in his work and Kitty remembered how she used to watch him. He had a special way with animals for they responded to his gentleness with trust and submission. He had always been kind, even to the ugly spider. There was not a single one of God's creatures that Jack didn't treat with respect, only the human. The War of Independence had shown Kitty that.

Jack inspected every inch of the horse, his face frowning with concentration as he checked for heat and swelling. At length he patted the horse's neck and Kitty could see from his expression that the problem was nothing serious. Elspeth, Peter and Mr Browne laughed at something he said then Elspeth came running over to Kitty. 'It's nothing to worry about,' she said. 'Jezebel just needs rest and poultices. Mr O'Leary is going to make her better. Sadly, I won't be taking her out for a while.'

'That's a shame, but at least she's going to get well,' said Kitty, trying to focus on her sister's earnest face and not to let her gaze wander back to Jack.

'Come inside. It's cold out here. Let's have a cup of tea. How's Florence? I hope she's recovered from her cold?'

'It was nothing,' Kitty replied distractedly.

A groom strode over to take Kitty's horse and she suddenly felt exposed without the warm body of the animal beside her. She hesitated a moment, wringing her hands, reluctant to follow Elspeth inside. She knew Jack didn't wish to speak to her. She wouldn't know what to say to him anyhow. He'd had enough of her apologies. She'd let him down too many times now to ever win back his trust. But she wasn't sure when she'd see him again and the anxiety of losing an opportunity began to suffocate her. She remained rooted to the spot, staring at him powerlessly, knowing that if she didn't move soon she'd arouse suspicion and anger him further.

'Are you coming, Kitty?' said Elspeth.

At that moment Jack looked at her again. He understood her too well not to read the desperation in her eyes. He knew exactly how she was feeling, and yet he remained coldly unresponsive and Kitty turned away and followed after her sister, nursing her wounded pride.

Emer had just put Liam to bed when Jack arrived home from O'Donovan's. She could smell the stout on him as he walked into the kitchen, pulled her against him and kissed her neck. She laughed and brushed him off, aware of the little eyes watching them from the kitchen table. Alana jumped up, abandoning her mug of hot milk, and embraced her father. Jack bent over to kiss the top of her head, finding comfort in the sweet smell of her hair. There was nothing like the love of a child to restore the broken spirit.

'How are you, my little Alana?' he asked.

'School was boring,' she replied.

'School is always boring,' Jack chuckled. 'If you listen you might learn something.'

'It was such a beautiful day. I wanted to escape into the hills again.'

'You'll be doing none of that,' said Jack, an uneasiness creeping over him as he thought of her running into JP Deverill again.

She grinned up at him, her cheeks glowing. 'I'll get lost just so that JP can find me.'

Jack shook his head. 'You stay away from those Deverills,' he warned tersely. 'They're bad news.'

Emer smiled at her daughter indulgently. 'He was handsome, I grant you that.'

'Handsome?' Jack exclaimed. 'Alana is ten years old. She shouldn't have an opinion about whether or not a man is handsome! I don't want to hear another word about JP Deverill, Alana. I'm going to say goodnight to Liam. Might he still be awake?'

'I'm sure he's waiting for you,' said Emer softly. 'Kiss Aileen, she'll feel it in her sleep.'

Jack left the room and climbed the stairs to the bedroom Liam shared with Alana. The boy's eyes could be seen glinting in the darkness. Jack smiled and sat on the edge of his bed and stroked his son's forehead tenderly. 'You have a good day, Liam?'

'Yes, Da,' the child replied.

'You been good for your ma?'

'Yes.'

'That's what I like to hear.'

'How was your day, Da?' the boy asked and Jack was touched. Alana never thought of anyone but herself while

Liam, who was only seven, was always concerned about those around him.

'Mag Keohane's dog Didleen swallowed a sock,' Jack told him.

'Did it die?' Liam asked.

'No, it didn't die. But I don't think Mag will want the sock back when it finally comes out, do you?' The little boy giggled. 'Badger Hanratty's goat has got a cough.'

'I didn't know animals got coughs.'

'They get coughs and colds just like us,' Jack told him.

'Will it die?'

'No, it will be fine. Then I went to see Mrs MacCartain's horse.'

'What did that have?'

'A sprain.'

'It won't die then?'

Jack gently pinched the boy's nose. 'What's all this about dying, Liam?'

'Everything dies in the end,' he said fearfully.

'Yes, it does. But that's God's plan, son.'

'Then what happens?'

'We go to Heaven and meet up with all the people we love who went before us. That's what catechism teaches us, doesn't it.'

'Yes,' said Liam and his eyes began to droop. 'I don't want you or Mam to die.'

'Neither do I,' said Jack and he bent down to kiss the boy's forehead. 'God bless you, son.' He watched his child sink into slumber. He remained a moment on the edge of the bed, gazing into the innocent face and wondering what life had in store for his boy. He hoped Fate would be kinder to Liam than it had been to *him*.

He thought of Kitty then. He saw her standing by her horse, her red hair falling in thick tendrils over her shoulders and down her back, her pale grey eyes gazing at him in defeat. He felt her sorrow and her regret as if he were inextricably tied to her by the heart and his misery flooded into his chest as it had done that day in the cottage after she had told him she wouldn't be running away with him to America. He had allowed her to leave, training his eyes on the sea with all the might he could muster in order to stop himself from chasing after her; from falling to his knees and begging her to change her mind. It had taken all his strength to remain there by the window, and only when he was sure that she had gone had he allowed his devastation to overwhelm him. He had sobbed until there was nothing left of him. Then he had picked up his suitcase and vowed never to return to Ballinakelly. Over the years that followed, his hurt had wrapped itself around his heart like scar tissue, thick and impenetrable. He had believed himself incapable of loving anyone else and yet Emer, with her gentle patience and unrestrained devotion, had proved him wrong.

Together they had built a life in America and then, later, when he was fleeing from the Mafia, in Buenos Aires, where he had bought an Irish pub, and she had never complained about his lifestyle or the gun he always kept under his pillow. She had followed him dutifully from America to Argentina and now to Ireland and she seemed to be happy wherever she was as long as she was with *him*. Kitty had chosen Ireland over their love and he could never forgive her for that. Emer deserved his affection and his loyalty. She deserved his devotion too.

After kissing Aileen, who slept in a cot in the next-door bedroom, he left the room purposefully, wanting suddenly to

hold his wife and thank her for her love, which was uncon-
ditional, unselfish and pure.

Cesare watched seventeen-year-old Niamh O'Donovan help
her mother behind the bar. The sight of the pale, lightly
freckled skin on her chest aroused him. She had large,
bouncy breasts, a small waist and a plump, rounded bottom
that wiggled when she walked. She wore her brown hair up,
which showed off her long neck and pretty ears, as exquisite
as little shells, and, in spite of her carefully applied crimson
lipstick, she still looked fresh and buxom as if she had just
crawled out of bed. She noticed him watching her and gave
him a playful smile.

Cesare had only been in Ballinakelly a few weeks but he'd
bedded enough women to ensure that the quiet Irish town
did not bore him. Grace Rowan-Hampton was too old now
to be of interest to him in that respect, but she was eager to
make herself useful. True to her word she had come up with
a list of people to invite to the summer ball. It would be a
way of introducing the Count and Countess to Co. Cork,
she had explained. Everyone would come out of curiosity
but leave full of admiration and affection. The thought of a
glittering ball full of lovely young women, ripe for seduction,
appealed to Cesare who had long since tired of making love
to his wife.

Cesare was sitting at a table in the corner of O'Donovan's
with Badger Hanratty, an old rascal with curly white hair
and a thick white beard and big, twinkling blue eyes, brim-
ming with mischief. He had introduced Cesare to the illegal
poteen that he brewed behind a hayrick on his farm and it
had nearly burned the insides of his gullet. On Badger's left
with his back to the room was Jack O'Leary, who was more

of a kindred spirit to Cesare for he had lived in America
and was closer to him in age. According to Bridie, Jack had
played an important part in the War of Independence and
killed many men along the road to freedom. Cesare didn't
doubt it. Jack had a darkness about the eyes and a suspicious
glint that shone through them whenever the door opened,
as if he expected his enemy to saunter into the public house
at any moment. On Jack's left was Paddy O'Scannell who
owned the general store and the post office, a big-bellied,
black-haired man with ruddy cheeks and a ready smile and a
penchant for endless tankards of stout. Cesare enjoyed playing cards with these men, because they treated him, as king
of the castle, with deference – and they provided a lot more
entertainment than Sean, Rosetta and Bridie. There was a
part of Cesare, a deep, intrinsic part of him, that connected
with the working-class man – a part of him that, at every
other time of the day, he was careful to keep hidden.

As they smoked, drank and chatted over their cards,
Cesare watched Niamh with lustful eyes. The challenge of
devising a way to get her on her own gave him a heady sense
of excitement. Mentally he peeled back her blouse and ran
his hands over her smooth breasts. He slid his hand up her
skirt and she opened her legs for him, eager for his touch. He
groaned at the image then brought his tankard to his lips and
drained his glass. 'Miss O'Donovan,' he called, holding it up.
Mrs O'Donovan glanced at her daughter and narrowed her
beady eyes. 'I'll go,' she said and to Cesare's disappointment
Niamh remained behind the bar, drying glasses with a tea
towel.

Mrs O'Donovan was not naïve like her daughter. She
knew men for what they were and she knew what they
wanted. Count di Marcantonio had already earned a

reputation in Ballinakelly for having an insatiable appetite for women. He might have counted on Irishwomen being easy on the eye but he had not counted on them being slippery of tongue. To Mrs O'Donovan, it seemed, among the less dignified of the girls, that the Count was a conquest to be proud of and they merrily shared the details of their encounters with an appalling lack of shame. She was not going to allow her daughter to fall into disrepute as they had.

Mrs O'Donovan felt sorry for poor Bridie Doyle that was. She might have married a rich man and moved into the castle where her mother had worked below stairs as the cook, but her husband was not a gentleman. Mrs O'Donovan knew a gentleman when she saw one and the Count was definitely not of that class. He had neither the dignity nor the bearing of Lord Deverill, or his father the previous Lord Deverill. The Count was foreign, which was enough to raise her suspicions, but he was indiscreet, which confirmed them. Gentlemen kept their affairs secret: the Count did not. Mrs O'Donovan sensed that it was not going to end well. After all, wasn't his brother-in-law the formidable Michael Doyle? Michael might be reformed and pious with high positions in the community and the Church, but he was at heart a brutal man who was not likely to tolerate the Count's bad behaviour. Mrs O'Donovan watched the Count knock back another tankard of stout and wink at her daughter and she shook her head. Yes, she thought, it was definitely going to end very badly for the Count.

By the time Cesare got up to leave, Badger could scarcely walk, Paddy was singing in a loud, tuneless voice, missing out the consonants altogether and whistling the notes he couldn't reach, and Jack was singing too, an entirely different song to Paddy, about a girl with Titian hair. Cesare watched them leave then sauntered up to the bar where Mrs O'Donovan was with her daughter putting away the glasses. He placed crisp notes on the bar, more than enough to pay for every drink in the house, and smiled at Niamh. He could feel the tension grow hot between them and could see the rise and fall of her breasts as her heart accelerated beneath them. Her cheeks flushed with pleasure and her eyes shone with lust and the curl in her lips told him that she'd be his if only he'd ask. But Mrs O'Donovan was watching them like a cat with a pair of mice and Cesare could only communicate his desire with the intensity of his gaze. 'It has been an entertaining evening,' he said, looking directly at Niamh. 'You have the best house in the whole of Co. Cork.'

'Thank you, sir,' Mrs O'Donovan replied tersely. 'Niamh, you can finish now. Off to bed. I'll close up.' Cesare put on his coat and hat and left the pub reluctantly. Once outside he looked up to the windows which were all dark except for one, glowing softly with the warmth of a single light. He stood in the street staring up at it, knowing that Niamh was inside. Knowing that she knew he was outside, waiting for her. He lit a cigarette and blew the smoke into the damp air. He waited, but he didn't have to wait long. She appeared, silhouetted against the thin curtains, a fulsome profile unbuttoning her blouse and slipping it over her shoulders. He inhaled and the tip of his cigarette glowed scarlet. She turned to the window and slowly opened the curtains. She stood in her camisole top and looked out into the night. He could make out her breasts beneath the delicate fabric and his loins ached with desire. He wanted to scale the wall and climb into her bedroom and take her there. She dropped her gaze and grinned at him, lifting her hand to unpin her hair so that it tumbled about her in tawny waves. Then the lights of the pub went out and Cesare imagined Mrs O'Donovan climbing the stairs, her tread heavy on the steps. Niamh glanced over her shoulder. She gave one final toss of her hair before closing the curtains. She stood for a moment with her back to the window then moved away. Cesare dropped his cigarette onto the ground and walked to his car. He was as lustful as a bull. Perhaps he'd make love to his wife tonight after all, he thought. If nothing else presented itself there was always Bridie. Sweet, submissive Bridie.

As he drove up the road towards the castle he resolved that he would have Niamh O'Donovan one way or another. It was simply a matter of time.

Chapter 10

It was raining when Martha and Mrs Goodwin arrived in Ballinakelly, and very late. Dark clouds obscured the stars and a blustery gale blew in off the ocean, but Martha didn't mind; she was close to JP and nothing else mattered. She sighed with pleasure for they had arrived at last after a long and tiring journey from London and tomorrow she would surprise JP. She had thought of nothing else since boarding the train at Paddington. Holding down their hats the two women hurried into the inn.

They were met in the small hall by a stout woman in a pair of thick spectacles. Behind the glass her eyes looked large and owlish, but her smile was friendly and she greeted them with motherly concern. 'Ye must be perished, ladies,' she said and her soft Irish brogue curled around her vowels as if they too needed warming up. 'I've lit a fire in your room so it should be nice and cosy now. Come in out of the rain. It's been at it all day, cats and dogs and everything else besides. My name is Mrs O'Sullivan and you must be Miss Wallace and Mrs Goodwin. I thought you'd be hungry so I've put some supper on the table, nothing grand, just soda bread and corned beef, but it will keep the wolf from the door. Come, let's not dally a moment longer. Let me show you to your room and we can talk all we like on the morrow.' Mrs O'Sullivan led them up the narrow staircase, her slippers treading softly on the wood, her stockings gathering in rings at her ankles. When she reached the landing she put her hand on her chest; she had all but lost her breath and paused a moment to find it.

'Here we are,' she said at length and opened the door. 'I hope you will find it comfortable. The bathroom is at the end of the corridor.' She handed them the key. Mrs Goodwin and Martha walked into the room, which was very small. A wooden cross hung on the white wall above the chest of drawers and a tatty Bible had been placed on the table between the beds. A turf fire threw smoke into the room but gave out little warmth. 'I'll see you tomorrow,' Mrs O'Sullivan said. 'I hope you sleep well.' She disappeared and a moment later a stubbly young man in a cap arrived with their suitcases. There was barely enough space in there for the three of them so he dropped the cases onto the rug and left, mumbling something neither woman understood.

Martha went to the window and opened the curtains. She looked through the glass at the glistening street below. The headlights of a car distracted her. It was a grand car, not the sort one would expect to see in a rural Irish town like Ballinakelly. She watched it pass slowly beneath her window. For all she knew Lord Deverill was inside with JP and her heart gave a sudden leap of excitement. 'Tomorrow I might find my mother,' she said aloud. 'And tomorrow I might see JP.' She closed the curtains and swung round to face Mrs Goodwin, who was already rummaging in the suitcases for their nightgowns. 'I can't wait for tomorrow!' she said with a sigh. 'I'm too excited to sleep. I'll just lie awake, dreaming of tomorrow.'

When tomorrow eventually arrived Martha was up and dressed at first light. Mrs Goodwin was aching all over from their journey, but she knew she couldn't lie in bed all day and leave Martha to wander the county on her own, so she too got up and dressed and went downstairs to fortify herself with breakfast.

They had decided that they would find JP first and ask him to help them find Lady Rowan-Hampton. It wouldn't be seemly to appear on Lady Rowan-Hampton's doorstep without an invitation. They hoped JP would provide them with one.

'JP Deverill?' said Mrs O'Sullivan when Mrs Goodwin asked after his address. 'Of course I can tell you how to get to the White House. Now, he should, by rights, live up at the castle.' She pursed her lips and shook her head, pouring tea from a big brass teapot into their cups. 'That castle belonged to the Deverills for nearly three hundred years. The first Lord Deverill of Ballinakelly would turn in his grave if he could see who lives there now. But I'm not one to gossip. JP Deverill lives with his half-sister, Mrs Trench.'

'Shouldn't we write and let them know that we are here?' said Mrs Goodwin, who was rather old-fashioned and did not believe in turning up without prior warning.

Martha laughed. 'We'll write a note and leave it with the housekeeper if he's not there,' she said. 'It's a sunny morning, we can walk.'

Mrs Goodwin sighed. She didn't feel like walking any-where. 'Is it far?' she asked anxiously.

'I tell you what, let's go by cab and walk back. How's that for an idea, Goodwin?' Martha suggested. If she could have had her way she would have run there.

And so it was, with excitement rising in her chest, that

Martha climbed into the cab and sat down beside Mrs Goodwin. She had taken great trouble with her appearance. Her hair curled over her shoulders in shiny waves, her hat was placed at a witty angle on her head and her plum-coloured lipstick contrasted prettily with her white skin. She wore her blue floral dress beneath a thick coat with a fur trim, and kid gloves. Although it was sunny, the wind had a chilly edge to it. She looked out of the window as the cab pulled away from the kerb and set off up the street.

As they left the town and headed off up a narrow lane that wound its way into the countryside, Martha was ready to be enchanted. The sun shone brightly upon the rocky hills that rolled on and on until they plunged sharply into the sea. Heather and woodbine grew in abundance among wild grasses and clover, black-faced sheep grazed in woolly groups and little whitewashed cottages with grey-tiled roofs gleamed cheerfully in the morning light. The quaintness of it appealed to Martha's heart and she sighed with happiness. *This* was where she belonged. She could feel it in her blood. Every inch of her seemed to respond to a silent call that came from deep within the land and she smiled with happiness because she knew she had come home.

Mrs Goodwin rubbed her hands together. She wasn't happy about appearing at Mrs Trench's house without an invitation. It seemed impolite and intrusive. But Martha, usually so reserved and prudent, seemed to have thrown all her good sense out of the window. She was in love and Mrs Goodwin knew that love, when it strikes, obliterates all reason. She had some experience of love. Not with Mr Goodwin, however. Indeed, Mr Goodwin had been a measured and sensible man not taken to flights of fancy.

Mrs Goodwin had never experienced passion for *him*. But she *had* once loved another, one she couldn't have, and that impossible love had driven her almost to madness. Oh, she most certainly knew what uncontrollable desire felt like and she saw it in Martha. There was no point in trying to guide her or restrain her. No hope at all. She could only watch with indulgence, and if the truth be told, a little unease, as Martha hurtled towards JP like a comet racing across the sky.

They arrived at the White House and the cab turned into the drive and motored up the hill towards it. Positioned against a backdrop of tall trees, the house gazed out to sea through shining glass windows. Martha was now as nervous as Mrs Goodwin. But she took a deep breath and climbed out, stepping onto the gravel with her lace-up brown suede shoes. Mrs Goodwin followed reluctantly. She would have preferred to have waited in the cab, but loyalty to Martha propelled her on. They stood side by side in front of the door as the cabbie set off down the drive in the direction of Ballinakelly and O'Donovan's.

Martha smiled nervously at Mrs Goodwin, who smiled back with encouragement. She lifted the brass knocker and banged it three times. They waited and Martha's heart began to thump. She was seized by a moment of doubt, wishing suddenly that she hadn't come, had taken Goodwin's advice and sent a note. But the door opened and a plump maid in a black uniform with a white apron peered out.

'Good morning,' said Martha. 'My name is Miss Wallace. I've come to call on Mr Deverill.'

The maid frowned and looked uncertain. Martha wondered whether she had been brought to the wrong address.

But after a second's hesitation the maid opened the door wider and invited them in. 'I'll let the mistress know that you are here,' she said.

'If it's inconvenient we can leave a note,' Mrs Goodwin suggested.

'The mistress is at home,' replied the maid. 'Please come in and I will let her know that you are here.' Mrs Goodwin and Martha were shown into the hall and told to wait while the maid hurried off to find her mistress. Martha glanced around. There was a large fire, which had not been lit, and a polished round table laden with books. Pictures of hunting scenes hung on the walls and a threadbare Persian rug covered the flagstone floor. Martha could see through to the sitting room on her right. On a table beside the window was a display of photographs in frames. She wondered whether JP featured in any of them but before she could sneak in and have a look a strikingly beautiful woman came marching down the corridor towards them in a pair of brown jodhpurs and riding boots, followed by a young black Labrador. Her red hair was loose and tumbling about her shoulders, reminding Martha of JP, for it was exactly the same colour as his. But there was something else, a familiarity that Martha couldn't put her finger on. She was certain she had never met her before but she felt she *knew* her somehow.

'Hello,' said the woman, smiling politely. 'I'm Mrs Trench. I gather you have come to see JP?' She extended her hand and Martha and Mrs Goodwin shook it and introduced themselves. When Martha said her name a spark of recognition lit up Kitty's face.

'You're Martha Wallace?' she said.

'Yes, I met Mr Deverill in Dublin and—'

'Of course you did. But JP isn't here.'

Martha was unable to hide her disappointment. 'Oh? Is he not?' she gasped.

'I believe he's gone to London to find *you*.'

Martha stared at Kitty in horror. 'Gone to London!'

Kitty felt sorry for the girl, who was now blushing profusely. 'Why don't you both come in and have some tea. I'll just go and change. Agnes!' The maid appeared. 'Light a fire in the sitting room and bring Mrs Goodwin and Miss Wallace some tea. I'll only be a minute. Please, make yourselves comfortable.'

Martha wanted to cry. She followed Mrs Goodwin into the sitting room and took off her hat, coat and gloves and gave them to Agnes. 'What a fool I am,' she said in a small voice. 'I should have waited for word from him. What are we going to do now?'

'We're going to find your mother!' said Mrs Goodwin firmly. 'That's why we came to Ireland in the first place. By the time JP returns you will have fulfilled that part of the plan. Maybe it's a blessing that he's not here to distract you.'

'But how will we find her?'

'Leave that to me.' Mrs Goodwin was only too happy to take back the reins of control. She strode over to the sofa and sat down with a sigh. While Agnes returned to light the fire Martha wandered around the room looking at the photographs she had spotted from the hall. There were many of JP, both as a little boy and as a young man, always smiling, always looking as if he was about to make a joke or play a prank. Her disappointment lifted when she saw his face beaming out at her. She was sure he would come home the minute he heard that she was here and they would be reunited.

It wasn't long before Kitty appeared in a pair of

wide-legged slacks and a navy-blue sweater. She hadn't bothered to brush her hair and it remained in wild curls down her back. Everything about her exuded energy, Martha thought. From the way she walked, with purpose, to the way she spoke, with candour. Her vigour enlivened Martha who, only a moment ago, had wanted to throw herself under a blanket and disappear. 'Now tell me, Martha, what brings you to Ireland, besides my brother, of course?' She laughed, showing lovely white teeth, and Martha felt her embarrassment dissolve in the radiance of this charismatic woman, who looked so like JP.

Martha told Kitty the same lie that she had told her father: that her parents had sent her to Ireland because her mother was originally from Clonakilty. 'That's very close by,' said Kitty.

'We will be sure to visit,' said Mrs Goodwin.

'But *you're* from England,' said Kitty, looking directly at Mrs Goodwin with her bright grey eyes.

'I am indeed,' said Mrs Goodwin and she told Kitty a little about herself as the maid returned with a tray of tea and cake.

'Well, while you're here why don't you join us for supper?' Kitty suggested. 'I'm dining with my father tonight and a few friends. My great-aunts will be there and they love playing cards. Do you play?' She directed her question at Mrs Goodwin.

'I grew up playing cards,' said Mrs Goodwin happily. 'I haven't played in a long time but I will readily make up a rubber of bridge.'

'Then that's settled. You must come. It will be an informal gathering and you've already met my father. I shall arrange for a cab to pick you up at seven. Where are you staying?'

'At the Seafort House.'

Kitty laughed. 'Ah, with the garrulous Mrs O'Sullivan. She's quite a character. Though you must be careful, whatever you tell her will be halfway round Ballinakelly before you can blink. Like most people who claim to be paragons of discretion she's a terrible old gossip.' Martha and Mrs Goodwin sipped their tea, enjoying being in Kitty's company. 'I will let JP know that you are here and that I am looking after you. What a ridiculous misunderstanding.'

'I should have waited for a letter from him,' said Martha bashfully.

'And he should have waited for word from you. I believe you are both as impulsive as each other.'

When Mrs Goodwin and Martha left the White House it was almost time for lunch. Kitty had told them of a nice place to eat on the harbour overlooking the little boats. What she didn't tell them was that it was the only café in Ballinakelly. 'I will ask her about Lady Rowan-Hampton tonight,' said Mrs Goodwin as they set off down the drive. 'We are getting close now,' she added, linking her arm through Martha's. 'And JP will be home soon. Everything is going to turn out all right. I can feel it.

'She's very like JP, isn't she?' said Martha.

'Very,' Mrs Goodwin agreed.

If I marry JP I'll be part of their family, Martha fantasized happily to herself. And with the thought of belonging to these colourful people she almost skipped down the road.

At seven o'clock Martha and Mrs Goodwin set off again in a cab, but this time they had an invitation to dine with Lord Deverill at the Hunting Lodge. Both women were excited and more than a little apprehensive. They felt they were inveigling their way into this family by dishonest means.

Taking advantage of their hospitality without coming clean about the real reason they were in Ballinakelly. 'I shall tell JP the truth as soon as he comes back,' said Martha, sensing that Mrs Goodwin was thinking the same thing.

'I think that would be prudent,' Mrs Goodwin agreed. 'With any luck you will have found Lady Rowan-Hampton by then. If he is the right man for you he won't think any less of you for the circumstances of your birth.'

'They are not dissimilar to his own,' said Martha.

'Something else you have in common.'

'I know, isn't it funny? It's as if we're destined to be together.' Martha grinned at Mrs Goodwin. 'You're not regretting you came?'

'On the contrary, my dear. It's an adventure. Who at my age has the opportunity to live another life? I thought my retirement would be an end, not a beginning.'

'What will you do when this is all over?'

Mrs Goodwin looked down at her hands, neatly knitted in her lap. 'I don't know, Martha. I think I shall be very sad. They say every old stocking finds its shoe, but not me by all accounts.'

The cab drew up outside the Hunting Lodge, which looked forbidding in the eerie light of the moon. Its pointed gables appeared to stab the sky, scattering it with a million twinkling stars. A butler in a black tailcoat opened the front door, throwing light onto the ground as the two women trod across it and mounted the steps. They heard the sound of voices coming from inside as they took off their coats. A sudden peal of laughter rose above the rumble and Martha glanced nervously at Mrs Goodwin. Mrs Goodwin took the lead and lifted her chin. It was always best, she thought, to appear more confident than one was.

The butler announced their arrival and everyone in the room fell silent. Martha's heart stalled as she felt momentarily assailed by the numerous pairs of eyes that scrutinized her curiously. But Lord Deverill leapt to his polished feet and welcomed them enthusiastically. 'Why, my dear Mrs Goodwin and Miss Wallace, what a pleasure to see you again.' He shook their hands keenly, engaging them with his pale grey eyes and charming smile. 'Now, let me see. You already know my daughter, Mrs Trench.' Kitty, resplendent in a floor-length blue dress with her hair pinned up and adorned with a black feather, stepped forward to greet them warmly. 'Now, you don't know my aunts, Miss Laurel Swanton and Miss Hazel Swanton.' He chuckled as two birdlike ladies waved from the sofa. They must have been in their eighties, Martha thought, and looked very much alike with sweet smiles and sparkling eyes and white hair carefully curled onto the top of their heads and held with small diamond clasps. 'And this is Lord Hunt,' Bertie continued, waving forward a tall, distinguished-looking gentleman with thick silver hair, intelligent brown eyes and a tidy moustache set over a sensual mouth.

'It's a pleasure to meet you both,' he said, taking their hands and lifting them to his lips.

'My daughter's husband, Mr Trench.' Martha was surprised that this diffident man, who seemed somehow less brilliant than everyone else, was Kitty's husband. Martha had expected someone with a more powerful personality, someone more like Kitty herself. Robert stepped forward and shook their hands formally. Martha noticed that he walked with a limp, but he was classically handsome with chiselled features, a long straight nose and intelligent, kind eyes looking through a pair of small round spectacles.

'Let's not forget Reverend Maddox,' said Bertie and a portly, pink-faced man of about sixty stepped forward. Martha could tell by his cheerful expression that this was a man with a good sense of humour who enjoyed his wine and his food. When he shook her hand she was not surprised to find his skin warm and his handshake firm yet fleshy.

'Welcome to Ballinakelly,' he said to Martha. 'And welcome to the *heart* of Ballinakelly, for surely it is right here in Lord Deverill's home that it beats the loudest.' Everyone laughed, except Mrs Goodwin. She was staring at Reverend Maddox with her mouth slightly parted, her cheeks flushing and her breath catching in her throat. Indeed, she could barely breathe at all.

'And welcome, Mrs Goodwin,' said Reverend Maddox, taking her hand. Then he stalled. He looked closer. 'Hermione?' he uttered hoarsely, disbelief draining his face of its pink glow.

'John,' she said shyly and the room seemed to still around her.

'Is it really you?' Reverend Maddox's voice had changed completely. It was no longer boisterous but gentle with a tenderness that only Mrs Goodwin recognized.

'Do you two know each other?' said Bertie, breaking the silence.

'We do,' said the Rector, without dropping Mrs Goodwin's hand. 'From a long time ago.'

'Well, isn't that a coincidence!' Bertie exclaimed happily.

Martha watched in amazement as Mrs Goodwin and Reverend Maddox continued to stare at each other.

There was a commotion in the hall as the final guest arrived. Everyone switched their attention to the door and the gust of cold wind that was sweeping through it. A moment later a woman, who was clearly not averse to making entrances, stood in the doorway. She was comely with light brown hair parted at the side and pinned with a small tiara, and falling in gentle undulations over one shoulder. Her green silk dress plunged at the front to reveal a creamy décolletage and pulled her in at the waist, falling to the floor in shiny folds. But it was her confidence that was arresting. She drew every eye in the room, which was obviously her intention. She smiled and her charm seemed to radiate around her like heat. Martha didn't think she'd ever seen anyone as glamorous except in the movies. Then a small, stocky man with ruddy cheeks and a balding head stepped in behind her. Even in his evening attire with the large gold signet ring shining on the little finger of his left hand he could not help but be eclipsed by his wife.

'Ah, Grace!' exclaimed Bertie happily. 'Sir Ronald, what a rare treat to see *you*!' Now it was Martha's turn to be stunned. Was it possible that the woman she had crossed the Atlantic to find had just stepped into the room? Crippled by fear and uncertainty she could do nothing but stand there mutely, watching the couple greet Lord Deverill with the affection of old friends.

Then Lord Deverill turned to her. 'May I introduce a new acquaintance,' he said, putting his hand on her arm to usher her forward. 'A friend of my son JP,' he added with a grin. 'Miss Wallace.'

Grace extended her hand and Martha took it.

'Lady Rowan-Hampton,' said Bertie.

'How do you do,' said Grace.

Martha stared into the woman's soft brown eyes but there was no spark of recognition there. 'It's a pleasure to meet you, Lady Rowan-Hampton,' she replied, astonished that the words came out so smoothly.

At the sound of that name Mrs Goodwin tore her gaze away from the Rector and stared, open-mouthed, at Grace. Never before, in all her life, had she so badly needed the fortification of a strong drink.

JP stood outside number 10 Ormonde Gate, hat in hand, heart in throat, and rang the bell. There was a long moment before the door opened and a parlour maid looked at him inquisitively. 'Good morning. I've come to call on Miss Wallace,' he declared and her name sounded sweeter when said out loud.

'I'm afraid Miss Wallace is no longer here, sir,' said the maid.

'Oh. When will she be back?'

'She's not coming back, sir. She and Mrs Goodwin left three days ago.'

JP was stung. 'Might I ask where they've gone?'

The maid edged closer and lowered her voice. She wouldn't normally be so indiscreet, but the gentleman had a certain way about him that made her want to please him – and he looked so sad. 'They've gone to Ireland,' she whispered. 'A small place called Ballina ... Ballinakilty or something like that.'

'Ballinakelly!'

'Yes, sir, that's it. They've gone there.'

'Good Lord!' he exclaimed, replacing his hat and giving her a grateful smile. 'How strange, we even *think* alike.' And he set off down the road, whistling merrily. The maid watched him go. *What a lucky girl she is, that Miss Wallace,* she thought to herself. *The luckiest girl in the world.*

Chapter 11

'I really must *do* something!' said Adeline anxiously, pacing the room.

'If you continue to walk up and down like that you're going to make us all dizzy,' Barton grumbled.

'But I can't remain silent. I just can't,' she said.

'My darling,' Hubert interjected from where he was sitting on the sofa with his fingers knitted over his paunch. 'Just because you can go anywhere you choose and witness events you really should not be privy to, does not mean you should interfere. If spirits interfered all the time the world would be in an even bigger muddle!'

Adeline glanced at him and frowned. 'That Martha and JP would fall in love was never a consideration. Of all the millions of people out there they had to choose each other!' she said, pacing again.

'Why the devil should it matter?' Egerton asked.

Adeline stopped pacing. 'Because they're twins,' she said, her voice heavy with worry.

Egerton and Barton were not surprised by much, but they were surprised by *this*. 'Twins?' they exclaimed in unison.

'They are Bertie's illegitimate children,' Adeline said and

she glanced at Hubert, who shook his head in exasperation at his son's folly.

'Good Lord,' said Egerton with a grin.

'And they have fallen in love?' said Barton.

'They recognize themselves in each other. I suppose one could call it narcissism,' said Adeline.

Barton laughed. 'Sounds very Shakespearean!'

'I never foresaw it,' she continued, pacing again. 'I wanted Martha to come to Ballinakelly to find her roots. She's a Deverill. She's one of us. It was right that she should come.'

'*You* made it happen,' said Hubert and there was an accusatory tone to his voice that saddened Adeline. Hubert had never adopted such a tone in life.

'No, my dear, Joan, her aunt, made it happen by telling Edith and Edith told Martha. Once Martha knew, she was always going to come and find her home. She only needed a little prompting. It turned out that she hadn't lost her sixth sense, after all. It had just lain dormant. She just needed a little prompting,' Adeline repeated. 'But I could never have predicted that she and JP would meet in Dublin, let alone fall in love.'

'There's little you can do about it,' said Hubert.

'Little is better than nothing,' said Adeline.

'What do you propose?' Barton asked. He was finding the situation highly amusing. Nothing of interest went on in their limbo so that the slightest ripple in the lives of the living was entertainment enough for the dead. He only wished it were going on in the castle then he could witness it too.

'I propose I warn Kitty,' Adeline replied, pausing her incessant pacing again.

'She'll find out soon enough,' said Egerton.

'But what if she doesn't! What if they marry? I can't bear to think of it!'

'Now *that* would be mighty fun,' Egerton added gleefully. 'It was fun here while the ridiculous Count was enjoying having his way with the maids, but now he spends all his time away from the castle, life has become dreary. Bridie is having no fun at all and that Rosetta has expanded like a prize cow at the Ballinakelly Fair!'

'Bridie loves her Count in spite of his faults,' said Adeline.

'She doesn't see them,' said Egerton. 'Women are blind when drugged by love.'

'Love!' Barton growled. 'It's a trick, a cruel trick. Who has ever been successful in love?'

Adeline settled her eyes tenderly on her husband. '*I* have,' she replied quietly. Hubert looked sheepish and smiled at her with gratitude.

'You're one of the rare few,' Barton added. 'The rest of us can but chew on the memories of love. Like bitter leaves they are sour to taste.'

'Will you ever share your story with us?' Adeline asked.

'No,' said Barton, then he threw his shaggy head back and gave a belly laugh. 'I'll take the secret with me to the grave!'

Leopoldo did not like his cousins. He did not like them one little bit. There were five of them. The oldest three, Emilio, Mariah and Joseph, being fourteen, twelve, and nine respectively, were too old to bully, and the six-year old Tomas too quick to complain to his father, but the little one, Eugenio, who was four, was timid and shy and easily controlled. Leopoldo liked him the least.

Leopoldo liked pulling the legs off spiders, torturing beetles with pins, baiting dogs and slapping horse's faces, but he enjoyed tormenting Eugenio most of all. It irritated him that the boy was sweet-natured and good, that his heart was always ready to fill up again as soon as Leopoldo had drained it with unkindness. It annoyed him that Eugenio got up when he kicked him down and that he was eager to find goodness in his cousin when Leopoldo was doing his best to show him that there was none. It really infuriated him that Eugenio was adorable. He hoped he'd grow up to be ugly.

Leopoldo was dark-haired like his uncle Michael, but unlike Michael he wasn't handsome. His face was long and narrow, his eyes too close together, too small and black, like little beads they were, always sliding about in search of trouble. His smile was sardonic, his humour only triggered by someone else's misfortune or pain, and his teeth were awry. He was most proud of his eye teeth which resembled a wolf's – had he been a wolf he would have had no compunction about tearing into his young cousin's flesh. As he couldn't very well do that, he hurt him with words instead. Drawing him into his confidence one minute, like reeling in a fish on a hook, then slapping him down with some cruelty the next. Each time, Eugenio would blink at his older cousin with glittering eyes, incredulous that he could really be so mean.

Cesare had been very clear about Leopoldo's superiority when Sean and Rosetta moved into the castle. Leopoldo was a prince, he reminded them, and should be treated as such. Therefore, he was served first at mealtimes, he sat in the best chair at the table and the other children had to do exactly what he wanted. Bridie should have had the wisdom to know that *that* kind of treatment would only raise a monster, but she was so blinkered by her love for her precious son that she couldn't see beyond it. She certainly didn't notice his cruelty.

To Bridie Leopoldo was perfect in every way. To Cesare, who saw him much less, he was a prince of the Barberini dynasty, a descendant of Pope Urban VIII. He made sure that, like him, his son was adorned with gold bees wherever possible. At the tender age of seven he wore gold bee cufflinks in his shirts and kept a gold pocket watch, engraved on the lid with the trio of Barberini bees, by his bedside. Leopoldo was very aware of his status, and the lack of status of his Doyle cousins (after all, his grandmother and uncle Michael lived in a hovel!). While Cesare and Bridie failed to see his faults, his uncle Sean saw every one of them, and so did his uncle Michael, but while they depended on their sister for so much, neither felt able to voice their concerns.

Like all bullies, Leopoldo was a coward. Never more was that apparent than when Egerton appeared in the middle of the night to rattle the doorknobs and creak the floorboards. The boy would shiver and whimper in his bed, too terrified to get out and run to his mother. In the morning he'd complain that his bedroom was haunted but Bridie would reassure him that there were no ghosts in Castle Deverill. He was too proud to admit his fear to his cousins. Instead, he told Eugenio about the ghosts with bravado, hoping that the child would tell him that he, too, was visited in the night, but Eugenio claimed to see nothing. He slept soundly. So Leopoldo thought he'd dress up as a ghost and frighten the boy himself.

The thought of creeping into Eugenio's bedroom and scaring the life out of him gave Leopoldo an enormous thrill. He lay in bed as the winter winds blew about the turrets, fantasizing about Eugenio's fear. He saw the boy's face puce with terror, his mouth wide in a scream and his knuckles white as he gripped the bedclothes. Every detail of Eugenio's torment delighted him. In fact, it delighted him so much that he began to forget his own fear. But he didn't know that he was being watched – that he was *always* being watched – by Egerton, who was determined to teach the scoundrel a lesson.

Leopoldo's excitement prevented him from sleeping, so when his pocket watch said midnight, he climbed out of bed and put on his dressing gown. He took a torch and pulled the sheet off his bed. He padded down the corridor to the east wing and stopped outside Eugenio's door. The children's bedrooms were far away from the grown-ups' and Leopoldo was sure that they wouldn't hear Eugenio scream – and if they did, Leopoldo would be back in his own bed before they even left their bedrooms.

He composed himself for a moment, taking a few deep breaths in an attempt to control the excitement that made him shiver like a horse in the starting block. Then he turned the knob.

The room was dark and quiet. Only the moaning wind could be heard outside. Heavy curtains blocked out any moonlight, but Leopoldo could just make out a small lump in the bed where Eugenio was sleeping peacefully. How Leopoldo envied his ability to sleep so serenely. Well, he was about to finish all that. After this, he didn't imagine Eugenio would ever sleep soundly again. With that thought he put the sheet over his head so that it covered him completely and switched on his torch. Then in a low voice he said, 'I am the ghost of Castle Deverill and I am going to kill you.'

He heard a rustle and then a scream. It was so loud and sudden that *he*, the ghost, nearly jumped out of his skin. Before he had time to switch off the torch and make his exit, Eugenio had shot out of bed and was running in terror down the corridor.

With a satisfied chuckle Leopoldo threw off the sheet. The bed was empty where Eugenio had been moments before. He stared at it, reliving his cousin's fright. Then the door, which Eugenio had left open, closed with a bang. Leopoldo stopped chuckling and spun round. The air had gone very cold. He felt a shiver travel over his skin, causing it to goose-bump. He caught his breath as he saw, very clearly, a shadow on the wall that was the exact shape of a man. Leopoldo shone his torch onto it, but it didn't disappear. It remained as if it were a stain on the paper. At the sight of a *real* ghost, Leopoldo's chest shrank with fear as he let out a wild howl.

It seemed like minutes before Bridie came running into the room, her face ashen. Leopoldo was crying, clutching the sheet and the torch, staring at the wall. 'What's happened?' she asked, switching on the light then gathering him into her arms. 'What's going on? Tell me, Leopoldo, what's going on?'

'I saw a ghost!' he wailed.

'What are you doing in Eugenio's bedroom?' Then she saw the sheet and the torch. 'What were you doing, Leopoldo?'

'I only wanted to scare him,' he whimpered.

Bridie glanced at the bed. 'Where *is* he?' she asked.

Then Cesare was in the doorway in his dressing gown and slippers, his expression grave. 'You had better come quickly,' he said. Then he shook his head dolefully at his son, and Leopoldo felt as if his father had taken his heart and given it a hard squeeze. Bridie followed her husband down the corridor to the staircase. Now the entire household seemed to be awake and standing in the hall around Rosetta, who was on her knees, cradling her son's limp body in her arms. Everyone stared, not knowing what to do.

Bridie saw her brother's stricken face and her hand shot to

her mouth. Holding on to the banisters for balance she hurried down the stairs, feeling as if at any minute her legs were going to give way, almost hoping that they would because she was too afraid to ask the question. Was Eugenio dead?

'The doctor is on his way,' said Sean.

'Is he . . . ? Is he . . . ?' she stammered. *Oh Lord, if you are a loving God, please don't take him.* She looked at Rosetta. Then she looked at the child. Then she saw his eyes open. He moved his arm. He tried to get up. Eugenio began to cry and Rosetta, so relieved that he had come round, cried too. *Thank you, God,* Bridie thought. *Thank you.* Then she turned to see Leopoldo standing at the top of the stairs. He was no longer holding the sheet and the torch.

'What happened, Leo?' his father demanded. 'What were you doing in Eugenio's bedroom?'

Bridie replied before her son had a chance to. 'He heard Eugenio screaming and hurried in to see what the matter was. Then he said he saw the same ghost that Eugenio saw. God save us, Cesare, but we must call Father Quinn at once and have him exorcise it. Whatever it is, it must go.' And she remembered Kitty's ghosts, the Deverill heirs, stuck in the castle until an O'Leary returned to claim the land, and she wondered whether Kitty had really seen ghosts. Whether they were here, in the castle, and whether Leopoldo was seeing them.

Leopoldo gazed down at his mother and nodded. 'The ghost that scared him scared me too,' he said.

Cesare's expression softened and Leopoldo felt his father's hand loosen its grip on his heart. 'You did well, Leopoldo,' he said. 'Now go back to bed.'

'I'll take him,' said Bridie, feeling sick for having lied.

When Leopoldo was tucked up in bed, his mother kissed

his forehead. 'My darling, sometimes well-intentioned games go wrong. This is one of those times. I know you didn't mean to frighten Eugenio like that and it's not your fault that he fell down the stairs. He'll be all right, I'm sure of it.'

Leopoldo bit his bottom lip. 'I didn't mean to scare him, Mam. He's like a brother to me. I wouldn't hurt him.'

'I know you wouldn't,' she soothed, stroking his dark hair off his forehead.

'Has he broken bones?'

'He might have.'

Leopoldo hid his delight at that possibility. 'He was really scared,' he said, masking his glee.

'He must have been.'

'I saw it too. It had three heads. It was a monster.'

'Whatever it was, Father Quinn will make it go away.'

'Will he come tomorrow?'

'I'm sure he will.' She kissed him again. 'You're a good boy, Leo. Don't worry about Eugenio. The doctor will be here soon and he'll put him right. You sleep well.'

And for the first time in weeks, he did.

Chapter 12

'Goodness! The shock of it. I'm still reeling!' said Mrs Goodwin, lying in bed as the early morning light shone in beams through the gaps in the curtains. Martha understood her to be speaking of Lady Rowan-Hampton, for the coincidence had been extraordinary, but Mrs Goodwin was thinking of John Maddox. She had believed that the part of her he had once awakened had died upon their parting, but last night he had brought it back to life with one tender look. She felt as if she was young again with her whole life ahead of her, and this time Mr Goodwin did not stand in the way, nor did her guilt or misplaced sense of duty. She was free. But she was old – was it possible that he still wanted her?

'I feel sick,' Martha groaned, rolling onto her side beneath the blanket to face Mrs Goodwin. 'I've felt sick ever since I laid eyes on her. She's more beautiful, more charismatic, more sure of herself than any woman I have ever met. She doesn't look like she's spent the last seventeen years pining for her lost daughter.'

Mrs Goodwin turned her attention to Martha. She wanted her to be as happy as *she* was. 'My dear, you don't know what's in her heart. You have no notion of how much she might have suffered. Seventeen years is a long time, long enough to come to terms with your grief and accept what you have and not what you have lost.' Mrs Goodwin knew *that* only too well. 'She was very friendly. After all, she invited you to call on her.' She propped herself up on her elbow. 'I thought her incredibly charming. She has a kind face, don't you think?'

'She does,' Martha agreed. 'I can't believe I've found my real mother. I thought I would feel ecstatic but I just feel scared.'

'What did you expect, Martha dear?'

'I don't know. An emotional reunion?' She smiled sadly at her own foolishness. 'When one thinks of a mother one conjures up a universal image of motherhood. Lady Rowan-Hampton is almost too beautiful to be that.'

'Go and see her this morning and tell her everything. After all, what have you got to lose?'

Martha sighed. 'Nothing I hadn't already lost seventeen years ago.'

Mrs O'Sullivan was only too happy to arrange a cab to take Martha to Lady Rowan-Hampton's house – Martha insisted to Mrs Goodwin that this was a meeting she had to endure alone. As she left the inn she bumped into Reverend Maddox striding purposefully towards it. He had a spring in his step and a broad smile on his lips and as he raised his hat and bade her good morning she didn't imagine it was the sunshine that had filled his heart with happiness. They exchanged a few hurried pleasantries because Martha was keen to get to her meeting and Reverend Maddox impatient to get to his. Martha climbed into the waiting cab as the Rector disappeared into the inn. She suddenly wished she hadn't been so self-absorbed and had asked Mrs Goodwin how she and Reverend Maddox knew each other.

The cab bounced along the winding lanes that meandered up the coast. The day could not have been more splendid but Martha barely noticed the sunshine bouncing off the water creating the illusion of a million jumping stars for her heart was full of doubt. Should she have come? Should she have dug into her past? Was this meeting going to give her the answers she craved? She thought of JP and wished he had come with her. She wondered whether she should turn round and go back to the inn and wait for him.

Before she could change her mind the cab turned off the lane and through a wide gap in an old stone wall. Lady Rowan-Hampton's grey manor was large and imposing, positioned at the end of a long sweeping drive. However, the sombre façade was softened by wisteria, which Martha imagined must look glorious when in flower, and the symmetry of the two wings which sandwiched the centre portion lent the house a pleasant harmony.

Martha took a breath as the cabbie walked round to open the door. She had arranged for him to wait. She wasn't sure how long the meeting would take. If it went well she would send him away; if it went badly she'd be out within minutes.

She rang the bell and was greeted by a snooty-looking butler in livery who showed her into an airy drawing room of comfortable sofas and chairs arranged around a fireplace. It appeared to Martha that Lady Rowan-Hampton entertained a lot because the fire was lit and crackled hospitably. Unsure whether to sit or stand she went and stood by the window that looked onto the lawn at the back of the house. As she waited, her ears straining for the sound of footsteps in the hall, she wrung her hands to stop them shaking.

Lady Rowan-Hampton swept into the room like a bird of prey, silently. Martha sensed she wasn't alone and swung round. 'I'm sorry, Lady Rowan-Hampton, I didn't hear you.'

The older woman smiled graciously. She looked less formidable this morning in a simple green floral dress and short purple cardigan with her hair clipped in an untidy knot at the back of her head. 'Please call me Grace, Martha,' she said and extended both hands. Martha took them and noticed how radiant her skin was without make-up. Free of the dramatic use of artificial shadow her eyes appeared more gentle too, as if she had been wearing a mask the night before and was now revealing her true face, which was soft and maternal. Martha was heartened. 'How lovely to see you,' she continued. 'Wasn't last night amusing? It's always frightfully jolly at Bertie's.'

'It was so kind of Lord Deverill to invite me,' said Martha. 'Any friend of JP's is a friend of his and consequently a friend of mine. Please, do sit down.' As Martha perched awkwardly on the edge of one of the sofas a couple of maids walked in with trays of tea, cake and biscuits. Martha was beginning to realize that it was customary in Ireland to offer more than just cups of tea. 'I've known JP since he was a little boy,' said Grace and as she reached for the teapot Martha noticed the pretty gold bracelets at her wrists and the glittering rings on her fingers. Everything about Lady Rowan-Hampton exuded elegance and good taste. 'He was such a little mischief, just like his father. They both have the same twinkle in their eyes.'

'Yes, they do,' Martha agreed. Grace handed her a delicate china cup of steaming tea. Martha took it and held it steadily, summoning all her strength to hide her trembling.

Once she had served herself Grace sat back in the armchair with a sigh. 'Tell me, how old are you, Martha?'

'Seventeen,' she replied.

'The same age as JP. Such a shame he dashed off to London just as you were dashing over here. Really, Fate could not have been more unkind! But he'll be back in Ballinakelly soon and I'm sure he'll take you into the hills. You know he's mad about horses. They all are, the Deverills. It's in the blood. Do you ride?'

'Oh yes, I adore it, but unlike the Deverills my family are not so keen on horses. My sister Edith can't bear them. But I feel something very magical when I'm on a horse at full gallop.'

'Then you must come and join the hunt.'

'I've never hunted before.'

'JP will show you the ropes. It's easy, you just follow the hounds and jump anything standing in your way.' They both laughed and Martha began to feel less nervous. 'How long are you planning on staying or is that a silly question to a girl who's just fallen in love?'

Martha blushed. 'I don't know ... I mean ... I'll wait and see how—'

'I understand, my dear. I might look like an old sack of potatoes, but I've been there myself.'

'You couldn't look less like a sack of potatoes, Grace,' said Martha.

'You must take your time but I always think one knows right away. If you have that sort of heart, which I think you probably do, you just know. Am I right? I think I am.' She laughed again and Martha imagined many hopeless men must have fallen in love with that smile over the years. It was irresistible. She wondered which of those men had fathered her.

Martha put down her teacup. 'I need to tell you some-thing, Grace,' she said and she must have paled for Grace was immediately concerned.

'Of course. Is there something I can help you with? Are you in trouble?'

'No, no, not in trouble. Did I tell you that my mother was born in Clonakilty?'

'No, you didn't.'

'Well, she and my father were not able to have children, at least not when they married. Edith came after, you see, and she was theirs.' Martha noticed the baffled expression on Grace's face and realized that she wasn't making much sense. She ploughed on nonetheless. 'They desperately wanted a child so they came here, to Ireland, and adopted a baby who was born in a convent in Dublin.' Grace placed her teacup on the little table beside her and carefully folded her hands in her lap. Martha didn't notice that she had begun to rub her thumbs together and that she was now looking more closely into her face. Martha was too frightened of her reaction to meet her eyes, so she dropped her gaze onto the carpet. 'I didn't know I was adopted until my aunt Joan told my sister, who told me. I found my birth certificate in a cupboard in my mother's bathroom . . .' Her voice cracked.

'My name is on the birth certificate,' said Grace smoothly.

'Yes,' Martha replied. Now she dared to look at Grace. The older woman sat very still and composed, as if she had been told nothing in the least surprising or out of the ordinary.

Grace inhaled deeply. 'My dear Martha, I'm afraid I am not your mother.'

Martha stared at her uncomprehendingly. 'You're not?'

Grace shook her head. 'No, I helped a young girl who had

got into trouble. I'm afraid the nuns used my name on the birth certificate so that the couple adopting would pay more. They specifically wanted a baby of noble birth.'

Martha didn't know what to say. She stared at the woman she had believed to be her mother and her heart caved in with disappointment. Grace got up and went to the window. She stood with her back to the room, gazing out over the garden as if searching for something hidden out there among the trees. Her hand rubbed the back of her neck and if Martha had been able to see her face she would have noticed a rigidity there as the need for self-preservation shifted into focus.

'An acquaintance of mine met your parents in London,' Grace continued without turning round. She had to think clearly for much was at stake here. 'She told me that they were looking to adopt a baby and I immediately thought of the young woman in my care. It was perfect timing.' Martha sat stiffly on the sofa feeling nauseous, as if she were staring into an abyss and suffering from vertigo. 'You were born and your parents came over to Ireland to collect you. The couple had said they wanted a baby of noble birth. They had been very specific about that. The young mother was adamant that her name was kept off the certificate, so I generously gave *my* name. It seemed the right thing to do. I never thought for one minute you would track me down years later, believing me to be your mother. I'm sorry to have disappointed you, Martha.'

'What was my mother's name?' she asked in a whisper.

'Oh, I can't recall.'

Martha thought it strange that Grace couldn't remember.

Grace turned round. She knew her lie didn't wash. 'I will look through my papers,' she said with a rush of enthusiasm. 'I will find her name for you. Leave it to me.' She smiled and Martha's hope reignited. 'I helped your mother, now I will help *you*. I know where you are staying. I will find you.'

'What was she like, my mother?' Martha asked, standing up.

'Like you,' said Grace and that was the truth. 'She looked just like you.'

When Martha had gone Grace hurried to the telephone. She asked the operator to put her through to the White House at once. When Kitty's voice came on the line Grace spoke plainly. 'Kitty, we have a terrible problem. I need to see you and your father at once without a moment's delay.'

'What is it, Grace?' Kitty asked.

'I cannot tell you over the telephone – those operators listen in and I don't want them hearing this. I'll meet you at the Hunting Lodge in half an hour. I hope your father is at home.'

Martha asked the cabbie to drop her near the beach. She decided she would walk back to Ballinakelly from there. Her heart had contracted into a tight ball in her chest. It felt like a stone, hard, cold and very small. She needed time alone to think before facing Mrs Goodwin and telling her the bad news. It had all seemed so positive when Grace had walked into Lord Deverill's drawing room the night before. There, at last, was her real mother, or so she had thought. But the tearful reunion she had dreamed of had been nothing but a mirage created by her wretched need to feel wanted. She should never have come, she thought now as she trudged through the long grasses down to the shore. She should have stayed in America instead of chasing this cloud. For that's what it was, a puff of vapour, nothing more. She doubted she'd ever find her mother now.

Martha walked over the sand with her shoulders hunched and her hands stuffed into her coat pockets. The wind raced up the beach in gusts, snatching her tears and turning her nose red with cold. She felt as if she had lost her real mother all over again, but this time it hurt because she thought she had found her. Grace's face floated into her mind and she cried all the more because she so wanted *her* to be her mother. Having thought her remote and unmaternal Martha now realized that she was perfect, in every way, and her loss felt even more acute for that.

Kitty and Bertie were waiting in the library when Grace hurried into the Hunting Lodge. They stood up when she entered and watched her close the door behind her. She waved away the offer of tea but requested a large glass of whiskey and when they suggested she sit down she refused that too, preferring to stand. Her face was taut, the skin between the eyes pinched with worry. Neither Bertie nor Kitty had seen her so distressed. Indeed, Grace had always been a woman who was able to keep her composure under pressure; a mistress of pretence, a queen of deceit. But now she seemed to be unravelling and the way she knocked back her glass of whiskey and asked for another filled both their hearts with foreboding. 'What is it, Grace?' Bertie asked gently, putting a hand on her arm. 'You must tell us at once.'

'Yes, Grace,' Kitty interjected, stepping closer. 'Don't keep us in suspense a moment longer.'

Grace looked from one to the other and her brown eyes appeared suddenly feral, like those of a cornered animal. 'I don't know how to say this,' she said quickly. 'I don't know how to tell you without turning you both against me forever.'

'What do you mean?' said Kitty. 'Our friendship has

survived some terrible things. Surely we can survive whatever it is you have to tell us.'

'I have done something unforgivable,' she said breathlessly. 'Something unspeakable. I have stooped lower than the lowest scum. I am full of shame, but I beg you not to turn away from me.' She appealed to Bertie, her eyes now welling with tears. 'My darling Bertie, please forgive me.'

'What is it?' he implored.

'JP wasn't the only baby Bridie gave birth to. There was a twin. A little girl. I told the nuns to tell Bridie that she had not survived.' Kitty and Bertie stared at her in amazement and disbelief. 'I put my name on the birth certificate because the couple, the couple who were to adopt her, wanted a child of noble birth and were willing to pay a very high price for her. The nuns insisted I do it, and I thought nothing of it. I believed I was helping the child *and* the adoptive parents. Now that girl has found me, believing me to be her mother.'

Kitty gasped and her hand flew to her mouth. 'Martha!' she exclaimed, horrified.

Bertie rubbed his forehead then walked over to the drinks cabinet to help himself to a glass of whiskey. He hadn't tasted alcohol since his cousin Digby had persuaded him to give it up almost fifteen years before, but now he needed a drink more than he ever had. *Dear God,* he thought, *Bridie gave birth to twins!* He had not *one* but *two* illegitimate children. He had believed he had outridden his shameful past but it was now catching up with him again and creeping over him like an ugly shadow. 'Martha is my daughter,' he said huskily, after taking a giant swig. He poured more whiskey from the crystal decanter with a shaking hand. 'By God, Grace!'

Grace recoiled from his burning stare. 'I'm sorry. I should have told you. But—'

'Martha is JP's twin sister,' Kitty interrupted, saving Grace from having to weave more lies. She went to the window for some air. 'But they look nothing alike.'

'They are non-identical twins,' said Grace. 'Martha and JP are as different as if they were born four years apart. But they arrived together, I can vouch for that.'

'My poor JP!' Kitty groaned, taking a gulp of air. 'What are we going to tell him?'

'Tell him the truth?' Grace suggested meekly.

Kitty swung round. 'The truth? Are you mad, Grace? I told JP that his mother was dead. You can't now tell him that she's alive and living in the castle. I forbid it.'

'She's right,' said Bertie quietly. 'We cannot tell Martha the truth. But we can tell her *some* of it.'

'Then we need to prepare our story,' said Grace, her voice suddenly steady for there was little that appealed to her more than a plot. 'I have told her nothing save the fact that I put my name on her birth certificate. I assured her that I would help her find her real mother. She will not rest until she finds her. Therefore, we must be watertight, the three of us, and work out with care what information we are going to divulge.'

'Let's sit down,' Bertie suggested, moving to the armchair by the fire. The women sat on the sofa, united once again in conspiracy. 'We must do what is best for JP,' he said firmly. 'This is more about damage limitation than anything else. JP believes his mother is dead so that is what we will tell Martha. Then we will tell her that I am her father. God help the poor girl with *that*.'

'But, Papa . . .' Kitty protested. 'This will finish off Mama for good.'

'There is no way to avoid it,' he replied dolefully. 'JP will have to know that Martha is his sister. Their romance must come to an end at once.'

Kitty put her hand to her throat. 'It will destroy him,' she said, panic rising. 'And what if Bridie hears of this? She might do something stupid. She might tell him the truth and he'll hate us for having hidden it from him. He'll learn that not only does he have a sister but a mother too! Oh God, the consequences could be hideous.'

Grace narrowed her eyes. 'Perhaps we can persuade Martha to keep it secret?' she suggested calmly. 'She's a sensible girl. She'll understand how delicate the situation is. She'll have found her father, at least. Why make it public? That's not why she's here. She's here because she wants to know who her real parents are.'

Kitty was quick to agree. 'Yes, she doesn't have to tell anyone,' she said, clutching at Grace's proposal like a drowning woman at a raft. 'It can be our secret, one we all share together.'

Bertie rubbed his chin thoughtfully. 'I have another daughter,' he said, still trying to make sense of it. 'She was here last night and I never knew.' He drained his glass. 'I had no idea.'

'She looks like Bridie,' said Grace. 'I should have noticed it at once, but I didn't.'

'Neither did I,' Kitty concurred. 'But how are we going to break it to JP? He believes he is in love. This is going to destroy him.'

'Hearts mend,' said Grace. She did not catch Bertie's eye, for once, many years ago, she had broken *his*.

'How did you pull it off, Grace?' Kitty asked.

Grace closed her eyes and shook her head. How could she explain to Kitty that she had been jealous of Bridie for her affair with Bertie, and taking control of the girl's destiny had given her the perfect opportunity for revenge? How could she articulate such a thing without looking like a monster? How could she confess that she hadn't acted out of a desire to rescue Bertie from scandal or indeed to save Bridie from ruin, but out of a need to be rid of Bridie and her children forever, for her own sake? With her artful skill of manipulation Grace had arranged for Bridie to disappear by sending her off to America. Grace had intended to arrange the adoption of the two illegitimate children as soon as possible and in so doing rid her world of all the evidence of her ex-lover's weakness, which was an affront to *her,* for Bridie had been but a maid, a lowly maid, and a plain one at that! But Michael Doyle had intervened, kidnapped JP and brought him to the Hunting Lodge in a creel – while the other twin was successfully spirited out of the convent and sent across the Atlantic with Larry and Pamela Wallace, who were very grateful indeed. Grace had never expected the child to come looking for *her.* Dear God, she thought with the deepest regret, what had possessed her to put her own name on the birth certificate?

'It wasn't hard to pull off,' she replied, opening her eyes. 'The nuns do this sort of thing all the time. They make a lot of money that way. It's not right but it's the way it is. They knew exactly what they were doing and they fooled Bridie into believing her daughter was dead. And Bridie? Poor girl, she was like a lamb, a lamb to the slaughter. God forgive me,' she whispered, suddenly overwhelmed with remorse. 'If I could turn back the clock and do it differently, I would.'

'Well, seeing as you can't, Grace, there is one thing you *must* do,' said Kitty. Bertie raised his eyes over his glass. 'Pretend you are as shocked and appalled as we are. You never knew there was a twin, the nuns never told you and they betrayed you all. The maid's name was Mary O'Connor, that's the name Papa and I agreed to tell JP, and she is buried in Dublin, you know not where. She died soon after giving birth from loss of blood. That way you protect yourself from JP's wrath and from Martha digging further.'

Grace took Kitty's hand and squeezed it. 'Thank you,' she said.

Kitty squeezed it back. 'We must be grateful,' she said. 'If you hadn't put your name on the birth certificate Martha would have come looking for Bridie Doyle and then we'd have been in a much deeper mess.' But in her heart she smothered her true feelings, that she was appalled by Grace's decision to split up the twins. How Grace could have done such a callous and pitiless thing was beyond her understanding.

Mrs Goodwin knew Martha's meeting had gone horribly wrong even before she saw her tear-stained face, for her list-less gait was of a person who had lost all hope. Mrs Goodwin, who was walking towards the inn from having spent the morning in the delightful company of John Maddox, pushed aside her happiness and hurried over to embrace her. Martha had walked back from the beach with her hat in her hand, so that her hair was now a tangled mess. She allowed Mrs Goodwin to wrap her arms around her and escort her into the inn and up the stairs before Mrs O'Sullivan appeared out of the shadows to ask awkward questions. When they were safely in their bedroom with the door closed Martha dropped onto the bed and tossed her hat onto the quilt. 'Grace is not my mother,' she said. 'She put her name on the adoption certificate in order for the nuns to make more money out of the deal. I suppose a baby of noble blood is going to be worth more than the baby of a simple maid.'

Mrs Goodwin perched on her bed, opposite Martha. 'Oh my dear girl, you must be so disappointed.'

'I thought I had found her, Goodwin. But I've found nothing but a phantom.'

'What did she say?'

'That my mother was a maid but she couldn't remember her name. She remembered my parents' names, though.'

Mrs Goodwin frowned. 'How did she know this maid? Was she working for her?'

'I don't know. She said she was young and in trouble and she took it upon herself to help her. She said she's going to find out. Then she's going to tell me.'

'I should have gone with you,' said Mrs Goodwin crossly. There *she* was, enjoying herself immensely, while Martha was facing the greatest disappointment of her life. She should have been more attentive.

'No, it was right that I went on my own. I just feel very let down.'

Mrs Goodwin smiled. 'You will find your mother, if Lady Rowan-Hampton is helping you. I imagine she is a woman who is capable of anything. And JP will be back soon. That will cheer you up.'

Martha rallied a little. 'Yes, it will. I feel I need him more than ever right now. I don't think I'm wrong in expecting him to understand.' She laughed sadly. 'I've been wrong about everything else, but I don't think I'm going to be wrong about *that*.'

Chapter 13

That evening Martha hid her disappointment as she and Mrs Goodwin dined at the White House. Kitty had sent an invitation through Mrs O'Sullivan, and Mrs Goodwin and Martha had supposed that she was eager to entertain them while they waited for JP to return from London. When they arrived Kitty embraced Martha affectionately as if she were a Deverill already and her husband Robert, who had been somewhat reserved the night before, was surprisingly genial, which Martha put down to him feeling more comfortable in his own home. Kitty's sister Elspeth MacCartain and her husband Peter, who had clearly had more than a tipple before arriving, were already in the drawing room, and the Rector, Reverend Maddox, who had sent Mrs Goodwin into such a fever of excitement the night before, was eagerly standing by the door as if he had been waiting for her to arrive all evening. Martha's spirits were resuscitated as Kitty made a great fuss of her and once or twice Martha caught her staring at her from the other end of the table. She wondered whether she was under scrutiny on account of JP and if that was so, whether she came up to scratch.

Martha had been wallowing in her own emotions all

afternoon so that it was only in the middle of dinner, when Mrs Goodwin laughed at something the Rector said, that Martha noticed something extraordinary was happening to her nanny. Martha had never heard her laugh with such abandon. As Martha looked closer she noticed too that the old woman's hair had come loose from its bun, leaving it to soften around her face in silvery waves. Indeed, she looked distinctly pretty as the candlelight blurred the lines on her skin and danced off her eyes. Was it possible, she wondered as Reverend Maddox leaned towards Mrs Goodwin and said something in a low and confidential voice, that Mrs Goodwin was in love? Martha hadn't imagined that grown-up people's hearts were the same as young people's. She had assumed that by the time they reached sixty they had wizened like dried prunes, but Mrs Goodwin's seemed to be as ripe as a new fruit. This was a very different Goodwin to the one who had raised her in the nursery. She laughed again and Martha envied her nanny's happiness. She longed for JP to come home so that she could be as happy as *she* was. *It won't be long*, Martha told herself. *And when we are eventually reunited I will tell him everything.*

'What a splendid dinner that was,' said Mrs Goodwin with satisfaction as she climbed into the cab when the evening was over. 'What charming company they keep here in Ballinakelly. Charming. I must say I am enjoying myself very much.'

'Tell me, Goodwin, how do you know Reverend Maddox?' Martha asked.

Mrs Goodwin turned her face towards the window as the cab set off down the drive. 'I met him a very long time ago in Brighton,' she said softly. 'He was yet to find his vocation. We were both of us very young.'

'Did you fall in love?' Martha worried that her question might be intrusive because Mrs Goodwin remained gazing out of the window without replying for a very long while.

Finally, she looked into her lap and answered. 'Yes, dear, I did.' Martha sensed that that was all Mrs Goodwin was prepared to share. She longed to ask whether she had met *Mr* Goodwin at that point but didn't want to embarrass her if the answer was yes, so she remained silent. Martha could tell that she was thinking of John Maddox. She knew that look because she'd seen it before in her own reflection; the look of wonder at a world so beautiful simply because *he* is in it. She sighed and let her gaze rest on the little beads of rain that had collected on the glass of her window. Beautiful, yes, because JP rendered everything so.

The following morning the two women set out to browse the shops. The skies were heavy with cloud and the air cold and damp with the promise of rain. There weren't many shops of interest in Ballinakelly for two women used to the abundance of America, but they needed something to do to while away the hours. After visiting a couple of shops selling trumpery and bric-a-brac they were drawn to the milliner's on account of the pretty coloured hats and trimmings in the window. They pushed open the door, nudging the little bell that tinkled heartily, and found that there were already a couple of women talking to the milliner at the other end of the shop. The milliner greeted Mrs Goodwin and Martha with a nod and a polite 'Good morning' but continued talking to the two other women who were finely dressed in elegant coats and hats. Martha paid them no attention and began to peruse the shelves. 'Look at this, Goodwin,' she said, lifting a teal-blue hat off the display. 'What a beautiful colour.'

On hearing the American accent Bridie turned round. She watched the young woman for a moment as she stood in front of the long mirror and exchanged her own brown hat for the teal one. 'What do you think, Goodwin?' the young woman asked.

'I think it's lovely,' said Goodwin. 'I think they're *all* lovely.'

Unable to restrain her curiosity Bridie walked across the shop floor to join them. 'You know, Mrs O'Leary can make anything you like,' she said. 'She's an artist. And you won't find that teal colour anywhere else. It's quite unique.'

Martha turned round and smiled at Bridie. 'Thank you,' she said. 'That's very kind of you.'

'Please forgive my intrusion but I can tell from your accent that you're from America,' Bridie continued, smiling. 'I lived in America for a good many years. If you don't mind me asking, where are you from?'

'Connecticut,' Martha replied.

Bridie's face lit up with surprise. 'What a coincidence! I lived there too.'

Mrs Goodwin tore herself away from the ravishing hats to listen. 'Goodwin, isn't this a remarkable coincidence?' said Martha. 'This nice lady—'

'Countess di Marcantonio,' Bridie interrupted and Martha was so startled that she was in the company of a countess that she came over all nervous, unsure whether or not to curtsy. But the Countess seemed uninterested in etiquette. 'May I introduce my friend, Mrs O'Leary,' she added. On hearing their names both Emer and the milliner turned round and Bridie laughed. 'There are two Mrs O'Learys,' she said. 'Mrs Jack O'Leary and Mrs Séamus O'Leary.'

'It's a pleasure to make your acquaintance,' said Martha

politely, now believing herself to be among royalty. 'I'm Miss Wallace and this is Mrs Goodwin.'

'Is this your first time in Ireland?' Bridie asked.

'Yes, it is,' said Martha. 'My mother is originally from Clonakilty.'

'So you've come to find your roots?'

'I have,' Martha answered and she was so used to telling the lie that she almost believed it herself.

Bridie narrowed her eyes and looked closely at Martha. 'You know, Miss Wallace,' she said. 'You and I have the same colouring and in my opinion the shade that suits us best is deep plum.' The milliner reached into the window and lifted a plum-coloured felt hat with a wide pink ribbon off its block and put it into Bridie's outstretched hand. Martha removed the teal one and let Bridie arrange the other onto her head. The two women stood in front of the mirror, Martha in the plum-coloured hat and Bridie in a more subdued beige one, and Mrs Goodwin gave a start because they were so very alike. Both had pale faces with cocoa-coloured eyes, a sprinkling of freckles over their noses and long, dark brown hair. 'Now that brings out the pink tone in your cheeks, do you see?' said Bridie. 'It lifts you. Indeed, Miss Wallace, you and I can look a little washed-out at times and this plum shade brings out the life in our faces.'

'The Countess is right,' the milliner agreed, nodding. 'And the cloche style is still very fashionable.'

Emer smiled in amusement. 'The two of you look very Irish,' she said. 'Don't you think, Mrs Goodwin? They couldn't be from anywhere else!'

Bridie laughed. 'Well, I'm from Ballinakelly and Miss Wallace is from Clonakilty. Who knows, we might even be related.'

Martha laughed, flattered. 'I love the hat, Countess. But we're on a very tight budget.' She took it off and handed it back to the milliner. 'The Countess is right. You are truly an artist, Mrs O'Leary.'

'But you must have it!' Bridie insisted. 'Don't you think so, Emer?'

'Oh, she must,' Emer agreed. 'But I understand a tight budget. How long are you staying?' she asked.

'A few more days, perhaps,' Mrs Goodwin replied. 'We're lodging at Seafort House, which is not too dear, and we're having such a nice time. We're in no rush to leave.'

'That's grand,' said Bridie. 'Perhaps you'll reconsider, Miss Wallace. Mrs O'Leary will put it aside for a day or two in case you change your mind, won't you, Loretta?'

'Of course I will,' said Loretta O'Leary, going behind the counter with the hat. She was willing to do anything for the Countess who had only been in Ballinakelly for a few weeks and had already commissioned more than a dozen hats.

'Then that's settled,' said Bridie with satisfaction. 'I think you'll look very elegant in Connecticut in that plum hat.'

Martha was blushing at the kindness of these strangers. People in Ireland were remarkably friendly, she thought. 'Well, it's been nice meeting you,' she said. 'Mrs Goodwin is keen to wander around the church before lunch,' she added. 'So, we'd better be off.'

'If you want to see something miraculous,' Bridie suggested, 'there's a statue of the Virgin on the hillside as you leave the town. It was built in 1828 to commemorate a young girl's vision. Occasionally it moves all by itself. People come from the world over to see it. You can't leave Ballinakelly without having a look. You never know, she might move for *you*.'

Martha looked at Mrs Goodwin. 'Shall we go and see it after lunch?' she said.

'That's a good idea,' Mrs Goodwin replied.

Martha turned to Bridie. 'Have *you* ever seen it move?'

'As a child I saw it move all the time,' she replied.

'Goodness, how extraordinary.'

'But I haven't seen it move since I've been back, but to be truthful, I haven't cast it more than a passing glance.'

'Does it bring good luck?' asked Martha.

Bridie sighed doubtfully. 'I don't know. I have had both bad luck and good luck in my life so far, so I couldn't say. But if the Virgin intervened in the lives of everyone she'd be run off her wings, don't you think – and I do believe we are left to make our own mistakes and to learn from them. I'm sure, Miss Wallace, that if she moves for you, it will bring you good luck.'

Martha and Mrs Goodwin left the milliner's in high spirits, remarking on how incredibly warm and gracious the people of Ballinakelly were. 'That lady must have married a foreign count,' said Mrs Goodwin as they walked up the street towards the church. 'She was very elegant, wasn't she? Did you notice the diamonds on her ears? They were the size of marigolds!'

Martha laughed. 'I didn't notice the diamonds, Goodwin. Is a countess like royalty?'

'Not a foreign one, my dear. They are two a penny.'

'Oh,' said Martha, disappointed.

'She said she grew up here in Ballinakelly and her Irish accent is very strong in spite of the years lived in America. I'll bet she wasn't a lady when she met him. If you ask me the Virgin brought her good luck in marrying a count.'

They reached the Protestant church of St Patrick just after

eleven. As they walked up the path towards the big doors
Mrs Goodwin quickened her pace, and not because it had
started to drizzle lightly but because, there, standing near
the entrance, was Reverend Maddox, carrying a cardboard
box of prayer books. He feigned surprise at seeing her but
Martha sensed their meeting had been pre-arranged. His
round face glowed the colour of cranberry jam and the string
of exclamations he ejected about coincidences was much too
theatrical to be spontaneous. He had planned his reaction and
was delivering it badly. Martha, keen not to be a spare wheel
in what was clearly the rekindling of an old romance, made
her excuses and left them alone, telling Mrs Goodwin that
she would meet her back at the inn at one for lunch. She then
set off down the road to explore the town. Glancing above
her she saw that not far away the clouds were thinning and
patches of blue were beginning to show.

Martha wandered up the street, taking pleasure from her
solitude. She enjoyed the old-fashioned sight of a horse pulling a cart full of sacks and a couple of lads in caps and jackets
weaving up the middle of the road on bicycles. Ballinakelly
was quiet and sleepy and seemingly from a bygone age. She
wondered what it had looked like when her mother was
a child. But having thought her roots were here she now
realized that she didn't belong in Ballinakelly after all. The
feeling of coming home had also been an illusion as unreal
as the tearful reunion with her mother that she had so often
repeated in her mind. For all she knew her mother had come
from the other end of the country. She might not have even
come from Ireland at all. Her heart grew heavy and her eyes
ceased to gaze about her in wonder but dropped disconsolately to the pavement.

After a while she looked up and noticed that she was

standing in front of the Catholic church of All Saints. It was
built of grey stone with a needle spire soaring up towards
Heaven and it seemed to loom out of the drizzle like a beacon
of solace. Drawn by the golden lights that shone through the
stained-glass windows and the certainty of somehow finding
comfort there, Martha wandered in. The Tobins, her mother
Pam's family, were Catholic but Martha had been brought
up in her father's faith, which was Presbyterian. However,
she didn't feel it improper to venture inside to have a look.
God was God, after all, she thought, whichever house one
chose to find Him in.

All Saints was a small church with rows of wooden pews,
white walls and statues of the Virgin and saints positioned in
the corners to inspire the parishioners with their fine exam-
ples. At the end of the aisle the altar sat in a pool of soft light
that streamed in misty beams through the colourful arched
window above. Up a small flight of stairs was a pulpit and
flickering on tall wooden stands were giant candles. Martha
wasn't alone. A few people were kneeling in the pews in
quiet contemplation, a little old lady in a long black dress and
shawl was lighting votive candles at a shrine which glowed
with tiny flames while a tall man with dark black curls was
talking in a low voice to the priest. The place smelt of incense
and candle wax and was so warm that Martha thought she'd
sit in one of the pews and enjoy the peace for a while.

The priest did not seem to mind. Martha saw him glance
in her direction and thought he must recognize her need for
solitude. She let her thoughts meander back to JP. He'd be
home tomorrow, she hoped. She looked forward to sharing
her troubles with him. As an illegitimate child himself he
would understand, she knew. If she never found her mother
at least she'd found JP.

Her thoughts were interrupted by the tall, curly-haired man and the old woman who were now walking slowly down the aisle in her direction. Martha watched them absent-mindedly. The woman was as fragile as a bird; beside her the man looked like a giant with his broad shoulders and powerful presence. Then he looked at her. For a moment Martha caught his eye but she quickly looked away. Then the old woman spoke. 'Bridie?' she said. Martha ignored her. 'Bridie?' she said again, this time with more insistence. The man bent down and mumbled something into her ear and the old woman gasped. 'God save us, Michael,' she said. 'I thought that was Bridie twenty years ago.' Martha lifted her gaze in time to catch the old woman's wizened face staring at her in bewilderment, as if she were a ghost. Then they were gone and Martha was alone and the priest left her to her meditation.

At last the day of JP's arrival dawned. An invitation was delivered via Mrs O'Sullivan at breakfast and Martha and Mrs Goodwin took a cab to the Hunting Lodge in great excitement directly after. The sun shone, the sea glistened, the little boats bobbed on the water like a flock of gulls and everything in the world seemed beautiful to both Martha and Mrs Goodwin. They were met by the butler who showed them into the drawing room where Lord Deverill and Grace Rowan-Hampton were waiting for them. However, it wasn't the anxious expressions on their faces that grabbed Martha's attention but the portrait hanging above the fireplace. It hadn't been there the other evening, but it was there now and Martha recognized the person in it at once. She stood in front of it and felt a strange dizziness come over her. But before she could work out *why* she knew the woman with red hair and pale grey eyes her attention was diverted by Kitty who was now walking in with JP.

When JP saw Martha his features, which had been taut with annoyance ever since Kitty had informed him that he couldn't see Martha until they had talked, all together, up at the Hunting Lodge, now softened and he took her hands and kissed her blushing cheek. There was nothing anyone could say, he thought, that would prevent him from marrying her. Nothing. He remembered the wish he had made on Ha'penny Bridge and knew that not even the disapproval of his family would discourage him to follow his heart. He had made a wish and his wish had been granted for he could see that the tenderness in her eyes was equal to his.

'Please sit down, JP,' said his father and his apprehension made his voice sound gruffer than he intended. JP was startled and his features hardened again with irritation. He greeted Mrs Goodwin and Grace then went and sat on the club fender so that Martha and her chaperone could have the sofa to themselves. He wondered why this conversation had to involve Grace. Surely Kitty or his father could have had a quiet word? Kitty sat beside Grace on the sofa opposite and Bertie sank into the armchair with a groan. 'We have something we need to tell you,' he began. The air in the room was oppressive and Martha was beginning to sweat. Through her mind raced the reasons why she might not have come up to scratch. Perhaps they thought she was Catholic, maybe they didn't approve of Americans ... 'Grace?' said Bertie and all eyes turned to Lady Rowan-Hampton.

'I don't know whether you are aware, Martha, but JP's mother died in childbirth,' Grace began.

JP's face flushed. 'What does that have to do with ... ?' he interrupted crossly.

Bertie put up his hand. 'Let her speak, goddamn it. It's important.' Again, his anguish gave his tone a sharp edge which took even *him* by surprise.

Grace continued gravely. 'JP was born in a convent in Dublin in January 1922 ...' Now it was Martha's turn to flush. She glanced at Mrs Goodwin who shot her a startled look. 'His mother was a housemaid for Lord Deverill. What no one realized until a couple of days ago when Martha paid me a visit was that the young woman gave birth not to one child but to two. Twins.' Martha stared at JP and her flush drained away with her hope, leaving her face as pale as death. JP blinked back at her in astonishment, a terrible disappointment seizing him by the throat. Of all the reasons two people might not be permitted to be together he had never imagined *this*. 'The nuns put my name on the birth certificate, knowing that an aristocratic mother would fetch a higher price,' Grace continued. 'But I am not your mother, Martha. I can tell you now that your mother was a sweet, gentle country girl called Mary O'Connor and it is a great pity that neither you nor JP ever knew her. But Lord Deverill is your father and you are siblings. I'm sorry that you cannot be together in the way you wish, but you came into the world together, it is a blessing that Fate has reunited you.' JP shook his head and clenched his hands and his face reddened as he tried very hard to stem his tears.

Martha stared at Lord Deverill, her father. She had only ever considered her mother, but here she was in the presence of the man who had fathered her, and she was overcome. There was to be no tearful embrace, no triumphant end to a lifelong search, no satisfactory conclusion. Lord Deverill gazed at her and she gazed at him and there was no spark of recognition, just a hollow and aching bewilderment. *How disappointed he must be to discover that he has another illegitimate child*, Martha thought – as disappointed as *she* was for having found, in the place of a loving mother, a confused and begrudging father.

Martha's attention was drawn to the portrait and it was as if the lady depicted in paint was not a picture at all but a real person, gazing down on her with real eyes. She stared at it as a memory resurfaced like a bubble that has been trapped for years beneath a rock at the bottom of the sea. It rose slowly into her consciousness then popped into her mind with startling clarity. She had seen the lady before. She had seen her many times and she had loved her. 'That's Adeline,' she said in a quiet voice. 'My grandmother.' And her eyes stung with tears.

'You know Adeline?' said Bertie, astonished. He too turned his gaze to the painting. Adeline gazed back and smiled sadly. *Yes, Martha, I have always been beside you even when you lost your ability to see me. I never left you and I will never leave you.* And Martha heard her words in a whisper that might have been the sound of the wind outside had they not been articulated so clearly.

'She's always been with me,' Martha replied, the portrait blurring now as she gave into her disillusionment.

Kitty rushed over and wrapped her arms around her, pulling her close. 'You really *are* my sister,' she said, feeling the girl stiffen in her embrace. 'You and I have inherited the gift of second sight from Adeline. I'm sorry you haven't found your mother, my darling, but you have found us and we're your family too.' Kitty's eyes stung with tears, not for herself, but for JP and the half-sister she had just discovered.

JP stood up. 'Please can you all leave us,' he said, looking at each in turn. 'I want to have a moment alone with

Martha.' With heavy hearts Bertie, Kitty, Grace and Mrs Goodwin left the room to reconvene in the library where they shared their unhappiness in hushed voices over large glasses of whiskey.

Martha and JP looked at each other, not knowing what to say. They knew they loved each other but neither had imagined that their attraction was fuelled by a deep unconscious recognition. By a magnetic pull that had started seventeen years before, in the womb. How could they express the devastation in their hearts while at the same time acknowledge the miracle of their reunion? As the full weight of Grace's revelation fell upon them they came together in a desperate embrace.

'We're leaving Ireland,' said Martha when she and Mrs Goodwin climbed once again into the cab. 'I can't stay here a moment longer. I need time to think. I need space to gather my thoughts. I have just suffered the greatest disappointment of my life and I don't know what to do with myself. I should never have come. Life was better in ignorance. I should have appreciated the family I had, not longed for a fantasy. I have been a fool, Goodwin.'

Mrs Goodwin drew Martha to her and rested her cheek against her hair. 'I don't know how to comfort you,' she said helplessly.

'Crying over my poor dead mother is simply crying over a lost dream, but JP was real. I don't think I'll ever recover from that loss, Goodwin. I don't know how I'm going to go on.' Her voice broke. 'I don't think I can. The world has changed. It was beautiful. Now it's hard and unfriendly and I'm frightened to be in it.'

They reached the inn. It seemed surreal that only a couple

of hours before they had left it in such a state of excitement. They pushed open the door and walked into the hall.

There, sitting in a chair, was Larry Wallace.

He stood up when he saw his daughter and a cloud of uncertainty swept across his face, but Martha ran to him and threw herself against him. 'Oh Daddy!' she sobbed. 'You're here!' He took her into his arms and glanced at Mrs Goodwin over her head. The old woman's miserable face told him that something dreadful had happened.

'Martha!' he soothed, stroking her hair. 'It's okay, I'm here now. Everything's going to be all right.'

'How did you find me?'

'Professor Partridge and a little detective work. It wasn't very difficult.'

'You came all the way from America for *me*?'

He squeezed her so tightly she could scarcely breathe. 'You're my girl, aren't you?'

'I am,' she sniffed. 'I *am* your girl. Take me home,' she said.

Larry Wallace closed his eyes and sighed deeply. 'That's what I was hoping you'd say.'

Martha was not sorry to leave Ballinakelly. She wanted to erase it from her experience. She wanted things to return to the way they were, before she had loved so deeply and lost so terribly. But Mrs Goodwin had made up her mind. *She* was not going anywhere.

The old nanny took Martha's hands and told her that even though their adventure had come to a devastating end she wouldn't have missed it for anything in the world. 'But my place is here, in Ballinakelly, with John,' she said. 'I have been given a second chance, my dear Martha, and I don't want to miss it.'

'Then you mustn't,' Martha replied. 'He's lucky to have found you again. At least one of us is happy. Thank you, Goodwin—'

'Don't say it,' Mrs Goodwin interrupted swiftly. 'We're beyond thank-yous. Go now before I start to cry too . . .'

Just as Martha was about to climb into the cab Mrs O'Sullivan hurried out, carrying a large hat box. 'This came for you this morning, Miss Wallace,' she said. Martha knew immediately what it was but she couldn't imagine why anyone would gift it to her. Overwhelmed, she opened the little white envelope and read the note. It said, simply: *Dear Miss Wallace. It was made for you. My best wishes, Countess di Marcantonio.* Why would a lady she'd only just met buy her a hat?

Then Martha was struck with an idea. 'There's something we have to see before we leave,' she said to her father as the cabbie put the hat box in the cab. 'It will only take a minute.'

Larry and Martha Wallace stood at the foot of the hill and looked up at the statue of the Virgin, who seemed to watch them serenely, if a little curiously, from her place in the grass. She wasn't as tall as Martha had imagined, only about four feet, dressed in a white gown with a blue cloak draped over her narrow shoulders. Her pale face was shiny and inclining slightly, as if she was ready to listen to the problems of the world with compassion and understanding. Larry didn't know why his daughter wanted to see the statue, but everything about his daughter had baffled him since he had read the note she had left in the hall and the subsequent letter she had written from London. It hadn't been hard to find her. The problem was trying to work out whether she'd *want* to be found. As it turned out, much to his relief, she did.

But he stood beside her now, patiently, wondering what she was waiting for.

And then the statue moved. Martha caught her breath. Larry blinked. 'Did that thing sway?' he asked. Martha nodded, afraid to speak unless she ruined it. It swayed again, indisputably so, from side to side. 'Is someone up there playing a prank?' Larry asked, wandering further up the road so that he could see behind it. But Martha knew. It wasn't a prank; it was the Virgin. She didn't know how and she didn't know when, but Martha was certain that, in the end, everything would turn out all right.

Maggie O'Leary

Ballinakelly, 1662

Maggie first laid eyes on Lord Deverill on a drizzly morning in early spring, when, accompanied by an entourage of about fifteen men, he entered the small hamlet of Ballinakelly. He was mounted on a majestic chestnut horse, dressed finely in a crimson cloak, a wide-brimmed hat with an extravagant plume, high leather boots and shining spurs. His hair was a rich brown and curled in fashionable waves onto his broad and confident shoulders. But Maggie didn't notice how handsome he was with his straight nose and pale grey eyes. Blinded by anger she stepped into the lane.

This man had stolen her family's land. Land the O'Learys had owned for generations. He had knocked down their home and built a castle there, seizing their magnificent view of the ocean and all the memories contained within it. High grey walls now soared towards the sky where once the smoke from their modest chimney had gently wafted. Towers and turrets formed powerful defences to protect this ennobled soldier from his enemies where, before, their small farmhouse had welcomed anyone who chose to stop by on their way up the coast. This castle was an affront to the people of Ballinakelly, an affront to the O'Learys – what was left of them – and a personal affront to Maggie, who was now responsible for her sister and her grandmother who had gone mad with despair in the ramshackle cabin Maggie had built in the woods.

There he sat, the newly appointed Lord Deverill of Ballinakelly, speaking English which Maggie did not understand. His voice had to compete with the wind that swept up the main street in insolent gusts as if it too wanted to see the back of him. Maggie stepped into the road, her Bandon cloak trailing in the mud at her feet. Lord Deverill stopped talking and watched her with interest. A man beside him raised his voice and placed his hand on the sword at his hip, but Lord Deverill lifted his glove to silence him and Maggie lowered her hood. She shook her head and her long dark locks of tangled hair fell about her face and over her shoulders in thick, wild waves. Her anger did not, however, blind her to the expression of wonder on his face. She stared at him with wide green eyes and spoke the curse that seemed not to come *from* her but *through* her from some supernatural force beyond her control. '*Is mise Peig Ni Laoghaire. A Tiarna Deverill, dhein tú éagóir orm agus ar mo shliocht trín ár dtalamh a thógáil agus ár spiorad a bhriseadh. Go dtí go gceartaíonn tú na h-éagóracha siúd, cuirim malacht ort féin agus d-oidhrí, I dtreo is go mbí sibh gan suaimhneas síoraí I ndomhan na n-anmharbh.*' As she spoke her voice took on a mellifluous tone like the hiss of an enchanted snake and she saw, to her delight, that Lord Deverill was mesmerized by it. When she was finished Lord Deverill turned to one of his men and Maggie assumed that he was demanding the translation for the man looked reluctant and his face was grey with fear, but he finally replied in a loud and quivering voice for the whole party to hear.

'Lord Deverill,' said the man and a small smile crept across Maggie's lips as she waited to see Lord Deverill's reaction. 'You have wronged me and my descendants by taking our land and breaking our spirits. Until you right those wrongs I curse you and your heirs to an eternity of unrest and to the world of the undead.' The men reached for their swords but Lord Deverill seemed to make light of those dark words. When he turned his face away Maggie lifted her skirts and with the agility of a young deer disappeared into the cluster of thatched hovels.

She only stopped running when she reached the safety of the forest. When she was certain that she was alone she sank to the ground at the foot of a tree. Her body shook with nervous laughter. It amused her to think that she had not only bewitched Lord Deverill but snatched his heart as well. *He has taken our land so I vow to take his heart and crush the life out of it with my own hands*, she thought, picking a little blue gentian and twirling it between her finger and thumb. Having felt impotent for so long she now had a sense of purpose and an exciting plan.

Like a predator Maggie stalked Lord Deverill. She lurked outside the castle gates and watched him when he left and when he returned. She even dared sneak right up to the castle walls to peer in through the windows on dark nights when the rooms blazed with candlelight. She marvelled at the luxury, she wondered at his privilege, but she didn't expect to grow fond of the man.

From her hiding place at the window she watched him pace the rooms, his forehead furrowed with worry. She watched him playing cards with his friends by the large, vivacious fire and she sensed that his laughter was only for show, for when he knocked back the wine she noticed sorrow in the careless way he did it. What could he have to be sad about? she wondered. How could he be unhappy in a magnificent castle with such a beautiful view to please him? But there was a sadness in him that caught her off guard. She had expected him to be grandiose and pompous but what she saw was a sensitive man with troubles on his mind and she found herself wanting to unfurrow his brow with her fingers and kiss those lips that so rarely smiled.

Sometimes he'd disappear for months and the candlelight glowed cheerlessly in only a few of the rooms in Castle Deverill as the servants looked after the place in his absence. Maggie suspected he'd gone back to London and wondered whether he had a wife there and how he spent his days. She imagined him dining with the King, which gave her a frisson of pleasure, but when she thought of his wife she grew jealous.

Years passed. Maggie knew not how many. She imparted messages from the dead and her name grew infamous in Co. Cork. They said she was a witch and those who visited did not stay long, but she didn't care. It was her duty to be a medium between this world and the next. She didn't think much about the curse she had put on Lord Deverill. It was long ago now and Lord Deverill had grown into such a large presence in her life that she had almost forgotten her plan to crush his heart because a tenderness had arisen and attached itself to his name. .

Then one day in late summer she was in the forest when she heard the rumbling of hooves and the sound of the huntsman's horn. Birds took to the air and small creatures dived for cover. Maggie saw a stag on a grassy knoll, a majestic, noble creature standing benign and pure. Then she saw the pointed barrel of Lord Deverill's musket and her horror at the thought of that splendid creature's destruction compelled her to act. Hitching her dress to her knees she hurried up the knoll and, as the stag leapt lithely away, the clouds parted and a beam of sunlight shone down upon her, as if some higher power was grateful for her intervention. Lord Deverill lowered the barrel and stared at her in amazement. The apples of his cheeks flushed and his lips parted and to her surprise her heart began to pound against her ribcage with desire as if it, too, had forgotten that he was the enemy who had stolen her land.

She lowered her hood and gazed back at him. Their eyes met and the forest fell silent around them like an invisible veil, hiding them from the world. Lord Deverill dismounted and threw the reins around a branch. As he walked purposefully towards her, Maggie hastened down the back of the knoll, knowing that he would follow; *hoping* that he would. She turned to see him on the top of the hill and smiled, inviting him to catch up with her while at the same time quickening her pace.

Deeper and deeper into the forest they went. The trees grew thicker, knitting their branches into a dark canopy above them. The birds ceased to twitter and only thin watery beams of light managed to make it through the small gaps in the leaves to illuminate their way.

Then he was upon her. He swung her round and pushed her against the trunk of an oak and pressed his lips to hers. She allowed his tongue to slide between her teeth and explore her mouth with an urgency that enthralled her. This was the first time she had ever been kissed and it aroused feelings in her that she had never experienced before. She felt a hot and aching sensation between her legs and a strong desire for him to touch her there. He was breathing heavily through his nose, like a horse who has galloped a great distance, and he fumbled with her laces to undo her shift. At last it came undone and he let it drop at her waist. Her breasts, now exposed, were white and soft and he cupped them with his hands and the sensation in her abdomen grew so strong as to be almost unbearable. He buried his face in her neck and licked her skin and Maggie let out a low moan from the bottom of her throat as the feeling of his thumbs grazing her nipples sent quivers of enjoyment like hot arrows into her belly. She lifted her chin and closed her eyes as his fingers found their way beneath her skirt into the dark centre of her longing. His touch was gentle and slippery and rhythmic and the aching intensified until she lost control of her actions and of the thoughts in her mind and was only aware of this pleasure, tormenting her and pleasing her in equal measure, building and building.

At last he unbuttoned his trousers and released himself. He lifted Maggie's leg and slid inside her where it was hot and wet. With a groan he began to move like a beast and the excruciating feeling in Maggie's belly began to build once again until she was aware only of that and the need to reach some sort of peak. Lord Deverill moved faster now and Maggie moved with him, then she gasped, as if the glorious sensation now spreading through her body was some kind of miracle, and let out a sharp cry. Every nerve seemed flooded with heat and she shuddered as Lord Deverill expelled his seed inside her. Slowly they came back to their senses, dazed and flushed, hearts pounding against the bones that separated them. They were drenched in sweat and bathed in bliss. Weak in the knees they sank onto the soft forest floor.

Maggie knelt and pushed down her skirts but she left her shift still hanging around her waist and her breasts exposed.

She gazed at him, holding him in her thrall for a long moment. He stared up at her and his expression was of a man lost to love and lust and she laughed. She couldn't help herself. 'Has Lord Deverill given me his heart?' she teased and he frowned because he didn't understand her native tongue. Her laugh alarmed him and he brought his left hand to his chest, where a gold band gleamed on his third finger. At the sight of the wedding band Maggie's anger grew inside her like a maddened creature, reminding her of her curse and her vow and she pulled a knife out of her skirt and pressed it to his throat. She could end it all now, she thought. She could destroy the thief who had stolen her land. She could murder the man who had taken *her* but was married to another. But the fear that darkened his face made her lose courage and she pulled the knife away, laughing at her own foolishness; bewildered by her cowardice. It wasn't compassion that prevented her from taking his life, but love.

Scared that he might turn the knife on *her*, she bolted into the forest.

PART TWO

Chapter 14

If Bridie had wanted her summer ball to be the most spectacular that Ballinakelly had ever seen she had succeeded. The driveway was lined with enormous flares and the rhododendrons were at their most magnificent. The lawn was strewn with lavender that gave off its sweet perfume as the guests walked over it, and the trees and bushes had been lit from beneath so that, as the sun set, they glowed with a golden radiance. At dusk the castle was illuminated with so many lights it was a wonder that the ESB powerhouse in Cork had not collapsed under the demand for electricity. Inside the castle, the displays of lilies and roses were larger and more beautiful than anyone had previously seen. The ballroom mirrors glittered with the reflection of five thousand candles and the great chandeliers, which had been polished until the glass pieces shone like diamonds, dominated in all their glory. Servants in livery attended to the guests' every need, refilling the crystal flutes with the finest champagne and taking around silver trays of the most exquisite little canapés anyone had ever tasted. But Bridie had had very little to do with the arrangements. Grace had suggested she hire the famous Violet Adair, who organized the most lavish parties in London, and insisted that Bridie leave everything to *her*, explaining that Mrs Adair was a woman of exceptional taste and, when unrestrained by miserly budgets, could create an earthly paradise that would dazzle even the most hardened party-goers. This elegant woman with a brisk, efficient manner and a perfectionist's eye had exceeded Bridie's expectations. And Cesare, with his hunger to be bigger and better than everyone else, had to admit that even *he* had never seen anything quite so impressive.

'My darling, you have made me the proudest man in the whole world,' he told Bridie, kissing her temple as they enjoyed one of the few moments they would have together in the entire evening. 'Our guests will be talking about this night for many years to come.'

She swelled with pleasure. Pleasing her husband had now become something of a vocation for Bridie who was aware that Ballinakelly had little to offer a cosmopolitan man like Cesare. The only thing he seemed to relish was the castle and playing cards in O'Donovan's. Bridie was grateful to Grace for inviting the guests and relieved that they had agreed to come. Grace had not doubted they would, they were curious to see who had bought the castle, she had told Bridie, as well as unable to resist the allure of money and a glamorous title. Well, if that's what it took to entertain her husband, Bridie was prepared to flaunt both her title and her fortune without restraint. She noticed that Cesare was running his eyes over the guests who were drinking champagne on the lawn. If she was aware that they lingered on the faces of the pretty young women, she chose to ignore it. Her husband *had* to be happy and that was all there was to it, regardless of the cost to herself or her purse.

With a deep breath, Bridie, in a green silk dress with a red rose in her hair, waded into the sea of strangers on the arm of her husband. She shook hands and smiled graciously, keen for Cesare to see that she was all that a hostess should be, and everyone smiled back with deference as if she were royalty, taking in the diamond earrings and the three-bees diamond brooch that embellished her dress. But soon Cesare had moved away, wandering deeper into the crowd, and she only saw his sleek black head rising above the rest as he introduced himself to the ladies. Without her husband at her side Bridie felt a sudden sense of drowning, of being out of her depth, and she searched anxiously for her brothers Michael and Sean, who were somewhere in the throng. She was sure that these new people who scrutinized her saw her for what she really was, the grubby-faced and shoeless daughter of a simple farmer and the castle's cook, and she felt exposed as a fraud. As long as she was in Ballinakelly she would never be free of her past – for she saw it reflected in the eyes of everyone who looked at her.

Bridie was relieved when at last she found Jack and Emer O'Leary and for a blessed moment she could relax and be herself again. Only Jack and her family, who had known her since childhood, made her feel comfortable in her skin, reminding her through memory of who she really was. She rested her gaze on her old friend and was suddenly gripped by an aching longing to be by the river again, hunting for frogs in the undergrowth with Kitty and Celia while Jack stood on the bank watching them with his dog at his heel and his pet hawk on his arm. Life had been simpler then when she had been sure of her place in the world. Who was she pretending to be? she asked herself. A countess in a grand castle! The very idea of it was preposterous but here she was acting the

lead in the most unlikely of plays. Who was she trying to
fool? Cesare? The Deverills? Herself? No amount of money
could change who she really was on the inside. Bridie took
a swig of champagne and laughed bitterly. But when Jack
asked what she was laughing at she couldn't tell him. How
could she explain that the last twenty years had been a farce?

Once everyone was assembled on the lawn the Count
positioned himself on the raised dais which had been put
there for this very moment, and lifted his chin importantly
as the chatter hushed and the guests turned to face him
expectantly. At that moment there was a flurry of activity at
the French doors behind him and Lady Rowan-Hampton,
escorted by a pair of servants, appeared in a stunning silk
gown of the palest duck-egg blue and stepped onto the terrace. Every eye moved from the Count to Grace, who was
no stranger to theatrical entrances. 'I'm so terribly sorry to be
late,' she said, beaming a wide and charming smile, hoping
that Michael Doyle was there among the many faces to see
her at her most splendid.

Cesare jumped off the dais and lifted her hand to his
mouth. 'My dear Lady Rowan-Hampton, the party was
incomplete without you,' he said smoothly, kissing her glove.

'I interrupted your speech,' she said.

'Not interrupted, no,' he replied with a grin. 'You have
introduced me perfectly. How could I have thought of beginning without you? But now you are here, I can welcome
our esteemed guests to our first summer ball.' He dropped
Grace's hand and retook his place on the dais. Grace stood
to one side and pretended to be listening intently, while
scanning the crowd and hoping that Michael might be close
and that she'd get a chance to speak to him. As the Count
spoke, enjoying the sound of his own voice and the sight of

all those distinguished people listening, Grace thought how incredibly pompous he was. He puffed out his chest with great importance as he alluded to his famous Barberini ancestor and Grace sensed once again that he was a brilliant fake. After all, who would know whether or not he was related to Maffeo Barberini? Who could say whether he was a count at all? She narrowed her lovely brown eyes and wondered whether, if she could discover some hidden truth about the Count, Michael might be keen to listen to her. She recalled that it had been the plot to murder Colonel Manley in the War of Independence that had first united them: might not another plot unite them again?

Rosetta watched Bridie as the Count droned on. Her friend's face was full of pride and admiration, and, Rosetta believed, fear: fear that he was too good for her; fear that he might run off with someone else; fear that she didn't have him quite where she wanted him; and fear, perhaps, that she would fall short and disappoint him. Rosetta hated this new fear that had crept into Bridie's heart. In Rosetta's opinion Cesare was arrogant, selfish and, from what she had heard from rumours circulating the town, an incorrigible womanizer. Apparently he had seduced Niamh O'Donovan, according to Rosetta's maid who was a delightful gossip, and plenty of other girls besides. She didn't imagine Bridie had heard these rumours; who would tell her? But she suspected Bridie knew, after all she wasn't a fool. And what did it matter anyway, Bridie would forgive him. In *her* eyes Cesare was perfect and beyond criticism. Rosetta wondered how much control Bridie had of her finances and wished Beaumont Williams, Bridie's attorney in New York, were around to advise her. From the odd comment Bridie had made it appeared that Cesare was going through her fortune

at a reckless speed. Rosetta wondered whether he had ever
had any money of his own before he had married money.
She very much doubted it. She was still bothered by the fact
that he didn't speak good Italian. For a man who claimed to
have spent his childhood in Italy his command of the language was surprisingly poor. She wished she had the tools to
do a little detective work, but she wouldn't know where to
begin. She needed someone with contacts, *international* contacts, to help her. She had a horrible feeling Bridie had been
ill-advised in marrying this handsome adventurer. Spending
all her money was one thing, robbing her of her self-respect
was quite another.

Just as dinner was announced, Grace spotted Michael.
He was talking to a group of men who were listening to
him attentively, as if every word he said was important.
Her heart gave a leap. It had been almost twenty years since
those exciting days during the Troubles when they had been
thrown together in their pursuit of freedom for Ireland, but
he was more handsome now than he had ever been. His black
curly hair was still wild, his dark eyes full of mystery and
danger, his powerful presence radiating around him as if his
very soul was too bright for his body. She felt the familiar
aching in her loins as the memory of his touch caused a ripple
to career over her skin. With the confidence of a woman
whose beauty has ensured that she is welcomed wherever
she presents herself, Grace glided over the grass to the small
group. 'Might the promise of a banquet be the only thing to
tempt you from your intriguing,' she said with a coquettish
smile so delightful the men diverted their attention at once
from Michael's deliverance and gazed on her with admiration. 'Mr Doyle, would you be kind and escort me into
dinner.' Michael, not at all astonished by Grace's boldness,

but surprised by her relentless pursuit of him, had no choice but to hold out his arm.

'I have a bad feeling about the Count,' said Grace as they ambled slowly towards the castle.

'What kind of bad feeling?' Michael asked.

'I sense a fake,' she said.

'Not just an adulterer then,' Michael replied and Grace's jaw stiffened for she was well aware that Michael's newfound faith had given him an abhorrence of adultery – theirs in particular.

'Oh, I'm sure he's that too.'

'Rumour has it.'

'Indeed it does and there is no smoke without fire.'

'You have been kind to Bridie,' he said and there was a tenderness in his voice that she hadn't heard in a long time.

'I'm fond of her, as you know, Michael. God has dealt her a tough hand of cards. I'm not sure the castle has made her as happy as she thought it would. It might have been more prudent to have stayed in America. But it is what it is and I feel responsible. I helped her when she was pregnant and alone and I set her up in America. Now she is here I want to make sure that she has friends. She needs all the friends she can get with that reprobate husband.'

Michael hesitated at the French doors of the castle. 'Grace,' he said in a low voice, holding her back a moment. 'I don't like him either. I don't like the way he treats Bridie and I don't like the rumours. Ballinakelly is a small town and he is indiscreet. If you choose to dig deeper I will be grateful for any information you can glean.' And once again Michael's eyes shone with menace.

Grace's heart gave another leap for he looked like the old Michael. The one she had loved before he had sobered up at

Mount Melleray and returned as pious as a priest. Once again they were united in a plot and she felt dizzy with happiness. 'You can rely on me, Michael,' she whispered.

'I know,' he said gravely. 'You're the one person I always could.'

The dinner was a sumptuous feast, more extravagant than any Deverill banquet had ever been before it. The noise of chatter was loud, the peals of laughter shrill and the sheer merriment of it all was strangely disconcerting to Bridie who, as the evening progressed, was feeling more and more choked with misery. She did not know how to talk to these people, these strangers invited by Grace, and their inquisitive questions sounded patronizing and prying to Bridie's distrustful ear.

As soon as she could she fled the castle. She wanted to hide. She wanted to disappear into the darkness where the watchful eyes of her guests could not find her. She wanted to sob where their vigilant ears could not hear her and take cover so that their critical tongues could not find fault in her to share. She wanted to scrabble about in the woods for the girl she had once been, now lost beneath her finery.

She lifted her skirts above her ankles and ran between the rhododendron bushes towards the gate at the end of the drive. Her shoes clattered on the gravel and the electric lights that shone through the foliage caught the smooth facets on her diamonds so that they sparkled like shooting stars. The anticipation of finding her freedom, even for a moment, gave vent to a loud moan that escaped her throat. She let it out and the feeling was such a relief that she let out another, until she began to weep with abandon.

Suddenly, she stopped running. She caught her breath

and stifled her sobbing. She saw, to her horror, the faces of people – *dozens* of people – staring at her through the bars of the gates while the guards in livery whom Cesare had hired in Dublin for the occasion made sure they remained outside the castle walls. They were gazing at her in the same way that *she* had gazed at the first-class passengers from the third-class deck of the boat that had carried her to America. She froze like a trapped animal with nowhere to run, and stared at them staring at her in bewilderment. Then she blinked and the faces shifted into focus and she recognized them. She recognized the people she had grown up with in Ballinakelly when she, like them, had been poor and shoeless and hungry. But now here she was in her jewels and silks on the other side of the gate while they looked in, eager to watch the spectacle that was this grand night of extravagances beyond their most fanciful longings.

Bridie wanted to throw open the gates and let them in, but she knew she couldn't. She thought of her mother then and her nanna, and her father's face seemed to appear there, among the crowd of locals, and gaze at her with a sad and disappointed air.

She spun round and hurried back to the castle and the life Fate had chosen for her, leaving the townspeople wondering whether they had really seen the Countess or whether she had been a Deverill ghost. After all, didn't they say the castle was haunted?

Rosetta didn't imagine that more sumptuous balls were even given by royalty. This was an extravaganza of extraordinary proportions, everyone said so. After dinner there was dancing in the ballroom and at midnight the heavens were lit up with the most breathtaking display of fireworks. She heard it muttered that the last time the skies above Ballinakelly had glowed so brightly was the terrible night the castle was burned to the ground.

Rosetta had watched Bridie drink glass after glass of champagne. It was *her* party but she didn't appear to be enjoying herself very much. The Count on the other hand was enjoying himself immensely. Every lady in the room wanted to dance with him and he was only too happy to oblige. His gleaming white smile dazzled and his green eyes seduced as he swept the adoring ladies around the ballroom with the nimbleness of a ballet dancer.

After midnight Rosetta went in search of Bridie. She hadn't seen her during the fireworks and she hadn't seen her on the dance floor. She had found Michael and asked him, but he hadn't seen her, nor had her husband Sean. Eventually Rosetta set off up the stairs towards Bridie's little sitting room to see if she was hiding out in there. However, a thudding noise alerted her to something going on at the end of a very dark corridor so she changed direction and headed off towards it. The sound of music from the band in the ballroom became muffled and distant, the voices of guests as soft as the murmur of bees far away. Rosetta could feel her heart beating wildly as an uneasiness crept over her, causing her skin to prickle. She dared not turn on any lights. She sensed that what she was going to find would not appreciate being exposed to the glare of electric light.

After a while Rosetta heard the sound of puffing and grunting coming from behind one of the big oak doors. She knew that she shouldn't look but she couldn't help herself. Her curiosity had now grown to such proportions as to be irrepressible. Slowly she turned the brass knob and pushed open the door. It moved on its hinges without making a sound. Gingerly she peered round it. There, making love on the bed, was the Count. The woman who was underneath with her ankles wrapped around his waist was not someone Rosetta recognized. Unaware of her presence they continued to take pleasure in what seemed to be the Count's most favourite pastime. Rosetta withdrew as quietly as she had entered and closed the door softly behind her. She was now more determined than ever to expose this man for what he was, an adventurer and a cad without whom Bridie would be *much* better off.

At last Rosetta found Bridie where she had imagined she would be, in her little sitting room. She was slumped in the corner of the sofa in her beautiful green dress, an empty champagne flute in her hand. Rosetta could see that she had been crying. 'Bridie, what are you doing in here?' she asked and for a sudden moment she feared Bridie knew about her husband. But she did not.

'I don't know what I'm doing here, Rosetta. I'm neither fish, fowl nor red herring. I don't know why I ever came back. I should have stayed in New York. At least I had a life there. I had friends. I didn't have to ask a friend to rent a crowd for me and she's not my friend anyway. Lady Rowan-Hampton will never be my friend.'

Rosetta sat on the sofa beside her. 'What has brought this on?' she asked.

'Who do I think I am, living in a grand castle? I was not raised for grand castles, Rosetta, unless to be working in one. As Mam says, "What is bred in the bone comes out in the marrow." Who am I to think that money can buy breeding?' A bitter chuckle rattled in her throat. 'No, it's Grace's party, not mine. She swept in and charmed them all and no one remembers that *I'm* the Countess and it's *my* castle. Cesare should have married someone like Grace. Not someone like me who doesn't know how to play the part.'

'You played the part beautifully tonight,' Rosetta insisted, putting a hand on her arm. 'No one would think you were anything other than a grand lady in a grand castle, throwing a grand ball.'

Bridie looked at her and smiled sadly. 'Do you really think so?'

'I do. The only people who might have reservations about you owning this place are the Deverills.'

'The Deverills.' Bridie shook her head. 'I loved them once. Kitty was like a sister to me. Celia was always happy, all the time. Her life was charmed, but then look what happened. Happiness is an elusive thing, Rosetta. It's like a cloud. You think you have it and then your hand goes straight through it. It's an illusion, happiness.' She sighed miserably.

'Come back to the party, Bridie.' Rosetta stood up. 'It *is* your party and *you* are the hostess. If you're going to make a life for yourself in Ballinakelly then you have to make friends with the people downstairs.'

Bridie pushed herself up with a groan. 'No, Rosetta. If I want to make a life for my *husband* in Ballinakelly, I have to make friends with the people downstairs. I have you and I have my family and I have Jack and Emer O'Leary. I don't need more friends.'

The ball was still going strong although the constant flow of champagne and dancing had made most of the guests look a lot less polished than they had looked when they arrived. Gowns were creased, bow ties loosened, make-up smudged and hair in need of a good comb. Rosetta left Bridie with her brother Sean and went to powder her face in the dressing room. As she was coming out she bumped into Grace.

'Ah, Rosetta, do you know where Bridie is?' she asked. 'I need to tell her what a success tonight has been. Everyone has told me how beautiful and charming she is and how utterly splendid the castle is.'

'She could do with a compliment,' said Rosetta.

Grace seized upon the suggestion that something was not right. 'Why? Is she unhappy?'

'Just a little insecure,' Rosetta replied, then she couldn't help but vent a little of her fury about the Count. 'Cesare has a nasty way of sapping her confidence.'

'Really,' said Grace. She took Rosetta by the arm and led her into a corner. 'I hear the rumours like everyone else and it vexes me greatly.'

'The rumours are all true,' said Rosetta in a low voice. 'He's not only bedding the girls in town but he's bedding one right now. I saw him with my own eyes.'

'What? Here? Tonight?'

'Quite so, Lady Rowan-Hampton. You wouldn't believe it, but it's true.'

'How insulting to his wife. Something must be done about it.' Grace conveniently overlooked the fact that *she* had once bedded Bertie Deverill right here in this castle at the Deverill Summer Ball, while his wife danced in the ballroom downstairs.

Rosetta looked at Lady Rowan-Hampton and she realized that here was the very person she needed to help her expose the Count. Rosetta had no idea, however, how eager Grace was to dig up dirt on the Count, or why.

'I don't believe he has anything to do with Italy, either,' Rosetta continued hurriedly. 'I have tried to speak Italian to him on many occasions and the little he has said reveals how little he knows.'

Grace narrowed her eyes. 'Are you sure?'

'Positive.'

'Are you telling me, Rosetta, that the Count is a fraud?'

'I believe he is.'

'Then where might he be from?'

'I don't know and I have no idea how to find out.'

'I can find out,' said Grace firmly, her excitement rising at the thought of a covert mission.

'There is one person I know who will be able to help you,' Rosetta said. 'One man who is very fond of Bridie and looked after her while she was in New York.'

'And who might he be?' Grace asked.

'Beaumont Williams, her attorney,' Rosetta replied. 'There is nothing he doesn't know about Bridie and nothing he won't do to protect her.'

Grace put a hand on Rosetta's. 'We are in this together because we love Bridie,' she said. 'There's nothing I won't do to protect her, either.'

Rosetta felt an enormous sense of relief. Here was a woman who had the means to expose the Count and she was prepared to help. In fact, she looked very determined indeed. Rosetta watched her walk off with the poise and confidence of a lady who has known only the grandest drawing rooms and the grandest people and she thought that if anyone was born to grand castles and grand titles it was *her*.

Grace entered the ballroom and swept her eyes over the revellers with purpose. Then her sharp, determined gaze rested on Michael.

Chapter 15

London

'How your mother has the audacity to bring her paramour to a family funeral is beyond me!' said Boysie Bancroft to Harry Deverill, whose mother Maud had just walked into the church in Kensington on the arm of Arthur Arlington.

'I can only deduce that she never much liked her husband's cousin,' Harry replied. 'I always found Augusta strident, overbearing and outspoken to the point of rudeness, but we were all marvellously entertained making fun of her behind her back. Mama clearly found her less amusing. I'm not sure what Papa is going to make of it. I dare say he won't be very happy.'

Boysie's beautiful mouth, almost too beautiful for a man, curled into a small smile. 'Goodie, funerals can be so dreary. I'm now counting on your parents to make a scene.'

Harry chuckled. 'Not very likely. They'll probably ignore each other.'

'No they won't,' said Boysie with certainty. 'Maud wouldn't have brought her lover if she didn't want some sort of reaction from Bertie.'

'My mother's a mystery. I've never really known what she's thinking.'

'Unlike her son,' said Boysie. 'I've always known *exactly* what *you're* thinking.'

Boysie was tall and elegant with sea-green eyes, sugar-brown hair and a boyishly handsome face. He had a languid, raffish air that betrayed long nights drinking cognac and smoking cigarettes, and a reputation for having one of the finest minds in London. Not only was he clever but he was a master of discretion, for he and Harry had been secret lovers for over seventeen years. 'So, what am I thinking now?' Harry demanded.

'That it's a pity it's up to you as an usher and a relative to show your mother and her paramour to their seats.'

Harry laughed. 'Well, that wasn't very difficult. But you're right. One must do one's duty.' He set off in the direction of his mother.

Maud, dressed expensively in Chanel and diamonds, was now in her late sixties, tall with a slim waist, jaw-length white hair and a face that had the remains of a once great beauty. The angular structure of her bones, which had made that beauty striking in youth, now served her well in her later years. She looked at least a decade younger than her contemporaries. Her wintry blue eyes were arrogant as she swept them over the congregation, silently challenging anyone to criticize her decision to bring Arthur, who had been her consort now for over ten years.

Harry greeted them politely. Arthur, shiny-faced and barrel-chested with skinny legs, small feet and piggy eyes swollen from years of excessive drinking and gambling, was delighted to see so many grand people in the congregation. Even though he was the younger brother of the Earl of Pendrith and plugged into the highest echelons of society, he was still very anxious about being with the 'right people'.

That many of those people disapproved of his very open relationship with a married woman, for Maud was still Lady Deverill if only in name, he was too thick-skinned and pompous to notice.

'Dear Augusta,' said Maud, her voice laden with a sorrow that had more to do with her own growing sense of mortality than her affection for her husband's dead cousin. 'She always talked about her own imminent death and look, she nearly reached a hundred!'

'A good innings,' chortled Arthur, his little eyes spotting one or two people he'd make a point of collaring at the reception afterwards.

'Is Beatrice here?' Maud asked Harry, for Beatrice Deverill, Augusta's daughter-in-law, had after her husband's death nearly a decade before retreated to her country home, where she had been living in mourning ever since.

'No,' Harry replied. 'She didn't feel up to coming.'

Maud lifted her chin. 'Really, *I* have suffered but *I* carry on,' she said, bringing the conversation round to herself, as is the habit of narcissists. 'Sometimes one simply has to bury one's sorrow and keep going! Come, Arthur darling. Harry, take us to our seats.'

'You're right at the front, Mama.'

'I should think so,' she replied.

Boysie watched Harry walk his mother down the aisle, followed by Arthur, who every few paces stopped to greet people. Boysie grinned as he observed the awkward smiles and tentative shaking of hands for Arthur was not well liked by anyone but Maud, and he wasn't even sure that *she* liked him that much. She liked the fact that he was aristocratic, of course, and she liked his wealth, what was left of it, but Boysie wondered whether his flattery and constant presence was what she liked best about the whole arrangement; Maud needed to be adored and she didn't like to be alone.

As for Harry, Boysie loved Harry more with every year that passed. Neither much liked their wives, they *endured* them, and they had both done their duty and fathered children, but what they both wanted more than anything in the world was something they could never have: each other. Years ago Harry's wife Charlotte had discovered them embracing at Celia's Summer Ball at Castle Deverill, but after an agonizing few months of tears and tantrums they had reached an agreement whereby Harry was allowed to see Boysie again, as a friend. Thus their friendship had resumed, albeit constrained by celibacy, and their affection for each other had been permitted to deepen. They had been well-behaved, *very* well-behaved, for years, but as Harry's fondness for his wife had diminished so had his resolve and his good intentions. He and Boysie had found each other again in that little nondescript hotel in Soho where they used to spend their mornings in bed together. Boysie had always told Harry that no one would think to look there, not even Charlotte with her habit of spying, and he was right. It wasn't ideal, but it was all they were allowed. One had to accept small mercies and *that* mercy was bigger than most. He watched Harry now as he showed his mother to her seat and the sight made him feel warm inside.

Harry had always been handsome. His blond hair had darkened with age to a wet-sand colour and his face had benefited from the lines that life had drawn into it; he looked less boyish these days and more distinguished. His blue eyes were the same shade as his mother's, but where hers were cold and hard like ice his were soft and twinkling like snow.

Boysie saw Harry laugh at something someone said and his heart gave a little leap.

The Irish Deverills were represented by Bertie, Kitty and Robert, Elspeth and Peter. Bertie had thought very hard about attending because he knew there was a fair chance that his wife would embarrass him by bringing Arthur, and he didn't want to find himself in the awkward position of having to meet the man, but the desire to lay eyes on Maud again outweighed his reservations. After years of estrangement Bertie's opinion of his wife had changed because his opinion of *himself* had changed. No longer casting his eye about for blame, he had come to recognize his faults, and there were, unfortunately, many. Because of these failings an insurmountable gulf had opened up between them and Bertie wondered whether it was futile to hope that she might one day bridge that gulf with forgiveness. If he hadn't given in to his desire and indulged in numerous affairs, if he hadn't fallen in love with Grace, if he hadn't impregnated that housemaid and brought JP and Martha into the world, if he had seen Maud and *only* Maud and watered her with affection like a fragile orchid, Maud might still love him. But if he never insinuated himself into her presence how would he ever convince her that he had changed?

After the service the reception was held in Deverill House, the magnificent Italianate mansion in Kensington built by Augusta's deceased son Digby, who had made his great fortune in the diamond and gold mines of South Africa only to lose it in the stock market crash of 1929. As his wife Beatrice was insisting on hiding out at Deverill Rising, their country estate in Wiltshire, it was left to her twin daughters, Leona and Vivien, to host the gathering of family and friends in the house they had so nearly had to sell had it not been for Beatrice's youngest daughter Celia, who had astonished everyone by travelling out to South Africa and mining an old farm her father had bought at the turn of the century, with surprising results. She had succeeded where everyone who knew her would have expected her to fail. She had established the Free State Deep Reef Mining Company and was fast restoring her father's fortune. Of course, Augusta claimed she had always seen grit in her youngest grandchild. 'A chip off the old block,' she had said not long before she died. 'But I was the only one who recognized those fine qualities. She was always going to surprise everyone, but of course she didn't surprise *me*, and, had her father lived, she wouldn't have surprised *him* either.' If her father had lived she'd never have had to go out to South Africa in the first place. But no one was talking about Digby, or Celia, or even Augusta. They were talking about the threat of war.

'If war comes,' said Maud to her daughter-in-law Charlotte, 'it will be a terrible war. It won't be like the last one. It will be much worse. The Germans are so technically advanced we shall all be obliterated within the first week.'

'I'm sure Chamberlain will do everything to avoid it,' said Charlotte hopefully.

'I'm afraid it's inevitable. There is no solution but to go to war and we shall once again sacrifice a generation of young men. Ireland will be neutral, of course. Clever them.' Maud lifted her eyes to find someone more interesting to talk to, because she found Charlotte very dim, and slid into Bertie's wistful gaze with a murmur of surprise.

Charlotte followed the line of her mother-in-law's vision and frowned. 'Shall we go and talk to Bertie? He's standing on his own,' she said.

'Well, I don't see why not,' Maud replied, casting her eye about for Arthur. She found him deep in conversation with the Earl of Shaftesbury and the Duke of Norfolk. Maud and Charlotte threaded their way through the crowd to where Bertie was standing alone with a glass of lime soda.

'Hello, Maud,' he said.

'It's been a while,' Maud replied. 'How are you, Bertie? You look well.'

'Getting old, Maud,' he replied with a smile. Maud looked around to see that she had lost Charlotte somewhere along the way, or perhaps Charlotte had lost *her* on purpose. Not so dim, after all, Maud thought wryly.

'How's life treating you in Ireland?'

'Ticking along,' said Bertie. He couldn't very well tell her that he had discovered *another* illegitimate child and that JP had run off to lodge with a friend in Dublin while he came to terms with the fact that the woman he loved was his long-lost sister. 'I see Arthur is still present in your life.'

Maud's jaw stiffened. 'He's a dear friend, Bertie,' she answered, but she knew Bertie was no fool. 'I need to talk to Victoria,' she said, changing the subject. 'If there's a war, which I'm very sure there will be, we will have to take refuge at Broadmere. We can't possibly stay in London. It's a shame we don't still have that castle of yours. The Germans won't bother bombing Ireland.'

'You are always welcome to come home, Maud,' said Bertie pointedly, hoping to remind her that they were still married. 'You can come back to the Hunting Lodge. If I recall we did enjoy many good times there.'

'I don't recall *many*,' she replied tersely.

'Come now, Maud. It wasn't all that bad living with me.'

She gave a small smile in response to his hopeful one. 'But one only remembers the bad.'

'Or one only *chooses* to,' he interjected. He lowered his voice, hoping that no one would come and interrupt them. 'Look, my dear, I apologize for being a shoddy husband. You deserved better.' Maud's expression softened at this unexpected apology. Encouraged by the minute dropping of her defences, he added, 'I have seen the error of my ways, Maud. The very many foolish errors that I made in the early years of our marriage. I didn't treasure you as I should have. I realize that now.' Maud's lips parted as if she was about to say something, but whatever that something was it never came and she just looked at him in bewilderment. Bertie found that the hardest part about apologizing was apologizing; once sorry had been said it was very easy to say it again, and again. 'I didn't realize how unhappy you were because I was only thinking of myself and my own pleasure,' he continued, warming to his theme. 'As a young man I was very selfish. Life was good and I had been spoiled. But since those days I have faced great loss and unhappiness, which would have been for nothing had I not learned something from them. I've learnt appreciation, Maud, of my home, of my family and of *you*. Yes, of *you* most of all.' Maud was now blushing. She didn't know what to say. She didn't know what to say because she didn't know how she felt. She stared at him with her frosty blue eyes and a long time seemed to pass before she blinked.

Bertie felt lighter of spirit than he had in a long time. Over the last twenty years he had shed his old self, slowly, layer by layer, like an onion. His cousin Digby had forced him to give up the drink and JP had shown him how to live again. The fire that had consumed his home and his father, his mother's death and the other terrible deaths that had depleted the Deverill clan had each relieved him of the darker elements of his ego. With every tragedy he felt less powerful and less ambitious to be so. He wanted little in his life now: his children, his grandchildren and Maud. He wanted Maud and the expression that was now breaking through the hardened contours of her face gave him hope. The sight of Arthur Arlington forcing his way clumsily through the crowd snatched that hope away. 'Think about what I have said to you, Maud,' he added quickly, touching her hand. 'War is coming and who knows what will become of us. Ireland is still your home and it would give me great pleasure to welcome you back.'

Maud watched him walk away. She felt weak in her knees. 'Oh Arthur,' she said when he reached her. 'I'm so glad you're here. I need to sit down.'

'Are you all right? I saw you talking to Bertie. What did he say? Did he upset you?'

'No, of course not. We were just talking about the children.'

'Ah,' said Arthur, relieved. She slipped her hand through his arm and let him lead her into a downstairs sitting room where one or two elderly people were nodding off on sofas. She could see through the windows into the garden where guests were gathered in small clusters on the grass, bathed in sunshine. As she settled into an armchair she saw Bertie walking up to Kitty, Elspeth and Harry and joining in their cheerful repartee. There was no ceremony, no formality or stiffness, in fact the four of them simply continued from where they had last left off and Maud felt a stab of jealousy; they belonged together and she was an outcast. Only Victoria, her eldest daughter, took any trouble with her at all. She turned to Arthur who responded to her need with a well-practised reply:

'You outshine every other woman in the room, Maud dearest,' he said and she smiled weakly and allowed his flattery to fill the emptiness inside.

Britain declared war on Germany at the beginning of September and a fever of fear and excitement swept the country. Old people remembered the Great War with horror while young people hurried to enlist, hungry for the thrill of adventure. London was at once transformed. Outside Buckingham Palace the King's Guard changed from peacetime scarlet to wartime khaki and the steel helmet replaced the bearskin. Hospitals were evacuated and schoolchildren sent to the safety of the countryside, labelled like parcels. Londoners continued their daily commutes to work but along with their briefcases they carried gas masks. They hoped they'd never have to use them.

The first air-raid siren had sounded twenty minutes after war had been declared and everyone had hurried to the bomb shelters, forming orderly queues without the slightest panic. Indeed, there was an air of calm typical of the British character. Maud, who thought it beneath her to cower with strangers in Underground stations and hovels, fled the city to stay with Victoria in her stately home in Kent, taking Harry's wife Charlotte and their children with her, while Harry insisted on offering his services to the government. Boysie sent his wife to the country to stay with an aunt, and enlisted too. Both men were in their mid-forties. Even though they had fought in the Great War they were now too old to rejoin their regiments, but they were determined to make themselves useful somehow, and determined to remain together.

War was a boon that came at the perfect time for JP. Sick in the heart and his soul tormented with longing, he saw it as a way to lose himself and his pain. He postponed his course at Trinity College, Dublin and wrote to the Air Ministry, telling them that he wanted to fly a plane. Having considered various options he had concluded that what he enjoyed more than anything in the world was galloping over the hills on a horse, which must be much like flying. The RAF sent him forms to fill out and a short while later he was invited to attend a selection board at Adastral House in Kingsway, London. His father, who had fought in the Great War, tried to dissuade him. JP was too young to understand what war meant, said Bertie, and certainly too young to fly a plane. But Robert, whose stiff leg had prevented him from fighting in the previous war, knew all about the desire to play one's part and although he feared for the boy's safety he did nothing to stop him going to London to interview. Kitty understood JP's need to run away from his disappointment. She had heard that he had turned to drink in Dublin, and, considering their father's habit of reaching for the bottle in times of distress, realized that his joining the Royal Air Force might possibly be the only way to save him from himself.

News spread fast that JP Deverill had enlisted to fight. No one in Ballinakelly was in the least surprised. JP was Anglo-Irish therefore it was normal to want to serve his king and country. However, one person was devastated that his life was going to be put in danger; one young girl who had lost her heart to him that morning out on the hills when he had rescued her on his horse like a knight in shining armour from a fairy tale.

Alana O'Leary was only eleven, too young to understand grown-up love, but she knew what she felt and the place in the centre of her chest where she felt it. She went to bed at night and lay with her eyes open, fantasizing about bumping into him again. She sat in class, gazing out of the window, picturing his smile and the way his grey eyes twinkled. She wandered back home at the end of the day with her gaze lost somewhere in the half-distance, imagining all the possible scenarios that might put her once again in his path. At Mass she prayed for God to keep JP safe. To preserve him from bombs and bullets, to bring him home in one piece. She prayed so hard that her hands turned white as she clamped them together. Knowing what her father thought of the Deverills, she spoke to no one about her infatuation. She guarded it close against her heart like a secret treasure. Knowing she had such a secret gave her pleasure – knowing JP was in the world, even though she had only seen him once, made its beauty more dazzling.

'Another war,' said Adeline sadly, folding her arms and staring out of the tower window. The evening shadows crept over the dewy lawn as the sun set over Castle Deverill. 'Human beings are so very stupid,' she added.

'They never learn,' said Hubert huffily. 'No doubt the Deverills will suffer more casualties. Death isn't so bad when viewed from this side.' He chuckled bitterly. 'In fact, when I consider our Rupert's death on the battlefield, I realize it was much worse for us than it was for him.'

'Death for most people is over very quickly,' Barton agreed from the armchair. 'But for us it just goes on and on and on . . .'

'Will we ever see Rupert again?' Hubert asked, his face crumpling with misery. 'I would so dearly love to see our boy again.'

'We will see Rupert,' said Adeline firmly.

'But, my dear, you could move on at any time . . .' said Hubert. 'You don't have to stay here with me.'

'I remain because I want to,' Adeline replied. She went and put her arms around him from behind the chair, pressing her face against his. 'Because I love you.'

Barton growled from the armchair. Egerton got up and left the room. Neither was comfortable with expressions of love even though their parched hearts craved them.

Chapter 16

Connecticut

When Martha returned home to Connecticut she was a very different person to the one who had left a couple of months before. Then her heart had been intact, now it was in pieces and she didn't know whether those pieces could ever be put back together again.

Pam, who had been devastated by her daughter's disappearance, embraced her with remorse and regret, searching for forgiveness in Martha's distant eyes. Edith had been suitably reprimanded, although due to her young age she hadn't been punished. It was Pam's sister-in-law Joan who had received the brunt of everyone's wrath because it had been *she* who had spilled the secret about Martha's adoption to Edith in the first place. Edith had exposed her in the first moments of her questioning and Joan had been revealed as manipulative and cruel. There was nothing Joan could say in her defence. She had done wrong and she had to accept the consequences of her actions. Ted Wallace was appalled because he abhorred dishonesty and his wife Diana was distraught that her favourite grandchild should have discovered the truth about her parentage in that blunt, insensitive way. Pam and Larry were anxious to reassure Martha that not only did they love her but also she had never ever been anything other than a Tobin and a Wallace, whatever she had uncovered in Ireland. But Martha was unable to share what she had discovered. She had gone to find her mother only to learn that she was dead. There was no possibility now of ever knowing her. She felt that she had also lost a part of herself along with her mother; the part that was so full of potential, yet to be discovered. She was still licking her wounds – and she wasn't yet ready to show them to anyone.

As for JP, she couldn't begin to tell them about him.

Martha's love for JP ran deep. So deep, in fact, that she didn't think she would ever recover from his loss. Their love hadn't been a superficial infatuation, and their strange recognition of each other, which they had interpreted in the way poets do, was now easily explained. It hadn't been the romantic falling in love of two people who had found each other, but the rekindling of an old love of two people who had lost each other. They had been conceived together, grown in the womb side by side and arrived into the world as a pair. Although they didn't look alike, there had been so much that was similar about them besides their love of milky tea and cake. The more she thought about him and replayed the scenes from their day in Dublin, the more their likenesses were revealed. They had laughed at the same things and been touched by the same things and both had wondered at these amazing parallels. Martha had thanked God for bringing two such well-suited people together; she didn't realize He was, in fact, reuniting them. Now she had lost both – the man she loved and her twin brother. The loss was double and it sliced through her heart twice as severely.

Without Goodwin Martha was bereft. Mrs Goodwin had always been there and in many ways Martha had been closer to her than to Pam, but now she was gone the house resonated gloomily with her absence. Martha's misery was compounded. She felt she had nothing left to live for. However much her parents tried to make up for having kept her history secret Martha's sense of betrayal was profound. Half of her wished she could turn back the clock because before her discovery she had been happy. The other half was grateful for her experience because she had known love and it had been beautiful. She would never know it again; she had no desire to.

Martha felt alienated from Edith. Her little sister had been part of the betrayal and Martha didn't think she could ever forgive her for that. The girl who had only seen the good in Edith now saw her for what she was: jealous, spoilt and vindictive. Martha's disappointment in life had turned her sour and her once open, generous heart was now slowly contracting. The old Martha had absolved Edith from all responsibility; the new Martha was less benevolent.

Larry had noticed the change in his daughter the moment he had found her in Ballinakelly. After their emotional reunion she had withdrawn, giving nothing away. When he'd asked whether she'd found her birth parents she had merely shrugged and mumbled something about it all being a huge disappointment. He had taken her home on the boat and they had talked about other things and occasionally the old Martha had shone through. He had glimpsed her in the rare moments she had laughed, or in her smile, when he had manged to coax one out of her, but mostly she had retreated somewhere far away where he was unable to reach her. He didn't know what had happened in Ireland, and Mrs

Goodwin was not there to ask, but he knew that, whatever it was, it had changed Martha irrevocably.

Pam made sure that she spent time with her eldest daughter. She went through the photo albums of Martha's childhood, recalling the funny things she had done and said as a small girl and the pleasure she had given them. Although Martha seemed outwardly to enjoy Pam's stories, Pam sensed her heaviness of heart and she was at a loss as to how to lighten it.

As much as Martha wanted to stop thinking about JP she was unable to. He dominated her thoughts day and night. Oh, that she could cut the cord that tied her heart to his! But as *he* pined for her at the flying school in Leicestershire so *she* pined for him and the pull on their hearts was constant and painful. Of all the men in the world, she should fall in love with her brother! But perhaps it wasn't so strange after all, she concluded finally. They were two halves of the same whole – wasn't that what lovers believed themselves to be, too?

Diana Wallace tried to prise some information out of her, but in spite of their closeness Martha could not begin to articulate how she felt. She was afraid to say the words out loud in case she opened a door onto her grief which she could never close. If she started to cry she might never stop. So, she remained silent and her family, both the Wallaces and the Tobins, worried about her deeply.

There was, however, one person Martha could always talk to; one person who didn't judge her or think less of her. One person who would always love her no matter what; and that was Adeline. Martha knew her Irish grandmother was with her in spirit. Although she couldn't see her as she had done as a child, the memory had been released and she remembered. She sensed her often. She felt enveloped in affection and tenderness and the feeling was as soft as down. Adeline understood because she had witnessed everything. She had watched Martha love and she had watched that love thwarted. Martha got into the habit of going to bed at night, switching off the light and handing herself over to Adeline. She let her grandmother take her – as if she were literally lifting her out of bed and carrying her somewhere quiet and peaceful, somewhere far away from her suffering; somewhere closer to God.

Martha prayed. She prayed for JP and she prayed for her dead mother, and as she grappled in the darkness of her soul for some light, she seized upon the radiant presence of God.

JP was content to be far away from Ireland and the memories of Martha, which hung over the place like a beautiful but elusive fog. At the Royal Air Force base in Desford in Leicestershire he could concentrate on his training and throw all his energy into this new skill rather than lounging about in Dublin's pubs, pining for his lost love. Here no one knew who he was; he could be somebody new, somebody *whole*. Most of the other trainees were Canadian, South African, Kiwi and Australian. Not all would pass. JP was confident that *he* would. The moment he had laid eyes on the dozens of Tiger Moths lined up on the tarmac he knew he had made the right choice and his deadened heart pulsated once again with life. He breathed in the smell of doped canvas, petrol and oil and felt a strange sense of purpose.

JP was not yet officially in the RAF. As a civilian pupil pilot he had to pass the flying course by completing fifty hours' flying time with an instructor. His first flight made a deep and lasting impression on him. With his instructor in the front seat and JP behind in his helmet and goggles, the parachute strapped to his back, the propeller was swung and the engine started. The plane moved swiftly over the grass, rattling like a toolbox and gaining speed until the noise stopped suddenly and a floating sensation took over. JP watched with wonder as the ground below him receded. The sight was beautiful and its beauty filled him with a warm and buoyant sense of awe. Up there he forgot about Martha. England's wintry landscape spread out beneath him with its toy-like villages and hamlets, farms and forests and fields. So small and insignificant to his distant eye – was this perhaps how God viewed the world? Were human beings as ants to a giant? Up there he felt as if he had left all his problems on the ground. Was this what it felt like to die and leave the world? he wondered. The thrill of flying thrust him into the present, and the past and future dissolved like mist in sunshine.

JP was quick to make friends with the other trainee pilots. Like his father he was genial and charming and people were drawn to the light he exuded that promised warmth and fun like a blazing pub window on a cold winter's night. He hid his torment behind jokes and laughter, cigarettes and beer, and told no one about Martha. But when he slept he lost control of his thoughts and she surfaced time and again in dreams to remind him of his pain.

JP hadn't really thought much about his biological mother, but recalling Martha's dark hair and dark eyes, which were nothing like his red hair and pale grey eyes, he wondered whether their mother had looked like her. For the first time in his life he wanted to know. He awoke from his dreams about Martha with the same questions pulling on his mind: *What was my mother like? Who was she? What were the circumstances of our births and of her death?* For the first time in his life he wished he knew. He didn't want to die in ignorance.

Flying was not as easy as JP had imagined. Taking off was difficult. The plane swerved all over the place and he simply couldn't steady it. Landing was even trickier and more often than not the instructor had to take over the controls in order to land the plane safely. JP suffered doubts. Perhaps he wasn't meant to be a pilot. Being adept on a horse did not necessarily mean he was going to be adept in a plane! After a few weeks of flying dual it didn't seem to be getting much better, and the thought of flying solo was a daunting one.

It didn't help that he failed to warm to his instructor, Brian McCarthy, who was a dour, straight-talking Scot with no apparent sense of humour. JP hadn't ever met anyone he couldn't win over with his infectious smile and easy charm. Brian was the first, and no amount of wit or self-deprecating humour could even put a crack in the man's impenetrable veneer. As the fifty-hour hurdle got closer, after which JP would be expected to fly solo, he began to get more anxious. It was no good being able to keep the plane steady in flight if he couldn't land or take off properly. Would they kick him out? If they did, what would he do? He had his heart set on being a pilot now. If he was going to fight in this war he was going to do it in the cockpit of a plane, come what may.

One night in the local pub, smoking cigarettes and drinking beer with two men he had grown close to over the few weeks they had been training, he voiced his concerns. 'You have to relax,' said Stanley Bradshaw, a brown-haired, cheeky-faced Yorkshireman of twenty-three. 'Don't try too hard.'

'The more you worry about it the more you seize up,' said Jimmy Robinson, a jaunty Australian who kept a photograph of his mother in his wallet. 'It's all about confidence.'

'You Irish like your horses, JP. Just pretend she's a horse.'

They all laughed and Stanley drained his pint, leaving a line of white foam on his upper lip.

'The truth is,' said JP, 'I've never doubted myself before. This is a first and I don't like it.'

'We all have doubts. Jesus knows I have mine,' said Jimmy. 'My take-off is like a kangaroo with a rocket up his arse.'

'Sounds much like mine,' said JP with a chuckle. There was nothing like the company of friends to make him feel better.

Stanley wiped away the foam with the back of his hand. 'You know, it won't be long before we're up there with more than just pigeons for company,' he said gravely. 'We'll be facing the bloody Germans.'

'Too right,' said Jimmy. They fell silent for a moment, each man uncomfortable with his fear.

Stanley glanced warily at JP. 'You're very young,' he said.

'Nearly eighteen,' JP replied.

'Green around the gills. A sprog,' Jimmy added and they all knew what he was thinking, that eighteen was too young to die in a war.

'I got a girl back home,' said Stanley wistfully.

Jimmy nodded. 'What's she called?'

'Phyllis.'

'Same name as my mother,' said Jimmy. Silence again.

JP thought of Martha. 'Well, I've got nothing to lose,' he said after a while, staring into the bottom of his glass.

'Or do you mean *no one*?' said Jimmy, and JP's eyes misted.

After that JP regained his confidence. He stopped trying so hard and he stopped trying to win over his instructor. His take-offs and landings became smoother and he managed to keep the plane steady during their circuits. Then one day, after a particularly deft landing, McCarthy levered himself out of the cockpit and stood at the side of the fuselage, close to JP, and shouted over the sound of the idling engine, 'Right, Deverill, try a circuit on your own.' And JP realized, to his amazement, that he was being given permission to fly solo.

JP would never forget his first solo flight. With a mixture of nervousness and excitement, JP took his little Tiger Moth into the sky, towards the feathery clouds and the great beyond. With the vibration of the bracing wires and the buffeting of the slipstream, he was suspended in the air with the wind in his face and the sunshine radiating all around him. It was more poignant because he was experiencing it alone. He thought of Martha then. He envisaged her sweet smile and the tender way she had looked at him that day on the bridge in Dublin. He remembered the feeling of her hand in his and the way he had held it all the way back to her hotel. He recalled their final meeting. He could almost feel her in his embrace, pressed against his chest, while he had fought the desire to kiss her. As he indulged in memories he had tried so hard to forget, his eyes stung with tears, but his heart inflated with the glory of the heavens, and the sorrow he felt in his heart was somehow exquisite.

When he landed and taxied to the apron, he felt lighter of spirit than he had in a long time. He loved Martha – he knew he would never *not* love Martha, but he had found an intense joy in flying that would sustain him while he learned to live without her.

JP passed the RAF flying tests and final examinations. Having never had to work very hard at home being tutored by Robert, he had relished knuckling down and studying for something he really wanted, and he found, to his satisfaction, that he was good at it. He was sent to Hastings with Stanley and Jimmy to go through the transition from civilian to officer of the Royal Air Force. Their uniforms arrived from the tailor's in London: blue tunic and trousers with a thin stripe, but they lacked gravitas without the gold RAF wings on the breast. JP looked forward to the moment he earned his wings. He hoped it wouldn't be long. The war was on and he was eager to play his part.

After a few weeks of drilling, marching and lectures, JP was selected for 'C' Flight, which was responsible for training pilots to fly single-engine planes, namely the North American Harvard. He was pleased to see that Jimmy and Stanley had been selected too. They were all aware that training to fly the Harvard meant that they were on the road to eventually flying single-engine fighter planes. They were going to be up there facing the Hun, after all. JP had no doubt that flying fighter planes was what he was destined to do.

The three men arrived at the Flight Training School in Little Rissington in the Cotswolds in February 1940. It was wet and cold and a damp fog lingered in the air. The symmetrical, somewhat austere building looked gloomy and forbidding. They collected their kit: a helmet which included a face mask and microphone, leather gloves, overalls, a suit and flying boots, then reported to 'C' Flight in the No 2 Hangar where the Flight Commander gave them a brusque introductory talk. Afterwards, JP's flight instructor presented himself. Flight Sergeant Dawson was a small, wiry man with the steady gaze of someone who has scanned the skies from many different cockpits all over the world. Although he didn't smile there was a gentle wisdom in his eyes that immediately won JP's respect. He led him to an enormous hangar and JP forgot all about the fog and the unfriendly place as he laid eyes for the first time on the formidable Harvard.

Flight Sergeant Dawson explained that the Harvard was the most advanced aeroplane in service. Bigger than a Tiger Moth it was a low-wing monoplane with a retractable under-carriage and flaps and a constant-speed airscrew. JP wasn't sure what a 'constant-speed airscrew' was but kept his mouth shut and hoped it would all make sense when he was in the plane. He was already aware of the Harvard's bad reputa-tion – a few experienced pilots had been killed in it – but he wasn't put off. Quite the opposite: he felt the determination rise in him the way it did out hunting when he was faced with a high hedge, and the challenge thrilled him.

The first weekend of the course they were given a couple of days' leave. JP took the train from Kingham to London Paddington to stay with his half-brother Harry in Belgravia. London was now a city on high alert. Children had been evacuated to the countryside, army uniforms were apparent everywhere, windows and doors were blacked out at sunset and men were encouraged to leave their shirt tails exposed when walking the streets at night so that they could be seen by cars whose lights had been deflected to the ground. Sandbags had been piled up in the doorways of shops and public buildings and bombs were expected to drop at any time. Everyone carried a gas mask and a certain wariness.

Harry was pleased to see JP and embraced him fiercely. The war had injected Harry with a sharp sense of urgency and a wistful longing for those peaceful days of his childhood at Castle Deverill. Days picnicking on the beach, riding out over the hills, sitting in front of the warm fire playing cards; croquet, tennis and badminton on the lawn in the golden glow of the late summer sun. He remembered the last war, indeed the shot wound to his shoulder still ached sometimes, and the memory of loss had surfaced to remind him of the fragility of life. He had lost his uncle Rupert, his cousin George and many friends. The anticipation of losing all over again was almost unbearable. Every moment was precious. Every dawn to be celebrated.

Charlotte and the children were at Broadmere, Victoria's estate in Kent, so the house was empty. Their few servants had joined the war effort leaving Harry on his own, forced to make his dinners himself, which consisted mostly of toast and boiled eggs, which Charlotte sent up from the estate farm where Victoria kept a large selection of exotic hens. Harry had been given a desk job in Whitehall, which was only marginally more interesting than working in a bank, while Boysie had been sent to work at a secret location in Buckinghamshire after having won a crossword competition in the newspaper. Both men were thriving because for the first time in their lives they could be together without considering their wives. They managed to see each other most weekends and had settled into a comfortable routine of lunches at White's, strolls around the Serpentine and quiet dinners and nights at the hotel in Soho – Harry wasn't going to risk Charlotte discovering them again by being careless at home.

JP's weekend leave did not put Harry out. It just so happened that Boysie had to work so Harry welcomed the company and treated his half-brother to a hearty lunch at his club. Harry said that he found London in good spirits. He even questioned whether the war was ever really going to happen. The bombs that had been expected never fell and the sirens that went off were false alarms. People were even beginning to leave their gas masks behind, he told JP. JP was secretly disappointed. He now harboured ambitions of taking to the skies in fighter planes – if the Germans didn't invade England he'd never get his chance.

But by April the climate had changed. Germany invaded Denmark and Norway and the war started in earnest. In May Germany invaded Holland, Belgium and Luxembourg and King George appointed Winston Churchill as Prime Minister, which delighted Maud because the Spencer-Churchills were close family friends. In May the Allied army was pushed back to Dunkirk where they were rescued from the beaches and harbour in a miraculous evacuation – with no help from Eric, Victoria's husband, who had set off from the coast of Kent in his fishing boat only to sink half a mile out due to a leak in the hull. But it was no victory and in June the French surrendered to Germany.

JP and his friends Stanley and Jimmy finally earned their wings and were sent to Warmwell for advanced training. However, they had been there but a week when the Flight Commander informed them that their training had been cut short. They were to join a squadron at Biggin Hill where they were going to fly Spitfires. It looked like the German invasion of Britain would happen after all, and *they* would have to stop it.

Chapter 17

The Battle of Britain had indeed begun and, at Biggin Hill, JP was on the front line. The RAF base in the south-east of London was built on a plateau that was known throughout Fighter Command as 'Biggin on the Bump'. Responsible for protecting the approaches to the capital, it already bore noticeable signs of war: craters where bombs had eaten chunks out of the ground, wrecked Spitfires and Harvards abandoned on the grass like fallen beasts, hangars burnt to the bone. But JP was now eighteen years old, a young man with a strong sense of his own immortality, a young man hungry for action. He'd trained for this. He'd worked hard for his wings. He was eager to play his part, even though he was aware that it could be the last part he ever played.

At first light he walked to his Spitfire with his squadron, which included Jimmy and Stanley. The plane looked almost delicate in comparison to the Harvard, like a mosquito as opposed to a fat fly. With his parachute slung over his shoulder and his helmet on his head JP made his way towards the two ground crew, who had been busy removing the cover and plugging in the starter trolley. This was his moment. The moment he had been waiting for since he joined the RAF the previous autumn. The adrenalin was pumping through his veins but his nervousness was fuelled by excitement, not fear. He was ready to turn all his fury at the unfairness of love onto the Germans.

The sky was clear, the air damp. There was a stillness to the morning as if it was holding its breath for the battle ahead. JP walked across the grass and the dew collected on his flying boots. For a moment a memory surfaced, of walking across the lawn outside the White House in Ballinakelly, but the shoes on his feet then were small and laced, those of a young boy.

The sound of Spitfires starting up broke the silence and JP's memory, which dispersed like a reflection in a puddle that is briskly agitated. The engines exploded to life with a burst of flame from the exhaust stubs. The air vibrated with the noise, behind the planes the grass was flattened by the slipstream and all around the ground trembled. JP glanced at Jimmy and Stanley and nine other men in his squadron and wondered which of them would fail to come back.

Leaving his parachute on the wing, he climbed into his cockpit and gave the plane a quick once-over: fuel, brake pressure, rudder, elevators, airscrew, then he had a short chat with the fitter and the rigger who had been waiting to brief him. The preparation completed, he returned to the hut, put on his life vest and lay on a bunk to wait for the call to scramble. Some of the men read magazines, others slept, no one talked much. The atmosphere was tense, the air thick with anticipation. A few hours later the telephone gave a shrill ring and they all jumped. Those who had been sleeping awoke with a start. JP's heart dropped like a cold weight. He looked at Jimmy, but Jimmy did not catch his eye.

'Squadron scramble base angels twelve,' said the orderly.

It was time.

JP ran towards his Spitfire. The ground crew were starting it up. He could see the engine fire. He found his parachute on the wing where he'd left it and climbed into the cockpit. The crew strapped him in. He put on his helmet, fixed the oxygen mask and felt the familiar vibrating of the engine as he took off the brakes and eased open the throttle. The squadron were all taxiing at once. He could see Jimmy and took up his position beside him, on his left according to his instructions.

Over the R/T Jimmy's voice was reassuring. 'You ready, sprog?' – which was the Aussie's particular nickname for him.

'Ready, Jim,' JP replied.

'Okay, here we go.' And together, with all pilots' eyes on the leader, the planes accelerated over the airfield and took off.

The Spitfires ascended into the skies. Cloudless, bright blue skies as dawn gave way to day. The controller's voice came over the R/T: 'Gannic leader, this is Sapper. One hundred and fifty plus approaching Dungeness at angels twelve. Vector 120. Over.' JP looked into the clear azure – the vast canopy of serenity and beauty that would at any moment become a battlefield of smoke and fire. It didn't seem right to mar God's magnificent sky in that violent way. It didn't seem right at all. But JP didn't have time to dwell on the heavens. The enemy was approaching. He saw them, like a swarm of hornets buzzing out of the blue and turning it black.

There were more than a hundred and fifty, JP thought, accompanied by Me 109s covering the bombers. The sight was breathtaking and frightening all at the same time. He glanced at the eleven little Spitfires and his resolve weakened.

How could they take on that lot, he thought. But they were together; they were a team and they were the only thing standing between the Germans and England.

'Gannic from leader. Okay, boys, in we go. A good first burst and away. Watch for 109s.'

JP looked down to see the German formation of Dorniers. Big beast aeroplanes but not as fast and nippy as the Spitfire. Noticing one was slightly out of line with the others he thought he'd have a crack at him. There were no 109s visible so he focused on his target and went in for the chase. Closer, closer and then he put his finger on the button and fired. His guns made a noise like tearing calico. His bullets made holes in the plane's fuselage. Got him! JP thought triumphantly. He watched the plane break away then spiral towards the sea, leaving a trail of black smoke behind him.

The squadron had dispersed now; it was every man for himself. JP was now at 3,000 feet below the Germans and racing at a terrific speed. He pulled the stick back and returned to the battle, flying in zigzags to avoid giving the Hun an easy target. There was chaos up there: planes everywhere, flying in all directions, men swinging on the ends of parachutes, black smoke, the odd burst of flames and planes plummeting towards the sea like shot birds.

JP fought for his life, remembering the golden rule not to fly straight and level for more than twenty seconds – if you did you were dead. He managed to hit a Heinkel, causing it to limp towards home with bullet holes in its belly. He missed a few and ducked the odd bullet himself and yet, in the middle of combat, JP thought of Martha. He thought of her and of not being allowed to love her, and a recklessness came over him in a furious red mist. He felt no fear. He didn't even fear dying. At that moment, with a hundred enemy planes all around him, he almost welcomed it as a respite from his sick heart.

Then JP spotted an Me 109 on his tail, turning as he turned, the glint from his cannon shining in the sunlight. He didn't feel terror. The anticipation of death stilled the world around him. The sound of his engine became muffled as if it were very far away already. He felt as if he were out of his body and someone else was doing the flying for him. Someone else was gritting his teeth and narrowing his eyes and smiling. Yes, someone else was smiling as if he was actually taking pleasure in the possibility of death.

Then JP was back in his body and he was turning the plane in tight circles, pursued closely by the 109. Knowing that the Spitfire could turn more tightly than the bigger German plane, he pulled it in even further, challenging the German to follow him if he dared. The little plane juddered but it didn't protest. JP's forehead began to perspire. He grew unbearably hot, but he was flying for his life and relishing the drama. The Hun fired at him again and missed. JP was elated. 'Just you bloody try!' he shouted, even though the pilot couldn't hear him. The German tried to tighten his turn but to no avail. That big plane was no match for the agile Spitfire, or the pilot for the daring of JP, who had been seized by wild fury, possessed by the indomitable Deverill spirit.

At last, when JP was beginning to panic that he was pushing his plane beyond its limit, the German plane was forced to bail out. It broke away and, most likely low on fuel, headed back out to sea. JP gave a manic laugh. He had won this small battle. He took a deep breath, shook his head and blinked the sweat out of his eyes. He glanced at his own level of fuel. It was time for him to head back to base as well. He'd survived his first battle.

When he landed, he discovered, to his horror, that Jimmy had not.

Losing their friend was a terrible blow to JP and Stanley. They had been a clique of three; now they were two. In that moment, when the reality of Jimmy's demise sunk in, JP felt that he had transitioned from a boy, a 'sprog' as Jimmy had called him, to a man; a man in a man's war. But he didn't dwell on Jimmy's death. None of them did. Losing comrades was soon to become too frequent to give in to grief. He just had to try to survive and then, when it was all over, he would take the time to mourn those who hadn't. In the meantime he had a war to fight and he had no other option than to get on with the job.

JP was in the Mess when he received Kitty's letter. He didn't realize how much he missed home until he read it.

My darling JP

I hope this finds you well and in good heart. We all miss you terribly here in Ballinakelly and wish the war would come to an end so that you could come home and start your studies in Dublin. I know flying planes is what you wanted to do, but I would rather you rode a horse and got your kicks that way! However, let me share some news.

Your great-aunt Hazel died yesterday, peacefully in her bed, but as you can imagine Laurel is beside herself. She says she wants to go too, even though she now has that old reprobate Ethelred all to herself! Our father is going to plant a hazel in her honour and Laurel says that when it's her time to go she wants a laurel planted right next to it. Ethelred is not a shrub so I don't suppose he's included in the plan.

*Mama is furious because the Army has requisitioned
Broadmere for a hospital and it's going to be filled with
wounded soldiers. It makes me smile because she can't abide
anything messy and all those bloodied bandages will drive
her to madness. Perhaps she will return home after all,
we all know that that is what Papa would like. God only
knows why! I'm not sure why he thinks they could be happy
after years of being very unhappy, but he is a law unto
himself. Victoria is keen to roll up her sleeves and be of use
in this war. I hear she has also taken a whole load of evacuee
children and has them all working on the farm. Who would
have thought the Countess of Elmrod would want to get
her hands dirty? Charlotte writes to me often, complaining
that Victoria marches about the place like a colonel bossing
everyone around. She has found her calling and is taking it
all very seriously. Apparently she has caught the eye of one
of the recuperating officers so Eric had better watch out, but
he is busy with the Home Guard, defending our coastline, so
I don't suppose he will notice.*

*Robert sends you lots of love. He's writing as usual. War
puts him in a very bad mood because it reminds him of the
last one, when he couldn't fight because of his stiff leg. He
feels useless all over again. Poor darling. I think that's the
subject of his new book. It will probably be his best. Florence
misses you. Although we are neutral, war has touched us
too. There is rationing and the Germans bombed Campile
in Co. Wexford, killing three people. It was a great shock to
everyone, as you can imagine, for no one believed that the
Luftwaffe would drop bombs on the Republic. But there it is.
We're surviving here. Life goes on, albeit rather anxiously.*

*Darling JP, I hope you have put your disappointment
behind you. I won't go on about it but I want you to know*

*that you are in my heart and on my mind, constantly. I pray
for your safety.*

  Your loving sister, Kitty

*PS A sweet little girl called Alana knocked on the door the
other day and gave me a letter for you. I asked her her name
but she just said Alana. She spoke with a rather strange
American accent so I imagine she must be Emer and Jack
O'Leary's daughter. Anyhow, she said you were her friend
and would I make sure this letter gets to you. I think you
have an admirer!*

JP enjoyed Kitty's letter, except for the news of Hazel's
death. It was good to hear from home. Ballinakelly seemed
so far away from Biggin Hill and another world entirely from
the daily battles he was fighting in the skies above Britain.
The bombing of Campile just made him more determined
to blast the Luftwaffe off the face of the planet.

He turned his attention to Alana's letter, written in neat,
looped handwriting, obviously with great care. He grinned
as he remembered the little girl he had rescued from the hills
and felt wistful for a moment as he recalled the peace up there
in that wild green landscape. Those weeks before Martha had
come to Ballinakelly had been innocent, full of anticipation
and excitement. Then it had all changed. Martha had gone
back to America, war had come and the world had slipped
on its axis, leaving everything looking different, distorted
and grim.

He read the girl's letter. It was long. There were pages
and pages, so he skimmed most of it. The ramblings of an
infatuated child, he thought, shaking his head in amusement. He'd write back to make her happy and because,

while he waited in the hut to scramble, there was not much else to do.

The summer passed and while JP took to the air in ever more intensive battles the Germans increased their attacks on British airfields and radar stations, pushing the Royal Air Force to the limit, outnumbering them four to one. Then in September the enemy changed tactic and turned their full might on London, blackening the skies with their bombers.

Harry had never imagined it would get to this. He had never imagined that the enemy would strike at the heart of London. Before, it had been a battle fought over the water, but now the battle was happening all around him. The attacks were nightly and the people of the city took shelter underground like small animals, emerging bleary-eyed at dawn to assess the damage.

It was the sounds of those raids that were the most terrifying. The menacing drone as the enemy planes approached overhead, the whistling of falling bombs, the banging of explosions, the rattling of anti-aircraft fire, the clattering of falling tiles, the crashing of breaking glass, the screaming of horses, the howling of dogs, the cries of people and the crackling of fires. Then the silence; the terrible silence in London's blacked-out city where every ear was strained in anticipation, hearing noises that weren't really there.

There seemed to be a lull over Christmas. Some of the evacuee children returned to their parents for the festivities and the churches were full of people, celebrating their festival as they always had. Harry spent the day at Broadmere, attending the little family church on the estate with his wife Charlotte and their children. From there he wrote to Kitty, reporting on the various hilarities with their mother and on

Victoria's obvious infatuation with the now much recovered Army officer. Harry returned to London on Boxing Day and spent the day with Boysie.

'I shouldn't admit this, old boy, after all, there's a war on,' he said to Boysie over dinner at the Savoy. 'But this year has been the best year of my life.'

Boysie grinned. 'Mine too. Let's drink to that.' They raised their champagne flutes. 'How will we ever survive when everything returns to normal?'

'Do you think it will?' Harry asked.

'I *know* it will,' Boysie replied and because Boysie had an important job in intelligence, Harry believed he knew something. They drained their glasses and gazed at each other with shiny eyes.

Harry put his hand on his heart. 'I'm emotional tonight,' he said. 'I don't think I can say the words.'

'Then don't,' Boysie replied. He put *his* hand on *his* heart. 'And I shan't either.' They smiled at each other with complete understanding, their hands pressed to their chests, and anyone who might have been watching would have thought they were making some kind of military salute rather than a declaration of devotion.

Boysie returned to his secret job at Bletchley Park and Harry to his desk job. Harry wondered whether the air raids were now over. Perhaps the Germans had turned their attention to another city, in another country far away, like Russia. There had been nothing for a fortnight and things were beginning to feel normal again. But then 29th December arrived.

The raid began at 5.30 that evening.

The city was in blackout, as usual. Darkness prevented the enemy from finding its target, but tonight they had a plan to light it up like a bonfire.

Harry was in a West End cinema watching a matinée of the new Charlie Chaplin film with a couple of friends from work when the bombs started to fall. The reel was stopped abruptly and a notice appeared on the screen, advising everyone to take to the shelters as quickly as possible. When they hurried into the street they discovered that they weren't the normal bombs at all, but small incendiary devices designed to start fires. These miniature bombs fell onto the roofs and into the streets with a clattering sound before exploding into a yellowy light and bursting into flames. Harry ran to put them out one by one, smothering them with his coat. Others followed suit, throwing whatever they could get their hands on over the flames and stamping them out with their feet. But there were too many. It seemed that the planes were dropping them in their thousands and each little flame grew into a fire and soon it seemed that the whole of the city was burning.

By 7.30 the first phase was done. Now London was lit up with hundreds of burning buildings the second wave of bombers could attack the city with ease. Thirty more planes approached London. Harry looked into the smoky sky to see bombs falling like giant hailstones caught in the spotlights being projected from the ground below. The sight stole his breath. He was awestruck and horrified. He wondered whether there'd be anything left of London in the morning.

Propelled by a sense of duty, Harry hurried to help in any way that he could. Fires needed putting out, people needed rescuing from fallen buildings, apparently St Paul's was in flames. The fire brigade's Green Goddesses were struggling to cope with the spreading fires and it didn't help that the wind was beginning to pick up.

And still the planes came, wave upon wave. There seemed to be no end to them.

Harry knew he should find a shelter but the thought of sitting it out was repugnant to him. London needed him. He thought of all those children who had come back from their temporary homes in the countryside to spend Christmas with their families and the desire rose in him in a great tide of humanity to save London from total destruction.

He worked through the night, running his hands over the rubble in search of survivors, rescuing people from under piles of debris, stamping out flames, assisting firefighters and ambulance men. The smoke filled his chest and the flames scorched his skin but he didn't stop. Not for a moment. He was on the ground being useful and he hadn't felt useful since the Great War when he'd fought in the battlefields of France.

Then he heard a high-pitched cry for help. A child screaming for his mother. It rose above the crackling sound, which was almost deafening, and was carried on the wind, which fanned the flames so that they grew even higher, like bright orange monsters, rising into the night. As Harry ran down the road he heard the whistling of a bomb above him. The crackling was silenced, the roar of flames stilled, only the whistling could be heard and then the quiet. The quiet, eerie sound of imminent death.

Harry didn't look up. He didn't need to. He kept running but there was no way to avoid it. He thought of Boysie, his children, of Kitty and his father and he felt sorry, because he was just beginning to make sense of his life and now it was going to be over.

The bomb fell in front of him and threw him ten feet into the air. But by the time he fell he was no longer in his body. He was standing beside it, looking down onto the broken man he had been. The broken man who had tried so valiantly to do good. *Bloody war*, he thought.

Then he saw Adeline. She was beside him, shining in a light that did not pertain to this desperate night. She smiled at him and he smiled back. 'So this is it,' he said, still unable to believe that he was no longer alive. He *felt* alive. More alive than ever.

'This is it, my darling. You've done your bit.'

'So, what now?' he asked, but before she could answer he saw a light that was brighter than any he had ever seen before. It was love, pulling him into its embrace.

Adeline watched in astonishment. Surely, as heir to Castle Deverill, Harry should be locked in limbo like all the Deverill heirs before him. But no, he was being enveloped by the light, melting into infinity, and there, in the dazzling radiance, Adeline could just about make out the shadowy figures of Digby and Hazel, Rupert and George, Stoke and Augusta, welcoming him home. For a moment her heart expanded with an almost overwhelming desire to join them, as if the light was pulling at her too, as if she was already part of that light and longed to become whole, but she resisted. She had much to do before she would be ready to leave this dimension.

So there was to be no limbo for Harry. There was only one reason why he might escape the curse, Adeline thought: he wasn't a Deverill heir – which meant that he wasn't a Deverill. Adeline reflected on Maud and remembered her affair with Eddie Rothmeade all those years ago. Adeline should have known. Harry wasn't Bertie's son, after all. He never had been. What a blessing to escape the dreadful limbo that was Hubert's fate.

Adeline watched Harry go. Then she looked down at his broken body and felt desperately sad for those still living who had loved him.

Chapter 18

Ballinakelly

News of Harry's death devastated his family. Kitty took to the hills on her horse, as she had always done when faced with great unhappiness, and galloped at high speed, crying at the injustice of the world. Bertie resisted the bottle and went to church instead, where he sat quietly in the pew, trying to remember what Adeline had taught him about death. Elspeth held her children close, thanking God that they weren't old enough to fight in the war. In Kent, Maud took to her bed as Beatrice had done after Digby died, wailing that her son Harry's death was God's punishment for her sins, while Victoria was more pragmatic: 'People die in war,' she said phlegmatically. 'It's unlucky that a bomb got Harry but not at all surprising.' She secretly wished it had got her boring husband Eric instead, but he was defending the coast with other old men in the Home Guard, and the closest he'd come to a bomb was hearing about them on the wireless.

Boysie's desolation was total. It was as if the bomb had destroyed his entire world, leaving a wilderness of isolation and misery. The worst thing was not being able to tell everyone how utterly distraught he was. He wanted to shout out his love and his terrible loss so that everyone would know what Harry had meant to him. He wanted to honour him in this way. But the existence of his wife and children prevented such imprudence. However much he wanted to acknowledge Harry he couldn't bear to hurt *them*. So he hid his pain and mourned his one true love as if Harry had been nothing more than a dear friend.

The funeral was a quiet, sombre affair in the church of St Patrick in Ballinakelly. The January skies were a clear watery blue, the winter sun low and bright, the wind cold and salty as it blew inland in gusts from over the water. It was here in this church that Kitty had witnessed the funerals of many of her loved ones. She had said goodbye to her uncle Rupert, who had died in the Great War, and to her grandparents, Hubert and Adeline, whom she had loved so fiercely. She had recently bidden farewell to her great-aunt Hazel and while she had prayed she had squeezed her eyes shut and asked God to spare JP in this war. She hadn't asked God to spare Harry, not that it would have made any difference for Harry's destiny was to die on that night; however, she still regretted not mentioning her brother in her prayers. She felt she had let him down. But here she was at his funeral and it was too late for prayers, and regrets were pointless.

Kitty had never expected to say goodbye to Harry so soon. He had been her ally and friend and now he was gone. Life had not been easy for him, she mused. She remembered discovering him in bed with Joseph the first footman when he was home on leave during the last war, and the time he had asked her for advice following Charlotte catching him kissing Boysie at Celia's Summer Ball. He wasn't made for marriage. He wasn't made for convention. But society had insisted on him fitting in and he had done his duty and conformed. She wondered how much it had cost him to toe the line. She wondered whether he had ever been truly happy in a world that did not allow him to be himself.

She couldn't look at Charlotte and the children. It was too awful to witness their suffering. Those children had lost their father and Charlotte had lost her husband, although Kitty knew that she hadn't really ever had him. His heart had always belonged to Boysie.

Kitty looked at Boysie then, who was sitting across the aisle beside his wife Deirdre. His profile was fixed in a rigid frown, his mouth downturned and his lips quivering and she knew that Boysie had loved Harry very deeply. He looked old suddenly, she thought, even though he was only in his mid-forties. He sensed her watching him and turned to look at her. Their eyes met and Kitty was shocked by his pain, so blatantly exposed. She gave him a sympathetic smile but he was too distraught to respond. He dropped his gaze into the prayer sheet that trembled in his hands. Kitty turned her attention back to Reverend Maddox who had grown fat on happiness ever since his marriage to Mrs Goodwin the previous spring.

After the service there was lunch at the Hunting Lodge. Maud and Bertie sat on the window seat and from the way Bertie was inclining his head and listening intently Kitty could tell that he was hoping Maud would come back to him. She wondered whether shared grief would unite them. Surely Arthur Arlington could not commiserate with Maud in the way that Bertie did.

Kitty spoke briefly to her sister Victoria, the formidable Countess of Elmrod, but the years had grown up between them like a thick forest and Kitty didn't have the energy to fight her way through it in search of the person she had once been, for she had never much liked that person to begin with. She talked to her twin cousins Leona and Vivien who told her that Celia was on her way back from South Africa without the children, who would remain in Johannesburg until the war was over. Kitty knew that news of Harry's death would have cut her to the quick. But the twins were very keen to tell Kitty how rich Celia had become – and by extension, how rich *they* had become. 'She's made a fortune mining gold,' said Leona proudly.

'A fortune!' repeated Vivien, and Kitty smiled for the first time since Harry's death because those snooty twins had always considered Celia a good-for-nothing.

Grace Rowan-Hampton was accompanied, for a change, by her husband Ronald, who was ruddier and more portly than ever. He handed Laurel his own handkerchief with a pudgy hand and the remaining Shrub dabbed her damp eyes with a dainty snivel. Lord Hunt was very attentive, patting Laurel's back sympathetically, and Kitty wondered why he didn't marry her now that Hazel was no longer with them, but the old rogue clearly had no intention of doing anything so conventional.

After a while Kitty found the smoky air in the drawing room stifling and wandered into the hall. She found Boysie sitting alone on the sofa there, staring into his glass of sherry. 'Hello, Boysie,' she said, sitting beside him.

Boysie shook his head. 'What was Harry doing in that part of town?' he asked. 'Why wasn't he in a shelter? What was he thinking?'

'I imagine he was trying to help,' Kitty replied.

'Fool,' said Boysie bitterly. There was a lengthy silence as they both considered Harry's foolishness.

'I know how much you loved him, Boysie,' said Kitty

quietly. 'Harry and I shared many secrets and that was one of them. I know how much he loved *you*.'

Boysie turned to her, his eyes shining with tears. 'Do you?'

'Yes, I do.'

His face reddened and he plunged his gaze back into his glass. 'I don't know how I'll go on,' he said. 'I don't know how to live now that Harry's gone.'

Kitty put her hand on his and gave it a gentle squeeze. 'You will because you have to. When you have no choice you somehow push yourself forward.'

He swallowed hard. 'I'm grateful for your understanding, Kitty.'

She smiled sympathetically. 'It helped Harry to know that he could talk to me and share his feelings. I dare say Celia was privy to your friendship too.'

'Celia,' he groaned. 'Where is she when I need her, eh? Mining for gold! Really, that's no occupation for a girl who always liked her nails beautifully manicured!' He chuckled joylessly.

'She's on her way back,' Kitty told him.

Boysie stared at her, astonished. 'She's coming back?'

'Her ghastly sisters just told me.'

'Why didn't she tell me herself?'

'She's a woman of mystery these days. Perhaps she wants to surprise you, or maybe she was just in a dreadful hurry to get home.'

'She must know how helpless I am without Harry,' he said and Kitty thought that he did look particularly helpless.

'Then she's returning to rescue you,' she replied. 'After all, she rescued herself after Archie's suicide, didn't she? Celia's a dab hand at survival.'

'Like all you Deverills. Tell me, Kitty. How do you do it?'

Kitty sighed, reflecting on the many times in her life when she had had to push herself off the floor, dust herself down and carry on. 'I don't know, Boysie. Because there's something inside us that refuses to break.'

'The Deverill spirit,' said Boysie. 'That's what Digby called it.'

'Yes, that's it. The Deverill spirit.'

He gave a wan smile. 'Can I have some of it, please?'

Kitty laughed and rested her head on his shoulder. 'You have your own spirit, Boysie. It's in there somewhere. You just have to find it.'

Losing Harry made Kitty nostalgic for the past, grateful for the present but anxious about the future, for she was more aware than ever that life was woefully short and precarious. Consequently, her wish to live it fully and for herself grew more intense. She rode out as usual but took to stopping on the top of a hill that gave her a clear view of the solitary cove below where the sea rolled onto a white horseshoe beach and Jack's house stood in isolation, nestled among bushes and short trees. She would remain there, watching the building in the hope of glimpsing the man she couldn't stop loving. She knew she shouldn't, she was well aware of what she'd lose if she gave into her heart, but she had loved him for so long she didn't know how to feel otherwise. And she suspected that, deep down in the secret caverns of his heart, beneath the resentment and the anger, he loved her too; because he always had.

Sometimes Kitty saw the small figure of Emer, Jack's wife, strolling up the beach with her children and she wished that it were *she* in Emer's place and that those children were *their* children. From her distant spot she watched them playing with the dog, running in the wind, laughing as they chased seagulls and mimicked them with their arms outstretched. Kitty suffered at the sight of Jack's family for surely Emer had stolen the life that should have been hers. She begrudged Emer her happiness and her good fortune. Why, when Fate had obstructed Kitty at every turn, had it assisted Emer? What had *she* done to deserve Jack when Kitty had loved him all her life? But when she saw Jack she had to turn her horse round and canter away because the sight of him with his wife caused her too much anguish.

Then, one evening in early spring up on the hill, Kitty turned her horse to find Jack there, on his. He had ridden up behind her and was looking at her with a serious expression on his face. Kitty's cheeks stung with shame at having been caught spying, but she was so surprised to see him that she couldn't think of an excuse as to why she was there. Therefore she said nothing.

Jack looked uncomfortable and Kitty sensed that *he* didn't know what to say either. 'I'm sorry about Harry,' he said at length. 'He was a good man.'

Kitty was relieved he wasn't going to tell her off for snooping. 'Thank you,' she replied.

'I've been wanting to tell you but . . .' He turned his gaze to the beach. It had been nearly four months since Harry had been killed and it had taken Jack all that time to engineer a way of meeting her.

'I understand,' Kitty interjected, looking down at the solitary house in the bay. 'Ride with me?' she asked suddenly, desperate to get him away from Emer and into the old familiar places he had once shared with *her*. She grinned at him in the challenging way she used to and one corner of his mouth curled into a small smile, as if he was weary of being furious with her; as if he couldn't be furious with her any longer.

They set off together, but not the way Kitty had come. She felt that old frisson of excitement which had always been present in the days when they had met in secret. When they had made love in his cottage or kissed up at the Fairy Ring. There had always been the danger of being discovered and that danger was here now, quivering in the air between them. Without saying a word they cantered over the hills, side by side, and the wind seemed to snatch their awkwardness and toss it away. In its place there slipped the old familiar sense of delight.

They drew their horses to a halt at the top of a cliff and dismounted. The sun was a blood orange that turned the sky pink and the sea below it a deep indigo. The waves lapped sleepily onto the sand as the tide slowly retreated and a pair of gulls squabbled over a small crustacean before flying off towards the cliffs. Besides the rhythmic sound of the sea and their horses' gentle breathing the evening was quiet and still.

The beauty of the moment caught in their chests as they stood together, gazing out over the ocean as they had done so many times in their youth, before Fate had stolen their dreams. They saw their pasts in the great horizon and their loss in the flimsy wisps of cloud that were darkening now as the sun sank lower, and all their longing and disappointment flooded their hearts with an aching tenderness. Kitty's throat tightened as the words she so longed to say swelled with emotion. She glanced at Jack's profile. It was hard and inscrutable. She wondered whether he was thinking of Emer as she had once thought of Robert. But she wasn't thinking of Robert now.

Jack turned to look at her and his eyes were full of sorrow.

His face was dark with the sun behind him but she could make out his pain in the downturn of his mouth. They stared at each other, knowing the next few moments would be decisive. Kitty felt the pressure build until it was almost unbearable. She wanted to tell him of her regret and her craving and of the endless hours she had stood on the hilltop gazing onto his home, hoping for a glimpse of him. Most ardently she wanted to brush away his sadness with her lips.

She took a step towards him. She barely dared breathe. After everything they had been through would he walk away from her now? But the beauty had penetrated deep into those hidden caverns of his heart where his love had never altered. He pulled her against him and kissed her.

Celia Mayberry arrived in a London she did not recognize. She had left for South Africa in the summer of 1932, when the glittering era of the 'Bright Young Things' who'd partied through the 1920s with a decadence that now made her blush was swiftly disappearing into the gloom of the Great Depression. London had changed then, but nothing in comparison to the change now. Windows were darkened, streets were virtually empty, buildings lay in ruins, a thick grey dust seemed to cover the streets and the smog hung heavy and damp in a lingering winter even though winter should have already made way for spring. There were no children playing in the parks and everyone walked briskly, with purpose. She noticed that the ticket collectors on the buses were women and when she chatted to the lady in the newsagent she was told that women had taken over many of the men's jobs, seeing as the men had gone off to fight. The woman also told her with great excitement of the bombings night after night and the escapades she'd had in her air-raid shelter. She also commented with a wink on the handsome men in Army uniforms.

Celia was very relieved when she found that Deverill House was still standing even though there were only a couple of old retainers left to look after it along with the cook and a couple of maids. Everyone else had gone to join the war effort, her sister Leona told her, and everyone who could get out of London had.

Besides Leona, who had briefly come to London not to see Celia but to have her hair done, Boysie was Celia's first real visitor. It had been almost ten years since they had lunched at Claridge's with Harry and said farewell. Celia hadn't intended to stay away so long and the monthly letters she had written in the early years had dwindled to one or two annually. Now Boysie stepped into the hall where Beatrice Deverill had once hosted her infamous Tuesday-evening Salons and feasted his eyes on his old friend with delight. Celia noticed how much he had aged and she was moved by the sorrowful downturn of his mouth, which had once been pouting and petulant. Boysie smiled with happiness to see her but behind his joy his grief was raw and smarting.

Celia threw her arms around him and held him tightly, breathing in his familiar scent, which reminded her of Harry. They cried then because of what Harry had meant to them both.

Celia had lit a fire in the upstairs drawing room and they settled into one of the sofas, Boysie with a large glass of whiskey, Celia with a more modest glass of sherry. She kicked off her shoes and curled up in the corner against the silk cushions. Boysie grinned at her and his enlivened eyes told of his relief that she had come home just when he needed her most. 'Darling girl,' he sighed. 'You're more beautiful than ever.

The years have done nothing to diminish you. If anything, you have a shrewd look about you which has only made you more attractive. Although I did adore the doe-eyed innocent you used to be.'

Celia took his hand. 'I've come a long way in a decade.'

'It had better have been worth it, because you sacrificed *us*,' said Boysie and they both thought of Harry again.

'How is Dreary Deirdre?' she asked mischievously.

'Dreary,' he replied with a feeble smile.

'She never knew?'

'Never.'

'Not even suspected?' He shook his head. 'Charlotte knew, didn't she? But she never breathed a word. She's good like that. A real trouper!'

'Charlotte allowed us a friendship and we did try, but I'm afraid we went beyond that in the end.'

'Was Harry happy, Boysie? He was always so restless, as if he was searching for some sort of meaningful way to live his life. I don't think he ever found it.'

'You're right, he was restless and rootless. Losing Castle Deverill hit him harder than any of us knew. He had grown up sure of his destiny and then suddenly that destiny was taken away from him and it left a void. He never found anything to fill it.'

'*You* filled it, Boysie.'

'I did, old girl, but only up to a point. A man defines himself by his work, which meant that Harry was never really sure of who he was. Before the war I found myself in the art world and now I've found myself at Government Communications Headquarters, which has been enormously satisfying. Harry wanted to be useful, but he ended up at a desk in some dull office in Whitehall. He loved his children and he was fond of Charlotte, but it's frustrating not being free to be yourself. Harry found the burden of living a double life unbearable.'

'I can only imagine,' said Celia.

'But what of you, darling? Tell me about *your* lovers. I hope you have lived an immoral life in Johannesburg.'

Her blue eyes twinkled. 'I've had lovers, certainly, but I will never fall in love again, Boysie. I don't wish to.'

'Really?' He wasn't convinced.

'I had a good marriage and I loved Archie. But he hurt me, Boysie. He hurt me deeply. I don't ever want to be hurt again.'

'I know all about hurt. I don't want to be hurt again either.'

She smiled affectionately. 'If you weren't married to Dreary Deirdre I'd marry you myself and we would live very happily on our memories and all the money I've made in the mines.'

'Don't tempt me, old girl.'

'So, what now?' Celia asked.

Boysie withdrew his hand from hers and pulled an enamel cigarette case out of the inside pocket of his jacket. He put one between his lips and Celia flicked the lighter. He puffed smoke into the room. 'I search for the Deverill spirit in me,' he replied with a grin. 'Kitty told me that if I look hard enough I might find it.'

'Darling Kitty.' Celia laughed. 'How is she?'

'Restless,' he replied, raising an eyebrow.

'Oh dear!'

'Yes, I sensed a restlessness which had nothing to do with Harry.'

'What do you make of it?'

'Perhaps we ought to go to Ireland together and find out.'

'Oh let's!' Celia exclaimed excitedly. 'Will they do without you at Government Communications Headquarters? Sounds jolly important.'

'We might have to wait until *after* the war.'

Celia lifted his arm and snuggled up beneath it. 'I'd like to go and see what the Countess di Marcantonio has done to my castle! Do you know when Kitty wrote and told me that the Countess was none other than Bridie Doyle I nearly threw up my breakfast! But it's only a castle. Bricks and stone and a great deal of Archie's money!'

'To Kitty it is much more than that,' Boysie reminded her.

Celia sighed. 'I know, but she won't be happy until she learns that home is wherever love is.'

Chapter 19

Ballinakelly

Alana lay on her bed with her dog Piglet, an adorable French bulldog bitch that Bridie had given her for her twelfth birthday the September before. So enamoured was she of her new friend that she took her everywhere, except to school where the nuns had recoiled in horror at the sight of a dog on the desk and sent them both home in disgrace. Nothing excited Alana more than returning to Piglet at the end of the day, except a letter from JP Deverill.

The first letter she received had arrived in July of the year before. Her mother had looked at the envelope closely and studied the handwriting, astonished that anyone had written to Alana. She had shown it to Jack, who had been reading the newspaper at the breakfast table, and he had studied it too, holding it up to the light and frowning. Then he had asked Alana directly and she had had no alternative but to tell them that she had written to JP and that this was his response. Both parents had stared at her in stunned silence. The child was only eleven, it was most unseemly to be writing to a young man she barely even knew. When they voiced these concerns Alana had grabbed the letter and fled the room in tears. Those tears had dried up pretty swiftly, however, on reading what JP had written. He had used *both* sides of the paper, thanking her for *her* letter and telling her as much about his life as a fighter pilot in the RAF as the censorship would allow. To Alana it sounded like the most glamorous life ever. She soon forgot about her parents' disapproval as her heart expanded with elation and she read it over and over again before hiding it inside the encyclopaedia her father had given her.

Alana had written back immediately. She had told JP about her parents' reaction to his letter and suggested that he send any letters to his sister Kitty's house instead. Alana had always been a bold child and her parents' disapproval only made her more determined. She had walked to the White House the following day after school and told Kitty of her plan. Kitty was amused by the child's pluck, being no stranger to schemes and plots herself, and had agreed to send Alana's letters for her and to leave any letters from JP under a stone just inside the wall that surrounded her property. Alana could not have imagined that once her father and Kitty had left notes for each other behind a stone in the vegetable-garden wall at Castle Deverill. The parallel was not lost on Kitty, however, and she had been only too ready to go along with the girl's plan.

Now, as Alana lay on her bed with Piglet snoring softly beside her, she read JP's most recent letter. He had written over two sides of paper, telling her stories of his childhood growing up in Ballinakelly when his days had been spent hunting and fishing and building a model railway with his father. He told her little about the daily battles in the sky, but from the small amount he was able to share she knew he was risking his life doing his duty and she feared for him. To

Alana he was a hero, defending Britain from the most fero-
cious enemy that small island had ever known. She poured
her anguish into her prayers, certain that God would do as
she asked and keep him safe.

JP always ended with *From your knight on horseback*, referring to the day he had rescued her in the hills. Alana could
feel him through his letters, as if his writing literally resonated with his life force. She pressed the paper to her heart
and closed her eyes, envisaging him on his horse, his grey
eyes twinkling at her from beneath the rim of his hat. She
remembered the feeling of her back nestled against his warm
body and his arms around her as he had taken the reins and
directed the horse home. She could recall the vibration of
his voice in his chest as they had talked and his smile when
he had lifted her down. She was now nearly thirteen but she
believed she loved him and she believed that, although she
was not yet a woman, one day he would love her back.

Alana was certain that her parents had forgotten all about
JP. After they had found the initial letter she had been careful
to hide all his correspondence from them. Neither had mentioned JP since and when Alana felt the need to talk about
him she whispered her feelings into Piglet's ear and Piglet
wagged her tail. Alana had now over a dozen letters full of
nostalgic recollections and amusing anecdotes. She might
be a child but JP treated her like an adult – she wondered
sometimes if he'd forgotten how young she really was. He
had even poured out his heart about Harry, his half-brother,
who had been killed in the Blitz, and Alana had cried for
him and his sorrow, which he had described so touchingly.

It was early summer now. The war had been going on for
nearly two years. In spite of their neutrality the Republic of
Ireland had not escaped the might of the German bombers.

Dublin had been attacked twice, first in January and then in May, when twenty-eight people had been killed. Alana worried for JP and Kitty grieved for Harry, but Alana's father Jack seemed, for the first time in years, to be free of concern. Alana had noticed a sudden lightness in him – a readiness to laugh, an energy that seemed to invigorate every limb and smiles that softened his face when he had no apparent reason to smile. It was as if summer had not only restored to life the hills and forests but her father as well. The house was full of sunshine, even when the sun wasn't shining, and her mother seemed to be affected by it too, for she laughed as well when he put on the music and danced with her around the kitchen table. Alana didn't wonder why – the adult world was a mystery to her which she didn't care to question – but she enjoyed the lift in atmosphere all the same.

At the White House Robert noticed a change in Kitty too. Despite her sadness at losing her beloved brother, she seemed to be finding pleasure in her life again. He wondered whether Harry's death had taught her to appreciate what she had, whether it had perhaps shown her that the people she loved were more important than bricks and mortar. She had not mentioned Bridie and the castle in a long time. It appeared that she had let that whole business go at last. How ironic it was, he mused, that it had taken the death of some-one dear to jolt her back to life.

Grace Rowan-Hampton put down the telephone and smiled. She remained a moment at her desk, taking pleasure from the thought of Michael Doyle. How he'll enjoy *this*, she thought to herself.

She wound her hand around the back of her neck and closed her eyes. How she longed for him. How her *body* longed for him. She was sixty-six years old and yet her lust was that of a woman half her age. She had always been sensual and Ronald had never satisfied her in the bedroom, even when they had been young; but many had. She reflected on the affairs she had enjoyed over the years. Some she only recalled vaguely, a few had been as passing storms in the night, but a small handful stood out. Among them there had been her long and amorous affair with Bertie Deverill, who had been a very adept lover, sensitive, mischievous and tender. Then there had been her torrid and passionate affair with Michael Doyle, who had pleased her in a way that no man ever had before. Later there had been her affair with the arrogant Count who had turned sexual pleasure into an art form. But out of those three very different men Michael Doyle was the one she was unable to let go.

Grace parted her lips and sighed. She would do anything for Michael Doyle, anything at all to spend another night in his arms. The years were passing and she was growing older. Her allure was fading. She wasn't the ripe young woman she had been when he had first taken her in the old farmhouse on the Dunashee Road. But she still had a certain appeal. She knew that. She saw it in his eyes when he looked at her, although he tried very hard to disguise it. She had failed in persuading Kitty to forgive him but she could deliver the Count. Yes, she thought resolutely, pushing herself up from her chair. She could deliver the Count.

The Count was where he was happiest: in bed with Niamh O'Donovan. He had rented a little cottage outside Drimoleague in the name of Mr McGill and taken to smuggling Niamh there hidden beneath a blanket on the back seat of his car. The skulduggery excited him as did Niamh, who had the most luscious body he had ever encountered and a shameless delight in letting him have it any which way he desired. She was quite a different woman now to the virgin he had first seduced two years before. In fact, he thought she could probably make even hardened professionals blush with some of the things he had taught her to do.

Ballinakelly did not offer him a great deal besides women – and he had pretty much made his way through the most attractive of them. He had tired of the sharp, brittle socialites of Manhattan and the brassy waitresses in Connecticut. He had been ready for a change and the castle had held a very powerful allure, but Ballinakelly was a small town with limited entertainment for a man who was used to the glamour of polo and the glitzy city soirées. Had Bridie been of a different stock he might have enjoyed hunting with the Deverills, but as it was he was restricted to a lesser class of person and they bored him. Niamh didn't bore him. There was something about her which kept him coming back for more. Besides her obvious sexuality she was witty with a natural cunning, and mischievous and playful like a voluptuous cat. He enjoyed talking to her. She had a delightful way of listening to him. Not like Bridie, whose eager face revealed an anxiety to please, which now bordered on fear. Niamh listened to him with great interest as if everything he said was intelligent and wise. Bridie made him feel unmanly because it was *her* money he was spending and *her* castle he was living in, even though he had gained control of her fortune over the years. But Niamh made him feel powerful. She didn't know that he had brought nothing into his marriage save a grand Italian title. Not only did she make him feel sexually proficient but clever too. He didn't know how long he was going to last in Ballinakelly, but when he left, which he surely would one day, he fantasized about taking Niamh with him.

The only thing stopping him from going anywhere was Leopoldo, his son. He loved the boy deeply. He would like to have had more children so that one day the Marcantonios of Ballinakelly would be a formidable dynasty. But his ambitions had been thwarted by Bridie's inability to conceive again. He didn't imagine *he* lacked fertility. He blamed Bridie entirely for that and now he didn't feel like making love to her any more. She bored him as much as Ballinakelly did. She hadn't been boring in America. She had been full of fun then, but Ballinakelly had turned her into someone else; someone who lacked courage and zest and spirit.

Michael Doyle was leaning on the stone wall by his farm-house when Grace drove up in her car. Mrs Doyle pulled back the curtain and peered through the window. She admired Lady Rowan-Hampton, who had spent many an hour in her kitchen being instructed in Catholicism, but that had been years ago. Now she attended Mass at the Cottage Hospital on the pretext of noblesse oblige. Mrs Doyle knew how sensitive her conversion had been and hadn't mentioned it to anyone. Only Michael knew of it but they had never discussed her. The old woman was surprised to see Lady Rowan-Hampton's car pull up and wondered what business she could possibly have with Michael.

Michael didn't move but watched Grace languidly from beneath his cap, blowing cigarette smoke into the air. Mrs Doyle thought that *that* was no way to greet a lady, but she wouldn't be telling Michael. He had been the head of the family ever since his father had been murdered by a tinker and Mrs Doyle knew better than to tell him anything. He watched Grace approach in her pale summer coat and hat. The wind caught the coat and flicked it up, exposing a flash of leg and the fine dress she was wearing. She was still attractive, there was no doubt about that.

'So, what brings you to my door, Grace?' he said quietly when she reached him.

She put a hand on her hat to stop it blowing away. The sunshine lit up her face, turning her skin to amber. 'I have news that might interest you,' she replied and her lips curled like a secretive cat.

'Go on.'

'I have used all my contacts, Michael, this side of the Atlantic as well as the other, and I have some information about your brother-in-law that might interest you.'

'If you're going to list the women he's bedded, you can save your breath because I already know.'

Grace smiled and Michael's interest was aroused for there was something of the old Grace in it, the one he had taken in the farmhouse on the Dunashee Road. He stood up and stubbed out his cigarette on the wall. 'The Count is not really a count at all,' she went on and watched Michael catch his breath. His surprise gave Grace a tremor of pleasure. 'In fact he's not even Italian,' she added.

'Jesus, Grace!' Michael shook his head.

'He's Albanian.'

'Albanian?'

'His family is from Tirana. But his father *did* move to Italy and Cesare *was* born there, but both his parents are Albanian and they were poor. It appears that his father, whose real name was Besmir Zaharia, was a gardener for the Barberini family in Rome. He got involved in some sort of shady business on the side, made some money, then left in a hurry, taking his wife and son with him. He owed money, apparently, and had to flee for his life. Besmir invented the title Count Benvenuto di Marcantonio when he moved to Argentina, and was obviously an accomplished con artist because he fooled everyone. He got involved in industry and farming, exporting beef and the like, but he was one of those entrepreneurs who quickly make a fortune then lose it. He's infamous in Buenos Aires for gambling and womanizing and, from what I hear, his wife, who claims to be an Italian princess, has left him. I doubt Cesare has had anything to do with his father for years. Cesare left Argentina and made a career out of leeching off rich people. He's got charm and charisma and a title.' She grinned knowingly. 'Americans love a title! I'm afraid they are as much related to the Popes of Rome as you or I. Those silly bees he's stuck above the door of the castle are nothing but fantasy.'

'A fantasy financed by my sister's money,' Michael added grudgingly.

'Speaking of her fortune, Cesare has managed to manipulate her into giving him total control of her money.'

'I thought as much. She's as blind to his faults as she is to his intentions.'

Grace arched an eyebrow. 'You think he's planning on running off with her money?'

'Do you think a man like him is going to spend the rest of his life in Ballinakelly? The only reason he's lasted so long is because of the war. Believe me, the moment it's over he'll be out of here like a devil on horseback.'

'Ruining Bridie in the process,' Grace added. Michael rubbed his chin thoughtfully. 'Who's to say his parents didn't dupe *him* along with everyone else,' Grace suggested. 'Perhaps he's an innocent.' She shrugged, as if giving him the benefit of the doubt, then dismissed the idea with a shake of her head. 'But if you ask me, Cesare is an adventurer and a fraud. I sensed he was so the first time I met him, but I didn't realize how deeply deceitful he was.' Then, remembering suddenly that she was speaking of Michael's sister's husband, she pulled a sympathetic face and added, 'I'm so sorry for Bridie, Michael. I fear Cesare has taken advantage of her.'

Michael didn't reply. Grace watched him and thought how the passing of the years had only enriched his allure. His skin was weathered, the lines around his mouth and eyes deeper and his hair now streaked with grey, but his eyes were still black and pernicious even though he claimed to be leading a pious life, serving the community and the Church. Grace was certain that his lust simmered beneath as it always had, like lava beneath a hard crust. She could almost feel it in the space between them, as if it seeped through the cracks in his chilly veneer.

'And you're sure about your sources?' Michael said at last.

'I'm very sure. I have sources in both Italy and Argentina.' She didn't mention Beaumont Williams, Bridie's attorney in New York, who had been only too happy to help for he had also had his reservations about the Count and done a little digging himself before Bridie had married him. He hadn't dug deeply enough the first time but the second time he had left no stone unturned. 'So, Cesare's real name is Zaharia,' she said. 'Cesare Zaharia. It doesn't have quite the same ring to it, does it?'

'It certainly doesn't,' Michael agreed. He rested his dark

eyes on Grace as if he were seeing her anew. 'You've done well. Back to your old form, aren't you?'

She smiled coyly. 'We had fun once, didn't we? Now we're reunited in another plot. Don't tell me you don't get a buzz out of it.' He chuckled and there was an intimacy in it that Grace hadn't seen in years. It was a chuckle that seemed to say, *How well you know me, Grace.* 'So, what are you going to do?' she asked him. 'Surely you're not going to let him get away with it?'

'I'm going to sleep on it,' he replied.

'Poor Bridie, I gather he's bedding Niamh O'Donovan,' she added.

'It appears so,' Michael said gravely. 'But this is no time to be rash. A foolish man would rush in and put a knife to his heart, but I'm not a foolish man. I will keep my powder dry. You did right in coming to see me.'

Grace gave him her most charming smile. 'We've been through a lot, you and I. I'm nothing if not loyal, Michael.' He gave her a look then that turned her stomach to jelly. It was a look that held within it the memory of long nights of pleasure, of a time when they had been co-conspirators and secret allies, when he had known every curve and crease of her body because he had tasted them all.

It required every ounce of will-power to walk away from him. If Mrs Doyle hadn't been spying on them through the window she might have thrown herself against him, but they were not alone and he was not ready for her yet. She had to make him believe he couldn't have her. She'd whetted his appetite; that was all. Like the old tinkers – he would become wanton when hungry.

Michael watched her go. She had an appeal that was born out of total self-belief. However, he had made a vow at

Mount Melleray to uphold God's Commandments and lead a reformed life. Grace was a married woman. It was going to take all his self-control to resist her, but resist her he would. As for Cesare, Grace was right; he would not let him get away with it. The question was, to what lengths would he go to stop him?

Chapter 20

Jack did not think about the future. In the past the future had been *all* he had thought about. He had dreamed of an independent Ireland and a life with Kitty. He had fought hard for both, but had only won a republic; Kitty had eluded him. He realized now that his youth had been wasted in dissatisfaction with the present. He had barely lived it, so busy was he thinking about what was to come and trying to manipulate it to his will. However, it is a fool who thinks he can control the future and Jack was no fool. His life was much too complicated to hope for a resolution with Kitty. His dream of their living together in a cottage overlooking the Celtic Sea was never going to materialize now. All he could do was love her and accept the limited amount of time he was able to be with her. He had her heart; he knew he must be grateful for that.

Jack loved Emer too and he adored his children. His family life gave him great joy and he was determined not to jeopardize it, but he couldn't resist Kitty. He had tried. He had *really* tried, and in America and Argentina distance had made it possible, but now he was back in Ballinakelly he just couldn't do it. He had thought his fury at her for not running away with him to America would have dampened his ardour.

He had thought that he and Emer would be strong enough to withstand the appeal of an old love. He had thought he had changed. But he was wrong.

The moment he had stepped onto Irish soil he had sensed Kitty's presence, as if her perfume lingered in the very air he breathed. It had assaulted him and he had felt light-headed with the sudden onslaught of memories. His heart had contracted with longing and he had become once again the man who had stood staring out of the window of his cottage, willing himself not to turn round as Kitty left the house, mounted her horse and cantered away. He had become the rejected lover he had been when he had boarded the boat and sailed off to a new life across the Atlantic, a life he had dreamed of living with Kitty. It had all come flooding back then, on disembarking in Ireland, and although he had a wife and children Kitty's shadow had wrapped itself around him like an invisible cloak and however hard he tried he could not shake her off.

Then he had seen her through the window of the milliner's and he realized that he had been looking out for her from the moment he had arrived in Ballinakelly, glancing anxiously down every street, into every window, half craving, half dreading seeing her again. But there she was behind the glass and the sight of her had rendered him powerless. Her face had been pale, her cheekbones more pronounced, her eyes darker, and on locking into his they had darkened further. He had tried to rouse his fury, to tell himself that she had hurt him, that she didn't deserve so much as a smile, and he had turned away. But how he had longed to march into that shop and shout at her for her broken promises and her callousness, then take her beautiful face in his hands and kiss her.

Later he had made love to his wife with a passion they

hadn't enjoyed since the early days of their marriage. Emer had laughed at his unexpected ardour but he had known that it was Kitty who had aroused him. As he had tried to throw off her image it had remained between them so that he had had to open his eyes and gaze into Emer's face, fearful that if he closed them again he would see Kitty.

Anger was the only way he could deal with the conflict of emotions that played tug of war in his heart. If he stayed angry surely he'd be able to repel her. He remembered her as she had been that morning, sitting across the table from him, confessing that she was pregnant with Robert's child and that she couldn't go with him to America. He had concentrated on that. Not on the flame-haired girl with the impulsive nature and mischievous smile who he had loved from the moment he became a man.

What had changed everything was Kitty's remorse. She hadn't had to explain herself; he had seen it in her eyes. Those grey eyes that he knew even better than his own. Her emotions had been laid bare as if she was saying, *Take my remorse and my sorrow and my regret. Take it all and do with it what you will, but I will never stop loving you, ever. Because I can't.*

He had seen her on her horse, on the crest of a distant hill, and he had heard her silent call as if it was carried on the wind. And resist her he couldn't; because he was unable to stop loving her either.

Now their notes to each other were left not behind a stone in the vegetable-garden wall at the castle, but up at the Fairy Ring, beneath a stone hidden in a shrub. Neither of them dreamed of 'what ifs', for those days were gone. They accepted what they had, which was very little: kisses stolen in the cave on Smuggler's Bay, embraces on the hillside concealed among the long grasses and gorse, snatched glances across the street in town. There was too much at stake to risk getting caught; too many people to hurt. And as impossible as loving two women seemed, Jack loved Emer and hurt her he wouldn't.

To Kitty the fact that Jack was hers again changed everything about the world. If only the war would end and JP come home then all would be well again. But the war didn't look like it was going to end any time soon. It seemed that the Germans had stepped up their air raids on British cities and Kitty feared for JP in his Spitfire.

JP hadn't been home since before war broke out, which was now over two years ago. The odd week's leave had been too short to spend in Ireland so he had stayed in Harry's house in London, meeting up with Boysie and Celia. The three of them had plotted their return to Ballinakelly as soon as the war was over and Kitty was heartened at the thought of being all together again, even though they would miss Harry dreadfully.

In the summer of 1942 Ethelred Hunt died, leaving Laurel alone without even her sister to comfort her. The shock aged her a decade in a day. She wasn't sure where she was or what her name was and Kitty, taking pity on her great-aunt, rashly suggested she move in with them until she felt stronger. Robert was appalled when Kitty told him, but didn't want to appear mean-spirited so agreed at once. Their daughter Florence on the other hand, who was now nearly sixteen, was delighted because she wanted to be a nurse and her parents had not allowed her to offer her services in England where women like her were in great demand. She'd have her patient at last, even though Laurel would turn out to be a very cantankerous one.

*

It was on a balmy July afternoon that the Biggin Wing had been detailed to fly to Northern France to escort the bombers home. As JP took off it occurred to him that he and Stanley had been in the squadron the longest of any of the men. It seemed like decades ago that he had gone for his interview at Adastral House in London. A lifetime ago that he had sat in a cockpit for the first time. He felt older than his years with the experience of a veteran. He barely recognized the boy he had once been. He thought of Jimmy then and the other men who had been killed in this senseless war and for a moment he was filled with trepidation. JP never thought about his own mortality because there was no point. Fear was not something he allowed himself to give in to. Fear bred rashness, which in turn bred fatal mistakes. But somehow this afternoon as the ground fell away beneath him, he thought about death.

Over France, just behind Lille, the skies darkened with Me 109s and it suddenly occurred to JP that this could be it. The thoughts of death had been a premonition, for sure. His time was up. He gazed at the enemy in dismay. There just seemed to be too many of them. He felt once again like a bee that has flown into a swarm of hornets and realizes it won't make it out. It is simply impossible on account of the sheer quantity of hornets. JP thought of the white cliffs and his heart was seized with longing. He wondered whether he'd seen them for the last time. The R/T went quiet as the squadron concentrated on the battle. They were too busy for chatter; too busy fighting for their lives.

Out of all the battles JP had fought this was without doubt the most perilous. Unable to focus on a target all he could do was avoid being one himself. He flew his plane harder than he had ever done, aware that it was gobbling up fuel and anxious that he might not have enough to get back home. Indeed, he was very far from home. He looked around for his number two, or any other friendly fighter, but saw nothing, just the enemy on all sides. It appeared as if he was alone against the entire Luftwaffe. Less than ten minutes into the battle he began to ache all over. His muscles were burning and the sweat was pouring down his face and blurring his vision. He noticed he had two yellow-nosed 109s on his tail and weaved frantically in an attempt to throw them off. They were persistent, however, and for all his twisting and turning he couldn't lose them. He was a target now, he thought with a sinking feeling, a dead man flying. 'I'll be joining you soon, Jimmy,' he said out loud and a serenity fell upon him like snow. 'I'll be joining you, too, Harry. Just make sure you're there at my arrival, because I won't know where to go.' Then he thought of Kitty, Robert, and his father, his niece Florence and little Alana who thought she loved him. He couldn't allow them to suffer. He just couldn't. Martha's tormented face surfaced in his fevered mind and his hand clenched on the joystick.

In one final, audacious move he turned, allowing the nose to drop. If he was going to go he'd sure as hell take those bloody Huns with him, he thought grimly. The plane juddered as he nearly stalled, but he managed to hold it together, just. He was facing the enemy now. He opened the throttle and went for them at 600 mph, firing madly. He knew he had taken them by surprise and grinned. Who would break first, he or they? Which of them had the balls to hold their course – or the madness? If they stuck it out there'd be one hell of an explosion.

But there was no explosion. No death. Just the intoxicating sense of relief as the Germans broke.

Glancing quickly at his instruments JP pulled back firmly on the stick and flew higher into the sky in a roll-over, hoping there wouldn't be anyone up there waiting for him. Keeping his eyes on the horizon he came out of his roll. No one was on his tail now. He was alone in the wide-open sky. Relief gave way to delayed fear and he began to shake all over. He headed for those white cliffs, which he could just make out gleaming at him through the evening mist.

JP arrived back at Biggin Hill, the fuel all but used up. He felt tired. Very tired. But this was a different sort of tiredness to the kind he was used to. It seemed very deep, right in the pith of his marrow. He was surprised and a little bewildered. After all, he'd fought many battles over the last couple of years and escaped death dozens of times. Why the nerves now? Why the trembling? Why the exhaustion? Why now?

That evening JP realized that he wasn't the only one to have noticed his tiredness. His Flight Commander informed him that he had done his time in battle and was to be sent to a new location to instruct. It was over.

'You're off ops,' he told him. 'We'll all be sorry to see you go but you've done bloody well.' JP was rendered speechless. He'd thought he'd be fighting until the end of the war. He'd never anticipated *this*. 'You've come to the end of the line, Deverill. It's time for you to move on,' his Flight Commander continued, noticing JP's disappointment. 'You've served and by God you've served us well.' His praise did not compensate for JP's aching sense of loss. This had been his life for the last two years. He had grown close to the men in his squadron and somewhat addicted to the adrenalin of battle. The thought of leaving hit him so hard he thought he was going to vomit. 'Come on now, JP. Snap out of it, laddie. The bar is open. How about we go and down a large glass of Scotch?'

In dispersal JP hung up his parachute in his locker for the last time. He was no longer a member of 92 Squadron. It was over. He was being posted somewhere else. Would he ever experience again the exhilaration of being in the front line in his Spitfire? Would he ever know the camaraderie of being in a group of men who set off to fight together day after day? Their fear unspoken, their grief unexpressed, but all tacitly understood because they shared it, every bit of it. This had become his life. He didn't know how to live otherwise. He was twenty years old and he was already washed up. He swallowed his desolation and went in search of that Scotch.

Kitty was astonished when she received a letter from JP informing her that he had been posted to 65 Squadron as a flight commander. Her relief was immense. He would be out of the fray, out of danger, and she thanked God for what she truly believed to be His intervention. JP didn't tell her how hard it was to adjust to life at his operational training unit at Aston Down, flying Hurricanes, he told Alana instead. Alana wrote back that she and Piglet were very happy that he was in a safe place but she still prayed for him, as she would do until the war was over.

JP missed the men at Biggin Hill and the routine that had been his life for two years. But he met a pretty barmaid called Gloria whose voluptuous body and brassy laugh did much to comfort him in the little inn where they routinely made love and talked about everything other than the war. When he was with Gloria he didn't think about Martha. Slowly Gloria began to unwind the yards of stress that had wound themselves around him and he started to find pleasure in his new life.

In February of 1944 JP was summoned to attend an investiture at Buckingham Palace. Kitty, Robert and Bertie came over from Ireland to witness the King honouring him with an enormous medal – Florence had had to remain at home to look after Laurel. They gathered in the grand crimson room at the palace with JP's old friends from Biggin Hill in their best blue uniforms. The military orchestra played and the King was softly spoken and sincere as he thanked JP for his duty and courage and pinned the medal to his chest. Kitty dabbed her eyes with a handkerchief as JP became Flight Lieutenant Jack Patrick Deverill, DFC.

When JP arrived back at the Mess he was surprised and delighted to see, greeting him with a 'Hello, JP, what a sight for sore eyes you are!', Stanley Bradshaw. The two men embraced and Jimmy Robinson's name resonated silently between them.

Kitty had been so preoccupied with her affair with Jack that she had barely spared a thought for Bridie Doyle and the castle. She had long given up on it ever being restored to her family and it surprised her that she could live only a few miles from it and yet never bump into its inhabitants. Bridie and she had not crossed paths in all the five years that Bridie had lived there. Kitty heard stories from her maid, who knew the maids working for the Countess and was only too ready to pass them on to Kitty: The Count shouted at the Countess; Leopoldo was a terror; Mr and Mrs Doyle (Sean and Rosetta) were at the end of their tether with the Count, whom they despised because of the way he treated his wife, and it seemed to be no secret that he had bedded many of the less virtuous girls in Ballinakelly and beyond – indeed, Kitty's maid took great relish in telling how he was even infamous in Cork! Kitty wondered whether Bridie knew and she would have felt sorry for her had she had time to dwell on the gossip. She didn't. She was much more concerned with thinking about JP, looking after Laurel and concealing her trysts with Jack from Robert.

So she was taken by surprise when, returning from town across the fields one early autumn evening, she bumped into Bridie. There was no way of avoiding her without being rude, and Kitty did not want to be rude, so she lifted her chin and continued walking until they came together on the bridge that straddled the stream where once, as children, they had searched for frogs in the undergrowth with Celia and Jack.

'Hello,' said Bridie.

'Hello, Bridie,' Kitty replied. They looked at each other steadily. Bridie's eyes were very black and her guarded expression showed no sign of yielding. Kitty searched for her old friend behind the frostiness but found nothing but resentment. JP would always be an obstacle to their reconciliation, Martha, if Bridie ever found out, the death of it. But Kitty was determined that Bridie would never know that the twin she believed had died lived. 'How are you?' she asked, hoping to get the pleasantries over with so she could be on her way and put an end to this awkward meeting. She had successfully managed to avoid Bridie for five years; she would make sure she avoided her for the following five.

'Well,' Bridie replied tightly. 'I trust *you* are well in the White House?'

Kitty was affronted at the implication. Did Bridie expect Kitty to be grateful to her for agreeing to the peppercorn rent that Celia had arranged with the Count? 'As you know, it has been my home for many years now. We are very happy there.' She didn't want Bridie to think that she was still hankering after the castle. It was woeful indeed that Bridie had the power to evict them at any moment.

'How is my son?' Bridie asked suddenly and the blackness in her eyes seemed to soften slightly with craving.

Kitty's heart caved in then for she could only imagine Bridie's agony. In spite of everything that had happened, JP was still Bridie's son and it was only natural that she should ask after him. 'He is a fighter pilot, Bridie,' she said softly, watching Bridie's face light up.

'He's flying planes?' she asked.

'Spitfires,' said Kitty. 'The King gave him a medal at Buckingham Palace.'

Bridie put her hand on her heart and her severe expression collapsed into a tender smile. 'A medal? God be praised.'

'He's a flight lieutenant with letters after his name,' Kitty continued proudly. Bridie was too moved to speak so Kitty went on. 'He's not fighting now. He's training men to fight. It's an important job and a safer one, I'm glad to say.' Bridie pursed her lips and nodded and Kitty noticed the tears welling in her eyes. 'How is Leopoldo?' she asked, changing the subject, which was much too thorny to take any further.

'He's the light of my life. I've been blessed,' said Bridie, recovering slightly.

'Well, I'm glad we have finally met and that, even if we can't be friends, we can at least be cordial,' said Kitty, edging past her. 'I will detain you no longer.'

Bridie looked disappointed, but Kitty couldn't imagine what more she had to say to her. However, Bridie hunched her shoulders and took a breath and Kitty dreaded the words she was about to deliver. 'If you hear any news, you know, about JP, you will let me know, won't you? I can count on you to show me kindness.'

'Of course,' said Kitty quickly.

'I know I can't ever be a mother to him, but he's still my blood. I have a right to know how he is.'

'Yes, you do,' Kitty agreed. Bridie held her gaze, as if she was determined to keep her there, but Kitty tore it away and marched through the field as fast as she could go. If JP ever found out the truth, would he forgive her? She couldn't bear to think about it. He simply *couldn't* know, not ever. Kitty would do everything in her power to prevent it.

Chapter 21

The following spring, as the war finally came to an end, Celia and Boysie joined the thousands of people who took to the streets of London in celebration of the Allied victory. But amidst the joy there was sadness as they remembered Harry. They had always been three and now they were two and the missing part was felt as keenly as a severed limb.

Maud returned to Chester Square much diminished. She looked old and defeated as if Harry had taken all her joy with him, leaving a black void where negativity and self-pity were left to fester. She found London battle-scarred and bruised and gazed onto the rubble with dismay. Once this had been the seat of her pleasure, but now it was the centre of her pain. She thought of Ballinakelly and the quiet town which had once bored her suddenly offered her refuge, comfort and relief. She remembered the peaceful hills and gently meandering streams, the sound of the ocean and the cries of gulls, and in her mind they took on an enchantment that they had never had in reality. Her spirit yearned for the protection of those thick castle walls, for the soggy grass and light summer rain and for the contentment to be found in her memories. How she longed to withdraw into those recollections. But when she suggested to Arthur that she take a short break in

the bosom of her family he got down on one knee and pro-
posed, stealing her breath and her intentions in the surprise.
'Ask Bertie for a divorce and I will make you my bride,'
he said pompously, as if he were at last granting Maud her
dearest wish. And Maud was momentarily distracted from
the deep longing that now ran in a hidden current in her
heart because Arthur offered her a diamond ring, security
and respectability. The vision of Ballinakelly was quickly forgotten in the more immediate relief of Arthur's proposal and
Maud withdrew from the lure of the past, focusing instead
on divorce and how she might obtain it.

Boysie felt nothing but resentment when his wife Deirdre
returned home. He resented her for not knowing of and
therefore not understanding his deep love for Harry. He
resented her for the sham that was their marriage and he
resented her for the limitations she unwittingly imposed
upon his lifestyle. While she had been safely out of London
he had worked through his grief in the only way he knew
how: in the arms of strangers. Men who could temporarily
alleviate his suffering during the long nights when Harry's
death caused him the greatest suffering. Now she was back,
fussing around their daughters who were seventeen and
fifteen years old and desperate to have some fun in London
after almost five years in the countryside toiling on their
grandfather's estate in the place of the men who had gone to
fight. Boysie's work at Bletchley Park came to an end with
the war and he returned to his old job at Christie's, and to
his old friend Celia, who understood him in a way his wife
never would.

Celia had moved back into Deverill House with her children who had come home from South Africa, and set up her
office in her father's old study, looking out onto the avenue

of tall plane trees where once Aurelius Dupree had stood menacingly in the shadows. The memory of that broken man served only to strengthen her desire to keep her father's atrocious past secret and to honour those who had helped her restore the fortune he had lost, like Duchess and her son Lucky Deverill. Without them the family would have surely sunk in debt. It gave her a deep sense of gratification to look after those two people her father had so callously abandoned.

When Celia reminded Boysie of their plan to return to Ballinakelly at the end of the war Boysie was only too ready to escape. He told his wife of their plan, which didn't include her, and braced himself for the customary tirade of hurt and accusation, but it never came. She accepted his decision with a smile and Boysie wondered whether five years of living apart had in some way been conducive to the kind of marriage he wanted to have: one where he was free to live as he chose, without being reproached for neglect and self-interest.

Kitty was delighted that she was going to see Celia again. She had missed her cousin dreadfully while she had been in South Africa and the thought of her returning to Ballinakelly with Boysie filled her with excitement. It would be just like the old days, she told herself, when they had enjoyed picnics on the beach and long evenings laughing and gossiping on the terrace at sunset. She felt a sudden regret at not being able to play croquet and tennis, which had been so much part of summer life at the castle, but it was gone as quickly as it had come for she had much to be thankful for. JP was coming home for the first time since he had left Ireland at the outbreak of the war, and she had Jack. Jack, whose love meant more to her than bricks and stones ever could.

*

JP returned to Ballinakelly with a sense of trepidation. The last time he had made this journey across the Irish Sea his heart had been full of excitement at seeing Martha again. Now painful memories hung over the coastline in a grey mist that threatened to engulf him for Martha was gone and every dream of happiness had gone with her. He was looking forward to arriving home and seeing his father, Robert and Kitty, but he dreaded the emptiness he would find there for it would surely resonate with Martha's absence.

JP had thought of Martha often during the war. Time and again she had crept into his consciousness undetected only to flower onto his mind with her endearing smile and tender gaze to remind him most cruelly of what he had lost. Now, as he approached the harbour, he wondered whether she had suffered as much as he had – whether she ever thought of him – whether she had managed to get on with her life, successfully putting him behind her, or whether, like him, she had been forever scarred by her loss. He still found it hard to comprehend that he had a twin. That he had, in a single moment, found her only to let her go. It didn't seem right that she lived on the other side of the world, that such a monumental discovery should be so readily discarded. And yet how could it be otherwise? He loved her in a way that was inappropriate for a brother to love his sister and he doubted that would ever change.

With these thoughts he stepped onto Irish soil. To his delight Kitty was on the quay to meet him with Robert smiling at her side. They waved vigorously and he dropped his bag and ran towards them to embrace them fiercely. It was only then, as he held them tightly, that he realized how much he had missed them. He had grown into a man in the five years he had been away, but inside there was still something of the boy he had left behind, and it was that small part that wept with relief because, after everything he had been through, he had made it home at last.

JP had endured many battles in the skies above Britain and France and stared into Death's dark face more times than he cared to remember, but home had always been at the root of his courage, steadying his resolve and giving him the strength to carry on when he might otherwise have given in. Home had been the point on the horizon towards which he had always dreamed he would one day navigate, once this bloody war was over. Now it was, he allowed himself to grieve for the friends he had lost in the arms of the woman who had raised him.

They set off in the motor car and Kitty explained that Florence had wanted very much to come and meet him too but was unable to leave Laurel on her own in the house. 'She's been bedridden for six months now,' she explained. 'And she's lost most of her marbles, but Florence is a saint for looking after her the way she does. I'm afraid I don't have the patience for it.'

'You do your bit too,' Robert interjected.

'Such as it is,' she laughed. 'I'm really not much help at all.'

Kitty had realized very soon after inviting her great-aunt to stay that she would never leave. As Jack had said with a grin, 'The only way she'll be going is feet first!' but Laurel was in no hurry to do so. There were times when Kitty's humour ran dry. Only Florence had the resources to care for her with patience and affection. The solemn girl was now eighteen years old but showed no inclination for parties and courtships. She sat at Laurel's bedside, read her poetry and stories and talked to her, even though the old lady was almost entirely lost in her befuddled imagination and called her Adeline or Hazel.

'Oh, but it's so lovely to have you back,' Kitty exclaimed, smiling at JP in the rear-view mirror. 'Papa is longing to see you.' She didn't add that since Harry's death Bertie had taken to the bottle again. She hoped that JP would restore his beleaguered spirit and give him a reason to stop drinking.

At last the car motored up the drive to the White House, which hadn't changed in the slightest since the last time JP had been there. He dislodged Martha from his thoughts as he hurriedly climbed out to embrace his niece who was waiting on the doorstep to welcome him home. JP had grown to well over six feet and towered above Florence. He lifted her off the ground in an affectionate hug so that her feet dangled in the air. She protested weakly, kicking them, while secretly enjoying her uncle's enthusiasm and the feeling of his strong arms around her. She too had missed him. When he put her down she pushed him playfully to hide her emotions. 'Just because you've been flying planes doesn't mean you can get above yourself,' she said, smiling through her tears. But she couldn't fail to notice the deep lines that had appeared around his mouth and at the corners of his eyes, fanning out across his temples, and the heaviness in his gaze. She realized then that the war had changed him profoundly. 'Let's go inside and have a cup of tea,' she suggested, walking back into the hall. 'I bet you're dying for a cup of Bewley's finest.'

As soon as she was home Kitty telephoned her father. Ten minutes later Bertie was marching into the house with his two big dogs panting behind him, calling out JP's name. 'JP, where the devil are you?' He strode into the sitting room to find JP, still in his RAF uniform, standing up to greet him. 'My dear boy!' said Bertie, pulling his son into his arms and patting his back with a firm hand. 'My dear, dear boy.' He took in JP's face with moistened eyes. 'Back from the war, thank the Lord. At least He saw fit to bring *one* of you home.'

'Have a cup of tea,' Kitty interjected, not wanting her father to dwell on Harry.

'Might you have anything stronger?' he asked. 'I think this requires a celebration, don't you?'

Kitty handed him a cup of tea. 'You can celebrate with this,' she said stiffly, as if talking to a child.

Bertie sat down in the armchair and JP returned to his place on the club fender where the ash remained cold from the last of the winter fires. 'How long are you home for?' Bertie asked, sipping his tea and wishing it was whiskey.

'I'm going to leave the RAF,' JP replied. His family looked at him in amazement. 'I want to go to Trinity College, Dublin and study as I always intended and then I don't know what I'm going to do.' He grinned. 'I'll take everything as it comes. I'm weary of obeying orders and I'm weary of war. I want peace. I know I can find that here.'

'That is wonderful news!' said Florence.

'Wonderful,' repeated Kitty, noticing suddenly how acutely tired he looked.

'You've made a wise choice, JP,' said Robert.

Bertie drained his teacup. 'I suggest you change out of that uniform then and put on your riding breeches. Start as you mean to go on, I say. There's nothing like the wind in your face to revive you. Of course you've had an awful lot of that in your plane, but it's quite different on horseback and a great deal safer.' He stood up and beamed at his son, the old twinkle restored to his grief-stricken eyes. 'How about it, JP?'

'Ready when you are,' JP replied, eager to get back on a horse where he felt most at home.

'Let's not dawdle then,' said Bertie, rubbing his hands together. 'I'll meet you at the stables in half an hour.'

JP had been back over a week before he turned his mind to Alana. He was out riding with Kitty when she reminded him of the girl's letters and the part *she* had played in enabling her to correspond with him. 'I think you should go and see her,' she suggested. 'She's a lovely girl and she's sweet on you. It would be polite to pass by and say hello.'

Having fantasized about riding round to her house and surprising her, JP felt differently now that the war was over. There was a strange sense of anti-climax and he had been taken over by a feeling of inertia. He was a little embarrassed too about the amount he had written to a person he had only met once, and a child at that. Alana knew things about him that he hadn't even shared with Kitty, his fears and his failings mostly. He had only told Kitty the good things. He had told Alana the bad things and had felt better for it, admittedly, but only because he had believed he would never see her again. He had unburdened himself of his dark thoughts as if in a confessional, but he hadn't really considered the person on the receiving end of his unburdening. She had certainly helped him get through the war. Her letters had entertained him and he had allowed himself to grow fond of her even though he couldn't remember for the life of him what she looked like. He realized now that she had been little more than a mirage in a desert. A vision of home during the bleak and lonely years of fighting. He didn't know what he'd say to her, but Kitty had a few suggestions.

'I think you should be kind and ask her about herself and her family. Thank her for her letters and tell her that she was a great comfort to you, giving you news of home. I'm sure she knows that the disparity in age, religion and class makes anything more than a friendship impossible.' Kitty was only too familiar with those obstacles herself.

'Yes, you're right,' he said with relief. 'I'll go now and get it over with. I hope I haven't led her on too much.'

'You were fighting a war,' said Kitty. 'I think you can be forgiven if you have.'

It was late afternoon when JP rode down the path to the house by the sea. The sun was low in a pale blue sky, the ocean calm and serene beneath wheeling gulls. He dismounted outside the white cottage and knocked on the door. A moment later Mrs O'Leary appeared. She smiled warmly when she saw him, but knowing nothing about his correspondence with her daughter, she assumed his visit had something to do with her husband. 'I'm afraid Mr O'Leary isn't here,' she said. 'Is it urgent?'

'No, actually . . .' and he hesitated because he didn't know how to ask for her daughter without appearing forward or inappropriate.

'I'm glad to see that you are safe,' she said. 'Your family must be very happy to have you home.'

'They are, very happy. And I'm happy to be home too.'

'Shall I tell my husband that you called? He's so busy these days. It seems that everyone has an animal that needs seeing to.'

'No need. Is Alana at home?'

Believing he had only asked about her daughter out of politeness, Emer smiled and thanked him. 'How kind you are to ask after Alana. I won't ever forget the day you rescued her and brought her home.'

'It was nothing,' he replied.

'Not to you but it was to us. It was very gallant of you. I will tell her you mentioned her. She's out walking Piglet.'

He laughed for he had read about Piglet in her letters. 'What a funny name for a dog,' he commented.

'That's Alana.' She gave a gentle laugh. 'I'll tell her you asked after her. She'll be pleased.'

He nodded and said goodbye, mounting his horse and waving as he made his way back up the path. He wondered whether he'd have to make another attempt or whether the fact that he had passed by and left a message with her mother would suffice. However, when he reached the top of the cliff he saw a small figure in the distance, walking in his direction. Close by, running in the long grasses, was a dog. He knew immediately that the figure was Alana, but it was too late to canter off without appearing rude. He had no alternative but to meet her.

Nothing could have prepared JP for the sight of Alana O'Leary. He barely remembered the girl he had rescued from the hills; however, the person now approaching was no longer that girl, but a young woman of almost seventeen – and a beautiful young woman at that. She walked towards him confidently with a light, buoyant gait and a carefree swinging of her arms and he could see that she was smiling. Her long fair hair was swept off her face and tied into a ponytail, revealing a slender neck and a flash of collarbone where her white shirt was unbuttoned. She wore a pair of beige slacks and walking shoes but he could see that she had a small waist and feminine hips from where her shirt was tucked into her trousers. A few moments later she was standing before him, her cheeks pink and her blue eyes sparkling with pleasure, and he was lost for words.

'You're home,' she said, taking the reins in one hand and

looking up at him happily. 'I prayed that God would spare you.'

JP remembered his manners and dismounted. She extended her hand and he took it, but it seemed woefully inadequate after the long letters they had written to each other so he leaned down and kissed her warm cheek. He wasn't sure whether her glow was due to a blush or the sunshine.

'And you've grown up,' he said, trying hard to take her all in with subtlety.

'Six years is a long time,' she replied. 'I would say that you've grown up too.'

'I don't suppose you get lost in the hills any more.'

She laughed and he found himself chuckling along with her for her laugh bubbled infectiously. 'I know these hills better than the sheep,' she said. 'I know every rise and fall and every bush and tree. I doubt I'd lose myself even in a thick fog.'

'Well, I'm going to have to get to know it all over again now,' he said. 'I've been away far too long.'

'Then I shall be the one to rescue you. Come, let me show you something.' She grinned and set off the way she had come. Piglet remained watching her in bewilderment. 'She's had enough now and wants to go home,' she told JP, turning round and putting her hands on her hips in mock exasperation. 'Come on, Piglet, you can have another sniff at that old badger set.' The dog gave a little grunt as if deciding that the badger set was a more exciting option than the hearth rug and trotted after them. JP walked beside her, leading his horse by the reins.

'Thank you for your letters,' he said. 'They got me through some of the darkest times.'

'I'm glad. I hoped they would. I thought you might be lonely up there in the sky.'

'I was, but you were always with me.' He wished now that he had read her letters more carefully and taken more trouble with his. He might not have been so ready to expose his fears and failures had he known what a lovely creature she had become.

'I enjoyed yours too,' she said. 'I imagine you must have had loads of adventures. Now you're no longer being censored you can tell me all about them. I bet you were very brave, JP.'

'I was because I had to be. There was no other option.'

'Of course there was. There was cowardice. But you chose to be brave.'

They followed a path that ran along the cliff top and JP was obliged to walk behind her for the track was too narrow for them to walk side by side. They continued to talk and fell into an easy conversation as if they had known each other for years. JP realized that their letters had lifted their friendship onto a more intimate level, for they had shared so much in them. He had confided in Alana and, without intending to, he had made her his confidante.

'Where are you taking me?' he asked after a while.

'Not far now and you won't regret it. The path widens in a moment. We're near the badger set so we might lose Piglet.' The little dog hurried on ahead, picking up the enticing scent of badger.

As they talked JP admired the confident way Alana spoke. She wasn't afraid to voice her opinions nor did she feel the need to soften her tone when she disagreed with him. For a girl not yet seventeen she was formidable. And every time he made her laugh he felt he had won something special.

At last she stopped. She told him to tether his horse to a

tree and then whistled for her dog. When Piglet reluctantly extricated herself from the badger set Alana scooped her into her arms. She lowered her voice. 'Follow me.'

They walked into a small coppice of hazel trees where the ground was soft with moss and last autumn's decomposing leaves. Fresh ferns and bracken unfurled their green tentacles in the shafts of sunshine that beamed through the branches and primroses grew in clusters among the burgeoning blue-bells. Alana sat down and placed Piglet on her lap. 'You be quiet now,' she whispered.

JP sat beside her, his curiosity mounting. 'What are we looking at?'

'Over there, you see that hole.'

The hole was visible on account of the loose earth at its mouth. JP recognized it instantly. 'A fox's den,' he said.

'She's had pups,' Alana told him. JP thought of the Ballina-kelly Foxhounds but didn't enlighten her on the hundreds of foxes he'd hunted and killed.

'You've seen them?'

'Yes, she's got six and they're adorable. They come out and play around this time.'

'You think they'll come out with Piglet sitting here wait-ing for them?'

'They don't mind Piglet. It's the hounds they mind.'

'Well, yes, I would imagine they're more of a threat than Piglet.'

She grinned at him knowingly. 'I'm not naïve, JP. I'm well aware that you hunt foxes and that they steal lambs and chickens and drive the farmers mad. But these are pups and while they're pups they're not doing any harm to anyone.'

'So, we just sit and wait until they decide to come out and entertain us?'

'Are you in a hurry to get back?' she asked and there was a mocking glint in her eyes.

'No,' he replied.

'Then they can take all the time they like because I've got nothing to hurry home for. Just helping Mam with the tea and I'd rather be here with you.' She gazed at him steadily and he was disarmed by her forwardness.

'And I'd rather be here with you,' he said and grinned.

They sat and waited and neither wanted the foxes to come out until dark.

Chapter 22

It was dark and raining heavily when Michael Doyle knocked on Father Quinn's door. There was a cold and ragged edge to the wind as it whipped around the walls of the priest's house, which stood in isolation behind the ancient church of All Saints. Michael waited, shoulders hunched against the cold, cap leaking water into his hair, and wondered why the old priest wanted to see him now, at this ungodly time. He was reminded of the secret meetings that had taken place here in the dead of night during the War of Independence, when Grace and Kitty had crept in through the back door to plot and scheme and betray their class. He grinned as he thought of Grace now, pressed up against the farmhouse wall, legs wrapped around his middle, upper lip glistening with sweat, moaning with wanton pleasure. He knew what lay beneath the ladylike veneer she presented to the world. He knew how deeply ran her lust and how hot and uncontrollably it boiled. He had enjoyed her immensely. The big door opened a crack and Father Quinn's wrinkly face peered through it, bringing Michael back to the present and to the matter at hand, which, judging by the priest's expression, was urgent.

Michael took off his jacket and cap and followed Father

Quinn into the parlour. There was a fire in the grate and a dim, cheerless light radiating weakly from a few tatty lamps placed on polished wooden tables positioned around the room. The parlour was dour and simple and lacked a woman's touch, Michael thought, but Father Quinn was a practical man who did not have the patience or the desire for embellishment. Michael was pleased to be out of the rain. He took the armchair beside the fire where he had sat so many times before and Father Quinn took the one opposite, which was placed directly beside one of the lamps so that he could read more easily. Michael noticed the almost empty glass of whiskey and the open book on the table.

Father Quinn took off his spectacles and looked at Michael gravely. 'I would not have invited you here at this time of the night had it not been of the greatest importance,' he said, folding his big, coarse hands in his lap.

'I thought as much. So what is it?' Michael replied.

'It's Ethan O'Donovan. He came to see me this evening. His daughter Niamh is planning to run away with the Count.'

Michael had been expecting this and showed no surprise. 'Did he say when?'

'He did not. But his wife found a packed bag beneath the maid's bed and when she questioned her the girl confessed. She told her that Niamh boasted that she is going to start a new life in America now that the war is over. I fear that the Countess has given her husband power over her riches.' Father Quinn had known Bridie when she had been a barefooted scrap of a girl in his congregation, but since she had acquired status and a great fortune he was not only respectful of her title but protective of her money, for she gave generously to his church as well as to local charities. He was not about to see it disappear across the Atlantic with her good-for-nothing husband.

'Does Mrs O'Donovan know that Ethan came to see you?'

'She does not,' said Father Quinn, knowing Michael well enough to understand where his questioning was leading.

'Does anyone else know that he came to see you?'

'I believe not. No one knows that you are here either, I don't imagine.'

'Then leave the matter with me.'

Father Quinn nodded his grey head and his rheumy, hooded eyes looked at Michael without blinking. 'Sometimes men of God such as we are have to take justice into our own hands. In this case the Countess is your sister and you have a right to protect her. I will absolve you of any sin.'

'I knew the sort of man the Count was the moment he arrived in Ballinakelly,' said Michael.

'I am afraid he is one of God's lost sheep.'

'But there's no shepherd to bring him into the flock, Father Quinn. He is a man who abides by his own rules and thinks he can act with impunity because of his title and his wealth. But let me tell you that he is not what he seems.'

'I have no doubt of it.'

'I will not let him ruin my sister.'

'I'm glad to hear it.'

'I will deal with him the Irish way.' Michael pushed himself up from the chair. 'You must tell Ethan that you cannot do anything to help besides giving advice and support and that his daughter is in God's hands now. What will be, will be, and it will be God's will.'

'I will talk to him tomorrow,' said Father Quinn.

'You must remain above suspicion, Father.'

Father Quinn grinned grimly. 'I always am, Michael.'

Michael left the priest in his armchair and let himself out. It was still raining but not as hard as when he had arrived. He pulled up his collar and walked briskly to his car.

The following morning Bridie received an unexpected visitor. She was sitting on the terrace with Rosetta, for the rain had passed and the sun was shining down with the enthusiasm of summer, when the butler stepped out to announce Mrs Maddox, the Rector's wife. Bridie raised an inquisitive eyebrow at Rosetta. What could the Rector's wife possibly want with her? She didn't imagine it was a social call, Catholics and Protestants did not mix, so she was curious as to what the woman's motive might be. A moment later the elderly lady was shown through the French doors.

Ballinakelly was a small town but Bridie did not venture there much and many of the people who had come to live there in recent years were strangers to her. Mrs Maddox, the former Mrs Goodwin, was one of those. But Bridie instantly recognized her, for it was impossible to forget that sweet, gentle face and unassuming smile. However, she couldn't remember where she had seen it, only that she had, at some time in her past, set eyes on it. 'Mrs Maddox, please join us here in the sunshine,' she said, playing for time while she racked her brain in search of her. 'Have you met my sister-in-law, Mrs Doyle?'

Mrs Maddox shook Rosetta's hand and then sat down on a garden chair made comfortable by pretty floral cushions. The butler disappeared to fetch a fresh pot of tea and another teacup. As soon as Mrs Maddox began to speak Bridie recalled the moment in the milliner's when she had met the pretty young girl trying on hats with her companion. In fact,

Bridie had been quite taken with her. Now that the girl's companion had come to call she would ask after her.

'What a lovely day,' said Mrs Maddox, whose life had turned into a veritable banquet of pleasure since marrying her old love John Maddox. Her joy rendered *everything* beautiful. Not a moment went by when she didn't count her blessings. Like her husband she had grown fat on happiness. The two of them resembled a jolly pair of portly partridges. But her chubbiness gave her a rosy, friendly demeanour, as well as restoring her youthful appearance, which years of silent longing had purloined, and Bridie and Rosetta were immediately charmed by her. 'This is the first time I have seen Castle Deverill in its entirety. Of course I've seen the towers peeping above the tree line and Mr Maddox showed it to me from the distant hills. I have to confess that the first sight of it stole my breath.' She put her hand on her chest and sighed. 'Indeed, it is quite magnificent.'

'We have met before, haven't we, Mrs Maddox,' said Bridie, pleased that she had recalled the memory in time.

'Oh yes, we have,' said Mrs Maddox.

'It was before the war,' Bridie told Rosetta. 'I was in Loretta's looking at hats with Emer when Mrs Maddox came in with a sweet girl with an American accent.'

'Miss Martha Wallace,' Mrs Maddox interjected helpfully. 'You very generously gifted her a hat.'

'She had to have it,' said Bridie, now remembering the moment well.

'She was delighted. I'm sure she wears it often. The colour was so becoming on her.'

'Did she return to America?' Bridie asked.

'Yes, she suffered a terrible disappointment and fled with her heart broken.'

The joy was swept from Mrs Maddox's face, replaced by a sad, regretful expression as she thought of her beloved, disconsolate Martha.

'I'm sorry to hear that,' said Bridie.

'Who broke her heart?' Rosetta asked, for while Bridie was too polite to pry Rosetta had no such compunction.

'Well, it's a very sad story,' Mrs Maddox began. She did not feel she would be betraying Martha if she were to confide in the Countess who had been so sweet to her. But just as she was about to share Martha's sorry tale the butler reappeared with a pot of fresh tea and a cake on a silver tray. She paused as he poured the tea. All the while the three women remained silent. In that prolonged moment Mrs Maddox had time to reconsider.

'Do go on,' said Rosetta, once the butler had gone back inside.

'You were about to tell us the girl's sad story,' said Bridie.

Mrs Maddox's lips hovered over the fine rim of her teacup. 'She had fallen hopelessly in love with Mr JP Deverill,' she said, then took a sip.

Now Bridie grew more interested. 'He didn't love her back?'

'He did,' said Mrs Maddox.

'So why the broken heart?'

Both women looked at her expectantly. The secret balanced precariously on the older woman's tongue. It was true that happiness had made her garrulous. She had been only too eager to throw off the constraints imposed upon her by her position as nanny in the Wallace household, discretion being one of them. Indeed, since marrying John Maddox she had become something of a gossip.

'They were *both* broken-hearted,' Mrs Maddox said carefully. 'I do believe they intended to marry.'

Bridie's eyes widened. 'But what stopped them?' she asked. 'They ...' Mrs Maddox hesitated. But just before she spilled the details of Martha and JP's parentage, she stopped herself. 'The Deverills forbade it,' she said instead, which was still a revelation to the two women who were now staring at her with their mouths open. 'They prohibited it on account of Martha's parentage.' *There,* she thought, *that's not exactly an untruth.* 'Martha was forced to leave. But your hat did much to raise her spirits,' she added and took a bite of cake.

As Bridie expected, Mrs Maddox had come to appeal for money for a charity she was hoping to set up through the Catholic and Protestant churches to unite children of both religions, but Bridie wasn't really listening. She was thinking about her son JP, and wondering about his broken heart. The thought of him suffering made another tear in her already ragged heart and she had to concentrate very hard on what Mrs Maddox was saying in order to stop her emotions from showing.

Bridie had heard from Emer O'Leary that JP was home. She had told Bridie how he had come looking for Jack but had asked very kindly after Alana. Not only was he hand-some to look at, Emer had said, but he had lovely manners too. 'Those Deverills have all the charm,' she told Bridie with unconcealed admiration.

'But they don't have their castle,' Bridie had replied.

Emer, who had heard all about the castle's history from her mother-in-law, had smiled and said nothing. According to Jack's mother, the land the castle was built on should still belong to the O'Learys.

Leopoldo was only thirteen, but he was taller than his mother and almost as tall as his father. He was spoilt and unpleasant and feared by everyone, from his tutors to his cousins. He had no friends, for his parents had brought him up to believe that as a prince he was superior to everyone else. Consequently, he was lonely and unhappy and his unhappiness made him mean. He seemed to find pleasure only in hurting creatures weaker than himself. The one creature he was unable to dominate was the horse and as a result he was terrified of it.

Cesare insisted he learn to ride so that he could hunt and play polo, but the boy's fear prevented him from mastering the beast that seemed to sense not only his terror but his disagreeable nature and responded by bucking and bolting and generally acting up. His riding instructor despaired, not least because the Count would not listen to reason and allow the boy to quit. He wanted Leopoldo to be a finer version of himself and was infuriated that he did not have all the qualities to make him proud. 'A prince does not fear anything!' he would shout and his ears would go red with fury and his lips would glisten with spittle. 'You are to be a prince of princes! The duty of a son is to exceed his father but you are a disappointment, Leopoldo.' Leopoldo would retaliate with equal vitriol, calling his father a tyrant and a bully; if he was a disappointment it was only because his father had made him so. The two of them would stare at each other and snort like a pair of bulls in a ring but Leopoldo was now too big for Cesare to smack so the Count would lower himself to use the only threat he knew had any impact. 'If you don't master the horse I will cut you off and you will be penniless and I will leave the castle to one of your cousins!' Leopoldo knew that there was no point appealing to his mother because his father held the financial strings. So he had no choice but to learn to ride because he enjoyed too much his material comforts and the promise of a future lording it up in the castle. There were times when his father shouted at his mother that Leopoldo wished he was dead.

A few days after Mrs Maddox had visited the Countess (and managed to leave with the promise of money and support for her charity) Leopoldo found his mother sobbing on her bed. In her hand she held a piece of paper. She was crying so loudly that she didn't notice him come in. By the time she did he had taken the letter out of her hand and was reading it. Leopoldo went white. 'You shouldn't have seen that, Leo,' Bridie said, sitting up and wiping her eyes with the sleeve of her dressing gown. 'It doesn't involve you.'

'Of course it involves me, Mama,' he snapped. 'If Papa wants to divorce you then he wants to rid himself of both of us.'

Bridie started to cry again. She put a hand to her mouth in an effort to stop herself but the tears tumbled down her cheeks all the same. She couldn't begin to explain to a thirteen-year-old boy that she had feared this moment for years. She had known Cesare was bored in Ballinakelly. In spite of her efforts to divert him he hadn't found the place or the people amusing. And what was worse, she knew *she* bored him. She had bored him from the moment they set foot in Ireland. 'We should never have left America,' she said regretfully. 'We were happy there.' *And I was lively and fun and entertaining.*

'Then why did you?' Leopoldo asked, an accusatory tone in his voice.

'Because I wanted to come home. I wanted to buy this castle and make a home for us.' *And I wanted to wreak revenge on the Deverills who had ruined my life.*

'Where is he?' Leopoldo demanded.

'He didn't come home last night. I found this when I woke up. He must have put it on my pillow while I slept, then crept away.'

'How cowardly not to tell you himself.'

'I expect he didn't want a scene.'

'Well, he's going to get one now! I'm going to find him.'

'No, Leo, please—'

'He's probably spent the night in one of those inns in Ballinakelly.' Bridie watched as he marched out of the room. She lay on her bed and cried into her pillow. She wished she'd taken Beaumont Williams' advice and kept control of her money. Everything was lost. Everything. But she wasn't thinking of herself because she knew what it was to be lowly. *My poor Leo*, she thought. *My poor, poor Leo.*

Leopoldo marched to the stables. He was going to master the horse now if it killed him, he decided, and gallop into Ballinakelly to find his father. So furious was he that he shoved aside his fear and saddled his father's grey mare. The grooms watched in bewilderment as the boy who was terrified of horses threw the saddle onto the horse's back and pulled the girth tightly round its belly. When they offered to help he barked. *I'm not going to be a coward like my father,* he thought to himself as he put on the bridle. *I'm going to show him just how fearless I can be.* He mounted with ease and, suppressing a moment's doubt, trotted out of the stable yard.

As he accelerated into a gallop across the field towards the hills he began to gain more confidence. The horse did not play up, nor did it try to buck him off. Leopoldo held the reins firmly and gritted his teeth, repeating to himself, *I am master of this horse. I am master of this horse.* He wondered whether the animal sensed the transformation in him, that he had changed from a frightened child into a furious young man, determined to confront his father and shame him into withdrawing his threat of divorce, for his mother's sake. He wondered whether the horse knew that he was boss.

Leopoldo arrived in Ballinakelly and went from inn to inn in search of his father. No one had seen him. When he entered O'Donovan's he found Mr O'Donovan talking to Father Quinn in a low voice. They stopped talking when he entered and in the silence Leopoldo was sure he could hear a woman sobbing upstairs. He asked whether they had seen the Count and they both shook their heads. 'He hasn't been in here for a few days,' said Mr O'Donovan and Leopoldo left because there was obviously a crisis going on in the O'Donovan household and he had one of his own to settle.

By the time he rode out of town his anger had abated. He was disappointed that he hadn't found his father. Disappointed that he hadn't shown him how masterful he was on a horse. He made his way slowly up the road then turned off into the field that led to the hills. He no longer felt afraid and wondered why he had allowed horses to terrorize him. He realized now that it was simply a question of showing them who was master.

In spite of the dramas playing out beneath it the sun shone heartily in a cornflower-blue sky. The green hills glistened vibrantly beneath it and Leopoldo began to enjoy himself. He kicked his heels into the horse's flanks and set off at a canter. The wind raked his hair and the sensation of speed lifted his spirits. *If Papa could see me now*, he thought triumphantly.

When he reached the cliff top he saw that the tide was out. The beach extended for miles, the pale white sand smooth and flawless in the morning light. Then he spotted a flock of birds pecking at something lying on the sand. It resembled a buoy, and seemed to attract every sort of bird from the greedy white gulls to the gannets and grebes. Leopoldo turned his horse and directed it down the path towards the beach. Perhaps something exciting had been washed up during the night, he thought, curious to see what it was.

The horse stepped onto the sand and they made their way across it towards the birds. As they approached, there was a noisy flapping of wings as the birds reluctantly took to the air. They didn't go far, however, but hovered above like vultures, unwilling to discard such a rare and tasty feast.

Leopoldo narrowed his eyes. He couldn't make it out. What *was* it? His pleasure mounted at the thought that some poor animal had been savaged and he gave the horse a kick to move it closer. Leopoldo saw then that it was a head, a *human* head. His horse noticed at the same time, gave a terrified whinny and reared. Leopoldo was thrown to the ground, landing with a dull thud. As he nursed his bruised hip the horse bolted up the beach in terror, leaving him alone on the sand. The sound of squawking birds grew louder as they flew closer to their meal.

Leopoldo got up and brushed himself down. He peered at the head, realizing that it belonged to a man who had been buried up to his neck. The tide must have come in and drowned him. What a horrid way to die, he thought, but fascination and a dark attraction to the macabre brought him even closer.

Suddenly Leopoldo recoiled. He cried out in panic as if the head itself had turned on him. It was his father's.

Leopoldo fell to his knees. Unable to tear his eyes from the bloodied, bloated face of the Count, he stared at him with loathing. He hated him. He hated the world and he hated God. Most of all he hated himself because in his father's eyes he had never been good enough, and now he never would be.

Bridie's world imploded when the inspector informed her of her husband's murder. The same anguish that had seized her when her father was stabbed by the tinker seized her now and she let out a desperate cry and sank to the floor. Her first thoughts were for their son. But Leopoldo's face was as hard as stone. 'He won't divorce you now,' he said as she clung to him. 'He won't hurt you ever again.'

However, Bridie had loved Cesare in spite of his faults – faults that had marred his character like shadows lingering about a beautiful painting. During his life Bridie had found it easy to overlook the shadows by focusing solely on the beauty, but now he was dead those shadows were relegated to the very back of her subconscious mind as if they had never been there and the beauty rose in stature like a magnificent, rearing stallion. She swiftly forgot his infidelity, which she had taken pains to ignore, and she forgot his indifference and his cold-heartedness. He grew out of all proportion in her eyes and her grief became unbearable because of the greatness and nobility of the man she had lost. Bridie was no fool but love had made a fool out of her. However, it is a happy fool who lives in ignorance of an ugly truth and Bridie believed she had been happy. The only way to go on without him was to continue being a fool.

What was inevitably a tragedy for Bridie was a triumph for Grace. Michael arrived at her door, having abandoned his virtuous intentions and with the lascivious glint restored to his eyes. Sinning is a slippery slope and as Michael had now gone and put his foot once again on that familiar incline he was quick to slide further towards Hell. He had refrained from sex for years, choosing to lead the pious life of a monk, but that kind of abstinence had ill suited him. He had returned to his old ways by arranging the murder of the Count and the thrill of wielding power over life and death gave him a profound sense of satisfaction that far exceeded the satisfaction of being moral. 'I knew you'd come for me,' Grace gushed hoarsely as he pushed her against her bedroom wall and lifted her skirt. He didn't care that she was old now and that she had lost the succulence of her youth; there was still something wild and wanton about her that appealed to him, and of course the memory of the woman she had once been was real to him. He kissed her passionately, bruising her lips and stifling her breath as the full weight of his body pressed against her chest. His beard scratched her skin, his coarse hands fondled her breasts, his fingers plunged inside her as he was impatient to savour every part of her and careless with his touch, but Grace relished the vigour in him. Nothing excited her more than the rough handling of a man, and no man excited her more than Michael Doyle.

Maggie O'Leary

Maggie stared into the flames and invoked every spirit she could think of. In her fury she called upon the spirits of the wind and the spirits of the sea, those of the darkness as well as the light, and those of the earth and the eternal sky, and she commanded them to rise up against Lord Deverill for the child he had planted in her belly that would never carry his name.

The fire crackled and burned, the golden flames licked the air with pointed tongues and Maggie was mesmerized. She stretched out her hands to catch the golden sparks that flew like fireflies about the pyre but they would not be caught. They spun and twirled in tiny dances just beyond the reach of her fingertips. Maggie watched, hypnotized by these small sparks of light, as the small spark inside her grew with a light of its own.

Maggie had boldly knocked on the castle door to appeal to Lord Deverill, but he had refused to receive her. She had stood at his window as the rain soaked through her shawl and he had seen her there and turned his back. She had shouted out her despair in a language she knew he didn't under-stand: *I beg of you, have mercy on my child.* And he had sent his men to take her away. She had done everything to get his attention but nothing had worked. Now she would strike at the very heart of his reputation and he would be forced to acknowledge what he had done to her in the woods and take responsibility for his seed.

Maggie gazed into the fire and called upon the Devil himself, for the Catholic God would not approve of her plan.

Lord Deverill left for London and Maggie roused the men of Co. Cork. It was not hard to incite a rebellion because the Irish bore a deep hatred for the British, but more powerful than their patriotic fervour was their fear; they believed Maggie to be a witch and a powerful one at that. When she demanded that they burn down the castle, which stood as a symbol of British greed and oppression, they picked up their weapons and lit their flares and marched behind Maggie in an army of five hundred men. It was a cold, damp night and Maggie imagined that from the castle walls their rabble must look like a burning snake winding its way up the lane towards it.

Maggie stood back and watched with excitement as the first flaming arrows flew over the walls of Castle Deverill. She watched the ramparts catch fire and she watched the panicked soldiers do their best to defend it when they had been caught off guard and their numbers were few. Indeed, Maggie was sure her mob would burn the castle to the ground. A handful of dozy soldiers was no match for the might of her rebel army. But then the King's army came with their fine horses and their banners depicting the arms of the Duke of Ormonde and Maggie's men scattered like crows.

Maggie did not resist when they captured her. She wanted to be caught. She wanted to be taken before Lord Deverill and for him to see her extended belly and to know that the child she was carrying was his, growing stronger every day. It would not be long now.

Maggie was locked in a room at the bottom of the castle and because of her condition she was given every comfort. She had a bed and blankets, candles and food and was more comfortable than she was at home in the wood. While she rested she waited for Lord Deverill to return from London. Her anticipation grew because she was certain he'd come and see her now. He'd be furious with her, of course, but he'd see that she was heavy with child, *his* child, and his heart would soften and he would forgive her. He would no longer be able to turn away.

Yet the child came early. Maggie writhed and heaved and bellowed and cried out as her body laboured and the soldiers brought Maggie's sister, Breda, to her side to bring the baby into the world. When at last he arrived, Maggie held him in her arms and gazed tenderly into his pink face. 'This is Lord Deverill's son,' she told Breda.

Her sister blanched. 'Lord Deverill?' she repeated, unable to comprehend that the English nobleman on horseback had lain with her sister.

'He took me in the wood and now he'll take me to be his wife.'

'But he already has a wife,' Breda reminded her.

Maggie turned on her crossly. 'I have given him a son!' she retorted.

'A *bastard* son,' said Breda. 'You think he'll let you keep him?'

Maggie stared at her in defiance. 'Of course he'll let me keep him.'

'He'll take him away and you'll never see him again. You think he's going to let a child of his grow up a peasant?'

'And what about *me*?'

'You? He'll have nothing to do with you, Maggie!'

Maggie's eyes filled with tears. She thrust the boy at her sister. 'Take him then. Keep him safe.'

Breda took the baby in her arms. 'If Lord Deverill finds out about this I cannot vouch for his safety. He might come looking for him. He might even kill him.' A gasp escaped Maggie's throat and the blood drained from her face. 'You have to make them believe he died,' Breda continued. 'Do you understand?'

'The guard already fears me,' said Maggie. 'It will not take much to bend him to my will. You must take my son, Breda, and look after him.'

'I promise,' said Breda. 'He's the last of the O'Leary men. What'll you call him, Maggie?'

'Liam O'Leary,' she said. 'After Father.'

Breda kissed her sister's cheek. 'I'll keep Liam safe until you come home. You *will* come home, won't you, Maggie?' she asked fearfully. She had heard what people were saying: that Maggie was a witch and she would burn at the stake.

'Of course I'll come home,' said Maggie.

But Fate thought otherwise.

Maggie waited to see Lord Deverill. She waited and she waited and she waited some more. She waited for weeks, but Lord Deverill never came. She wondered whether he was somewhere in the castle above her, oblivious that she was below, locked in a room, waiting for him to receive her.

Maggie was put on trial for witchcraft and it didn't take long to sentence her. She had cast a spell on the men of Co. Cork and incited them to rebel. Every surviving man had confirmed it and as a reward for their information they had been spared. As for Maggie, the punishment for witchcraft was death by fire. She smiled grimly as she recalled the spirits she had invoked with fire. What had begun in the flames would end in them, she thought. They asked her if she had anything to say. *I want to see Lord Deverill*, she said, and they laughed and took her away. She was incarcerated in the village of Ballinakelly and the day of her execution was set.

When that day dawned the sky was slate-grey and the wind was cold, as if it carried within it blades sharp enough to tear the skin. Crows and rooks cawed from the rooftops as the great pyre was built in the square and the people slowly gathered to watch the spectacle. In her cell Maggie prayed. She didn't pray to her pagan spirits and she didn't pray to the Devil, she prayed to God and asked for His forgiveness. She didn't fear death because she knew it was false and that the soul lived on. Yet she feared the pain of burning in the fire. She feared that more than anything.

They came to fetch her. They tied her like a pig and lifted her into a cart. She knelt in a white robe a good woman had given her and looked out through the curtain of knotted, dirty hair that hung in front of her face. She swept her eyes over the faces of the people she had known all her life, many of whose broken hearts she had healed by passing on messages from the dead, and many of whom had fought beside her father and brothers against Cromwell's mighty armies. Maggie saw their fear, raw and unconcealed, as they watched the cart move slowly past them. No one said a word. No one jeered. She wondered whether they were too frightened that she'd wield a final spell or two before dying – or that she'd come back after she had gone and harm them then. They stood back and formed a clear path that led directly to the pyre.

Still Maggie looked for Lord Deverill. She was certain he would come. She was certain that if he knew of her execution he would come and stop it.

Just as she was lifted off the cart a young boy bolted out of the crowd and ran at her. He was small and nimble and the soldiers were slow to react. He fell against her and thrust a small leather bag into her hand. Before they could catch him he had scampered away. Maggie squeezed the bag tightly behind her back and wondered what was in it.

They tied her to the stake and bound her hands behind it and they seemed to be so afraid themselves that they didn't notice the bag in her grasp, or, if they did, they chose to ignore it.

Maggie did not resist. There was no point. She was in God's hands now.

The priest read out her crime and then said a prayer in Latin, which Maggie did not understand. A soldier came with a flare and lit the pyre. Maggie raised her eyes above the crowd. Then she saw him. She saw him there and her heart gave a leap of hope.

Lord Deverill was mounted on his horse in his fine clothes and plumed hat. He was accompanied by his men but Maggie saw only him, watching her impassively, one gloved hand on the reins, the other on his thigh. He did not move. He just stared at her and she did not know what he was thinking.

She thought then of their son, of Liam O'Leary, and hoped that he was safe. She hoped he would grow up strong and have a better life than she'd had. Then the flames began to grow and the smoke began to billow out from the pyre and the heat began to intensify beneath her. She did not withdraw her eyes from the man she loved. From the man she loved and loathed in equal measure.

She gazed at Lord Deverill and he gazed back, but although he had the power to stop the burning, he did not.

The flames reached her feet and she gave a low moan. The moan became a scream that pierced the air. Maddened with agony she lost all reason. Then the little bag of gunpowder exploded in her hand and she was released.

Maggie stood beside the pyre and watched the remains of her body burn. Then she saw Lord Deverill turn away. She knew he had given the boy the gunpowder, but that was little consolation now that her life was over. He led his horse back through the hamlet, back to the castle and back to his wife, leaving her ashes to scatter on the wind.

Maggie searched for the light but it never came. She listened for God's calling but it never came. The world was dark and gloomy and her spirit seemed to be stuck in it. She wondered how long she'd have to stay in this limbo. She wondered what she had to do to free herself.

PART THREE

Chapter 23

Connecticut 1945

It was a typical Sunday in June at the Wallaces' palatial home in Connecticut. Joan Wallace was lying on the sun lounger in a fashionable red-and-white polka-dot two-piece bathing suit. Her red hair was curled to her shoulders, her manicured nails painted crimson and her pouting lips Max Factor scarlet. She held a smouldering Virginia Slims cigarette between her long white fingers and looked decidedly bored. Dorothy Wallace was on the sun lounger beside her sister-in-law in a more demure one-piece bathing suit, which she felt was more appropriate for her age, while Pam Wallace had deliberately taken the lounger on the other side of the pool. She was wearing a green polka-dot one-piece suit, for although she admired and copied Joan's style she wasn't brave enough to show her midriff – and she didn't think Joan should be either. Their mother-in-law Diana, in a straw hat and floral sundress, was sitting at a small round table at the other end of the pool beneath a large parasol, talking to her granddaughter Martha over large glasses of iced tea. They had been conversing for some time, confidentially and quietly. In the distance the sound of a men's tennis four could be heard beyond the rose garden as Joan's husband Charles played with his brothers Larry and Stephen, and his eldest son Joe. A small group of the Wallace grandchildren were playing croquet on the lawn with their spouses, a few were in the pool and one or two were out riding. The youngest great-grandchild was asleep in a pram beneath an apple tree. Ted Wallace, patriarch of the family, was in an armchair beneath the veranda, reading the newspapers and enjoying the peace before guests would descend on the house at 12.30 for lunch in the garden.

Joan watched Diana and Martha through her dark sunglasses. Pam watched Joan and suspected she was plotting or at least bitching. Ever since she had told Edith that Martha was adopted Pam had mistrusted her and with good reason. Martha had never divulged what happened in Ireland but the trip had altered her irrevocably. She had been quite a different person when she had eventually come home: solemn, ponderous and sad. Even now, six years on, she had yet to fall in love, marry and live the normal life of a girl her age. Most worryingly she had taken to spending hours in her bedroom reading the Bible, or at church. Pam blamed Joan for the massive change in her daughter and would never forgive her. It was only because Larry had begged her to at least tolerate her sister-in-law that she had managed to dissemble enough to be civil.

'You know, I've often wondered what went on in Ireland,' Joan said to Dorothy, without taking her eyes off Martha and Diana. 'Do you think she's confided in Diana?'

'Most likely,' said Dorothy without looking up from her magazine. The whole Martha business had been so unpleasant Dorothy didn't really want to be seen colluding with the person who had started it. Only the formidable presence of Ted Wallace had prevented the family breaking in two.

'Martha should find a nice man to marry,' said Joan, blowing out a puff of smoke. 'She's pretty enough,' she added reluctantly. She thought of her own children and their highly successful marriages and felt very smug. 'But no one's going to marry her if she doesn't put on some make-up and a nice frock and smile a little. If she continues to go about with a face like a boot she'll end up an old maid like Aunt Vera.' No one in the family wanted to end up like Aunt Vera who had died alone aged ninety-six and gone into family legend for being drab, brittle, miserable and lonely. Joan watched Martha and Diana talking with their expressions grave and their heads almost touching, and was more curious than ever.

But not in Joan's wildest dreams could she have imagined what they were discussing. Now that the war in Europe was over Martha wanted to leave America and return to Ireland. But what she wanted to do there no one could ever have predicted.

The previous night Martha had told her grandmother everything. She hadn't planned to. In fact, she had vowed to herself that she would never tell a living soul about the Deverills and JP. But her grandmother had been unwell, nothing more serious than a cold, and the thought of losing her had propelled Martha to share the burden of her secret. She needed her grandmother's support for an idea that had been brewing for some time. She knew that no one else in her family, least of all her parents, would understand or indeed favour her plan.

Diana had listened as Martha had sat on the edge of her bed and, hesitantly at first, then in a torrent of emotional outpouring, confided her sorry tale. Diana had taken her hand, gazed on her with compassion and listened without interrupting once. Only when Martha had finished did

Diana speak. 'My poor child, no wonder you returned as if the stuffing had been kicked out of you. But you have had six years to think this over, Martha dear. What is it that you wish to do?' And Martha had told her. It wasn't something that had come to her in a rush of inspiration but something that had insinuated itself into her consciousness over the many days and nights she had searched her soul for an answer and the Bible for reprieve. Diana had been surprised, but she had not tried to dissuade her. Most importantly she had not judged her. 'If that is what you want to do with your life, my dear,' she had said a little sadly, 'then you have my blessing. Who is to say what our purposes on earth are to be? Ultimately we are all searching for meaning.' She had stroked her granddaughter's cheek and smiled. 'I suggest you and I sleep on it tonight and discuss it in the morning. We will need to tread carefully.' There was no way on earth that Larry and Pam would accept Martha's proposal. They would do everything in their power to stop her returning to Ireland unless they were sheltered from the truth. Diana was all for telling white lies if the circumstances demanded them.

Joan's attention was diverted from Diana and Martha to the four men who now came to the pool to cool off after their tennis. They changed out of their whites in the pool house and dived into the water. A few minutes later the rest of the family were drawn to the scene from every corner of the estate like animals to a watering hole. They all fell into the pool with squeals of pleasure and Martha's plotting with her grandmother came to a natural close.

Martha did not want to swim and she did not want to have to make polite conversation with the guests who were coming for lunch. She longed for a quiet life. More than ever she felt dislocated from her home and awkward in the

THE LAST SECRET OF THE DEVERILLS

company of those who should have been her most natural companions. She had always had a sense of isolation, but since Ireland that sense had grown stronger. She still yearned for JP Deverill with all her heart. Sometimes she feared that it would never heal and she'd suffer that searing, aching pain forever. Her mother and aunts were constantly trying to set her up with well-connected, wealthy young men, but their meddling got them nowhere; Martha was not interested. None of those young men compared to JP and none of them was enough to distract her from pining. In fact, those disastrous, disappointing dates only left her feeling ever more bereft and desperate to find some way out of her suffering.

That evening, after the guests had finally departed, when the men were exhausted after further sets of tennis and Pam, Dorothy and Joan pink from too much sunbathing, Diana spoke with Larry. Martha remained in the garden while they sat in the swing chair on the veranda, talking as the sun set over the rose garden, but she knew exactly what her grandmother was going to say to him for they had planned it carefully that morning by the pool. Once they had finished Larry suggested he and Martha take a stroll, just the two of them, and she waited anxiously for him to initiate the conversation.

As the light bounced off the water in a thousand golden stars and the gentle chirruping of crickets rang out from the undergrowth, Larry spoke. 'Your grandmother and I have been talking about your future, Martha,' he said and Martha pretended she knew nothing about it.

'What future?' she asked. 'Please don't tell me you've arranged for me to marry some rich but chinless son of one of your friends,' she said with a smile.

'No, of course not. That's your mother's department. She

and your aunts seem to be making quite a hash of it,' he replied.

'I have no desire to marry, Daddy.'

Larry did not believe her. All girls married, except the rare few like his aunt Vera, and he didn't envisage a pretty girl like Martha ending up like her. 'You will when the time is right,' he said. 'But you're young. You don't need to rush into anything. But I want to make a suggestion to you before I suggest it to your mother.'

'All right,' she said, folding her arms as they slowed their pace.

'Your grandmother and I agree that ever since you came back from Ireland you have been unhappy. The war is over now and people are beginning to travel again so she suggested you go to London and work at the Embassy. It wouldn't be hard to arrange because I know the Ambassador's family well. You could go for a year or two, do something constructive and interesting and live an independent life. It would do you good. Who knows, you might even meet someone over there and put your mother and aunts out of business!'

Martha knew that would never happen. 'I think I'd like to go to London,' she said, as if now was the first time she'd thought of it. 'I would miss you all but Grandma is probably right. It would do me good to throw myself into something constructive. The Embassy would be a fascinating place to work and my secretarial skills are good. I could make myself useful there, serving the country.' She glanced at her father and hoped that she hadn't gone too far. She didn't feel in the least patriotic.

'Your mother won't be happy, but I'm sure I can persuade her if you really want to go.'

'I do,' said Martha. *More than you can imagine.*

'Then leave it with me,' Larry said, putting his hands in his pockets and gazing out over the water. 'I know you never told me what happened in Ireland and I'm not asking you to tell me now, but I've lived longer than you and I can tell you on good authority that letting heartbreak go is the only way to move forward in life. Hurting is part of living, Martha. It's part of God's great purpose, to drive us deeper and to teach us about compassion so that we can better understand ourselves and other people. But healing is also part of the lesson. You mustn't ignore that.' He looked at her and smiled kindly. 'I'll let you go to London if you promise me you will try and live a little.'

'I will try,' she replied with a small smile.

'I can't ask any more of you than that,' he said and he put his hand on the small of her back and turned to walk home the way they had come.

Only Diana and Martha knew the full extent of her plan. Going to London was simply the first step. Diana secretly hoped that time in London would change Martha's mind before she took the more drastic second step and went to Ireland. Being a traditional woman Diana believed in marriage and procreation and she considered the workplace the domain of men. What Martha planned to do was a leap too far from convention for Diana's peace of mind. But Martha seemed determined and it was her duty, as her grandmother, to see that she found her way, whatever that way was.

Martha left for London at the end of the summer. Pam had tried to prevent her leaving but her tears and protestations had not weakened Martha's resolve. She had set her heart on going and Pam sensed that she would not be coming back. Larry told her that it was her fear speaking, but Pam shook her head. She knew she was right. Martha had grown distant over the past six years and now she was taking herself off and there was nothing Pam could do or say to hold her back. She had lost her and it was all thanks to Joan and her jealous, evil tongue.

Pam looked back to that precious time when she had first held the small baby in the Convent of Our Lady Queen of Heaven and felt a terrible wrench in the middle of her chest. She could never have imagined then that she would only have her for twenty-three years. If only Martha could understand the depth of Pam's longing to be a mother. If only she could know how deep and sincere her love was, then maybe she'd stay. But Pam had tried to tell her and her words had fallen short, for there was no adequate way to express something so powerful. She hoped that time abroad would make Martha appreciate what she had left behind. As Larry had told her dozens of times: *Life is long. There is time enough for reconciliation. God writes straight on crooked lines.* But Pam did not share his faith. Martha was leaving and it felt terribly final.

Martha arrived in London and settled into her new lodgings near the Embassy in Grosvenor Square. The lady who had agreed to take her in was the personal secretary to the Ambassador himself. Miss Moberly was a spinster in her late fifties with short white hair, an elegant physique and a busy, efficient air. She was classy and intelligent and plain-talking, kind but not effusive, and Martha was grateful for her hospitality and her readiness to show her the ropes in her new job, which consisted of typing, making the coffee and running small errands when Miss Moberly was too busy to go out. Martha was paid very little but she didn't mind. Her father subsidised her income so that she could buy nice dresses and go on dates. He was certain that it wouldn't be long before she shook off her misery and started to behave like other girls her age. He had told Pam that he predicted she'd be married within the year. The Ambassador had assured him that his wife would take care of that. She knew all the young men in London on account of their own daughter who had recently come of age.

But Martha had no intention of going on dates. As soon as she arrived and settled into her bedroom she sat at the wooden desk in front of the tall sash window overlooking a communal garden and laid two pieces of ivory paper before her. She proceeded to write to Goodwin. She wrote occasionally to her old nanny, sharing her thoughts and feelings, and wanted to let her know that she was now in London and that it wouldn't be long before she returned to Ireland to visit her. She didn't, however, share her ultimate intention. She wasn't sure that Goodwin would approve. Instead, for that sensitive matter, she wrote to the Countess. She had only met her once, at the milliner's in Ballinakelly, but she had obviously liked her enough to gift her a hat. Martha had treasured it but she had never worn it. She would now, when she went to see the Countess. But before she did she needed to remind her who she was and ask whether she might be permitted to call on her. She needed her help and she was certain that, once she knew the whole story, she would give it. It wasn't a lot to ask, but it would mean everything to Martha. She bit the end of her ink pen as she pondered how best to start her letter.

Chapter 24

Ballinakelly

JP had never believed he would fall in love again. He had never believed that there existed another woman as lovely as Martha, but Alana had swiftly swept away all vestiges of her like a spring breeze blowing away the lingering leaves of autumn. The darkness that surrounded memories of his old love was now consumed by the light of his new one and he thought no more of Martha. It was as if the cord that had joined them had been severed and his heart brimmed with tenderness for Alana.

After their initial meeting on the cliff top JP had taken every opportunity to see her for the remaining days of his leave. He had walked with her through the heather, ridden with her over the hills, even taken her out to sea in his father's little rowing boat. They had talked about everything and nothing, laughed with the delight of old friends reunited and kissed with the thrill of two young people setting out on the greatest adventure of all.

Alana was nothing like Martha, who had been shy and timid and sweet. Alana was bold, outspoken and confident. She dazzled JP with her wit, mesmerized him with her charm and always disarmed him with her wide, engaging smile. While he wanted to parade her through the town for everyone to see, she warned him that her father did not like the Deverills and would not permit her to be courted by one. 'It must remain secret,' she insisted, 'until the right moment presents itself to tell him.' JP didn't doubt that Alana would fight for him if she needed to, and that she would win – he only knew one other woman with her strength of character and that was Kitty. He was certain that those two would instantly like each other if they had the opportunity to get acquainted.

At the end of his leave JP returned to the RAF only to hand in his notice. His superiors were disappointed that such a skilled pilot had decided not to continue flying planes, but JP was eager to return home to Alana whom he intended to marry when he had finished his studies in Dublin. This time nothing would thwart his plan. If anyone objected on account of the differences of their religion or class he would run away with her and he didn't doubt that she would go with him; Alana was a girl who knew her heart and was brave enough to follow it. While he was away from her JP reread her letters, many of which he had barely glanced over the first time, and as he did so he saw from the content and style of her writing that, as the letters progressed, she had blossomed into a woman before his eyes and he had never even noticed.

While JP was still in England Boysie and Celia arrived in Ballinakelly to stay with Kitty and Robert at the White House. Their reunion was bittersweet, for Harry had always been so much part of their group and now he was gone. But Celia and Kitty embraced keenly and as they did they could not help but reflect on the family tragedies that had risen up around them like giant waves and yet still they remained, side by side, heads above the water; embodiments of the Deverill spirit. 'Don't ever go away like that again,' said Kitty, holding her cousin tightly by the hands. 'We survivors must stick together.'

Robert liked Celia and Boysie, for together they were electrifying, but he was not part of their intimate group, which included his wife, and he felt it. It wasn't just that they reminisced about a past that excluded *him*, but also that they almost seemed to speak another language, which he did not understand. With them Kitty became a more concentrated version of herself. She seemed to shed all the Trench traits she had acquired during their marriage and become a Deverill once again. He could not accuse her of being unkind, for she tried to include him in everything, but her euphoria in their company made their life together seem relatively dull. Robert felt drab and uninteresting and looked forward to their departure so that life could return to normal once again, and so could Kitty.

'I have something I need to tell you,' said Boysie as he sat with Celia and Kitty on the beach finishing his picnic tea. Robert had chosen to remain behind in his study, working on his novel.

'I hope it's something exciting,' said Celia. 'There hasn't been nearly enough excitement since I came back from South Africa.'

'I'm going to divorce Deirdre,' he said and the smile vanished from Celia's face.

'Oh darling, I didn't mean *that* sort of excitement!' she said, putting a hand to her mouth.

'When did you decide?' Kitty asked, knowing it had something to do with Harry.

'Back in the spring, when she returned to London. I don't want to live this sham any more.' Boysie popped a cigarette between his lips and turned out of the wind to light it.

'I feel mean calling her Dreary Deirdre now,' said Celia.

'I wouldn't worry about that, old girl. It's a very appropriate name,' he said, dragging on his cigarette so that the little end glowed crimson.

'Does she know?' Kitty asked.

Boysie shook his head of tousled sugar-brown hair, which had only recently started to turn grey, and looked at them with sad green eyes, once considered the most beautiful pair of eyes in London. 'I don't think she has a clue, poor darling. But then Deirdre has never really had a clue about anything. While Charlotte was forced into recognizing that her husband's heart was elsewhere, Deirdre was never given such an opportunity. I'll never know whether she would have been as open-minded and as generous as Charlotte was towards Harry. But I cannot live with someone who doesn't know me, you see. I cannot be with someone who doesn't understand me. I cannot be truly myself and I'm tired of being someone else. Really, I'm too old now for pretence. I've been living a lie my entire life and I'm weary of it. Harry and I crept about in the shadows like a pair of thieves but I won't do it any more.' He took a deep breath.

'She'll kick you out of the house, Boysie,' said Celia with a grin. 'So, come and live with me. I'm rattling around in Deverill House and I'd adore you to keep me company. It's almost like home to you already. Do you remember Mother's Tuesday-evening Salons?'

'She was a dreadful social climber, your mama,' said Boysie with a smile. 'Such a shame your father's death knocked the wind out of her, otherwise who knows who she'd be entertaining now? King George and Queen Elizabeth? She'd have been quick to embrace terrible old Wallis and would have relished the waves she'd have created! Really, she missed a trick there.'

'She has no desire to go anywhere now,' said Celia sadly. 'She's a miserable recluse. But I feel sorry for her. She adored my father.'

'She'll rise from the dead, mark my words,' said Boysie.

'I don't think she will,' said Celia.

'Perhaps you can restore her Salons,' Kitty suggested. 'You can make waves of your own.'

'I don't have what it takes.'

'A very fast propeller on your rear, my dear,' laughed Boysie. 'And a sharp eye for who is on the up and who is on the down.'

'If Boysie lives with you, Celia, you can do it together.'

'Yes, that might bring your mama back from the dead,' said Boysie.

Celia grinned. She liked that thought. 'Will you come and live with me, Boysie?'

He took her hand and squeezed it and Kitty suddenly felt a ripple career over her skin, causing the little hairs to stand on end. 'I'd love to, old girl,' he replied, looking at Celia steadily. Indeed the two of them gazed at each other as if Kitty wasn't there.

That night Laurel woke up with the sound of voices in her head. There were two and they were calling to her from somewhere far away. 'Come on, Laurel. It's fun over here. Do hurry and join us!'

'Yes, come on!' It was Lord Hunt, unmistakably. 'We're waiting for you on the beach. Do hurry.'

Laurel climbed out of bed. She put on her dressing gown and slippers but left her glasses on the bedside table. She wouldn't be needing those where she was going. She crept out of her bedroom, closing the door softly behind her, and padded down the stairs. The household was asleep. She didn't want to wake anyone, least of all Florence who looked after her so tenderly. That dear, compassionate girl needed her sleep. It was tiring work being a full-time nurse and Laurel knew that she wasn't an easy patient. She had lost her mind, she was aware of that, but right now she felt more lucid than ever.

Laurel wandered out of the front door and down the drive. The garden was lit up by the moon so that it looked like dawn was breaking but with a cold, silvery light. She wrapped her dressing gown around her and hurried down the slope to the gate at the end. She could see the ocean glittering beneath the luminous indigo sky and the stars were glittering too; in fact the whole world seemed to be glittering and Laurel felt her spirits rise in anticipation, because surely Heaven glittered too.

The voices grew louder and more insistent. She was getting closer now. She took the narrow lane between a cluster of white cottages, in the direction of the harbour where little boats bobbed about on the calm water. Everything was quiet. A black cat jumped lithely from one rooftop to another but Laurel trotted on, her little feet swift in her excitement to join her sister and Ethelred. The fact that they were waiting for her spurred her on. She had believed they had gone without her, which was very mean considering she and her sister had always been inseparable. 'Come on, Laurel!' Hazel called. 'It's so jolly over here. I'm longing for you to see for yourself.'

'It's not complete without *you*,' said Ethelred Hunt. 'We've been waiting but we don't want to wait any more. You have to come now. Come on!'

Laurel wanted to shout that she was coming, but she was panting so heavily now that she couldn't get the words out. She wanted to tell them to wait a little more, that she wouldn't be long, that she was hurrying as fast as she could.

At last she reached the quay. 'Don't be afraid, Laurel. It's really very easy,' Hazel was saying.

'Just put your toe in. It's not cold. It's lovely!' said Ethelred. Because she trusted him Laurel stretched out her foot. She lost her balance at once and fell into the water with a splash. The shock of it was terrible. But Lord Hunt was right. After the initial jolt she found that it wasn't cold after all; it was warm and soft like treacle. She didn't struggle. She simply gave in as the water closed around her and filled her lungs. Then she saw their faces, smiling at her with triumph as if she had achieved something miraculous, and Lord Hunt was holding out his hand in the gallant way he always used to. She took it and allowed him to lift her out of the sea into the sky of twinkling stars. She didn't look back to where her body now floated on the small waves that lapped against the side of the wharf, because she was moving on into a place where she no longer needed it. She felt light as if a great weight had been lifted from her, and happy, so *deeply* happy, that she could barely contain herself. She took Hazel's hand and beamed at her. 'And Adeline?' she asked.

'Adeline isn't ready to come with us yet,' said Hazel. 'But it won't be long.'

'I do so wish to see her again,' said Laurel.

'And so you shall, but just for a minute, then you must

come. You have completed your life. She has much yet to do.'
And for a brief moment Laurel saw Adeline standing on the
shore, cocooned in a bright golden radiance, smiling at her
with love. 'Come now, Laurel. Ethelred and I have waited
long enough for this.' And together the three of them floated
towards the greater light.

Adeline watched them go and wondered how long it would
be before she and Hubert were able to join them. Her heart
momentarily caved in, for the allure of that light touched her
right at the root of her soul and it was becoming increasingly
hard to resist. But the thought of her dear husband stuck in
the castle strengthened her resolve. She would not leave him
there; not ever. Only when he was liberated would she free
herself, and together they would leave this shady limbo for
that sublime light.

No one was more upset by Laurel's death than Florence.
She blamed herself for not locking her bedroom door. If she
had been doing her duty, she said, Laurel would not have
died. But Kitty wrapped her arms around her daughter and
reassured her that, at ninety-eight, Laurel had lived a very
long and happy life. 'She had to go sometime,' she said. But
Florence feared the loss of purpose which would come now
that her patient had gone. Who would she look after now?

   JP returned to Ballinakelly in time for Laurel's funeral and
for the ceremonial planting of the laurel bush, which Bertie
had promised to place next to the hazel. Kitty mischievously
positioned a red-cheeked garden gnome between them in
honour of Lord Hunt but Bertie tactfully removed it a couple
of days later in case his daughter, Lady Rowan-Hampton,
happened to see it and take offence.

Grace Rowan-Hampton was busy with Michael Doyle. The murder of the Count had once again embroiled them in conspiracy, and, as had so often happened in the past, the only way they could give vent to all that surplus energy was by making love. Michael had abstained from sex for so long he had almost forgotten how delicious it was. He kept Grace a willing prisoner in her bedroom and they both forgot about *her* husband and *his* vows as they sank even further into iniquity.

JP resumed his courtship of Alana, which continued to be a secret and would have remained so had Fate not interceded. It was the end of the summer and JP and Alana had sneaked up to the Fairy Ring to watch the sunset. They had taken a small picnic and JP's horse had carried the two of them like a knight and his lady of legend. They were sitting on the grass, leaning against one of the ancient stones, chatting quietly, when Jack and Kitty came upon them. So shocked were JP and Alana at being caught that they did not question why Jack and Kitty were out riding together. They were intending to do what JP and Alana were doing, except without the picnic. They had met hundreds of times at the Fairy Ring and never encountered anyone. The two of them stared at the young people in bewilderment. JP scrambled to his feet and began to explain.

'I'm sorry that I didn't ask your permission to court your daughter,' he said, looking up at Jack on his horse with a mixture of remorse and determination. 'But I love her and I intend to marry her.'

Jack looked from JP to Alana and didn't know what to say. He certainly had no reason to prevent his daughter marrying a Deverill when all his life he had loved one. Alana now stood beside JP and took his hand. 'I love him too, Da, and if he asks me to marry him I will accept.' She glanced at JP and grinned and he couldn't help but grin back, for she had agreed to marry him.

Kitty smiled as JP and Alana quivered with excitement. 'Well, I can't imagine why anyone would object,' she said. 'Mr O'Leary?' she added, suddenly remembering that Jack was the vet and she should, in public, treat him like one.

'Mrs Trench, I see no reason either. Alana, why ever did you think I'd stand in the way of your happiness?' he asked.

'Because you hate the Deverills,' she replied.

Jack glanced at Kitty. 'I do not.'

'Then you'll allow us to marry?'

Jack looked at JP and tried to be serious. 'Mr Deverill, if you would be so good as to come to my house tomorrow morning, I will receive you and you can ask me then, formally, for my daughter's hand.' Kitty envied JP for the ease with which he would marry the woman he loved. She looked at Jack and knew that he was thinking the same thing. Kitty's brother and Jack's daughter would enjoy the life together in Ballinakelly which *they* had been denied. It was impossible not to notice the irony and to be a little saddened by it.

'We will leave you,' said Jack, pulling his horse away. 'Mrs Trench has taken the trouble to find me, I must not delay her any longer.' But JP and Alana couldn't have cared less about Jack and Kitty's business; they only had eyes for each other.

When they were once more alone JP took Alana's hands and smiled at her tenderly. 'Will you marry me?' he asked.

Alana's face flushed. 'Yes, I'll marry you,' she replied, her eyes welling with tears. 'I've always known I would marry you, JP. From the moment you rescued me in the hills I was yours.'

'Then I don't want us to have any secrets,' he said, kissing her. 'I want to tell you everything and for you to know that you have healed me.' He took her hand and they sat down again on the rug by the giant stone. He told her the whole story, of his birth in the convent, the death of his mother and the survival of his twin sister. He didn't spare her any details, but told her frankly and dispassionately. All the while he held her hand and she listened without interrupting. 'Martha went back to America and I went into the RAF. I never thought I would love again. But you wrote to me and I found myself sharing things with you that I never shared with anyone else, even Kitty. When I came to find you in the spring, I didn't expect to fall in love with you. The last time I saw you, you were a little girl. But I fell in love with you the moment I laid eyes on you and every day I have grown to love you more. I want you to know everything, Alana, because I don't want there to be space between us. Do you understand? I don't want anything to ever come between us from secrets or misunderstandings. I want to always tell you the truth.'

'And I will always tell *you* the truth,' she replied, gazing deeply into his eyes.

'You're not shocked by my story?'

She shook her head. 'No. It doesn't change who you are. I'm sorry you were hurt over Martha. Perhaps you'll meet again one day and be able to enjoy a normal relationship of brother and sister. I don't own your past, JP, but I want to own your present. At least, I want to be the only woman you love now.'

'And you are,' he said.

'And the only woman you'll love in your future.'

'And you will be,' he added.

'Then I give you my heart forever and always.'

'And I will treasure it.'

'And I will treasure yours, JP. You won't ever suffer again in love, I promise.'

Chapter 25

In the last week of August two Americans arrived in Ballinakelly, a father and son returning to find their roots. The father was in his early fifties, handsome with a low brow, thick grey hair and a moustache. His eyes were deep-set and as blue as a lagoon. His son looked nothing like him. He was dark-haired and skinny with a long weaselly face, swarthy skin and small hazel eyes. They wandered into O'Donovan's and ordered stout and the room was silenced. Mrs O'Donovan was not one to hold her tongue. 'So, where are you gentlemen from in America?' she asked, putting two glasses of Guinness on the counter.

'Boston,' said the older man. 'My grandfather was from round here,' he added by way of an explanation.

'Really? From where?'

'From here,' he replied. 'Ballinakelly.'

'What's your name then?' she asked.

'Callaghan,' he said. 'Jim Callaghan.'

'Well, there are many with that name here.' She raised her eyes and beckoned over an old man in a brown cap and jacket. His white hair curled about his large ears and in bushy sideburns on his cheeks. 'This here is Fergus O'Callaghan,' she said.

The old man approached the bar stiffly. 'Jim Callaghan,' said the American, extending his hand. 'This is my son, Paul.'

Fergus O'Callaghan wiped his hand on his jacket then shook theirs. He grinned, revealing shiny gums and a few remaining yellow teeth. 'Well, seeing as we're related, you can buy me a drink!' he said, staring at the American boldly and a little unsteadily. Mrs O'Donovan cackled and a roar of laughter erupted from the locals behind them.

'Seeing as we are, I will,' said Jim with a grin that charmed Mrs O'Donovan and disarmed Fergus O'Callaghan. 'One for my cousin,' he said.

Mrs O'Donovan shook her head. 'Isn't that grand,' she said, reaching for a glass. 'There's nothing like the generosity of family!'

'I suppose ye'll be looking for a pair of colleens to carry back to Amerikay,' said Fergus, watching Mrs O'Donovan fill his glass.

'Aye, you could travel farther and fare worse, lads,' Mrs O'Donovan added. The older American laughed but the younger one just scowled and wet his lips with Guinness.

Fergus O'Callaghan took his stout and shuffled back to the round table by the window where his friends were waiting for him. The chatter resumed and father and son settled onto their bar stools with their Guinness.

'So where are you staying?' Mrs O'Donovan enquired, because after they'd gone she didn't want everyone asking her questions she couldn't answer.

'At Vickery's Inn,' the older man replied, which was a few minutes' walk from the pub.

'And how long will you be staying?'

'Only a week.'

'That's grand,' she said. 'You didn't come all the way from America just to find your roots, did you?'

'No, I had other business to see to in Dublin, so we thought we'd do a detour.'

'That's grand,' she repeated. Then she looked at the young man. 'Does your lad talk?'

'I do,' said Paul, glancing shiftily at the door.

'So he does,' said Mrs O'Donovan. 'Must be the stout.'

'I was told that this is the heart of the town,' said Paul, and Mrs O'Donovan thought he was only making conversation to prove that he did indeed have a tongue.

'Aye, it is,' she said. 'Everyone comes here.' She glanced at the young man's father and smiled. 'You might meet some more relations.'

He smiled back. 'Then I'll depart a poor man!'

'Do you know where your kin used to live?'

'It was a farmhouse on the hill but it's not there any more,' he replied vaguely.

'Farmers, were they?'

'Yes, I think so.'

'Your grandfather, you said?'

'Yes.'

'Well, I hope you find what you're looking for.'

'Thank you, Mrs—'

'O'Donovan. This is my husband's pub.'

'And a very charming pub it is too.'

She smiled. 'Thank you.'

A couple of nights later Jack went to O'Donovan's for a game of cards. Paddy O'Scannell and Badger Hanratty, who was now so old he needed a magnifying glass to see the numbers on the cards, were already at the table. They had substituted the Count with a young lad called Tim Nesbit, who had the best poker face in town and a keen eye for the ladies, but he didn't buy the locals rounds of stout like the Count had and the flamboyant Italian was sorely missed.

Everyone in Ballinakelly knew that Michael Doyle was behind the murder of Cesare di Marcantonio, everyone, it seemed, except Bridie, who, although aware of Michael's sinister past, would never have believed her brother to brutally murder the man she loved. Those old enough to remember the War of Independence and the Civil War that followed knew exactly what Michael Doyle was capable of. The fact that he had reinvented himself as a pious man of the Church fooled no one. The high positions he held in the community simply disguised his ruthlessness and everyone was as frightened of him now as they had been then. Niamh had disappeared the night the Count was murdered and the O'Donovans' explanation of having sent their daughter away to stay with relatives in Co. Wicklow did not convince anyone that the two events were not connected. The story got out and gossip boiled and bubbled and the Garda came round asking questions, but no one was going to rat on Michael Doyle; no one dared.

Emer had been a great comfort to Bridie, who was inconsolable. If Bridie knew the truth she didn't have to face it because Michael weaved a likely tale of Cesare's gambling and falling into debt and she was ready to believe that her husband had lost his life because of his refusal to pay the reprobates to whom he owed money. She turned a blind eye to the fact that Cesare had never had any qualms about squandering her fortune or, indeed, running off with it. Michael promised he would track down the criminals who murdered him and kill them himself, and Bridie believed him. She vowed to wear black for the rest of her life and found solace in church, much to Father Quinn's delight, for with the Countess's gratitude came large and frequent donations.

That night Jack found O'Donovan's abuzz with talk of the two Americans who had bought a drink for Fergus a couple of evenings before. 'Just say you're called O'Callaghan,' Paddy told Jack as he dealt the cards. 'And you'll get a free pint!'

'What are they doing here?' Jack asked Paddy, who had heard it all from Mrs O'Donovan.

'Looking for relatives, it seems,' said Paddy. 'They're from Boston.'

Jack frowned and rubbed his chin. There was nothing unusual about Americans coming to Co. Cork in search of their roots, but Jack's suspicions were raised all the same. He put a cigarette between his lips and lit it pensively. It was years since he'd left New York in fear of his life after the plot to kill 'Lucky' Luciano had failed. He didn't imagine anyone was after him now, but 'Bugsy' Siegel had put a high price on his head, so there was always a chance of some dogged bounty hunter tracking him down. He studied his hand of cards and dismissed his suspicions as paranoia. It was crazy to suspect the worst of every stranger who came to Ballinakelly.

Behind the partition, in the snug, the six women of the Legion of Mary, known as the Weeping Women of Jerusalem, sat in a row on the bench, drinking glasses of Bulmer's Cidona and nibbling on Mikado biscuits like dainty mice. They were more excited about the arrival of the Americans than anyone else, for it gave them something new to gossip about. 'The lad who looks like Clark Gable is a daily communicant,' said Nellie Clifford. 'They keep the faith,' she added approvingly.

'They go to Mass every morning,' said Joan Murphy.

'Indeed, they're already great pals with Father Quinn,' said Mag Keohane, whose elderly mongrel Didleen lay sleeping at her feet. 'They've promised to put electric lights in the church and electrify the organ. It will be America at home. And to top it all they are keeping him supplied in whiskey, God save us!'

Maureen Hurley shook her grey curls. 'Ain't it amazing, Mag, the call of St Patrick brings them all back to the land of the Shamrock.'

But that night when Jack went to bed he couldn't sleep. He couldn't stop thinking about the American tourists and he couldn't ignore the uneasy feeling that tugged at his gut. He didn't want to frighten Emer with his own fears, so he kept his suspicions to himself, but he took her hand and held it until dawn.

The following morning Jack was summoned to see three lame horses, two bloated ponies and a goat that had eaten an azalea bush. Everywhere he went people were talking about Jim and Paul Callaghan. The women's cheeks blushed as they repeated the compliments the older man had given them and even the most hardened farmers were touched by their interest in their way of life. *'Tis true what they say, you can take the boy out of the bogs but you can't take the bogs out of the boy*, they said. *There isn't an ounce of grandeur in the two Yanks and they must have a fortune to be able to stay in Vickery's Inn ... I knew a Mossie O'Callaghan from Killarney when I was a young girl and the older one is the dead stamp of him.* They nodded admiringly and Jack's suspicions were aroused even further, for these two men seemed to be making an effort to talk to everyone in Ballinakelly.

It was true that there had been no tourism during the war

and it was exciting to see new people visiting the area once again, especially from as far away as America. On top of that the Irish had a rose-tinted view of America because so many of them had emigrated there and sent money back to their poor relatives along with descriptions of the material comforts and marvellous opportunities they had found. But Jim and Paul Callaghan were, in Jack's opinion, asking too many questions.

When Jack arrived home Emer was waiting up in the kitchen, darning.

'We need to talk,' she said, putting down her work, and by the expression on her face he could see that she was upset.

'What about?' he asked, hanging up his jacket and cap.

'It was something your mother said to me today about a comment *she* had heard Nora O'Scannell make.' Nora O'Scannell was Paddy's wife and she worked the telephone switchboard.

'What did she say?' Jack hoped she wasn't gossiping about him and Kitty.

'You know those two Americans everyone is talking about?' she said.

Jack's blood went cold. 'Aye.'

'Well, your mother told me that Nora, who we all know likes earwigging down the line, was listening in on that Jim Callaghan making a call to America. I bet she wanted to find out whether he's married or not. She's sweet on him, you know. Says he looks like a film star. Anyway, she heard him say that he was going to give Jack O'Leary his present by the end of the week.' Emer looked at him anxiously. 'Nora went up and told Julia with great excitement, wanting to know why the Yank is going to give you a present and what it might be. But I know what it is. It's time, isn't it, Jack?'

The ground seemed to spin away from him. He pulled out the chair and sat down at the table. 'I thought as much,' he said, putting his head in his hands.

'They've come looking for you, haven't they?' She turned to gaze out of the window, into the black night, so he couldn't see the fear in her eyes. 'I thought we were safe here in Ballinakelly, but we're never going to be safe. We're always going to be looking over our shoulders, until you're dead.'

Jack gazed at her steadily. 'Then I have to get them first,' he said.

Neither Emer nor Jack slept well that night. While Jack tried to think of a way to outwit the Americans, Emer prayed that they wouldn't have to run away again. She liked Ballinakelly. She didn't want to go and start a new life somewhere else. But in the dark she reached for Jack's hand and he took it.

For the first time in years Jack felt fear. It was cold and hard, like a wall closing in around him, and he squeezed Emer's fingers hard. 'I love you, Jack,' she whispered.

Jack felt sick in his stomach for having betrayed her with Kitty. His life shifted into sharp focus at the terrifying thought of losing it, and all he saw was Alana, Liam, Aileen and Emer. Emer, his lovely Emer who had followed him unquestioningly from one country to the next. 'And I love you, Emer,' he croaked. 'God help me. I've done some stupid things. Made some foolish decisions and yet you've never left my side. You've been my better half, Emer, and I don't deserve you.'

'Now you're being silly,' she whispered, snuggling up to him. 'Any woman worth her salt would do the same.'

But Jack knew that wasn't true. 'No, Emer, they wouldn't.

You're not like other women. You're better.' He pressed his lips to her forehead. 'You're better,' he repeated. *And I've been an eejit not to notice.*

In the morning Jack kissed Emer goodbye and took his car straight to Michael Doyle's farmhouse. He and Michael had fought side by side in the War of Independence and yet those years which should have bonded them had set them at each other's throats on account of Kitty Deverill, who they both loved. After all that had happened in the past Jack and Michael could never be friends, but they had at least come to a mutual understanding. Jack knew that Michael was the only person who could help him and, because of the dark things they had shared in their past, he would be ready to do so. However, when Jack entered the cottage he found Mrs Doyle on her rocking chair, smoking a clay pipe and reading a tatty old Bible in the dim light through a pair of thick spectacles. 'Michael's gone to see Badger,' she informed him when he enquired after her son. 'He's good like that, is Michael. Poor Badger has no kin. Michael is everything to him now. But he'll be back soon. He visits Badger every morning just to check he wakes up,' she added with a toothless grin. 'You're welcome to wait. I can wet the tea.'

Jack took a chair at the table and accepted the mug of tea. He remembered the many times he had sat at that very table, with Michael, his brother Sean, Father Quinn and a few others, to plan strategies during the War of Independence. The place still smelt the same, of wood smoke, cows from the farm next door and cooking. Bridie had sat by the fire with her mother and grandmother while they had conspired against the British, and Jack wondered whether she had listened to every detail so she could go back and tell her lover, then Mr Deverill, all about it. Nothing was ever simple and few could be trusted.

The sound of Michael's car drawing up outside dragged him away from the past. A moment later Michael's presence darkened the door. He saw Jack and nodded. 'Hello, Jack,' he said, taking off his cap. Michael looked at his mother. 'Badger's gone,' he added.

Mrs Doyle's mouth opened in surprise. 'Gone? Badger?'

'I'm afraid so, Mam. He must have died in the night for he's as cold as ice this morning.' Michael shook his head sadly. 'He was an honest man, was Badger, and there are precious few of those.'

Mrs Doyle crossed herself vigorously. 'I will light a candle for his soul,' she said. 'May he rest in peace.'

'I'll go and tell Father Quinn,' said Michael.

'I'll come back later,' said Jack, getting up.

Michael sighed. 'No, you can talk to me now, Jack. Badger's not likely to go anywhere, after all.' Michael took a chair opposite Jack. 'What can I do for you?'

Mrs Doyle started to read her Bible again and Jack leaned across the table and lowered his voice. 'I need your help,' he said.

Michael grinned grimly. 'Go on.'

'Those Yanks are after *me*,' Jack said.

'Are they now?' said Michael. 'And why would they be after you?'

'They're working for the Mafia. When I was in New York I got into trouble and had to flee for my life. I took Emer down to Argentina. I only came back because I thought it was safe to do so.'

'But they've found you, have they?'

'Nora O'Scannell eavesdropped on a conversation one of

them had to America. They're going to do me in, Michael. So, *I* need to do *them* in first,' he said and his jaw stiffened with resolve.

Michael pulled a cigarette packet out of his breast pocket and tapped it with his finger. He popped a cigarette between his lips and dipped the end into the little flame of his lighter and puffed. All the while he looked at Jack through narrowed eyes. Michael wasn't clever in an educated way, but he was cunning in a feral way. More cunning even than the most highly educated. He now smoked languidly and Jack could almost hear his mind whirring with ideas. After a long while, during which time Jack drained his mug of tea, Michael smiled crookedly. 'Do you want to get rid of them well and good?' he asked.

'Well and good,' Jack repeated.

'Then listen to me and I'll tell you exactly how we're going to do it.' He turned to his mother. 'Forget what I told you about Badger, Mam.' Mrs Doyle, who was used to her son's intriguing, nodded her head solemnly before turning back to her Bible. 'For it to work, Jack, you have to do *exactly* what I say.'

Emer was at the castle having tea with Bridie when the butler announced that the Garda were at the door asking after Mrs O'Leary. Bridie looked at Emer and frowned anxiously. It was obviously urgent if they had tracked her down to the castle. 'Please show them in,' she said.

Emer had gone pale. 'Sweet Jesus, Bridie. It's Jack.' She stood up and hurried to the door, her breath burning her lungs with panic. She grabbed her neck with a white hand as the two men walked in with their hats in their hands.

'Mrs O'Leary?' said the first one gravely. Emer nodded.

'My name is Inspector Cremin. I think you might like to sit down.'

Bridie now stood beside her. 'What's happened?' she demanded. 'Speak up, for the love of Jesus.'

'I'm afraid there's been an accident,' he said. 'Your husband's car came off the road at Malin Point and fell onto the rocks below. I'm sorry to tell you, but your husband is dead.'

Emer swooned and the two men and Bridie helped her into an armchair. 'How is that possible?' Bridie asked.

'I don't know, Countess, but the car caught flames and the poor lad didn't have a chance.'

Emer started to howl, 'I know who did this!' she cried. She grabbed Bridie's skirt. 'I know who killed him!'

'I'm afraid it looks like an accident, Mrs O'Leary,' said the other inspector.

'Of course it looks like an accident,' she snapped, eyes blazing. 'They *want* it to look like an accident!'

'*Who* wants it to look like an accident?' asked Inspector Cremin gently, taking out his notebook.

'Those Yanks. They wanted him dead.' She began to sob uncontrollably. Bridie stroked Emer's arm as her grief overwhelmed her. When at last she had calmed down enough to speak, she added, 'They said they'd deliver the present to Jack O'Leary by the end of the week. Ask Nora O'Scannell. She'll tell you.' The two Gardai looked at each other in bewilderment, then Inspector Cremin put away his pad.

'We'll come back when you've had time to grieve, Mrs O'Leary,' he said and his tone was deeply sympathetic, as if he was talking to a distraught child.

'I'm sorry for your loss,' said the other and they departed.

Bridie asked a maid for two large glasses of brandy and crouched by Emer's chair. 'Why would those Yanks want Jack dead?' she asked, her eyes glittering with tears.

'Because Jack was running from them. That's why we fled New York and went to live in Argentina. We've been running for years. I thought we didn't have to run any more, but I was wrong. They got him.'

'Who are *they*?'

'The Mafia,' said Emer, and the way she looked at Bridie made her wonder whether, in her anguish, she had gone a little mad.

Bridie put her arm around Emer who cried softly onto her shoulder. 'What are you going to tell the children?' she asked.

But Emer didn't hear her. 'I'm going to get them,' she said. 'I'm going to find those two bastards and kill them with my bare hands.'

Chapter 26

The brandy did little to calm Emer's nerves. She sat sobbing in Bridie's drawing room, unable to comprehend that Jack was gone. Jack whom she loved so dearly. At last she asked Bridie to drive her home. 'I think I'd better go and break the news to the children before they hear it from someone else. Aileen is with Julia, the other two ...' Her voice trailed off. No mother wants to tell her children that their father is dead. Bridie recalled her own sense of desolation at the death of her father and her heart went out to those poor children. She helped Emer up and led her out to the car. She would go with her. Emer wasn't in any fit state to go anywhere alone.

The chauffeur drove the car down the drive and along the meandering lanes towards Ballinakelly. The golden light bounced off the water and the beauty of it made Emer cry all the more. The two women sat in silence. Bridie gazed out of the window, remembering the time Jack had made love to her in New York only to leave in the night without a word. She had grieved for him once already; now she was grieving for him again.

Ballinakelly was quiet, bathed in the grainy pink veil of dusk. The car motored down the main street and Bridie wondered how long it would take for everyone to know that Jack O'Leary was dead. It seemed strange to watch people going about their usual business, unaware of the tragedy that had just struck at the heart of their community. Suddenly Emer shouted at the chauffeur to stop the car. He slammed on the brakes and Bridie and Emer were thrown forward as the car came to an abrupt halt. Before Bridie realized what was happening Emer had opened the door and was scrambling out into the road. Bridie watched in bewilderment as she rushed at two men who were standing on the pavement. Emer threw herself upon them like a raging lioness, scratching and screeching, and Bridie realized they were the Yanks Emer accused of murdering her husband.

Bridie climbed out of the car, but by the time she reached Emer the men who had been drinking in O'Donovan's had already been drawn into the street by the commotion and were trying to break up the fight. 'You've murdered Jack!' Emer was shouting at the top of her voice. 'You've murdered my husband! I won't let you get away with it. I have proof! It wasn't a bloody accident. I know who you are and where you're from and you won't get away with it! I'll see you swinging from the gallows, if it's the last thing I do!' Paddy O'Scannell managed to tear her away but her nails had already scratched Jim Callaghan's face, leaving an angry red line from his eye to his mouth. His son Paul looked terrified. He was visibly trembling. Emer shook Paddy off and lifted her chin. 'You're from the Mafia and you came to murder my husband. You're not tourists at all. You have no connection with Ireland, I'd bet my life on it.' Jim and Paul Callaghan glanced at each other nervously. Paddy and the local men stared at the two foreigners with suspicion.

'I don't know what she's talking about,' said Jim Callaghan, backing away. 'I'm sorry for your loss, ma'am. Someone should take you home so you don't assault anyone else.' He touched his cheek and observed the blood on his fingers. 'When you calm down and realize your error, I'll be happy to hear your apology.' The two Americans pushed through the throng and set off at an urgent pace up the pavement in the direction of Vickery's Inn.

By now Mrs O'Donovan had come out onto the pavement. On hearing the shocking news she pulled Emer against her large bosom and stroked her hair. 'Let's get you home,' she said softly. 'Someone call Father Quinn at once and tell him to come without delay.' She patted Emer's trembling back. 'If those two men had anything to do with it, my dear, they'll swing.'

'We'll lynch them ourselves before the hangman has a chance,' added Paddy O'Scannell darkly.

News of Jack's death spread through the town quicker than an airborne disease. Kitty was at the supper table with Florence and Robert when it reached her. 'Jack O'Leary's been killed,' the maid said tearfully, bringing in a dish of cold meat. 'His car went off the road at Malin Point and crashed onto the rocks below. They say the Yanks did it. They say they're not tourists at all but Mafia.' Kitty felt the world give way beneath her chair as if a great hole had opened up in the floor and she was falling into it.

'That's Alana's father!' said Florence, blind to her mother's shock. 'JP must go to her at once,' she added. 'We must telephone him. He's with Grandpa.'

Robert stood up. 'I'll do it,' he said. He glanced at Kitty, who had gone as white as death itself. He assumed she was distressed on JP's behalf. He touched her shoulder. 'Two murders in Ballinakelly in the space of a few months. It's like the Troubles all over again.' Kitty didn't hear him. The blood had rushed to her ears and was pounding against them, drowning out any sound. Unable to speak she pushed out her chair and staggered to the door.

'Are you all right, Mama?' Florence asked. Kitty swayed in the doorframe and then fell softly, like a doll discarded on the nursery floor. She didn't want to wake up. She didn't want to ever wake up.

As soon as JP heard the news he borrowed his father's car and drove over to see Alana. When he arrived it was nearly dark. He recognized the priest's small Ford and the shiny racing-green automobile belonging to the Countess di Marcantonio. He knocked on the door and waited. A moment later Mrs O'Donovan appeared, her face both distraught and imperious, leaving JP in no doubt that she was in charge of the situation. She didn't say a word but nodded in acknowledgement and opened the door wider to let him pass.

JP stepped into the small hall. He could see into the sitting room where Mrs O'Leary was being comforted by Father Quinn. The Countess sat beside her, holding the widow's hand. She looked distraught and JP suddenly remembered to take off his hat. It was only a few months ago that the Countess had lost her own husband and JP felt sorry for her. As if sensing his compassion Bridie raised her eyes and looked at her son. Ignorant of the invisible bond that would always connect them, he bowed slightly – he was not sure how else to show his respect. Bridie's features softened, and her heart, made all the more fragile by loss, seemed to cave in as she watched him watching her. She nodded in response and suppressed her longing. Then Alana stepped between them and the moment was gone.

There was a quiet dignity to Alana's grief. JP knew she was being strong for her mother's sake and for the sake of her brother and sister. Her face was flushed and her eyes sparkled with recent tears, but she lifted her chin and held her shoulders back with surprising control for one so young. JP was a man who was not unacquainted with death. He had lost his brother Harry in the Blitz and many friends besides, and he knew how deeply cut the wounds of such losses. He drew her into his arms and held her there until her stiff body sagged a little and she allowed him to unburden her of some of her restraint.

The following day dawned as it always does. In the O'Leary cottage by the sea the women sat around the coffin, which had been placed in the front room, bathed in candlelight and prayer. The coffin was closed on account of the terrible state of the body within, which happened to be Badger Hanratty's corpse that had been put in Jack's car and pushed over the edge at Malin Point. The car had caught fire and Badger's body had burnt beyond all recognition. 'If you kill the Yanks there will only be more from where they come from,' Michael had told Jack. 'You need to kill *yourself* in order to shake them off your tail once and for all.' So together with Father Quinn, the three of them had planned Jack's death. Putting his family through agony for a hoax was better than putting them through it for real. Once they were sure that the Americans had fled, Jack would be permitted to come out of hiding and start his life anew.

Outside the cottage the men were smoking and drinking and sharing stories about Jack. Michael had explained Badger's disappearance by telling everyone that Father Quinn had sent him to Mount Mellaray to cure him of the booze and no one suspected any trickery. After all, Badger had brewed his own brand of potentially lethal poteen for years and was one of the only men in Ballinakelly who had a liver strong enough to take it. Mrs Doyle kept her lips tightly shut as Michael had instructed her to do.

Inside, the women gossiped and drank whiskey. Julia, Jack's mother, sobbed into a sodden handkerchief, whimpering that her life was over. Alana comforted her while Emer and the two Nellies, Nellie Clifford and Nellie Moxley, who had no body to lay out, kept themselves busy making sure everyone had enough to eat and drink. Mrs O'Donovan, exhausted with the effort of taking command, topped up her whiskey glass and sat down beside Mrs O'Scannell with a long-suffering sigh.

The Weeping Women of Jerusalem had by now drowned their grief in whiskey and unfettered their tongues. 'I wonder will Miss Deverill that was turn up,' said Joan Murphy in a loud whisper.

'Kitty Deverill? Why wouldn't she?' Maureen Hurley asked.

Joan sniffed through dilated nostrils and lowered her voice. 'Didn't Mag Keohane spot Jack putting a note in the kitchen-garden wall up at the castle and may God forgive her, didn't she read it. It was a love letter to Kitty and it looked as if they were going to run away together. Poor Mag wasn't in the better of it for weeks. It was a terrible burden to be carrying,' she said.

'What was she doing in the kitchen garden?' asked Nellie Moxley, hoping there was some mistake.

'She'd business there. 'Twas when Frank Nyhan was gardener for Lady Deverill,' Joan informed her. 'A long time ago now, but one doesn't forget hearing something like that. Mag's not one to pry but curiosity got the better of her.'

'Another drop of whiskey and a fag when you're passing, please, Nellie Clifford. They say that a drunken woman speaks a sober mind – God help us,' said Maureen Hurley, cackling softly.

Kit Downey was not to be outdone when it came to gossip. She lowered her voice and narrowed her eyes. 'Sure, that might have happened long ago, but I have a more recent tale to tell. When I was blackberrying last year up at the stone circle, didn't I see the pair of them canoodling. Jesus, I don't know how I got home with the shock of it. And I've kept it buried inside meself ever since, God save us. I'm like a tomb when it comes to keeping secrets.' A tomb that was now positively unlocked, thought Nellie Moxley wryly.

Joan Murphy gasped. 'In the name of God will ye hold yer tongues or Emer will hear and it will kill her outright on the spot, God help us.'

In their drunken state they hadn't noticed that Alana had heard every word.

Jack anxiously paced the floor of Badger Hanratty's farm-house. The thought of his family's suffering was unbearable. He couldn't eat and he couldn't sleep and he only drank because stout dulled his senses and took the edge off his own suffering. His regret at having resumed his affair with Kitty gnawed at his conscience until it felt as if it had bitten a hole right through it; a hole that ached and burned and stung. How could he have allowed himself to be seduced by the past when his present was more radiant than the embers of an old passion could ever be? How could he have been blinded to the woman at his side whose love was unsullied and pure? He loved two women, of that there was no doubt, but he had made his choice. He only wished he had made it years ago, before he had found Kitty on the cliffs and broken his marriage vows. He was certain now, more certain than he had ever been: it was time to give up Kitty. He drained his glass and banged it down on the table. Kitty was a mirage, a ghost from bygone times, the sweet allure of nostalgia, nothing more. Emer was real.

Jack shrugged on his jacket, pulled his cap low over his head and stole out into the night. He crept through the darkness, careful to keep off the roads and tracks so as not to be seen by anybody, although few were awake at this dead hour. The moon was high in the sky and bright. It illuminated his way with its watery light and he hurried deftly over the shadows without stumbling. When he saw his home, nestled in the embrace of high rocky cliffs and lulled by the gentle sound of waves breaking onto the beach, his heart lurched with longing. He yearned with every cell in his body to walk through the door and into the warm, familiar kitchen and to find his lovely Emer there, smiling at him from the stove and gazing at him with her kind and trusting eyes. He cowered behind shrubs and gazed up at the dark windows where his family slept, believing him dead. He felt like a ghost, unable to make contact with the living, and he shivered, recalling the two American men and how close he had come to death.

He remained hidden in the darkness for a long while, wondering how long he'd have to continue this pretence, wishing he could end it now and start his life anew. Then his attention was alerted to a movement in an upstairs bedroom. *His* bedroom. The bedroom he shared with his wife. He stopped breathing for a moment and stared hard as the curtain twitched and a pale arm pushed open the window. Emer's face was visible in the silver moonlight and he could see, even from where he hid, that his death had altered her.

Indeed, her features were so pinched and twisted with pain that she looked like an old woman. He opened his mouth in shock and groaned. He would have given his right arm to cry out to her then, but it was his life they wanted and he could not give them that, so he remained concealed and wracked with craving until she disappeared and closed the curtains.

Jack returned to the farmhouse with a heavy tread. He threw himself onto the bed and closed his eyes and it wasn't Kitty he saw, but Emer, with her tender smile and gentle gaze, and he sobbed as he thought how close he had come to losing her through recklessness and self-indulgence. Never again would he be so careless with her heart.

Alana had slept fitfully. Grief had exhausted her but her fury had made her restless. She could not forget what she had overheard at the wake. Was it true that her father had been carrying on with Kitty Trench? Or was it just malicious gossip? Alana knew what those old women were like, and she didn't want to malign her dead father if malicious gossip was all it was. But it pained her to think of her poor devoted mother being nothing but a loyal and loving wife while her husband was having an affair with another woman. And Kitty Deverill wasn't just *any* woman, she was JP's half-sister and soon to be Alana's sister-in-law.

Dawn was merely a glow in the eastern sky when Alana tiptoed into the little room that had been her father's study and began to quietly open drawers in search of evidence. She wasn't sure what to look for, and she hoped she'd find nothing to incriminate him, but she had to know one way or another if she was going to marry a Deverill.

There were no secret compartments in her father's desk, no love letters buried among his papers, no notes written in a woman's hand that were not from her mother. Then there was only his veterinarian's bag and it was locked as it always was to keep Aileen from playing with the medicines inside. Alana began to open it with her father's silver letter opener. It was a surprisingly easy task for the bag was old and the catch weak and she was able to do it without breaking it.

Alana took everything out piece by piece and laid it all on the desk. Once the bag was empty she delved into the two pockets that were sewn into the sides. In them she found two separate bundles of letters tied together with string. With her heart full of dread she analysed them closely. There were about a dozen, ranging from small notes of just a few words to long letters of many lines, and they were not from her mother. Alana sank into the armchair and read every one.

It was clear that her father had loved Kitty his whole life. They had fallen in love as teenagers and that love had blossomed into the all-consuming love of adults. There were hasty notes arranging meetings at the Fairy Ring and gushing love letters sent to him in prison, reassuring him that she would wait until his release. From the dates on the letters it appeared that the years in America and Argentina were the only ones when Jack had truly belonged to her mother, but Alana wondered whether, even there, he had pined for his old love. Alana wished they had never come to Ballinakelly. From Kitty's recent notes she deduced that their affair had resumed not long after he had set foot on Irish soil and she felt sick to her stomach that he had betrayed her mother who was only ever sweet and kind and saw goodness in everyone.

One thing she knew for certain was that her mother must never know. Alana threw all the notes, barring the latest and most incriminating one, into the grate and struck a match. It took only a minute for them to be destroyed. She wished her father were alive so she could confront him and tell him what she thought of him. But she would confront Kitty instead, after the funeral. She had held onto one letter for that very meeting.

Kitty was standing at her bedroom window, staring disconsolately out to sea, when Alana walked slowly up the drive. Kitty's heart went out to the girl whose every laborious step revealed her pain and she hurried down the stairs to greet her.

But the young woman who confronted her on her doorstep was not the gentle creature Kitty knew Alana to be, but a fiend, consumed with rage and loathing and full of accusation. Alana pulled the letter from her pocket and held it out in her trembling hand.

'How could you!' she seethed. 'How could you carry on with my father when all the while my mother thought he was devoted to *her*? Have you no shame? You have a husband of your own and a daughter, what were you thinking?'

Robert was drawn out of his study by the scene unfolding on the doorstep. When he reached the door Alana shouted at him too. 'Did you know your wife was having an affair with my father?'

'Excuse me ...' he began, fully prepared to defend his wife. But he saw the letter and two red stains flourished on his cheeks. He took it and glanced at the familiar writing. Then he looked back at Alana with his jaw clenched and his gaze steady.

'Your wife has been sleeping with my father and it seems that everyone in Ballinakelly knows about it but us. I've burned the rest, a dozen of them, there were, and I hope to

God Mam doesn't find out because it will break her heart, truly it will. It will break her in half. She loved my father more than any other.' Alana glared at them both. 'Well, he's dead now, so you can no longer get your claws on him.' She put her hand to her mouth to suppress a sob. 'And if you think I'm going to marry a Deverill, you've got another think coming,' she added as she set off down the drive. 'The Deverills have bad blood and I want none of it!'

'Is this true?' Robert asked Kitty.

'Yes,' said Kitty, dropping her gaze to her feet. There was no point in lying. Robert was holding the letter to prove it.

'Come inside,' he said in a calm voice, which Kitty knew was only a prelude to the storm to come. 'We need to talk.'

Just as Alana was striding through the gate into the lane, JP was walking towards it. He saw her stricken face and hurried to comfort her, but Alana stiffened and pushed him away. 'Did you know about your sister and my father?' she rounded on him and JP was so shocked by the hard fury in her features that he was lost for words. 'Your sister Kitty and my father were having an affair,' she hissed. 'Did you know about it? Did everyone know about it but us?'

JP took her by the shoulders. 'What are you talking about?'

'I found evidence. Letters declaring their love.' She began to cry. 'Ask Kitty and she'll tell you herself.'

'I'm sure there's some mistake.'

'There's no mistake. It's true.'

'My darling . . .' he began, attempting to embrace her and confounded by her rejection.

'If Mam finds out about this it will destroy her. I'll never forgive Kitty for seducing my father for as long as I live.' She pushed him away again. 'And I cannot marry you.'

JP stared at her, bewildered by her coldness. 'You cannot blame me for my sister's misconduct,' he argued.

'I don't blame you, JP. But I won't have anything to do with the Deverills and I will not carry their cursed name.'

He reached out to take her hand but she snatched it away. 'Please, Alana, you're not thinking straight. You can't destroy our happiness—'

She cut him off briskly. 'I'm not destroying our happiness, Kitty is.'

'But you are letting her.'

'I have no choice. I have to go.' She marched past him and set off down the lane. JP stood there for a moment, hoping that she'd stop and reconsider, and when she did, that she'd be the warm and affectionate woman he loved. But she did not stop and she did not reconsider.

'I will let you go, Alana, but I will not accept your decision,' he cried after her, his heart breaking. 'I'll wait until you see reason, which you will, in time.'

'Wait all you like,' she shouted without a backwards glance. 'You will die an old man waiting.'

He watched her go and with it his happiness. Then he strode up the drive towards the house and Kitty.

At last the funeral was over and the Americans had left; it was safe for Jack to come out of hiding. He knew he'd have a lot of explaining to do and poor Badger would have to have a proper funeral, but now Jack would be able to live without always glancing over his shoulder, expecting his enemies to appear at any moment.

Hiding out in Badger's farmhouse knowing his family

thought him dead had been the hardest thing he had ever had to do in his life and he had almost quit, but Michael and Father Quinn had convinced him to carry through their plan. 'You can only pretend to die once,' Michael had told him. 'Those Yanks have to leave Ireland believing you're dead or they'll finish you off themselves. This is the only way.' So Jack had stuck it out in the hills, pacing the floor of Badger's kitchen, while Badger was buried in his stead.

Jack reached home and flung open the door. Emer was in the kitchen laying the table when she looked up to see him standing in the doorframe. She froze. Then she dropped the plates, which crashed on the floorboards and shattered, and stared at him in disbelief. 'Emer,' he said, taking off his cap. 'It's over. They'll not be after me now.' He moved towards her.

Emer's face went white, her knees buckled and she began to slowly sink to the ground. Jack hurried to catch her and she grabbed his jacket to stop herself from falling and let out a loud wail.

The three children ran into the kitchen to see what the commotion was about. They saw their father back from the dead, lifting their mother into his arms and embracing her tightly. Like a rag doll, she was, limp and sobbing. 'It's all right. I'm back,' he was saying, pressing his face against hers. 'I'm back and I'll not be leaving you again. Not ever. I'm sorry. I'm sorry.'

After a moment's hesitation Aileen and Liam cried out with joy and raced to wrap their arms around their beloved da, risen like Lazarus, but Alana hung back. Love was swelling in her chest, expanding into every corner of her being, chasing away the resentment, but she clung on to her fury with all her might, reluctant to give it up, determined not to forget what her father had done with Kitty.

Jack saw her standing there, ashen, and he mistook her pallor for shock. He assumed she would come to him in her own time. It was only fair to give her space to digest the fact that he had come back. 'I'm sorry,' he kept saying and Emer smiled through her tears and covered his wet face with kisses, understanding why he had done it and forgiving him.

Alana watched from the shadows. *She* would never forgive him. Not ever.

Chapter 27

So it was true. Kitty had been having an affair with Alana's father. Robert was devastated, Florence in tears and Kitty herself refused to come out of her bedroom. In despair JP went to see his father, who was the only person he felt he could talk to. He wished he'd died up there in his Spitfire rather than suffering as he was now. Hadn't Alana promised him he would never suffer in love again? 'We are cursed,' he told his father. 'The Deverills are cursed.'

'Don't believe that, JP,' said Bertie from his armchair in the library where he liked to sit after dinner. He had become quite the creature of habit in his old age. He reached for his tea, which he still would have preferred to be whiskey, but he was not going to throw himself into a bottle again, not if he wanted to win back Maud. 'We make our own luck and your sister has done a very good job of making *bad* luck. One learns, as one gets older, that one simply can't have everything in life. Some things have to be denied for the greater good. I learned too late and lost my darling Maud. Kitty will learn now, but what is the cost of that lesson, eh? The destruction of not only her own happiness but yours and Alana's too. It all boils down to selfishness in the end. If we were all less selfish the world would be a kinder place.'

'But Alana won't marry me, Father. I've lost her.'

'No, you haven't. She's young and impulsive. Give her time. Go to Dublin and get on with your education. Leave the dust to settle here. It will. It always does in the end.'

JP looked at his father sadly. 'Will Robert leave Kitty?'

In this respect Bertie wasn't so positive. 'I suspect he will, I'm afraid. I doubt he'll be able to carry on, knowing that Kitty's heart has always been elsewhere. He's a proud man.'

JP groaned and put his head in his hands. 'This is a disaster.'

'I dare say some good will come out of the ashes, but I can't see what that might be in their case.'

'We are cursed,' JP repeated. 'Ever since Barton Deverill built his castle on O'Leary land we've been cursed. Can't you see? The Deverills have reeled from one disaster to the next. When will it all end? When an O'Leary returns to claim the land? Will that ever happen?'

Bertie chuckled cynically. 'I don't believe in curses nor do I believe in prophecies. We make our own fortune. It's up to you to make yours, JP.'

Adeline watched JP leave. It was all very sad, this strange turn of events. She smiled on her son, for he had grown wise with the years. *Bertie will be believing in ghosts soon enough,* she thought with amusement. But JP had a point. The Deverills did seem to be cursed. Adeline had never thought beyond the part of Maggie's curse that condemned the Deverill heirs to live in limbo within the castle walls, but her husband's family did seem to suffer terrible misfortune. She watched Bertie pick up his book and start to read, but she knew he wasn't seeing the words. He was thinking of Maud and contemplating his own troubles. How much hard luck had he brought upon himself and how much had been imposed upon him? Had he not seduced Bridie Doyle, Michael Doyle would not have burned the castle to the ground. Had Michael not burned the castle to the ground, Kitty would not have sought him out in the farmhouse and he would not have violated her. *Every action has a consequence,* she pondered. *A small stone thrown into a pond sends out ripples that reach far and wide and every ripple touches something that affects something else and on it goes. Life is all about learning lessons and each adversity is designed to instruct. What will Kitty learn from this?*

It wasn't long before the whole of Ballinakelly had heard about Jack's sudden reappearance. The Weeping Women of Jerusalem deemed it a miracle and crossed themselves vigorously, but the truth about the Yanks and Jack's involvement with the Mafia soon dispatched any illusions of divine intervention.

Kitty's joy at the news was tempered by the realization that she could never go near him again. It was over; this time for good. And her heart buckled beneath the weight of so much sadness. She had lost everything.

Unable to withstand her family's fury and Robert's hurt Kitty packed her bag and took the boat to England to seek refuge with Celia. She settled into Deverill House, where Celia was living with her children and Boysie. In the drawing room over a large glass of wine and an openness that was not typical of her more secretive nature, Kitty told her cousin and her old friend about Jack, from the very beginning.

'Gracious, Kitty,' said Boysie, reeling from the drama he had known nothing about. 'What happens now?'

'Yes, what happens now?' Celia repeated, curled up into the corner of the sofa, riveted by every detail of Kitty's extraordinary life, which made her own seem ordinary by comparison.

'JP has gone to Dublin, blaming me for Alana's refusal to marry him. Florence has taken Robert's side and is at home comforting him. Robert is devastated. I don't know whether he'll leave me. I don't blame him if he does. I've ruined everything.' She looked helplessly at her friends. 'As for Jack, what can I say? I love him. Not being able to have him won't change that. Nothing will. But if I've learned anything from this terrible situation it's that one can't have everything one wants in life. Some things are out of reach and should remain so. I was only thinking of myself. But no man is an island. When I saw Alana's distraught face I realized how selfish I'd been. I'll never forget her unhappiness. It will stay with me forever.' Kitty put her hand to her heart and her eyes filled with tears. 'No precious moment with Jack is worth that. If I could rewind the clock I would save Alana from that moment and I'd save myself from seeing it. I'd let Jack go. I truly believe I would.'

Kitty wasn't surprised by JP's reaction to her affair with Alana's father and she wasn't surprised by Robert's fury, but she *was* surprised by her mother's understanding. Maud and Kitty had never understood one another, ever. When Kitty had taken it upon herself to raise JP, Maud had all but disowned her. Now she turned up at Deverill House unannounced and full of compassion. What had life taught *her* for this sudden change of heart to take place? Kitty wondered as she followed her into the garden.

Maud suggested she and Kitty sit on the bench. It was early autumn and still warm and the pink hydrangeas were only just beginning to turn brown. Since losing Harry Maud had aged considerably. Her skin sagged around the mouth where bitterness had been allowed to fester and her hands betrayed her age with a tangle of blue veins and sprinkling of brown spots. Her eyes, however, were that piercing, icy blue that had won her admirers all through her life, yet they seemed to have softened slightly, as if suffering had instilled some empathy.

'Bertie has told me the whole sorry story,' Maud said once they were sitting down. 'I had no idea you were such a dark horse, Kitty.' She wrapped her shawl around her shoulders, not because she was cold, but because she felt awkward being a mother to this child who had always made her feel deficient and foolish. 'I had an affair, Kitty.'

'*You* had an affair?' Kitty exclaimed. It shouldn't have surprised her. After all, she had discovered her father making love to Grace Rowan-Hampton when she was a child, so why should her mother have been any different? Perhaps everyone was at it.

'I loved a man, a friend of your father's, and I loved him for years.'

'Why did it end?'

'Because I got pregnant with you.' She looked at Kitty and smiled apologetically. 'I think I probably blamed you for that, although now, in my dotage, I realize that he probably seized the opportunity to end it. You weren't to be blamed, how could you be?'

'You were devastated, naturally.'

'I was. Your father was carrying on with any pretty face that presented itself, but while I had Eddie, I was content. When he left me, I had to suffer your father's affairs without anyone to look after *me*.'

'Whatever became of him?'

'Eddie? Oh, he married and had children and moved to India. The point is, Kitty, I know what forbidden love feels like and so I understand what you're going through. I haven't been a good mother. In fact, I admit that I haven't been much of a mother to you at all. I regret that.'

'Don't regret, Mother. I wasn't an easy child.'

'No, you weren't easy, but I should have been less selfish.' Kitty was stunned by her mother's candour. Maud had only ever thought of herself. Kitty wondered what had inspired her to change. 'So, what are you going to do now?' Maud asked.

'I'm going to hide here and hope that Robert forgives me. I know that is asking too much. I've done a terrible thing and I regret hurting him. He's a good man and he doesn't deserve a wife like me.'

'I know you're comfortable here with Celia, you two have always been close, but you're welcome to come and live with me. The door is open should you wish to step through it.'

'Thank you,' Kitty replied politely, although the idea of living with Maud was not an appealing one.

'Tell me about your father. How is he?'

Kitty told her mother that her father had settled into a comfortable routine and found contentment at last, living in the Hunting Lodge and taking consolation from his memories. 'Losing Harry has been unbearable for all of us,' said Maud. 'I understand why Beatrice dived beneath the blankets and refused to see anyone after Digby died. That's how I felt after Harry was killed. Utter despair. Blackness. A void that you know will never be filled because Harry was irreplaceable.' Maud reached out and took Kitty's hand. Kitty did not resist, although her mother's touch felt very odd. 'I couldn't bear to lose you or Victoria or Elspeth.

I couldn't bear to lose Bertie, either. I don't think my heart could take any more loss. What I'm trying to say, and badly at that, is how much I regret the years we have drifted. You're forty-five now and I'm at an unspeakable age, and I look back and kick myself for the wasted years.'

'Nothing is wasted if you learn from your mistakes,' said Kitty. 'And mistakes have been made by all of us. None of us is blameless. You put up with a great deal: Papa's affair with the maid and the illegitimate child he raised as his own. You had every right to be appalled.'

'What is JP like?' Maud asked. 'Is he like Bertie?'

'Very,' Kitty replied. 'He's a Deverill through and through.'

Maud smiled wistfully and Kitty frowned. If Maud was now smiling at the thought of JP, something cataclysmic was taking place.

And at last Maud revealed what it was.

'Arthur has asked me to marry him,' she said. 'He's asked me to divorce Bertie and to marry *him.*'

Kitty's heart sank for her father, who still held a torch for Maud and who still harboured a fragile hope that she would one day go back to him. 'Have you told Papa?' Kitty asked.

'Not yet.'

'When are you going to tell him?'

'Soon.'

'He'll be very sad.'

'No he won't,' said Maud with certainty.

'Oh, he will.'

'Not when I tell him I'm coming home.'

Kitty gasped. She didn't think she was capable of happiness under the circumstances, but this made her deadbeat heart splutter back to life. 'You're not going to marry Arthur?'

'How can I marry Arthur when I love Bertie,' said Maud, and Kitty was sure that she could see her mother's eyes glistening with tears. 'It's taken me a very long time to know myself, but now I do, I'm going to ask Bertie if he'll take me back.'

'He *will* take you back. I know he will,' said Kitty, laughing. 'Oh Mama, that's the best news I've heard in such a long time.'

'And you need some good news,' Maud said, squeezing her daughter's hand.

'We all do,' Kitty added. 'But no one deserves it more than Papa.'

Martha had been in London for six weeks, working at the American Embassy, when she received a letter from Countess di Marcantonio. It was written on ivory-coloured paper with three bees embossed at the top in gold and black. In neat, deliberate handwriting she thanked Martha for her letter and invited her to stay at the castle so that they could discuss her plans in more detail. *I'm just the right person to approach about this,* she wrote. *I'm so pleased that you felt you could write to me. You must come at once so we can start the process. Your job sounds very interesting in London, but I fear it is not conducive to your goal. You must stay with me for as long as you need to.*

Martha was elated. She was more determined than ever to change her life radically and she knew exactly what she wanted to do. The fact that the Countess had invited her to stay in the castle was more than she had hoped. She gave in her notice at the Embassy and bought a passage to Queenstown.

Ireland was as beautiful as it had been when Martha had left it just before the war. A thin mist hung over the coastline as the boat approached the harbour. The sun shone through it causing the little particles of water to sparkle like glitter. She watched in awe and delight as the boat motored into its midst and she was at once enveloped in the magic of it.

It had been almost seven years since she had arrived with her heart full of anticipation and excitement at the thought of seeing JP. Seven years since she had left with her heart in pieces. But she had sought comfort in God and He had delivered. Now Martha felt a serenity she hadn't felt before, as if the wings of God's angels were wrapping themselves around her, protecting her from the ghosts of the past. She concentrated on the beauty of the landscape, on the soft green hills and the clean, damp air and let the mysticism that runs through Ireland like deep underground rivulets carry away the memory of her pain. She was returning to Ballinakelly but, with God's help, she would be impervious to the emotions she had left there.

The Countess had sent her chauffeur to pick Martha up at the port. He waited beside her shiny green car in a pristine uniform complete with gloves and cap. The drive was comfortable and Martha gazed out of the window with her spirits high on the excitement of being once again in the country which, in spite of the sorrow she had suffered there, had not lost its power to enchant.

As the car motored up the drive, between the lustrous rhododendron bushes, Martha thought of Lord Deverill, her real father, who had once lived in this castle. It seemed strange to think that she had a connection to this place – that her parents had conceived her here. How different might her life have been had her mother raised her in Ballinakelly. She gazed at the formidable stone walls, towers and turrets, chimneys and ramparts of Castle Deverill and marvelled at the long history of this once powerful family of which she was part.

When she arrived she found the Countess much changed. She seemed smaller than she had been that morning in the milliner's, and she wore black from head to toe, which Martha later discovered was due to the recent death of her husband. Bridie embraced her like an old friend, asking her dozens of questions as she led her upstairs to a sumptuous bedroom overlooking a large box garden below. While a maid unpacked her bag Bridie sat with her in her little upstairs sitting room where a fire burned heartily in the grate and tea was served on a silver tray. She introduced Martha to her sister-in-law Rosetta, who was as fat as lard but as sweet as summer fruit, and the three women talked without pause as if they had known each other forever.

'I have arranged for Father Quinn to come to the castle tomorrow at eleven,' said Bridie. 'I have told him about you and he is ready to start.'

'That's wonderful news,' said Martha. 'I'm so grateful to you, Countess, for your kindness.'

'Please, call me Bridie. That title has never suited me.'

'Bridie then,' said Martha. 'You are very kind to go to so much trouble.'

'It is no trouble at all, is it, Rosetta?'

'Bridie needs a project,' said Rosetta, as if she were talking about a restless child. 'Even before Cesare passed away she was bored.'

'You see, when I lived in America there was so much to do. There were so many parties and life was such fun. Here, it's so quiet. I tried to entertain Cesare, but Ballinakelly was too small for such a larger-than-life character.' Bridie's voice faltered then. 'I wish you could have met my husband. He was the most wonderful man. A true gem and I was lucky to have found him. I miss him every day, but thank the Lord that I had so many happy years with him. Truly, there is no man alive who can compare to my darling Cesare.'

Rosetta smiled stiffly. 'He was unique,' she said tightly.

'But now you are here, Martha, and I am in the fortunate position of being able to help you. My life has been an extraordinary adventure. I started here as a child born into poverty and made my way to America where I made a fortune. But I have never lost my faith. Indeed, my faith has been the one thing that has supported me through all the difficult times, and there have been many, many, believe me. God has never forsaken me. You said in your letter that God has shone His light into your dark and troubled soul and shown you the way. I have been there, Martha. I have been to very dark and troubled places and God has always shown me the light. So, I want to help you convert to Catholicism, which, as you told me in your letter, is the religion of your mother's family, the Tobins. And I want to help you achieve your ultimate goal.'

Martha was close to tears at Bridie's moving speech. She put her hand on her heart and sighed. 'You will really do this for me?' she asked.

'Of course. You see, I know the perfect convent for you.' Bridie couldn't imagine why she had suddenly decided to mention the convent where she had suffered such unhappiness. But it just felt right to do so.

'You do?' said Martha.

'Yes, it is the Convent of Our Lady Queen of Heaven in Dublin.'

Martha stared at Bridie in wonder, for that was the very convent where she was born and where she had later gone in search of her mother. At that extraordinary coincidence, she began to weep.

'Have I upset you?' Bridie asked, concerned. She looked at Rosetta who shrugged.

Martha shook her head. 'No, I'm just so touched. It feels like Fate. It feels like I'm *meant* to be here, with you. It feels like God Himself has led me to you.'

Bridie smiled with satisfaction. 'He *has* led you to me, Martha. And I am ready to do His work and help you become a nun.'

Chapter 28

It was a cold November afternoon in Ballinakelly but the skies were clear and the light was golden as the sun sank slowly behind the trees, casting long shadows across the damp ground. Bertie was in the garden talking to Mr Flynn the gardener, casting his eyes in dismay over the untidy shrubs and elder, which seemed to have taken over every border, and wondering whether Mr Flynn did any work at all besides chopping logs and laying them in neat piles in the barn, which had become something of an obsession. Bertie had grown benign in his old age and didn't reprimand the man, after all, *he* didn't show much interest in the garden so he couldn't really expect his gardener to be inspired. *If only Maud were here,* he thought. *She'd enjoy creating a beautiful garden and Mr Flynn would be motivated to do a little more than chop logs.*

Bertie's two big wolfhounds, who accompanied him everywhere, raised their heads and pricked their ears. 'Well, who's that?' Bertie asked with a good-natured chuckle. He'd already taken them on a long walk over the hills and shot a rabbit for his dinner. 'I think what's needed is a lot of cutting back,' said Bertie, rubbing his chin. The gardener nodded and frowned. It was a big job for one man. The dogs began to bark and the rumbling sound of a car grew louder.

It was a cab. Bertie wasn't expecting anyone. 'That'll be all, Mr Flynn,' he said, putting his hands in his coat pockets and heading off towards the front of the house. 'Who's that then?' he asked the dogs again who, excited by their master's tone of voice, shot off at a run.

The car was just drawing up when Bertie reached it. The cabbie got out and went to open the passenger door. Bertie watched as one elegant ankle in a shiny black court shoe stepped out onto the gravel. 'Good Lord!' he gasped. 'It can't be!' But it was.

'Hello, Bertie,' said Maud, and the smile she gave him lifted his heart higher than it had been for a very long time.

'Maud. Why the devil didn't you telephone?'

'I wanted to tell you to your face, not down a wire,' she said, straightening her hat, which didn't need straightening. As usual, everything about Maud's appearance was flawless.

Bertie walked up to her, his face flushing. 'What did you want to tell me?' He noticed the cabbie putting five suitcases onto the steps. 'Maud? What's going on?'

'I've come home,' she said with a sigh.

'You mean . . . ?'

She looked at him and her eyes betrayed her uncertainty. 'If you'll have me, of course.'

Bertie beamed. 'Oh Maud! You've made me the happiest man alive!'

Then she gave him the sort of smile for which she had once been celebrated, the sort of smile men had gone to great lengths to deserve, the sort of smile she hadn't given Bertie in forty years. He took her hand and pressed it to his lips. 'I promise you, Maud, that everything will be different now. I will love you and value you and never let you down. I have changed.'

'And I have changed too,' said Maud.

Their attention was at once diverted by the cabbie, who was now standing by the car, looking at them uncomfortably. 'Oh, I see, of course,' said Bertie, putting his hand in his pocket. He grinned as Maud walked into the house. *She hasn't changed that much*, he thought joyfully as he handed the cabbie his fare.

Jack felt as if he had been born again. With this new beginning came the gift of choice: the chance to change for the better, to choose right over wrong. With this fresh start came a renewed and heightened perception. He not only felt different on the inside but the world looked different on the outside as well. The hills were greener and more vibrant, the sea a deeper shade of blue and Emer, his precious and beloved Emer, radiated a sublime beauty. Jack's heart overflowed with gratitude for all the small things he had previously taken for granted. He was grateful for his family, his home and the beautiful country of his birth. He needed nothing more and the idea that he had put it all in jeopardy for the love of another woman now appalled him. Kitty was part of him, there was no denying it, but a part of his youth and there she must stay.

Jack's love for his wife intensified in the light of her forgiveness. She didn't berate him for putting them through such agonies and she didn't torment him with tales of their despair. She let the matter go altogether and stood firmly in the present, treasuring as he did their newfound freedom from fear and uncertainty and their appreciation of each other. Now, at last, they could finally live in peace.

Liam and Aileen quickly forgot the unhappy episode as they accompanied their father on his visits around the county. Life swiftly returned to normal and the memory faded. For Alana, however, it was an entirely different matter. She could not forget the love letters she had found in his bag.

Jack assumed that his eldest child's resentment was due to the misery he had put her through. He believed she lacked her mother's maturity, so he did not expect forgiveness to come easily, and she lacked her siblings' naïvety, which enabled them to accept so readily and move on. He resolved to give her time.

It wasn't until he noticed the absence of Kitty's letters in his veterinary bag that the truth was finally revealed. He hadn't realized they were missing because he hadn't gone looking for them. It was only after waking up in the middle of the night with the thought of what those letters could potentially do that he crept downstairs to find them and destroy them. He was horrified to discover that they weren't there. Of course he had only kept some of them in his bag and was relieved to find the other bundles where he had hidden them. After burning those he realized that Alana must have found the ones in his bag. If Emer had come across them would she have welcomed him back so warmly? If Alana hadn't, would she resent him so? He couldn't imagine what had motivated her to go searching in his veterinary bag and he deeply regretted having kept such incriminating evidence there; but so it was and he had to somehow put it right.

Now he knew the reason for Alana's unhappiness he understood why she had broken off her engagement to JP Deverill and why she had not confided in her mother, and he was wracked with guilt. It all made sense. Alana was suffering alone and he couldn't allow it to go on.

He found her at the Fairy Ring. He knew she'd be there.

It was no longer his and Kitty's special place; it was Alana and JP's.

It was late afternoon and the winter sun was low in the sky, casting long, eerie shadows across the damp grass at the foot of the megaliths. There was a brisk wind blowing in off the water and below the waves crashed loudly against the rocks. Alana was surprised to see her father. She'd been gazing out to sea, thinking about JP and trying to find a way through her unhappiness. Jack was the last person she expected to see, and the last person she *wanted* to see. She folded her arms defensively and turned her face back into the wind.

'We need to talk,' he said, standing beside her. Alana said nothing. 'You found the letters, didn't you?' he continued. She looked at him in surprise and his suspicions were confirmed. 'I thought so,' he said. She chewed her lip, not knowing what to say. He sighed and thrust his hands into his coat pockets. 'I'm not going to deny that Kitty and I loved each other—'

'Then don't,' Alana snapped. 'I don't want to hear your excuses.'

'But it's over. I've been an eejit, Alana, and I regret it more than I can say. I made a mistake. A massive mistake.' He turned to face her and Alana tried hard to keep her gaze trained on the horizon so as not to weaken. She was determined to make him suffer for his infidelity, to make him suffer for the distress he'd caused *her*, even though his remorse might be sincere and heartfelt. 'When I was hiding out at Badger's I had a lot of time to think,' he went on. 'I realized then that Kitty was nothing more than nostalgia. It was your mother who meant the world to me. I didn't think of Kitty grieving at the news of my death, but I thought of Emer and you and Liam and Aileen, and it tormented me. It drove me to madness. I knew then that what I had with Kitty was not real, that I had been selfish and self-indulgent. I resolved to change and I have, Alana. I see the world with different eyes now. I thank God for your mother, my wife. I know I don't deserve her. I don't expect you to forgive me, but I hope at least you'll understand.'

Alana looked at him steadily. 'Mam must never know,' she said. 'You must never tell her. Promise me you'll never tell her. It will break her heart.'

Jack nodded and Alana had to turn away again because it hurt her to see his eyes so full of regret, regret that was genuine. 'I hate to ask you to harbour a secret such as this,' he said. 'You're too young to be burdened with my sin.'

'I will do it for Mam,' she replied tightly.

'And what about you? JP played no part in this. He is as innocent as you are.'

'He's a Deverill,' she retorted. 'They're bad blood. You said so yourself.'

'Don't blame him for Kitty's wrongdoing, Alana. Don't cut off your nose to spite your face. You and he deserve to be happy.'

'I don't want anything to do with that family.'

'I don't imagine JP has declared that he'll have nothing to do with an O'Leary. He has just as much right as you to resent us. I doubt he does though. I think he loves you for you. You should return him the same courtesy and love him for himself.' Alana did not yield. 'Think about it,' he added. Then he walked away.

Alana's jaw stiffened. Only her hair gave in to the wind. She felt no better for having talked with her father. She thought of her poor, betrayed mother and felt just as miserable as she had before.

*

Robert Trench had never suspected his wife of infidelity. He had never had any cause. Kitty had always been loving, attentive and seemingly content with her life. Sure, there had been times when she had been distracted, like when Bridie Doyle bought the castle, and he had had to have words, but he'd never doubted their unity as a couple. Now he realized that their marriage hadn't been the only relationship she had committed to over the years. He had won her hand but Jack O'Leary had long ago won her heart, years, in fact, before Robert had even set foot in the White House. Their bond had been forged over decades of shared experience, strengthened by conspiracy and sealed by the constant intervention of Fate that thwarted them at every turn. Robert believed it was the fact that they could never have each other that made their longing so intense.

After Alana had revealed Kitty's love letters Kitty had confessed everything. Robert wondered whether she was perhaps a little relieved to share it with him, for as she had recounted her story, from their childhood friendship to their involvement in the War of Independence and later their plan to run off to America and start a new life together with JP, Robert saw the passion unconcealed in her eyes as if the fire of her love for this man could not be doused even by the shame of exposure. It had wounded him deeply.

Now Kitty had run off to London to lick her wounds with her cousin Celia while Robert decided what to do. He wasn't a fool. He knew that she loved him in her own way. He was well aware that it was possible to love more than one person at a time – he'd written about that in one of his novels, after all – but it was the fact that she had given into that forbidden love and broken her marriage vows that upset him the most. He was of the belief that once a person committed to another it was only right that they should honour that commitment, and in Kitty's case, sacrifice a love they couldn't have. Not only had she betrayed her husband, she had let her daughter down and JP as well. She had torn out not only their hearts but the heart of her family. He wouldn't have believed her capable of such selfishness. That wasn't the behaviour of the woman he had married. How could he have shared a bed with her for so long and never really known her? So, what was he to do?

Robert didn't believe in divorce and he didn't believe in giving in or giving up. Jack was back from the dead. What was to stop their affair from resuming? Robert certainly was not prepared to give Kitty what she wanted after she had behaved so abysmally. He wanted her to pay for the suffering she had caused *him*. Yet beneath the hurt and the desire for revenge, in the secret recesses of his soul, he wanted her to love him with the ardour with which she loved Jack.

Robert sat in the garden eating a sandwich and watched the crows pecking at the earth. It had rained for most of the day and the skies were heavy and grey, and yet there was something intrinsically beautiful about the place: even in the dullest light the hills radiated with a vibrant, spiritual energy. He loved Ireland and he loved his family. Florence meant the world to him and JP was like a son. He loved Kitty too. He shook his head and tossed a piece of bread at the crows. *Goddamn it*, he thought, *I love Kitty too.*

Mrs Maddox was amazed when Martha knocked on her door. She hadn't seen Martha since before the war and her letters, which had at first arrived monthly, had dwindled to a few a year and short ones at that. She had often wondered how Martha was and whether she had at last found happiness.

Then she had received a letter only a few weeks ago, sent from London, informing her that Martha was planning on coming to Ireland. Mrs Maddox had been both surprised and elated. But Martha hadn't been more specific about her timing. The sight of the young woman now standing on her doorstep took her breath away.

'Oh, I missed you, Goodwin!' Martha gushed, embracing her old nanny fiercely. The two women held each other and the years of separation melted away in the warmth of their enduring affection. Martha looked at the older woman with tenderness. 'You've changed, Goodwin. You've grown younger and plumper. Marriage suits you.'

Mrs Maddox smiled. 'Well, I have to admit I'm very happy. And what about you? What are you doing here? Why didn't you tell me you were coming?' Martha grinned secretively. 'You're not going to tell me on the doorstep, I don't suppose,' Mrs Maddox added. 'Come inside then and I'll ask Molly to make a nice pot of tea. John is out so we have the house to ourselves.'

The house was a pretty rectory made of grey stone with a grey-tiled roof and large windows placed symmetrically either side of the front door and on the floor above. It looked much like Reverend Maddox, Martha thought, cheerful and smiling, if a little pleased with itself.

Mrs Maddox showed Martha into a square sitting room where a turf fire burned beneath a mantelpiece of knick-knacks and black-and-white photographs in ornate frames. Above was a large mirror where Martha now checked herself. She couldn't help but notice that she had changed too. She looked older and wiser, a little gaunt in the face perhaps, but nothing that Irish potatoes wouldn't fill out. She wondered whether Goodwin would notice too.

Mrs Maddox asked Molly to bring them tea and porter cake. 'The Irish love porter cake,' she said, then she laughed remembering Martha's comment about her fuller figure. 'I suppose I eat much too much of it.'

'Life is good,' said Martha.

'Oh, it is,' Mrs Maddox replied. 'It really is. To think I thought I would die alone.'

'It is funny how life can suddenly turn on its head in the blink of an eye.'

'Well, it did that night I found John again.'

'I'm happy for you, Goodwin. I really am.'

'Enough about me. Tell me about you. Your parents? Are they well?' At the mention of Larry and Pam Wallace Mrs Maddox's face lost its gaiety and she looked at Martha anxiously. 'You didn't give much away in your letters.'

Martha shrugged. 'Life went back to normal very quickly,' she told her. 'Of course, it could never really go back. But I never told them what I'd found here. I only shared it with my grandmother and only recently. I didn't feel I could tell my parents. I didn't want to hurt them and I didn't want to relive it. It was too painful.'

'So, you just swept the entire episode under the carpet?'

'I suppose I did.'

'And they didn't ask?'

'They told me they loved me and made every effort to make up for having kept it secret.'

'And Edith?'

'She was young. She didn't know any better. But I'm still struggling to forgive Joan, Goodwin. That's the truth. I understand why my parents kept it quiet, but I fail to understand why Joan told Edith. I'm not a good person, but I'm trying to be.'

'My dear Martha, you have every right to be hurt and angry—' Mrs Maddox began but Martha cut her off.

'No, I'm trying to walk in God's light, Goodwin. I need to learn to forgive.'

Mrs Maddox frowned. The maid brought in the tray and they paused their conversation while she put it on the table and poured the tea. When at last she left, Mrs Maddox put her fine china cup to her lips and looked at Martha steadily. Something was different about her, besides ageing seven years, but she couldn't work out what it was. 'My dear, where are you staying?'

'At the castle. The Countess invited me.'

Mrs Maddox was surprised. 'Really? She just invited you and you came all the way from America?'

Martha laughed. Goodwin did seem a little put out. 'No, I came to work at the American Embassy in London, which Daddy arranged for me, but I wrote to the Countess asking for her help.'

'With what?' Mrs Maddox asked, intrigued.

'With my conversion to Catholicism,' Martha replied.

Mrs Maddox put down her teacup. 'You're converting to Catholicism?'

'Yes, it was my mother's religion, after all.' Mrs Maddox wasn't sure which mother she was talking about, but she could safely assume that both had been Catholic.

'Why would you want to do that? It's the same God, after all.'

'Because I have found my calling.'

Mrs Maddox now looked a little afraid. 'Your calling?'

'Yes, God has called me and I am going to become a nun.'

There was a long and heavy pause. Martha sipped her tea and Mrs Maddox struggled to find the words. Martha watched her old nanny's face flush and smiled sympatheti-cally. 'I know this has come as a shock to you, Goodwin, but I've had years to prepare myself. I know I'm doing the right thing. I'm following my heart.'

'Is it because JP broke it?'

'No,' Martha stated firmly. 'I won't pretend JP wasn't the catalyst. I should thank him, really. If it wasn't for him I would never have found my true vocation.'

'But you'll never marry and have children.'

'*You* never had children, Goodwin, and yet you were happy, weren't you?'

'I'm happy now with the man I love. I would have adored to have children. It's what we're made for. But it wasn't to be. Now I have John, I'm complete. I want that for you, Martha.'

'But I don't want it for myself.'

'So, how do you become a nun?'

'It will take years, but Bridie is helping me. She arranged for me to meet Father Quinn, who is supervising my con-version. When I am Catholic I'll go to Dublin and with the Countess's recommendation I will start the process at the Convent of Our Lady Queen of Heaven.'

'The one where you were born?' Mrs Maddox asked in surprise.

'Yes, isn't that extraordinary! Bridie has connections there and can recommend me. You see,' Martha said with satisfac-tion. 'God works in mysterious ways.'

'And I suppose the Countess will finance you?' said Mrs Maddox and her tone betrayed her disapproval. She corrected it swiftly by adding, 'She's a very generous woman. She gave money to a charity of mine and a considerable amount at that. One cannot say that she's not generous.'

'I'm going to work, Goodwin. I'm going to teach the

children. Father Quinn is going to arrange for me to help in the school.'

'I don't imagine you'll get paid as much as you did at the Embassy.'

'I'll be rich in satisfaction,' Martha told her. 'And I'll keep Bridie company. I think she's lonely.'

'Really? How sad,' Goodwin sighed. Loneliness was a terrible thing.

'She lives in that enormous place with her sister-in-law and brother and they have lots of children, but I feel she's desperate to be loved. There's something rather pathetic about her which makes me want to be kind to her. I think she's suffered a lot.'

'You know, she lost her husband in the most dreadful way not that long ago. He was murdered and found buried in the sand up to his neck. It was awful.'

'That's terrible. Who did it?'

'They never found out, but rumour has it that he was running off with O'Donovan's daughter.'

'Rumours are often false,' said Martha.

'Of course, I don't listen to rumour, but one can't help hearing it. Ballinakelly is a small town. But that isn't all. Let me tell you about Kitty . . .' Mrs Maddox was relieved to be able to change the subject and talk about something other than Martha's desire to become a nun. She hoped the girl would realize her folly, or meet a delightful man and fall in love. That would put an end to her silly idea. Really, the way to get over heartbreak was *not* to become a nun!

Chapter 29

On the anniversary of Cesare's death Bridie took Martha to the church of All Saints to visit his grave. It was a bright summer's morning. Birds twittered playfully in the trees, whose delicate green leaves were now fully unfurled, and the sun bathed the graveyard in its jubilant light. Cesare's grave was at the far end in the shade of a large horse chestnut tree. They placed flowers at his headstone and Bridie said a few words of prayer with her head bowed and her eyes closed. Martha did the same and prayed for the man she had never met who had died in such a horrible way and asked God to take care of his soul. It was tranquil there among the dead and she inhaled the scent of cut grass and flowers and felt the serenity of the place infuse her spirit with peace. Since she had arrived in Ballinakelly she had felt a surprising sense of belonging, as if she really had found her roots at last. She didn't know what to make of it, because she had assumed that any such feeling had been connected to JP. Now she was here without JP and still the place appealed to her on a deep, unconscious level. It just felt right.

Martha thought of Adeline often. She felt her presence everywhere, as if she was in the sunshine and the rain, her voice brought to her in whispers on the wind. Most of all she felt her in the castle. Sometimes the feeling was so strong it was as if she was standing right beside her, only Martha couldn't see her. How she wished she could. Now she felt her again, here in this graveyard, and there was something insistent about her, as if she was willing Martha to do something, but Martha couldn't work out what. She looked at Bridie, her head bowed and her hands clasped as she remembered her dead husband, and Martha's heart swelled with compassion.

'I loved him in spite of his faults,' said Bridie when her prayers were done. 'He was vain and proud and pleasure-seeking, but one cannot choose who one falls in love with. The heart doesn't listen to the head, but works on its own and is often wilful, at least mine was. But I won't give it away again.' She put her hand on her chest and smiled at Martha. Bridie had never acknowledged Cesare's shortcomings to anyone, not even to Rosetta, but she felt she could tell Martha anything and that she would not judge her, or think less of her husband. 'I don't believe there's a man alive worthy of my heart like Cesare was,' she added softly.

'I don't think a woman needs a man to be happy,' said Martha.

'Indeed, I shall be very happy living out my widowhood here in the place where I grew up. But you're young, Martha, and your heart is tender. You must be very certain that you don't need a man's love to give up the possibility of it forever.'

'I am certain, Bridie,' she replied firmly. She hesitated and frowned and a shadow of hurt darkened her face. 'I loved a man once but I couldn't have him,' she said quietly. Bridie knew of whom Martha was speaking, but she revealed nothing of what Mrs Maddox had told her. 'I'll never love another, I'm sure of that,' Martha continued. 'I believe one has to know that kind of love in order to reject it, so loving JP taught me a valuable lesson and through my suffering I heard God's calling.'

Bridie had to pretend this was a revelation. 'You loved JP Deverill?' she asked.

'I did.' Martha sighed. She was surprised at how easy it was to share her feelings with Bridie. 'He was my first love and my last. It wasn't to be.'

Bridie took her hand and held it fiercely. 'I'm so sorry,' she said with feeling. She wondered whether JP was the reason why the two of them had bonded so swiftly: they both loved him, and, although in very different ways, they had both been rejected by him. 'I know what it feels like to love someone you cannot have.' Bridie caught herself before she revealed too much. Yet the emotion bubbled into her chest. 'I have suffered terribly because of that.'

Martha recognized the pain in Bridie's eyes, for she had seen it too many times in her own. Impulsively, she put her arms around her. Bridie opened her heart and allowed the grief to trickle out slowly and quietly as Martha held her close. It felt good to cry and it felt right to do it in Martha's embrace. Martha had come into her life like an angel and swiftly banished the loneliness. Bridie silently thanked God for His intervention. Surely He had brought Martha to her for that very reason.

Martha had shared her story with her grandmother, now she wanted to share it with Bridie. She knew Bridie would understand. She knew she wouldn't be appalled or horrified. She trusted that Bridie would be compassionate and kind. But now was not the time. It was a long story and Martha didn't feel strong enough to tell it. She wasn't sure Bridie was strong enough to hear it. Bridie was remembering her husband and Martha did not want to distract her from that. The moment would come and then she would unburden her heart to Bridie.

Martha now realized, as she rested her head on Bridie's shoulder, that for all her beauty and glamour Grace Rowan-Hampton had fallen short of the mother Martha had longed for her to be.

If my mother had lived, Martha thought, closing her eyes and speaking silently to Bridie, *I'd like her to have been just like* you.

Adeline was moved. She had never given much thought to Bridie Doyle, and she felt sorry for that. If death had taught her anything it was that love is the only thing that truly matters. Martha was not just a Deverill, she was a Doyle too and Adeline had been wilfully blind to that fact. It was right, no, it was *imperative*, Adeline thought resolutely, that Bridie should know the truth; that her daughter hadn't died at birth but was beside her now, as ignorant of their relationship as Bridie was. Adeline had hinted and urged as much as she could from where she was and she knew that Martha was sensing her influence, but she could do no more than that. It was deeply frustrating. She hoped that Martha would confide in Bridie eventually. Of course such knowledge would really put the cat among the pigeons, and put Kitty and Bertie in a very difficult position, but it could not be helped. The pigeons would all settle in the end, Adeline was sure of that. *Oh what an unnecessary mess we humans make of our lives!* she thought.

Kitty dreaded returning to Ballinakelly. She hadn't spoken to Robert or Florence since she had left and JP had run off to Dublin without a backwards glance. If she had known what devastation her love for Jack would cause she would have nipped it in the bud years ago. She was not proud of herself, but what could she do? She couldn't hide out with Celia and Boysie forever. She loved her daughter and she loved Robert (although she hadn't done a very good job in convincing him of that) and she loved JP. It pained her to have hurt them and it pained her more to have lost them. There was only one thing to do and that was to ask for their forgiveness.

Kitty had spent Christmas at Deverill Rising with Beatrice, Celia, Leona and Vivien and their families. Boysie came too, now divorced from Deirdre, who, as it turned out, had been enjoying an affair of her own and was only too happy to be set free. Beatrice, who had been a virtual recluse since Digby died, was drawn out into the light by Celia and Boysie, whose ebullience was infectious. Even Leona and Vivien joined in the games Boysie made them all play. If it hadn't been for Kitty's misery it would have been the very best Christmas.

Besides Celia, the one person who gave Kitty her total support was Maud. Installed once again in the Hunting Lodge, which had been revived with a good deal of plaster and a fresh coat of paint, Maud, who now lived in blissful harmony with the husband she had once despised, telephoned Kitty every few days. Kitty wasn't sure whether their relationship was improved because Kitty *needed* her or because Maud was happy. It was certainly enhanced by the fact that Maud was a voice down the wire rather than a physical presence – that way their friendship was allowed to develop slowly. Kitty shared her feelings with her mother and for the first time in her life her mother listened.

Now Kitty arrived back in Ballinakelly full of dread. She took a cab from the station to her home, and asked the cabbie to drop her at the gate. She stood a while at the bottom of the hill looking up at the house she had lived in for over twenty years and wondered whether she'd ever live there again. She envisaged JP as a little boy, running towards her with his arms outstretched, and Florence as a small girl making daisy chains on the lawn. Then she imagined Robert, laughing at the window as he watched them frolic on the grass. They had been happy times. Even when she had pined for Jack, her family had always given her joy.

Kitty remembered her grandmother Adeline telling her that she was a child of the planet Mars on account of having been born on the ninth day of the ninth month and that her life would be full of conflict. Well, she didn't want to be a child of Mars any longer. She wanted to be a child of peace and she wanted her life to be full of harmony. She unhinged the gate and walked through it. With a heavy tread she made her way up the drive towards the house.

Kitty was so busy looking at her shoes that she didn't notice Florence who had seen her from the window and was now hurrying towards her. She heard the footsteps and raised her eyes. Florence was approaching with a serious look on her face. Kitty stopped. She didn't have the energy or the will to fight. She put down her bag and waited for her daughter to throw accusations at her, knowing that she would accept them whatever they were. But Florence didn't. She put her arms around her astonished mother with a sob. Neither said a word. They didn't have to. Florence knew her mother was sorry and Kitty knew she was forgiven.

It wasn't as easy with Robert.

Robert's heart had hardened towards his wife. Hurt had wrapped itself around it like weeds around a flower and sti-fled the love inside it. Yet he didn't ask for a divorce and he didn't request that she leave. 'We are man and wife,' he said. '*Those whom God hath joined together let no man put asunder,*' he added, quoting from their marriage service. Kitty's relief was intense. It wasn't ideal but it was better than what she deserved.

'Give Papa time,' Florence told her gently. 'He may yet forgive you.'

'And JP?' Kitty asked sadly.

Florence shook her head. 'I don't know. I think that all depends on Alana.'

Yet Alana's heart had hardened too. She received JP's letters but she put them unopened into a drawer.

As the months went by unhappiness became a way of life for Alana. She barely noticed it any longer because it became so much part of her. She forgot how to laugh and she forgot how to love. She went through her days mechanically and as she laid her head down at night she was too tired to ponder on her self-imposed exile from joy and how she might free herself. She thought only of her father's betrayal and of JP.

Emer was deeply worried about the change in her daughter. She knew she was pining for JP and she assumed that she still blamed her father for what he had put them through, but she sensed something else besides, an unnecessary stubbornness there, as if Alana had somehow got herself stuck in a rut and didn't know how to climb out. So one day when they were alone in the kitchen Emer decided she'd reach out and hope that her daughter would take her hand.

'You used to derive such pleasure from summer,' Emer said, putting a bunch of wild flowers into a vase and placing them on the windowsill. 'I don't think even nature's magic can rouse you from your unhappiness.' She sighed and looked at her daughter with concern.

'I don't know what you mean,' Alana replied.

Emer smiled as her daughter turned her back and began to knead the dough at the table. 'You can fool most people, Alana, but you can't fool your mother. Stop doing that for a moment and come and look at me.'

Alana wiped her hands on her apron and reluctantly joined her mother by the window. Emer held her gaze and Alana's eyes began to glisten.

'My darling, many things happen in our lives that are beyond our control, but we always have the choice of how we react to those things. We can decide to be unhappy or we can decide to let our unhappiness go and move on. We don't have to let circumstances control how we feel. Often it takes a great force of will, but most of the time it can be done. I don't know why you and JP argued and perhaps you will never make up, but you don't have to let him ruin your life. You are young and you have a long road ahead. You can choose to plod up that road with heavy feet or you can choose to skip up it. It's your choice to live in the moment or to imprison yourself in the past.' When Alana didn't speak, Emer put her hands on her shoulders and continued. 'As for your father, he did what he had to do to survive. We suffered, and I won't deny it was horrendous, but it's over now. You have to let that go too.'

Alana began to cry. The strain of keeping such a terrible secret from her mother had become intolerable. She couldn't do it any longer. She had to let it out in order to let it go. 'I know something I shouldn't know and it's eating away at me,' Alana whispered and her voice was so soft Emer had to lean in to hear it.

'What do you know, my darling?' Emer watched her daughter's face contort with pain and felt a rising sense of panic. She tightened her grip on her daughter's arms. 'Tell me, what do you know?'

Alana took a deep breath. She felt as if she were inhaling concrete. She didn't want to hurt her mother but she knew she couldn't carry the secret any more. 'Da had an affair, Mam. I found letters in his bag when I thought he was dead. They were from Kitty Trench.' Her shoulders shuddered and she began to sob. 'Forgive me.'

Emer's face relaxed as the panic drained away. She pulled Alana into her arms and held her tightly. 'I know,' she whispered at Alana's ear. 'I know he had an affair.'

Alana pulled away and stared at her mother in amazement. 'You know?' she gasped.

Emer smiled at her serenely and nodded. 'I'd have to be deaf not to hear the gossip in this town. Of course I know. I'm only sorry that you had to find out and that you kept it a secret in order to protect my feelings.'

'Aren't you furious?' Alana couldn't believe her mother's tranquillity. 'Or did you just choose not to be?' she said, wiping her eyes with her hand.

Emer gave a little laugh. 'What is the point of being furious? I know your father loves me. He loved Kitty too, once, and when we came back to Ireland he believed he loved her still. So, I turned a blind eye and hoped that it would burn itself out. Which it did.'

'Does he know you know?'

'Of course not. And we must never tell him. We women have to be cleverer than them.' She ran a thumb across her daughter's cheek. 'Don't live in the past, Alana. It's gone. What matters is now. It's the way you behave in the present that will determine your future.' Alana gazed into her mother's gentle eyes and felt her whole body lift, as if it was filling with something warm and effervescent. 'The three most powerful tools for a happy life are gratitude, forgiveness and love. If you can appreciate the small things, forgive those who wrong you and fill your heart with love you will always be content.'

Alana began to cry again, but this time with relief. 'I will try, Mam. I really will.'

'That's a good girl.' Emer glanced over at the dough, which was hardening on the table. 'Now, you'd better start again or we'll all break our teeth on the pie.'

'Thank you, Mam,' Alana said and she embraced her fiercely. 'I love you so much.'

'And I love you, too.' She kissed her daughter's temple. 'Now you be good to your da because he's been suffering on account of your coldness.'

'I will,' Alana replied and she resolved to do as her mother did and love him unconditionally.

Chapter 30

Dublin, 1947

JP had been at Trinity College, Dublin for just over eighteen months. He hadn't spoken to Kitty since he had left Ballinakelly and he'd stopped writing to Alana. He loved her but was done making a fool of himself. If she changed her mind, she knew where to find him.

His father occasionally came to Dublin and they had lunch together at the Kildare Street Club. It had come as an enormous surprise when Bertie had brought Maud. JP and Maud had never been formally introduced. JP knew who she was by sight, owing to the rare times she had come to Ballinakelly, and Maud probably knew him by sight, he imagined, but they had never spoken. JP knew very well what she thought of him and he didn't blame her. But she seemed to have forgiven Bertie, for the two of them had behaved like young lovers who had come alive in each other's company. Indeed Maud had been quite a different woman to the one Kitty talked about. More like the woman Bertie had been so nostalgic about. She'd been gracious and charming and interested in everything JP had to say even though he found her curiosity a little alarming. Under the scrutiny of her intense blue eyes he'd felt like a creature being studied beneath a microscope. He couldn't help wondering what Kitty would have to say about the three of them getting along so well together.

JP threw himself into his studies with alacrity. He knew that the only way to get over Alana was to focus on something else. There was plenty to do at College. He made friends easily, attracted many admirers who fought hard for his heart and played sport. He spent weekends in Galway hunting with 'the Blazers', as the famous hunt was known, and in the summer he joined house parties in Connemara and Co. Wicklow. JP was never short of invitations; he was one of those charismatic people everyone wants at their table. He hid his heartache well. He was determined not to let Alana dampen his enjoyment of life as Martha had done.

It was a particularly bright spring morning in Dublin when JP saw Martha. At first he wasn't sure it was her. Her features were the same, but her air was different. Of course, eight years had passed since he had last seen her; they had both been young then. He followed her as she walked with a female companion up the street in the direction of St Stephen's Green. She was wearing a simple blue dress with her hair pinned at the back of her head and sensible shoes. He recognized the way she walked and the shape of the body inside the dress, but he couldn't be sure he wasn't mistaken. Why would she have come back to Ireland and why Dublin? It seemed unlikely, somehow.

He followed the two of them into the Green and decided to take a different path and come at her from the opposite direction; that way he'd have the opportunity to take a good look at her face. As he strode beneath the plane trees he recalled the time he had walked with her there. It seemed a lifetime ago now. The war had changed the person he was. If she was indeed Martha, she would have changed too, he thought.

Now he joined her path a short distance ahead of her. He ambled slowly, hands in pockets, trying not to stare too obviously as the two women walked towards him. She laughed at something her friend said and he recognized that smile. He recognized the sweetness in it. His heart gave a little skip. When she replied he heard her voice with its distinctive American accent. He knew at once that she was Martha, after all. He hadn't been wrong. As they came closer she glanced at him, in the same way she might perhaps glance at any stranger, before her gaze drifted away. But then her eyes snapped back sharply and she stopped. She recognized him too.

'JP?' she exclaimed and blushed a deep scarlet. Her friend looked at JP and then looked at Martha.

'Hello, Martha,' he said and he felt a sudden, overwhelming delight in seeing her. He bent down and kissed her cheek.

'Jane, this is my old friend, JP Deverill,' Martha said unsteadily. 'JP, this is my new friend, Jane Keaton.' The two shook hands.

'What are you doing in Dublin?' he asked, ignoring Jane Keaton who looked from one to the other in puzzlement.

'Oh, it's such a long story . . .' Martha began.

Jane put her hand on Martha's arm. 'I'll leave you to catch up,' she said tactfully.

'Really, you don't have to,' Martha began, but she was grateful when her friend headed off, leaving her alone with JP.

JP looked down at Martha and smiled, the old tenderness returning in a rush as he took in her features, which were so pleasingly familiar to him. 'Let's go and sit down,' he suggested. 'Come, I know a nice bench.' They sat in the shade of a horse chestnut tree, both astonished how immediately comfortable they felt in each other's company, in spite of everything that had happened.

'Oh, it's so good to see you,' said Martha truthfully.

'How long have you been here?' he asked.

'I arrived in Ireland a year and a half ago but I've only been living in Dublin for four months.'

'A year and a half ago?' JP gazed at her in amazement, aware that it was wrong of him to take offence at her not having got in touch. 'What are you doing here?'

She hesitated. 'I'm joining the convent,' she said carefully and watched the surprise sweep over his face. 'I know that must sound odd to you, that I'm going to become a nun, but I made up my mind a long time ago. I'm very happy with my decision, JP.'

JP didn't want to make her feel uncomfortable. 'I'm sorry, I'm just a little taken aback. It was the last thing I expected.'

'I'm going to join the convent where we were born,' she told him. She took his hand then. It didn't give her the jolt of electricity it once had, but something different; something deeper. 'When I returned to America, JP, I thought my life had ended. I didn't think I could live without you. But in my despair I found God. It sounds silly, I know, but I want to thank you for opening that door for me.'

'It doesn't sound silly,' he said, sandwiching her hand between his. 'It doesn't sound silly at all.'

She looked into his gentle eyes and felt encouraged. 'I left the man I loved in Ireland but I feel now, as I sit with you here, that I have returned and found my brother.'

JP put his arms around her and drew her close. 'And

I've found my sister,' he said softly. 'Just when I needed her most.'

'*Do* you need me, JP?' she asked.

He let her go and sighed heavily. 'I don't know where to begin,' he said and she noticed a bolt of pain flash across his eyes.

'Why not start at the beginning,' she suggested with a smile, and JP realized that, out of all the people in his life, Martha was the only person he could share his story with.

He told her everything. From his experiences in the war to Harry dying, falling in love with Alana and Kitty's affair with Jack O'Leary. She listened and she didn't interrupt, but let him tell it at his own pace. For JP it was cathartic to talk through his troubles and the sympathetic look on Martha's face made him feel understood. She didn't flinch when he told her about Alana and he didn't spare her any details. Life had continued since their parting and they had both found new paths; he sensed that she didn't resent him for finding Alana along *his*.

'I have let her go,' JP told Martha when he came to the end of his story. 'She doesn't want to marry me so I have no choice but to move on.' He leaned forward with his elbows on his knees and stared into his knitted fingers.

Martha didn't agree. She silently asked God for guidance so that she could give him the best advice. 'I don't think you should give up,' she said after a moment. 'Time is a great healer. Perhaps all Alana needed was time.'

'I've given her eighteen months.'

'But you haven't seen her in all that time, have you?'

'No,' he replied.

'And you stopped writing to her?'

'Yes.'

'Then you need to go and see her,' she said. 'If you truly love her you won't give up on her until you have exhausted every avenue.'

'She won't want to see me,' he said, dropping his gaze in defeat.

'Then you have to make her. You have to fight for her. You have to stand on her doorstep until she has no choice but to see you. At least, if she tells you then that it's over, you will know that you did your best. If you give up now there will always be uncertainty. You'll never be sure and that's a horrid thing to live with.'

He pondered on her words. A young couple walked by hand in hand and JP watched them enviously.

'All right,' he conceded. 'I'll go back home.'

'Good,' she said. 'That's better.'

'Thank you, Martha. You're like a guardian angel. You appeared just when I needed you.'

'I'm glad,' she said happily, her heart swelling with satisfaction.

'But what about you?' he asked. 'Now you've found me, will you come and see Papa?'

'I don't know, JP,' she said. 'I already have parents who love me. I'm not sure that trying to build a relationship with your father, *our* father, is a wise thing to do. I have found my twin and that's enough for me.' She smiled resignedly. 'If he desperately wanted to know me, I would open my arms to him, but he doesn't. I don't want to engineer something that isn't there. Do you understand?' JP nodded. 'Isn't life complicated?' She laughed at the absurdity of theirs. 'It's hard making sense of it sometimes. I think you should forgive Kitty. She must be hurting so much because you're like a son to her. Go back and make it up with her. Don't sit in judgement over her. That's not your place. That's God's place. You must find it in your heart to understand her. Then tell Alana that you love her. I believe it is only with forgiveness and love that you can right those wrongs. In fact, there is no other way.'

JP took her hand again. 'And now we have found each other, will you promise me you won't run away again?'

'I'm not going anywhere, JP. I'm going to be here for the rest of my life.'

Kitty was in the garden on her knees pulling out elder from the border when JP appeared. She put down her trowel and stared at him fearfully. She could tell from his expression that he wasn't furious with her any more and her heart flooded with relief. He didn't speak. He walked up to her, and once she had scrambled to her feet he almost squeezed the life out of her in an impassioned embrace. Kitty closed her eyes and let his forgiveness wash away her pain.

Alana was in the kitchen slicing apples for the pie when there came a knock on the door. She wiped her hands on her apron and went to answer it. A scruffy young boy in a jacket and cap presented her with a bouquet of wild flowers. 'This is from JP Deverill,' he said importantly.

Alana stared at him in shock. 'What did you say?'

'I said, this is from JP Deverill,' he repeated.

Alana ignored the flowers. 'Where is he?' she asked eagerly, putting a hand on the boy's shoulder. 'Is he here?' The child blinked as he tried to remember what he'd been told to say. 'Speak up, boy!' she demanded. 'Where is he?'

The child thrust the flowers into her hands. Alana barely looked at them. 'He wants to know if you will see him,' he said.

'Of course I'll see him,' she replied impatiently. 'Where is he?'

The boy put his fingers in his mouth and gave a loud wolf whistle. Alana's hand shot to her heart as JP came round the corner on his horse. The sight was so astonishing. There he was, her knight on horseback, as he had been that day in the hills when she had first lost her heart to him. Suddenly she remembered how to laugh and she remembered how to love and the tears blurred her vision so that JP became a dark smudge that was getting bigger and bigger as he approached. When at last he dismounted, she rushed at him. 'I've been an eejit!' she said, falling into his arms. 'Will you ever forgive me?'

JP remembered Martha's advice. *It is only with forgiveness and love that you can right those wrongs.* 'Of course, I forgive you,' he said. 'Even though there's nothing to forgive.' He kissed her ardently and Alana felt as if his kiss was lifting her out of a very dark place and carrying her into the light. 'Come ride with me,' he said.

'But I'm in the middle of baking,' she replied.

'Leave the baking. Come into the hills. I want to be alone with you.'

Aileen suddenly appeared in the doorway. She stared at JP as if she'd just seen a ghost. 'Oh Aileen,' said Alana. 'Here, take these flowers, would you, and put them in water and hook my apron on the back of the door,' she added, untying it and raising it over her head.

'Where are you going?' Aileen asked as JP helped her sister onto his horse.

'I'm going into the hills with my fiancé,' Alana replied proudly and Aileen grinned.

JP swung into position behind her and took the reins.

'My knight in shining armour,' said Alana happily. 'I prayed you'd come back,' she told him as the horse walked slowly up the beach.

'You did?' he asked.

'I did,' she replied, then she lifted her chin and grinned. 'But what took you so long?'

JP and Alana were married in the summer of 1950 after a long engagement. JP had finished his course at Trinity College, Dublin and moved back down to Cork, where he started work as an architect. He had always loved building things with his father as a boy and he discovered that the pleasure had never left him.

JP was Protestant and Alana Catholic, but they were not going to allow religion or anything else to come between them. JP promised to bring up any children they might have in the Catholic faith and they were married in the sacristy of the Catholic church of All Saints.

Before the ceremony Alana was sitting at her mother's dressing table while Aileen threaded flowers into her hair when her father came into the room. He swept his eyes over the ivory dress that his cousin's wife Loretta had made for her and noticed she was wearing Emer's veil that she had brought all the way from America for this very day. 'You look beautiful, Alana,' he said and a lump lodged in his throat, thinning his voice. He coughed to clear it. 'The image of your mother.'

'Thank you, Da,' she said, glancing at her reflection. 'Don't make me cry. I've already cried twice already, haven't I, Aileen.'

'She has, Da, and twice I've had to repair her make-up.'

'I have something for you,' he said, stepping closer. He held out a velvet pouch.

'What is this?' She untied the string and poured a pretty

silver and lapis rosary into the palm of her hand. 'It's beautiful,' she said, welling up again.

'I can't pretend it's an heirloom, Alana, but it caught my eye in Dublin and I thought you'd like it.'

'Oh Da, I'm going to cry again.'

Aileen shot her father a disapproving look and reached for a tissue. She handed it to her sister and sighed. 'We should have left your make-up to the last minute,' she said.

Alana dabbed beneath her eyes. 'Thank you, Da. This means the world to me.'

'I hope you'll have something for *me* on *my* wedding day,' said Aileen.

Her father patted her back. 'Don't you worry, Aileen. I'll find something just as pretty for you too. But today is Alana's.' He looked at his watch. 'Are you nearly ready?'

'It's tradition for the bride to be late,' said Alana.

'And it's tradition for the father of the bride to wait at the bottom of the stairs,' Aileen added pointedly.

Jack nodded and grinned. 'Very well. I'm proud of *both* my girls,' he said.

Aileen smiled. 'You can be proud at the bottom of the stairs,' she said firmly and watched him leave the room. 'If he carries on like this I'm going to be after ruining *my* make-up as well!'

Jack found Emer in the kitchen toying with Alana's bouquet. She was wearing a caramel-coloured dress with a discreet hat. When she saw him she looked up and smiled. 'Did she like it?' she asked.

He nodded. 'Very much.'

'Good.'

He put his arm around her waist and kissed her. 'I can't believe our little girl is getting married,' he said.

'Neither can I. Doesn't seem very long ago that she was playing truant and running off into the hills.'

He gazed at her steadily. 'I don't know what you said to her, Emer, and I've never asked. But your words brought her back to JP – and to me. Yes, they brought her back to me and I'm grateful to you for that.'

Emer put her hand on his cheek and returned his gaze with her usual serenity. 'She chose to come back, Jack,' she said. *As you chose to come back to me.* 'And she chose to be happy,' she added. *As did I.*

Kitty had not spoken to Jack since Alana had confronted her about the letters. She had avoided him on purpose, as *he* had avoided *her*. The rare times they had found themselves in the same place at the same time they had hastily retreated or simply turned the other way. Kitty had grieved for Jack, but she knew that the only way to survive in her marriage was to give him up completely. And, as hard as it was to accept, she knew that he had given her up too. He had once held the roots of her heart with a fierce and forceful grip. Now he did not.

Kitty sat in the church sandwiched between Florence and Robert as Jack walked down the aisle with Alana. The music began, played on the fine electric organ Bridie had donated, and Kitty kept her eyes on her prayer book. Robert sat stiffly beside her in the front row with his straight leg stretched out. Their marriage wasn't as warm and intimate as it had once been, but it was cordial enough and she was grateful that they were still together. Perhaps in time he'd come to forgive her. Kitty saw the bride and her father out of the corner of her eye, but she didn't look, and she knew Jack wouldn't be looking in her direction either. Her heart was thumping beneath her dress and her hands were growing damp inside her gloves.

Bertie and Maud also sat in the front row and Maud almost eclipsed the bride with her glamour and beauty. She had given permission to Bertie to sell her house in Belgravia and a line had been drawn under their separation. She now sat in a pale blue dress and matching hat, which brought out the exquisite blue of her eyes. Deverill diamonds sparkled on her ears and around her neck and Bertie took her hand and squeezed it. Had she not been wearing gloves the large engagement ring, which had been absent during her affair with Arthur, would have been on display, glittering on the third finger of her left hand. Bertie and Maud gazed at each other with affection and Bertie felt an enormous sense of pride at having won her back. He resolved to treat her like his most precious treasure for the rest of his life and so ensure that he never lost her again.

Bridie sat with her mother and Leopoldo, Michael, Sean, Rosetta and their children. She glanced at Kitty and was suddenly seized by a great sorrow. It came from somewhere so deep and was so unexpected that she had to press her handkerchief to her mouth to stifle the sob that came with it. It was all too much. Her son's wedding was making her emotional and she was assaulted by wave upon wave of nostalgia and a searing longing for her past when she and Kitty had been as bonded as sisters. Over the years Bridie had made various friends: Rosetta and her attorney's wife Elaine Williams in New York, and later Emer, but none of them shared the history that she and Kitty shared. No one went as far back as they did. And Bridie felt desperately sad that one foolish episode with Lord Deverill all those years ago had set off a chain of events that had driven them apart and turned them into enemies. She wanted so badly to reconcile; she longed for it with all her heart. But she couldn't imagine how that might be achieved.

Father Quinn performed the marriage ceremony and JP and Alana vowed to love each other until death parted them. They gazed into each other's eyes and knew that, after everything that had happened, they would never allow anything to come between them again.

At the end of the service they walked up the aisle hand in hand to the faltering chords of Mrs Reagan, who was having trouble getting to grips with this swanky new organ. Kitty stepped into the aisle and found herself beside Jack. She caught Emer's eye, for his wife was right behind him, and panicked. But Jack smiled confidently and held out his hand. Kitty had no option but to give him hers. He slipped it smoothly around his arm and proceeded to lead her onwards. Kitty's breathing was shallow as she walked towards the door. She focused on the light at the end of the aisle and lifted her chin. Behind them Emer walked with her children, Robert walked with Florence, Bertie with Maud and Bridie with Leopoldo. They stepped out into the sunshine and Jack turned and smiled wistfully down at Kitty. In his eyes she saw his regret and his sorrow, but most of all she saw affection. 'We had our time,' he said softly. 'And it was special. But Emer is my future and Robert is yours. They both deserve our love and our loyalty.'

Kitty swallowed back her tears. She nodded. *I'll always love you,* she said silently and he nodded, as if he had heard. As if he had heard and had said the same to her: *I love you, Kitty Deverill, and I always will.* Then he let go of her hand and walked away.

Chapter 31

As the snow began to fall in big feathery flakes the grandest ladies and gentlemen of the city arrived at Deverill House in their chauffeur-driven cars, along with starlets of the silver screen, literary giants and newspaper proprietors, politicians, artists and minor royalty. Beatrice Deverill sat in the upstairs drawing room holding court in a lavish velvet gown, her neck and wrists glittering with diamonds from which her late husband, Sir Digby, had made his great fortune. In the event of her eightieth birthday no one cared to remember that he had lost that fortune or that his daughter Celia had travelled out to South Africa to find it. All anyone cared about was that Lady D's Salons were the place to be on a Tuesday evening and it didn't matter how one acquired an invitation so long as one did.

Beatrice had awoken from her stupor, taken off her widow's weeds and returned to London with aplomb. Celia knew that it had all started that Christmas when Kitty had come to stay. Boysie had just divorced Dreary Deirdre and he had been on such ebullient form that he had enticed Celia's mother from her mourning like a snail from its shell. Reluctant at first and then curious, Beatrice had discovered that there was fun to be had out of life still. She realized she was growing old and she did not want to die miserable. 'I shall join my darling Digby soon enough, I might as well enjoy myself as much as I can before I go.' She had been true to her word. She had left her misery behind and accompanied Celia and Boysie to London. With their encouragement she had resumed her Tuesday-evening Salons and it hadn't taken long for them to regain their reputation. The war had changed much in London but it hadn't diminished people's desire for entertainment, champagne and frivolity. There was an air of positivity, optimism and opportunity, and Beatrice had always had a talent for throwing the most unlikely people together. For Celia and Boysie it was a joy to see the brash and somewhat vulgar Beatrice again. How they had missed her.

The pianist played 'Anything Goes' and Boysie found Celia and pulled her into the middle of the room and started dancing with her. Celia squealed with laughter as Boysie, who had a natural sense of rhythm, led her across the floor. Soon it seemed that everyone was dancing. 'It's just like old times,' Celia shouted above the noise.

'I suppose you're going to say it's a riot!' Boysie shouted back.

Celia giggled. 'Well, it is!'

'It's more than a riot.' Boysie grimaced as someone stood on his foot. 'I need some air. Will you come outside?' he asked, limping in the direction of the balcony, which looked out over the front of the house and onto Kensington Palace Gardens. They escaped through the French doors and Boysie took off his jacket and draped it over Celia's shoulders. He burrowed inside the pocket and found his cigarettes and lighter. 'Fancy a smoke, old girl?'

'Love one, darling,' she said and watched him light it for her. 'Isn't it glorious, out here in the snow? It looks like a winter wonderland.'

'Divine,' said Boysie, handing her the cigarette. She took it between her crimson lips and inhaled.

'Do you know, I haven't been this happy in a long time. Not since before Archie killed himself. Really, I feel blessed. You're here and Mama is well again and I've managed to rebuild some of Papa's fortune. If I had a glass of champagne, I'd make a toast to you, Boysie. You've been such a dear friend for so many years. Think of what we've both been through and how we've survived.'

'Hang on a moment,' said Boysie and he dived into the sitting room to emerge a second later with two flutes of champagne. 'Say that again, it was beautiful.'

'Oh really, you're such a tease,' she said.

'No, I mean it. What you said was beautiful. The bit about you and me.'

She laughed and took a sip. 'You're a dear friend, that's what I mean to say.' They clinked glasses.

'So, anyone catch your eye tonight?' she asked.

Boysie laughed. 'There's a rather delicious brunette I have my eye on.'

'Ooh, not that Cavendish boy?'

'Yes, that's the one.'

'Darling, are you sure he's one of you?'

'Certain. I have a nose for it, don't forget.'

'All right. Well, do be careful.' She smiled at him fondly. Then she turned and looked out over the drive where the snow was now settling and forming a flawless blanket of white. 'Darling, I have an idea. I've been thinking about it for some time.'

'I love your ideas. Are we going to Ireland or South Africa?'

'No, it's something else—'

'Go on, old girl. I'm all ears.'

She turned and looked at him earnestly. 'You love me, don't you, Boysie?'

'I love you more than I love anyone else in the world,' he said, not wanting to complicate things by including his children.

'And I love you. You know that, don't you?'

'What's this all about, old girl?'

She beamed a smile and gazed at him with doe eyes. 'Let's get married.'

Boysie grew serious suddenly. 'But, darling—'

'I know, *I* don't want to sleep with *you* either. Well, I wouldn't mind if you kept to your side of the bed. No, I mean it. We're perfect together. You can have your affairs and I can have mine, but at the end of the day we'll have each other to come home to. I don't ever want you to leave. It's not like you're going to marry anyone else, is it?' She put her glass on the balustrade then turned and brushed the snow off his shoulder. 'I understand you, Boysie. I know you and I know exactly what you are. I love you as God made you and I want to spend the rest of my life with you. I don't want to *make* love to you, but I want to wrap my arms around you and kiss your brow and *love* you. There, I've said it. What do you say?'

Boysie frowned. 'God, Celia, you do bowl a fast ball.'

'You like me that way.'

He nodded and grinned. 'I do. I really do.' He put his champagne glass next to hers and wound his hand around her waist. 'I'd adore to be your husband,' he said, kissing her forehead. He rested his cheek there a moment and sighed. 'Wouldn't Harry laugh if he could see us now.'

'I'm sure he can see us now,' she said, 'but I doubt he's laughing. Knowing Harry, he'll be moved to tears.'

'Very true,' Boysie agreed. 'Harry cried at the smallest thing.'

'Celia Bancroft,' said Celia happily. 'That has a lovely ring to it, don't you think?'

'No one can say you're a conventional woman,' said Boysie.

Celia laughed. 'You see, you're just the sort of man for me!'

However, there was one young man who was not included in Lady Deverill's Salons and that was the now notorious Count Leopoldo di Marcantonio, who was residing in London and fast making a name for himself at the gambling tables of Mayfair and in the brothels of Soho.

Leopoldo was twenty-one years old. His doting mother had sent him to London with a generous allowance and yet he still telephoned her every month asking for more. Bridie was indulgent and forgiving of his shortcomings. She never blamed him for being irresponsible or careless and always found excuses for his lack of purpose. Whatever disaster befell Leopoldo, it was *never* his fault.

Leopoldo believed he was special. His father had told him he was better than everyone else and his mother had never held him accountable for his actions. Thus he treated women with disrespect, bullied those weaker than himself, got drunk at the gambling table and wasted money because he always knew his mother would give him more.

Ballinakelly bored Leopoldo but London dazzled him. He

attached himself to a fast group of privileged young people who 'did' the London Season, partied on the Riviera in the summer and skied in St. Moritz in the winter. They played polo on the manicured grounds of Cirencester and Windsor, shot pheasants in England and grouse in Scotland, stayed in grand houses, went to the races and danced until sunrise in the fashionable London clubs. Desperate to belong to this glamorous scene, yet aware that he had neither the education nor the breeding to fully qualify, Leopoldo threw his money around instead. When the bill came his new friends were quick to turn to Leopoldo. 'You are a darling!' they gushed, pushing it beneath his nose. 'What would we do without Leo! He's adorable!' they'd say, and Leo would inflate with happiness and feel he was truly part of this exclusive world as he wrote out a large cheque. Yet, in spite of buying the right clothes and becoming a member of the right clubs, he always felt he was somewhat falling short. Everyone seemed to speak a language he didn't understand, even though the words were the same. They seemed to exist behind a veil and however much money he threw at it, it never lifted. But as long as he was writing the cheques these privileged young people were only too delighted to include him.

But Leopoldo had a grand foreign title and a magnificent castle as well as money, which compensated for his unpleasant character. There were plenty of avaricious girls who hoped to marry him and Leopoldo chose the most insecure of them to go out with: that way he always felt powerful. He bought them clothes and jewellery and bragged about his heritage, that he was related to Pope Urban VIII, Maffeo Barberini, and showed off his diamond bee cufflinks, inherited from his father. He bragged about the castle his mother had bought from the illustrious Deverill family, who, he was quick to add, were now tenants. One day it would be his. He did not like to be reminded that his mother had come from peasant stock or that his father had been murdered.

London Society despised him. They mocked him behind his back and the press nicknamed him the Count of Monte Twitsko. His mother had once been a notorious socialite in New York; now her son received equal, but less positive attention. He was photographed leaving the Savoy drunk, crashing his car outside the Ritz and getting into a fight in the street after he refused to honour his losses at the gambling table. He was thrown into a cell for punching a policeman and fined for swimming naked in the Serpentine after the park was closed. His antics made entertaining reading for everyone except Bridie, who blamed the crowd with whom he was now mixing for leading him astray.

Leopoldo rarely went home and he rarely telephoned his mother. He was much too busy pleasing himself, but Bridie didn't mind. 'As long as he's well, I'm happy,' she told Rosetta, who believed that Leopoldo was selfish and undeserving of his mother's love. 'Poor boy has lost his father and his role model. He has to go out into the world and find himself now, as I had to do. But I had no one to look after me. Leo is lucky. I'll always be there for him, come what may. I'll love him whatever he does.' Rosetta suspected that Bridie only knew the half of what Leo did.

It was in the spring of 1953 that Bridie got sick. She hadn't felt well for a long time. At first she'd thought it was just weariness, then she'd thought she was simply getting old. The aches and pains were perhaps part of the menopause, she'd told herself, or more likely the result of a lifetime of sorrow, and, because she had never had any reason to visit a doctor, she soldiered on. She did not want to worry Leo by telling him. 'Let him have his fun without fretting about me,' she told Rosetta, and Rosetta resented Leopoldo all the more for not taking more trouble with his mother, for surely if he bothered to come home he'd see her sickness for himself. And Bridie did not want to worry her mother or bore Emer and Martha with her complaints. She managed to disguise her fading health behind a smile and dismissed their concern with excuses of tiredness and quips about growing old. Rosetta urged her to see a doctor, but Bridie told her that not even the most gifted doctor could mend her heart, which had broken the morning she had learned of her husband's murder. It was only natural that grief would take its toll eventually.

It was only when she collapsed at the top of the stairs that Rosetta took matters into her own hands. She called the local doctor who came to the castle. He looked grave, scratched his whiskers and shook his head, then referred her to a doctor in Cork. The doctor in Cork was equally troubled and sent her to a hospital in Dublin for tests. She travelled by train and Rosetta went with her for support. For the first time Rosetta feared, as Bridie seemed to be getting smaller, weaker and paler before her very eyes, that Bridie was dying.

The train journey back to Cork was a sombre one. Bridie stared out of the glass, but she didn't see the countryside sweeping past her window. Instead she saw scenes replayed from her life. She saw the farmhouse where she had grown up, her grandmother, Old Mrs Nagle, smoking her clay pipe by the fire, her mother saying the family rosary and the angelus at the table, her father dancing with her around the kitchen while their friends clapped and shouted, 'Mind the dresser.' She saw the convent where Martha was training to become a nun, she saw her babies and she saw herself losing them. She saw the boat that took her to America and the New York skyline as she had laid eyes on it for the first time, with optimism and hope and a deep sadness for what she had left behind. She saw Mrs Grimsby, who had bequeathed her a fortune and Miss Ferrel and Mr Gordon who had always been suspicious of her. She saw her attorney and ally Beaumont Williams, and his wife Elaine, who had been a dear and loyal friend. She saw her first husband Walter Lockwood, who had been so kind to her, and his family who had accused her of being a gold-digger. She saw her apartment on Park Avenue and her beloved Cesare, the man she had loved above all others. She saw Leopoldo as a boy, and the castle, which she had never felt really belonged to her, and she wondered now, as it was all going to end, whether the jealousies and feuds had really been worth it. In the light of her departure they seemed so trivial somehow.

'I have cancer,' she told Rosetta at last. She could no longer smile to hide the truth. She dropped her shoulders and sighed. Rosetta put down her magazine and gazed at her friend with sadness. She had suspected as much, but the words surprised her all the same; they seemed so much darker when said out loud. Bridie dropped her gaze into her hands and Rosetta tried to remain strong, but a tear escaped and trickled down her cheek. She swiftly brushed it away. 'I must accept what God has given me,' Bridie continued. 'I have suffered much in my life but I have never lost my faith. I will not lose it now. There is consolation in the promise of seeing my father again, Nanna and Cesare. I'll not be alone in Heaven.' And she thought of her baby daughter and her battered heart gave a little flutter of anticipated joy.

'Oh Bridie,' Rosetta croaked, moving to the empty seat beside her and taking her hand. '*I* will nurse you back to health.'

'I am beyond nursing now,' said Bridie. Her eyes shone as she looked at Rosetta with gratitude, as if she was suddenly seeing her anew. She pressed her hand against her cheek. 'You have been my dearest friend, Rosetta. You have stood by me through the toughest times. I have not always chosen the smoothest path, but you have never complained. I am glad you married my brother. You made him happy and you made me happy by becoming my sister. No one knows me like you do and I know that you love me for the person I am, in spite of all my faults. I have taken you for granted because you have been so steadfast and loyal. I have mourned my losses without appreciating what I have. So, I thank you, Rosetta, from the bottom of my heart, what is left of it.' She chuckled as the tears ran in rivulets down her face. 'I don't want to go without telling you. Without thanking you.'

Rosetta was too moved to reply. She gathered her frail friend into her arms and hugged her tightly.

Bridie did not want anyone besides her family and Father Quinn to know that she was dying. She told only Michael, her mother and Sean, and finally Leopoldo, who hurried back to Ballinakelly to be at her side. However, it was as hard to keep a secret in Ballinakelly as it is to pin down a cloud and soon the whole town knew. 'She might have risen to great heights but she's always been our Bridie,' said Mag Keohane in the snug.

'Oh, she has indeed. She's always had a heart of gold,' added Nellie Moxley.

'And a purse full of it,' said Nellie Clifford. 'Ballinakelly has never known such generosity.'

'Thanks to the electric organ Bridie donated to the church old Molly Reagan was able to give up the pumping of the old one. Do you remember how the poor old creature had to take to her bed after the sung Mass?'

'I do indeed,' said Maureen Hurley. 'Nothing but a drop-een of whiskey would revive her, God help us.'

They all went quiet for a moment, then Mag Keohane said in a low and portentous voice, 'That Leopoldo will inherit the castle.' She shook her head. 'I have a Christian heart and you won't find a better Christian virgin outside of the convent walls than me, but God forgive me, I have nothing good to say about *him*.'

Kitty was shocked to find Michael Doyle at her door. He stood with his cap in his hand and a sheepish look on his dark face. She didn't ask him in. She didn't want Michael Doyle to cross her threshold, but he didn't look menacing, he looked as if it had taken courage for him to come.

'Hello, Kitty,' he said.

Kitty lifted her chin. 'Michael.'

'I've come with news.' Kitty immediately thought of Bridie and pressed her hand to her heart.

'What's happened?' she asked, forgetting their history and thinking only of her old friend.

'Bridie is dying,' he said and his eyes looked at her wearily.

Kitty gasped in horror. 'Dying? But of what?'

'Cancer,' he told her. 'She's riddled with it. She's only there while she's there now. I know the two of you haven't had a relationship for many years, but I know Bridie would like to reconcile, even if she hasn't said so. She won't want to go with anger in her soul.'

Kitty nodded. 'Of course. I will go to her at once.'

He hesitated and this big, powerful, formidable man suddenly looked small and uncertain. He took a breath and Kitty felt his remorse as if it emanated from his every pore. 'I'm sorry, Kitty, for what I did to you,' he said softly. 'I understand that you can't forgive me. What I did was unforgivable. But I want you to know that I regretted it even as I did it. I was young, but that's not an excuse.' He averted his gaze because he couldn't bear to see the condemnation in hers.

But Kitty reached out and touched his hand. 'I forgive you, Michael,' she said and she couldn't believe she had said it. She couldn't believe she really *felt* it. After so many years of resentment and resistance, something was released in her and the feeling was exquisite. A warmth flooded her chest and rose into her constricting throat. Tears stung. But the joy in her heart was overwhelming.

Michael stared at her, uncomprehending. 'I forgive you, Michael,' she repeated and smiled.

Michael took her hand and squeezed it between his. He was too moved to speak, too full of humility to stand any longer in her presence. He nodded and put on his cap. Then he walked away.

Kitty watched him go and marvelled at how easy forgiving him had been. *Is it really necessary to hold on to past pain when the possibility of letting it go is within our grasp?* She thought of Adeline, for that was just the sort of thing her grandmother would have said. As Kitty thought of her she felt her presence and sensed her approval, and then she heard her, as if her words were spoken straight to her heart.

It was time now to ask forgiveness of Bridie.

Chapter 32

Bridie had taken to her bed. The fire was lit, but the autumn sunshine beamed through the window, bringing with it the cheerful song of birds and the scent of damp grass. Her world had been reduced to that small room but she wasn't sorry. She had never felt comfortable in the rest of the castle anyway. Now she lay in her nightdress propped up on pillows, waiting to die.

Leopoldo had come back from London. His presence had lifted her spirits more than anything else could. The very sight of him had restored the colour to her cheeks and the sparkle to her eyes. He had sat by her bed and held her hands and told her of all the things he had got up to in London and she had laughed because in her opinion everything he did was brilliant and clever and bold. Then he had left to seek entertainment in town.

Bridie had not expected to see Kitty. She had thought about her old friend often and memories of their childhood had served only to make her desperately sad. Now Kitty appeared in the doorway, afraid to step into the room in case she wasn't welcome. However, the prospect of death only made life more valuable and Bridie smiled. 'Kitty, I'm glad you've come,' she said, reaching out her hand.

Kitty pulled up the chair which had been placed near the bed and sat down. She gazed into Bridie's thin face and thought how terribly pale she looked. Dark shadows circled her eyes and collected in pools in the hollows of her cheeks. Kitty felt a tugging in her heart and a tightness in her throat. It pained her to see what Bridie had been reduced to and she took her friend's hand and pressed it to her cheek.

'How did we get here, Bridie?' she asked. 'How did we allow our estrangement to happen?'

'Because we are both stubborn,' Bridie replied.

'We are both fools!' Kitty exclaimed. 'We love JP equally and yet we allowed that love to destroy the love we had for each other. I feel sick to the stomach when I think of what we have lost.' Kitty's eyes brimmed with tears.

'You did what you believed was right, Kitty. You looked after my son and for that I thank you. You raised him well. He's a fine lad.'

'But he's *your* son and he must know,' said Kitty. 'I'm going to tell him the truth, Bridie. I'm going to tell him that you didn't want to give him up, but you had to. I'll tell him that you came back to get him, but I stood in your way. I will tell him what I *should* have told him long ago.'

'No, you mustn't, Kitty. Don't destroy his happiness and don't give him reason to resent you.'

'He has a right to know who his mother is,' Kitty insisted.

Bridie's face creased into a frown and she suddenly looked scared. 'I don't want him to see me like this, Kitty. I don't want him to meet his mother on her deathbed.'

At the mention of death Kitty stood up and went to the window. She didn't know how to tell Bridie that she had a daughter too, but she knew she had to and she was prepared to face the consequences. She gazed out onto the gardens and searched for guidance there in the place where she had grown up. 'Bridie,' she began. 'I need to tell you something else.' She turned round and looked at the small woman in the bed who had once been so full of mischief and vitality. 'You don't only have a son, you have a daughter too.'

Bridie stared at Kitty, confused. 'What do you mean, I have a daughter? I think I'd know about it if I did.'

'The twin you believed died at birth was in fact alive. She was taken from you and adopted by an American couple.' Kitty wrung her hands. 'Oh Bridie, forgive me. I should have told you earlier.'

Bridie pushed herself up into sitting position. She didn't take her eyes off Kitty. Her confusion had turned to fear. 'My little girl is not dead?' She looked so distraught that Kitty hurried to her side and sat on the bed to hold her.

'Your little girl grew up to be a beautiful young woman, Bridie.'

'My baby didn't die? How is that possible? I saw her. I saw her and she was blue!' Bridie was trembling now.

'She wasn't breathing, but she wasn't dead.'

'In the name of God, how could anyone do that?' Bridie gasped, sobbing onto Kitty's breast. 'How could anyone steal a baby straight from her mother's womb?' Kitty thought of Grace Rowan-Hampton and it was as if Bridie read her mind. She pushed Kitty away as it suddenly dawned on her who was behind such an appalling act. There could only be one person. There had always only ever *been* one person, whose manipulative fingers had repeatedly tied her life in knots. 'Grace,' she said, wide-eyed and alert. 'It was Grace, wasn't it?' Kitty nodded, stunned that Bridie had instantly thought of her. 'I should have known. I should never have trusted her. She was only ever self-serving, right from the beginning. But where is my daughter now, Kitty? What is her name? Is she happy?'

'You already know your daughter, Bridie. She's Martha.'

Bridie put a hand to her mouth and gasped loudly. 'Martha *Wallace*? *My* friend Martha?'

'Your friend Martha,' Kitty replied. 'She came to Ballinakelly in search of you, but because Grace had put her own name on her birth certificate in order to fetch a greater price, she found Grace instead. That is when I found out. When Grace came to tell me. She lied to Martha and told her that her mother had died giving birth to her.'

'Martha thinks I'm dead? Oh, that's dreadful!'

'I'm so sorry, Bridie. I collaborated to save JP from discovering the truth. I lied to you too to save my own skin and I regret it bitterly. I'm as guilty as she is.'

'Of course, that's why Martha and JP could never marry,' said Bridie, struggling in her agitation to put the pieces together. 'Does she know? She never even mentioned that she was adopted. We talked about everything, but she never told me that.'

'And I assume that you never told her that you had given birth to two babies who were taken from you,' said Kitty sensibly.

'No, it's true. I didn't. Neither one of us told the other the truth, which would have united us as mother and daughter.'

'I think Martha should know that you're her mother.'

Bridie sighed and lay back against the cushions and thought of Martha, the delightful girl who had brought her companionship and joy. 'I could never have asked for a more wonderful daughter,' she said, suddenly dizzy with happiness. 'She and I are so alike, you know, Kitty. We think the same and find the same things funny. We are like two peas in a pod, we are. To think we never knew . . .'

'And she's joined the convent where you gave birth to her,' Kitty reminded her.

'Indeed she has. What a strange twist of Fate.' Bridie took Kitty's hand. 'Thank you, Kitty. I have lived my whole life believing my daughter dead and now you have told me that she didn't die, but enjoyed a good life in America. I'm grateful that she grew up in a happy place.' Bridie wiped away a tear with the back of her hand. 'I'm glad that she has parents who love her.'

Kitty had not expected Bridie to react like this. She had expected to be shouted at and banished from the castle. She had not expected understanding. She was humbled. 'I should never have kept secrets from you or JP,' she said. 'We should all have been open with each other.'

'Sometimes the truth is not the wisest path, Kitty, at least, there is a time for it. I forgive you. After all, if you had told Martha I was her mother, you would have had to tell JP. What a tangle of secrets and lies we've created.' Her face hardened as she considered the woman who, like a beautiful, beguiling spider, had spun all the lies. 'But I will never forgive Grace,' she said. 'Not in this world or the next.'

'I think you should meet JP and Martha together,' Kitty suggested. 'There is a time for truth and it is now. I will tell them and bring them to you.'

Bridie shook her head and smiled beatifically. 'I don't want them to see me like this, Kitty, a woman with one foot in the grave. I want Martha to remember me the way I was when she stayed here. I don't want her to remember a dying woman. And I don't want JP to meet his mother who he believed dead, only then to lose her. Perhaps it's selfish of me, but I don't think I could take it, Kitty, the awkwardness of it. JP doesn't know me, after all. Better that he holds on to the image he already has of me. An angel in Heaven perhaps. I'll write them each a letter explaining everything and you can deliver them when I'm gone.'

'Don't say that,' said Kitty, appalled. 'You're not going to go.'

'Kitty Deverill, since when have *you* been afraid of death? Weren't you the one who told me that there is no such thing?'

'But I've just found you again and now I'm going to lose you.' Kitty began to cry. 'Oh, please don't leave me, Bridie.'

'Had I not been dying you would never have come to see me. I'm glad I'm dying because I've not only found my old friend, but I've found my daughter too.' Bridie's eyes glistened with contentment. 'Do you remember when we were little girls here at Castle Deverill ...' she began and Kitty reminisced with her, for how could she ever forget those blissful, innocent days of their youth?

When Michael heard from Bridie what Kitty had told her he was filled with a violent and uncontrollable rage. He downed half a bottle of whiskey then drove to Grace's manor house, chewing on his lover's betrayal as the car swerved dangerously in the darkening road.

He banged on the front door and shouted her name. At length a butler opened it, but Michael didn't wait to be invited in. He pushed past the man who had on so many previous occasions welcomed him in without hesitation and marched across the hall and down the corridor towards the drawing room, from where he heard the sound of sedate voices.

Grace looked up in alarm from the sofa when Michael appeared in the doorframe. He looked terrifying with his wild black hair and his angry black eyes. He was so tall and broad and his energy so intense that he seemed to fill the entire room and Grace was afraid. The butler caught up with him and tried to persuade him to wait in the hall. 'Lady Rowan-Hampton is with guests,' he exclaimed in exasperation. But Michael wasn't listening. He was staring at Grace and she was wilting beneath his gaze.

'What the devil is this all about?' Sir Ronald demanded. The portly old gentleman was standing in front of the fireplace dressed in a green velvet dinner jacket and embroidered slippers, holding a crystal glass half full of whiskey. His face had flushed pink with indignation that this uncouth man was interrupting his dinner party, but he looked incongruous there in his finery, like a fat parrot squawking at a giant eagle. The two couples who had been invited to dinner glanced at each other in shock and embarrassment. There they were enjoying a dignified drink before dinner and now, without any warning, a drunken madman had burst into the drawing room insisting on seeing Grace. If this had happened thirty years before they would have feared for their lives; as it was they feared for Grace's honour as the very coarse man began to launch a persuasive attack on her character.

'How well do you know your wife?' Michael asked Sir Ronald.

'I think you should leave,' said Sir Ronald bravely. The other two men stood up and rallied beside their host, albeit a little nervously.

'Oh, I'll leave, but not till I'm done.' Michael staggered to the tray of drinks, which had been placed on one of the tables, and helped himself to a glass of whiskey from a crystal decanter. He downed it in one and poured another.

'Michael . . .' Grace began, but she recognized the deep colour of his face and the cruel twist to his mouth and knew that trying to appease him would be futile: she was lost.

'Did you know that your Anglo-Irish, Protestant wife fought on *our* side during the War of Independence? In fact, it was *she* who lured Colonel Manley to that farmhouse on the Dunashee Road so that we could kill him. We couldn't have done it without her. Did she tell you that?'

'What nonsense,' Sir Ronald scoffed.

'Or what about her conversion to Catholicism?' Sir Ronald made a huffing sound. 'She never told you that, either? I didn't think so. She's a dark horse, your wife. But even *I* didn't know how much of a dark horse she was.'

'Get out!' Sir Ronald shouted, losing all temper. His face swelled like a ripe tomato. 'Call the Garda!' he bellowed to his butler. 'Goddamn it!'

'Michael, please . . .' Grace whispered, but Michael ignored her.

He narrowed his eyes and spat out the words with vitriol. The three men stepped back as Michael edged towards them. 'But to steal a baby barely out of her mother's womb and sell her to an American couple, well, that's something I would never have believed her capable of.' He turned on Grace and like a great bear rose to his full height. The two female guests blanched. 'But you did that, didn't you, Grace? You told Bridie her daughter was dead and she's lived her whole life mourning her child.' Michael was swaying now, pointing shakily with his finger and glaring at Grace with burning eyes. 'Did they name a chapel after you at the convent? Did they pay you handsomely? What did *you* get out of the deal?

Oh, sorry, I forgot an important piece of the puzzle. You were sleeping with Lord Deverill, weren't you? You couldn't bear it that he had seduced my sister and impregnated her. So you wanted those babies out of the way, and you wanted my sister out of the way too. As far away from your lover as was possible. Was America far enough?' The two female guests gasped and turned to Grace with their mouths agape like a pair of trout. 'How could you do it, Grace? How could you do it and live with yourself? Bridie trusted you. She thought you were her friend. But when her daughter came looking for her mother *you* told her that her mother was dead! Why? Because you didn't want your dirty little secret exposed.'

'This is preposterous!' Sir Ronald spluttered weakly. But he glanced uncertainly at Grace. 'How dare you insult my wife like this?'

Michael laughed maliciously. 'She won't deny it. She can't. Kitty Deverill has told us the whole story. Yes, Kitty Deverill betrayed *you,* Grace, like *you* betrayed *her* all those years ago, many times. We betrayed her together. For sure *I'm* going to Hell, but when I go I'm taking *you* with me.'

Sir Ronald turned to his wife. 'Grace?' he said. 'What do you say to this man?'

Grace hung her head. Michael could see that the glass she held in her hand was trembling. 'Grace? This isn't true. Tell me this isn't true.' But Sir Ronald stared helplessly at his wife and from the bewildered look on his face it was plain that he now doubted the woman he thought he knew.

Michael heard the footsteps approaching up the corridor. A moment later a pair of Gardai entered the room. He put up his hands and laughed as he tossed Grace a final glance. 'She's a good fuck, I will give her that.'

*

When Bridie left the world she did so in peace. Leopoldo sat on the chair and held her hand while her mother held the other, begging God in mumbled prayers to forgive her daughter's sins and open wide the gates of Heaven. Michael, Sean and Rosetta stood by her bed and at length the fire burnt out in the grate and the light faded from Bridie's eyes. She knew that Kitty was right, she was going to see Cesare, her father and her nanna, so there was nothing to be afraid of: they would show her the way home.

There was no resistance when she left, just an easy drifting into the next world. As she rose out of her physical body she felt as if she was a breeze lightly slipping out of the window into the night, a velvet night, and she marvelled at how very bright the stars were. How very bright the moon was, too, shining over Castle Deverill as it had done the night of the Deverill Summer Ball. Bridie only remembered the love. As she made her final journey she suddenly realized that *that* was what it had all been about: love. How very foolish of her not to have known.

Martha received Bridie's letter in the convent. She sat down in a shady corner of the courtyard and read it.

My dear Martha

There is no easy way to tell you that I am dying. But you more than most will understand that my heart is full of joy because I am going to see the face of God. Before I die, there is something I want to share with you. When I was a young maid working at Castle Deverill, I had a brief affair of the heart with Kitty's father, who was then Mr Deverill. I loved him and I believed he loved me. I got pregnant and was sent to Dublin to have my child in the convent where you are now working towards becoming a nun. I gave birth to not one but two babies. My son survived, but my daughter, they told me, had died. They took her away before I could press my lips to her brow and say a prayer for her poor soul. I was sent to America to make a new life. Later my brother Michael took my son from the nuns by devious means and put him on the doorstep of the Hunting Lodge so that Kitty would raise him as her own. This Kitty did and I bless her from the bottom of my heart for her kindness. Kitty called him Jack Patrick (JP) and later her father recognized him as his son. My daughter, I always believed, was buried in the gardens of the convent. Four years later I came back to Ireland for my son. When I was at the convent I asked to know where my daughter had been buried. There wasn't a headstone, they told me, for babies not baptized were buried in unmarked graves. I went to Ballinakelly and saw my son. I realized that he was happy where he was. With a grieving heart I returned to America and tried to forget him. But I never did and I never forgot my daughter either. I prayed for her soul and I suffered daily because of the two children I had brought into the world yet lost so cruelly.

The reason I tell you this, Martha, is because I have discovered, to my joy, that you are my daughter, the child I thought was dead — now a beautiful young woman. I thank God that we had some time together, even though we didn't know we were so closely related. I am happy to know that you have found your vocation and that it fulfils you so. Your grandmother is a devout woman who cherishes her faith, as her mother, your great-grandmother, did before her. You must have inherited that from them.

I don't want you to see me sick. I want you to remember me as I was. I want you to remember the laughter and the love, because I loved you then and I love you now, and I didn't know why, at the time, you penetrated my heart, but now I do. We have come a long way, the two of us, and we have God to thank for allowing our paths to cross.

I have asked Kitty to give you this letter after I am gone and the solicitor's letter, because I have provided for you in my will. You have my blessing to donate it to the convent.

Live well, Martha. Be strong, bold, fearless and full of love.

Your mother, Bridie

Martha stared at the letter until her vision clouded with tears and the words became black smudges on the paper. She pressed the page to her lips and closed her eyes.

JP read the letter Bridie had written for him with a strange detachment as if he were reading something meant for someone else. Bridie told him her story and explained why Kitty had kept her identity secret all those years. He had always believed that his mother was dead, but he was desperately sad that he had had the opportunity to know her and missed it. What hit him like a bolt between the eyes, however, was the solicitor's letter that informed him of his inheritance. He read it again just to make sure. Then he telephoned Kitty.

'The Countess has left me Castle Deverill,' he said, his voice quivering. Kitty had to sit down. 'Are you there, Kitty?'

'I'm here,' she replied quietly.

'And a fortune. Kitty, she's left me a fortune!'

Kitty's heart was thumping so hard she could barely hear herself think. If Bridie had left JP the castle that meant that the moment he moved in the Deverill heirs would be set free because his wife Alana was an O'Leary. 'I can't believe it,' she gasped, but JP wasn't thinking of the poor Deverill spirits, he was thinking of his father and the joy it would bring him to see his beloved Castle Deverill restored to his family.

'I must telephone Papa,' he said.

'He will be as happy as I am,' said Kitty, putting down the telephone. *Poor Leopoldo*, she thought. *This must have come as a terrible shock.*

Leopoldo was furious. He had always believed the castle would be his. Sean tried to explain that his mother had left him an enormous amount of money. 'But it's in trust!' Leopoldo cried. 'I have to ask you and Michael before I can have any of it. How am I going to have fun in London if I have to ask you for money all the time?' he asked.

'Perhaps you'll just have to have *less* fun,' said Sean reasonably. Rosetta watched Leopoldo storm out of the room, slamming the door behind him. Bridie hadn't been so oblivious, after all, she thought with a smile.

'Do you know, I never really liked this castle anyway,' she said. 'I dream of a little house by the sea, just for us and the children.'

'Then you shall have it,' Sean told her, taking her hand. 'The sooner the better.'

Bridie was buried in the churchyard beside her husband. It was the last golden day of autumn, before the winter gales would rob the trees of their leaves and the icy winds would blow in off the ocean. A day that, everyone would later agree, was charmed.

It seemed as if the entire town had come to say goodbye. The church had been so full that many members of the congregation had had to stand outside. Now, at the burial, JP Deverill stood beside his sister Martha and watched the coffin being lowered into the hole in the ground. He was going to be master of Castle Deverill; a great responsibility, which he would not take lightly. He remembered attempting to make a model of it with his father when he was a boy and fantasizing that one day, perhaps, he might have the money to buy it back. Well, he didn't have to now; he'd been *given* it. He wondered at the unpredictability of Fate.

Kitty knew that Bridie was not in the wooden coffin, but in the sunlight, watching her children with pride and love as she should have been allowed to do in life. She silently thanked her friend for returning the castle to the Deverills and thought how fitting it was because JP really belonged to both of them. Having been the reason for their animosity, he had become the catalyst for their reconciliation. Had Bridie lived the two women would have taken equal pride in him. Now Bridie had not only healed the wounds of the past by restoring the castle to the Deverills, but also she would release the spirits. Kitty was impatient to see that happen.

Mrs Doyle held on to Michael tightly and sobbed quietly into a handkerchief, hoping that the Lord had answered her prayers and reunited her daughter with her father and her nanna. Sean stood on his mother's other side with Rosetta and their children and wondered what would become of his nephew now that he had lost both parents – the only two people who had championed him. Leopoldo made a great show of his grief, which, in the opinions of the Weeping Women of Jerusalem, was overdramatic and mollyish in a young man. Everyone but Leopoldo was delighted that JP Deverill had been left the castle. There would be much celebrating in O'Donovan's tonight. Michael, who had fallen off the wagon with a spectacular thud, would drink with the best of them and, he thought with satisfaction, start looking for a wife. Released by Kitty, liberated from Grace and from his own inflated sense of piety, it was time to live again.

'I thought a nun was meant to wear a habit,' said JP, looking at Martha's elegant black dress and coat. 'Or perhaps this is what nuns wear these days.' He grinned and the freckles spread across his cheeks.

'I'm not going to be a nun,' she replied.

'Oh.' JP was surprised. She had been so dedicated to the notion.

'I realized that I was running away from life,' she told him with a sigh. 'I needed time to learn to live again, like a crippled person must learn to walk again. The convent gave me that time and that peace and with God's help I have healed. When Bridie wrote and told me that she was our mother, something shifted inside me. It was as if a great weight had been lifted from my chest. I don't know how to explain it.' She looked at him bashfully. 'Let's just say, I no longer fear love.'

'You're too beautiful to hide away in a convent, you know. You'll make some man very fortunate one day.'

'I intend to. And I intend to be a good mother to my children.' Her eyes shone and JP gave her his handkerchief. 'Thank you. It's been a rather emotional few days.' She dabbed her eyes. 'If I love my children half as much as Bridie loved us, I will be the luckiest mother in the world.'

JP drew his sister into an embrace and realized with a surge of tenderness that it was possible after all to love Martha, only now in a different way. 'Will you come and stay at the castle once we've moved in?' he asked.

'I would love to,' she replied as he released her. 'I would love to, very much.'

Alana came and slipped her hand around her husband's arm. 'Are you going to stay for a while?' she asked Martha. 'You're always welcome to stay with us.'

'Thank you. That's so kind of you,' Martha replied. 'But I will be leaving tomorrow. I'm going to America first. I have a few bridges to rebuild over there. Then I don't know where I'll go.' She smiled with optimism and shrugged. 'I'm a woman of means now. I can go anywhere I like!'

Chapter 33

'Well, why are you still here?' Adeline asked, looking in bewilderment at the expectant faces of the Deverill heirs who had gathered in the hall of the castle to await their release. 'An O'Leary has now taken possession of the castle,' she said. 'I don't understand. You shouldn't still be here.'

Barton looked at Egerton who looked at Hubert who in turn looked at Adeline. The disappointment on his face was enough to break her heart into a thousand pieces. It wasn't possible, she thought in desperation. The curse specifically said, *Until you right those wrongs I curse you and your heirs to an eternity of unrest and to the world of the undead.* Surely, now that the land had been restored to an O'Leary, the curse should be broken?

They watched JP and Alana walk excitedly up the stairs, hand in hand, while Kitty, Bertie and Maud looked on with delight from the hall. It was a moment of triumph, but it should also have been a moment of redemption, Adeline thought. She knew that Kitty could feel them there and was as confused as they were.

Adeline felt sick. Terribly sick. Not the kind of sickness one feels when one is in one's body, but a sickness in the soul, which is a very different kind of sickness altogether, and infinitely worse. It shrank her, as if a great, unseen weight was bearing down upon her. It was a dreadful sense of disappointment and fear. Disappointment for Hubert, who it seemed was destined never to leave this place, and fear for herself, for having willingly tied her soul to his. If he couldn't be freed, then neither could she. Love tied them to each other: that was their Fate.

Suddenly Barton fell to his knees. His face was contorted with anguish. He opened his arms and squeezed his eyes shut. 'Oh Maggie!' he cried out and the room must have turned cold for Kitty and Maud both shivered and Maud pulled her cardigan tightly about her. 'Maggie! Forgive me for taking your land. Forgive me for taking your innocence and forgive me for burning you when it was within my power to save you. Oh Maggie! I have carried my guilt for long enough. I can't take it any more. I can't hide my love for you. It is destroying my soul. I will gladly remain within these walls for eternity because it is what I deserve. It is *better* than I deserve. I lived a lie in life and I've lived a lie in death. But now I appeal to you, Maggie. Forgive me so that I may at least spend eternity with your forgiveness to comfort me.' He put his face in his hands and began to sob loudly. His heirs gazed at him in horrified astonishment. If their illustrious ancestor, the first Lord Deverill of Ballinakelly, had lost all hope, what chance did they have?

The room grew colder still. Maud and Bertie decided to go into the library where there was a fire in the grate and tea in the pot, just like there always used to be. JP would join them after he'd shown his wife around their new home. Kitty chose to linger in the hall, for now another spirit was floating into their midst, and as Kitty focused, she was able to see her.

It was Maggie O'Leary herself in a long white dress, with

her flowing black hair moving about her head as if she were underwater. She was even more striking in death than she had been in life and the spirits stared at her in wonder. For a moment she looked as amazed as they did, as if she hadn't expected to find herself here, in this hall, with so many eyes upon her. For reasons she did not understand, she had been released from her own dark limbo and brought to this place; the place where it had all begun, centuries before.

Maggie rested her gaze on Barton and her lips parted and her expression softened. She stopped in front of him and reached out her hands to peel his fingers from his eyes. He blinked up at her in surprise and a little fear, because of what he had done to her in the woods and because of what he had allowed to happen on the pyre. She held his hands in her elegant white ones and looked into his face with tenderness. 'You gave me gunpowder to shorten my suffering. I should have known then that you had not forsaken me,' she said. 'I know now that you did not turn away because you wanted to, but because you had to. I understand you, Barton Deverill, and I understand myself. Centuries of dwelling between worlds have not been for nothing. They have given me understanding.'

The gloom in the hall slowly began to brighten. It started with a glow emanating from the joined hands of Barton Deverill and Maggie O'Leary and began to grow. As they locked eyes the light grew more intense until it filled the entire room with a dazzling golden radiance. Kitty knew it wasn't sunshine that illuminated the hall because outside the winter's day was dull and overcast. It was otherworldly and it was beautiful.

'I forgive you, Lord Deverill,' Maggie said and she smiled serenely. 'Will *you* forgive *me* for the curse I placed upon you and your heirs?'

'I forgive you, Maggie,' Barton replied, standing up. 'I forgive you from the depths of my soul.'

'Then let us go in love,' she said. 'The blood of the O'Learys flows through Alana's veins, but also the blood of the Deverills. *Our* blood, Barton.'

Barton frowned. '*Our* blood?' he repeated.

'Our child, Barton,' she whispered and he understood.

Barton pressed Maggie's hand to his heart. 'My offence is all the more cruel,' he groaned, but Maggie kissed his hand.

'It is as it should be,' she said. 'The past is gone and all wrongdoing has been forgiven. Now let us rest in peace.'

Suddenly Adeline realized that the curse had never really been about land, but about forgiveness, and it had never really had anything to do with anyone else but Barton and Maggie. How very unlike her not to have worked it out before.

The light became so bright that Kitty had to close her eyes. She sensed the spirits leaving, one by one, as if they were each dissolving in that glorious light. When at last she opened her eyes she found herself alone. Well, almost. There, standing before her, was Adeline.

'It is done,' said her grandmother with satisfaction. 'Now it's up to you, Kitty, to live well, with an open heart and a readiness to forgive, because it is only through forgiveness that wrongs can be put right. Don't ever forget that.'

'I won't,' said Kitty as her grandmother began to fade.

'And don't cry, my child. I'm only a thought away.'

Then she was gone.

'Who are you talking to?' JP asked as he came down the stairs with Alana close behind him.

'No one,' Kitty replied, wiping her eye. 'Let's go and have a cup of tea,' she suggested quickly.

'What a good idea,' said JP, taking his wife's hand. They walked towards the library where Maud was laughing heartily at something Bertie had said.

JP grinned at Kitty. 'Do you think Maud's found some of Adeline's cannabis?'

'How do you know about Adeline's cannabis?' Kitty asked.

'Celia told me. Adeline was a right witch!' He laughed.

'She certainly was,' Kitty agreed, walking into the library with a buoyant step. 'The very *best* kind of witch.'

Acknowledgments

This book would not have been written without the following invaluable people. I thank them with all my heart.

My dear friend and co-conspirator, Tim Kelly.

My wonderful agent, Sheila Crowley, and her brilliant team at Curtis Brown: Abbie Greaves, Rebecca Ritchie, Alice Lutyens, Luke Speed, Enrichetta Frezzato, Katie McGowan, Anne Bihan and Mairi Friesen-Escandell.

My boss, Ian Chapman. My exceptionally talented editor, Suzanne Baboneau, and her superb team at Simon & Schuster who work so hard on my behalf: Clare Hey, Dawn Burnett, Emma Harrow, Gill Richardson, Rumana Haider, Laura Hough, Dominic Brendon, Sally Wilks and Sara-Jade Virtue.

I would also like to thank my brilliant publishing team in Canada who have taken so much time and trouble to produce these beautiful books. So much thought has gone in to them and the result is really exciting. The covers are absolutely stunning and I'm thrilled. So, thank you, Simon & Schuster Canada, for your talent and enthusiasm: Nita Pronovost, Felicia Quon, Kevin Hanson, Shara Alexa, Patricia Ocampo, Greg Tilney, Catherine Whiteside, Siobhan Doody. You're amazing and I'm so grateful!

My parents, Charles and Patty Palmer-Tomkinson, my mother-in-law, April Sebag-Montefiore.

My husband, Sebag, and our two children, Lily and Sasha.

About the Author

Photograph by Eliane Fattal

Santa Montefiore's books have been translated into twenty languages and have sold more than six million copies. She is married to the writer Simon Sebag Montefiore. They live with their two children, Lily and Sasha, in London.

Montefiore was born in Winchester and spent her childhood on her family's idyllic farm in Hampshire and Leicestershire. From the age of twelve, she attended the Sherborne School for Girls in Dorset, where she excelled in English and wrote stories for her friends, imagining romances between them and the young men they fancied at Sherborne Boys' School. From a young age, Montefiore gravitated towards writing. After Sherborne, she studied Spanish and Italian at Exeter University before taking a gap year that was to change her life forever.

At the age of nineteen, Montefiore travelled for the first time to Argentina, where she found her first good story. The wild and earthy beauty of rural Argentina – with its humid plains, colonial farmhouses and air redolent with the scent of jasmine – and the heady allure of its cities, with their distinct architecture, music and people – left a profound impression on Montefiore. It was to the memories of these places that she would return for inspiration for five of her novels.

Argentina is not the only location that has a special place in Santa Montefiore's heart. The British Isles, with their sweeping cliffs and pastoral villages, assume a central role in her oeuvre, their duality of ruggedness and charm almost a foil for the colourful characters who inhabit the books.

Before becoming a full-time writer, Montefiore built a career in public relations and retail. It was after she published her first novel and experienced great success that she embarked on her literary career. Since 2001, she has written almost without a break, publishing at least one novel a year. Besides the historical and contemporary fiction for which she is known, Montefiore has also embarked on children's books, with the Royal Rabbits of London series, which she penned with her husband.

Montefiore's twentieth book comes out next year. She counts as her literary influences greats such as Alexandre Dumas, Gabriel García Márquez, Daphne du Maurier and Isabel Allende.

Visit her at SantaMontefiore.co.uk.

The Last Secret *of the* Deverills

Santa Montefiore

Dear Reader,

I hope you enjoyed reading *The Last Secret of the Deverills* as much as I enjoyed writing it. Ever since I chanced upon a road sign directing people to Longbridge Deverill, a hamlet in rural Wiltshire, the name resonated with me. It evoked in my mind images of an old, imposing castle belonging to the equally impressive and commanding Deverill family that inhabited it. Through the stories of Kitty, Bridie and Celia, I wanted to explore not just themes of friendship and love, but also those of home and belonging.

I wanted to explore not just themes of friendship and love, but also those of home and belonging.

The Last Secret of the Deverills is, in many ways, a continuation of the exploration of those themes. A lot has changed in the lives of the series' main characters since the conclusion of *Daughters of Castle Deverill*. Kitty, who once called Castle Deverill home, doesn't live in it anymore. Celia, who once owned the castle, has been forced to sell it, and Bridie, who was once but a housemaid in the castle, is now its owner. This paradigm shift in the circumstances of Kitty, Bridie and Celia is only exacerbated by the people they have loved and lost. Some losses are too painful to overcome. So even after Bridie returns to Ballinakelly and assumes residence at Castle Deverill with her husband and son, old resentments resurface. Even when her former best friend, Kitty, lives so close by, she is far from reach for Bridie. While the theme of home is explored through Kitty and Bridie, the themes of love and friendship are explored through Kitty's adopted – and Bridie's biological – son, JP. Both JP and Martha, whom he falls in love with, don't know who their real mothers are and it is not just this that binds them together, but rather a deeper sense of kinship, love and belonging.

The Last Secret of the Deverills was in many ways supposed to be my swan song in the Deverill Chronicles. But I knew the stories of my characters weren't over.

But I knew the stories of my characters weren't over.

There was as much to look forward to as there was to look back upon. And so, in the next Deverill Chronicle – tentatively titled *The Forgotten Deverill* – I am going back in time. This book starts nine years before *Songs of Love and War* begins and follows the life of Arethusa Deverill, Bertie and Rupert Deverill's sister. Needless to say, a big family secret is unraveled that puts many of the stories we already know into perspective. It is currently scheduled to come out in the summer of 2019, and I can't wait for you to read it!

I wrote it from my home in County Cork (so to speak). After a long spout of travelling, it was so wonderful to be back in Ireland, in the town I invented called Ballinakelly, writing about my favourite characters again. I had you, dear readers, very much in mind as I wrote this one, because I want to give those who enjoyed the trilogy a fabulously entertaining read, and not disappoint them! I listened to Howard Shore and David Arkenstone as I sat at the kitchen table (near the fridge and the Nespresso machine!), whose Celtic soundtracks transport me to the rugged hills above Ballinakelly, and I really felt I was there. I met a guru in India who told me, when I lamented that I meditate very rarely these days because life is too busy, that writing my book *is* a meditation.

Writing my book is *a meditation.*

That made me feel better and gave me the energy and spirit to return to my desk to write.

It's always daunting starting a new novel, but the secret is not to think beyond the page you are writing. If you tell yourself you have 120,000 words to write, you risk losing heart and giving up! I start each writing day with the words: 'I'm going to really entertain my readers today' and set about doing just that. As long as I feel this inspired and enthusiastic, I'll keep on doing it.

Thank you for always being such avid readers. I love my characters and it fills me with great joy when I see how much they mean to you too.

I love my characters and it fills me with great joy when I see how much they mean to you too.

I can't wait to take you on yet another journey to Ballina-kelly!

Love to you all and thank you again for your continuing support!

XXX Santa

For Discussion

1. Discuss JP's first encounter with Martha. JP describes it as 'a bond, a connection, an understanding,' (p. 14). Is it love at first sight, or something that runs deeper?

2. Castle Deverill is a character in itself throughout the Deverill series. What symbolism does the castle hold for the Deverills? What symbolism does the castle hold for Bridie?

3. Discuss the relationship between Bridie and Cesare. Would you call their relationship strained? Typical? Problematic? Do you think the two were ever truly in love? Why or why not?

4. Discuss the three-part structure of the novel. What symbolism can you glean from this structure? How does the compression of time in the novel influence the characters' decisions?

5. How significant are the various secrets kept by the characters in the novel? Do you agree with Grace's decision not to tell Martha about her true parentage? Why do you suppose Bertie never revealed the true identity of JP's mother despite their close relationship?

6. What role does class play in the novel? How much of that influence is inherited versus learned?

7. The novel is rich with detailed descriptions of the Irish countryside. Is there a particular passage or scene that stood

out to you? What role does the natural world play in the characters' lives?

8. Which characters won your sympathy and why? Did this change over the course of the novel? Did your notion of what was best or right shift as you read?

9. Discuss the way that motherhood is portrayed in *The Last Secret of the Deverills*. Which characters are biological mothers, and which take on the responsibility of mothering despite a lack of blood bond?

10. Martha was raised by Pam and Larry Wallace, but by the end of the novel she finally learns the truth about her biological mother. How differently do you think her life would have turned out if she had never been given up for adoption?

Enhance Your Book Club

1. *Songs of Love and War* is the first novel in the Deverill Chronicles. If you haven't already, go back and read *Songs of Love and War* with your book club. Compare and contrast the author's style and the characters across the series.

2. The castle is itself a character in the novel. Have you seen many castles in your travels? Are you drawn to them? Talk as a group about the appeal of these historic buildings. Why do you think they are so romantic and compelling?

3. Who would you cast in the film version of *The Last Secret of the Deverills*? How would you cast Kitty, Bridie and Celia?

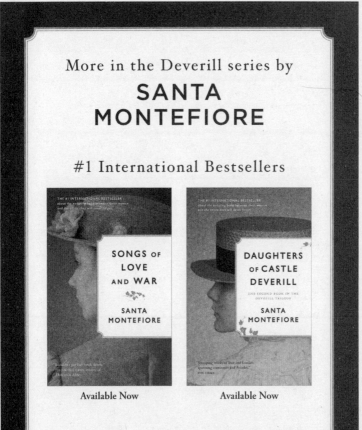